BOOK VII

# The End

They say there is divinity in odd numbers,
Either in nativity, chance, or death.
—William Shakespeare, *The Merry Wives of Windsor*

It doesn't matter how beautiful your theory is, it doesn't matter
how smart you are. If it doesn't agree with experiment, it's
wrong.

—Richard Feynman

## Praise for *Middlegame*

"McGuire has an uncanny knack for taking the worst things that lurk in the shadows and weaving them into an absolute delight."

—Becky Chambers

"It's the kind of book where you want to reach into the page just to help them out, to warn them of what's coming. It *blossoms*."

—NPR

"This is a fascinating novel by an author of consummate skill."

—*Publishers Weekly* (starred review)

"Satisfying on all levels of the reading experience: thrilling, emotionally resonant, and cerebral."     —*Kirkus Reviews* (starred review)

"This singular work keeps readers thinking long after the final page."

—*Library Journal* (starred review)

"An excellent recommendation for those who enjoyed Lev Grossman's *The Magicians* and Lauren Oliver's *Replica*."

—*School Library Journal* (starred review)

"Readers should come for the tightly constructed world and stay for the pleasure of watching the twins choose each other, come what may."     —*Shelf Awareness*

"What a story to read (and reread). If you've got a love for fantasy, you should read *Middlegame*."     —*Entertainment Weekly*

"This tragic, triumphant novel will break your brain and your heart . . . The finest work to date from an author of consistently fine works."

—*B&N Sci-fi & Fantasy Blog*

## ALSO BY SEANAN McGUIRE

*Dusk or Dark or Dawn or Day*
*Deadlands: Boneyard*

THE WAYWARD
CHILDREN SERIES
*Every Heart a Doorway*
*Down Among the Sticks and Bones*
*Beneath the Sugar Sky*
*In an Absent Dream*
*Come Tumbling Down*

THE OCTOBER DAYE SERIES
*Rosemary and Rue*
*A Local Habitation*
*An Artificial Night*
*Late Eclipses*
*One Salt Sea*
*Ashes of Honor*
*Chimes at Midnight*
*The Winter Long*
*A Red-Rose Chain*
*Once Broken Faith*
*The Brightest Fell*
*Night and Silence*
*The Unkindest Tide*

THE INCRYPTID SERIES
*Discount Armageddon*
*Midnight Blue-Light Special*
*Half-Off Ragnarok*
*Pocket Apocalypse*
*Chaos Choreography*
*Magic for Nothing*
*Tricks for Free*
*That Ain't Witchcraft*

THE GHOST ROADS SERIES
*Sparrow Hill Road*
*The Girl in the Green Silk Gown*

THE INDEXING SERIES
*Indexing*
*Indexing: Reflections*

AS MIRA GRANT

THE NEWSFLESH SERIES
*Feed*
*Deadline*
*Blackout*
*Feedback*
*Rise: The Complete Newsflesh
Collection* (short stories)

THE PARASITOLOGY SERIES
*Parasite*
*Symbiont*
*Chimera*

*Rolling in the Deep*
*Into the Drowning Deep*

*Final Girls*
*Kingdom of Needle and Bone*
*Alien: Echo*

SEANAN McGUIRE

# Middlegame

A TOM DOHERTY ASSOCIATES BOOK

NEW YORK

MIDDLEGAME

Copyright © 2019 by Seanan McGuire

All rights reserved.

Lyrics to "Erased" by Michelle Dockrey and "The Doctrine of Ethos" by Dr. Mary Crowell used with the permission of the original copyright holders.

A Tor.com Book
Published by Tom Doherty Associates
120 Broadway
New York, NY 10271

www.tor.com

Tor® is a registered trademark of Macmillan Publishing Group, LLC.

The Library of Congress has cataloged the hardcover edition as follows:

McGuire, Seanan, author.
Middlegame / Seanan McGuire.—First edition.
    p. cm.
"A Tom Doherty Associates book."
ISBN 978-1-250-19552-4 (hardcover)
ISBN 978-1-250-19551-7 (ebook)
1. Twins—Fiction. 2. Alchemy—Fiction. 3. FICTION / Fantasy / Contemporary.—
Fiction. I. Title.
PS3607.R36395
813'.6—dc23

2019285075

ISBN 978-1-250-23420-9 (trade paperback)

Our books may be purchased in bulk for promotional, educational, or business use. Please contact your local bookseller or the Macmillan Corporate and Premium Sales Department at 1-800-221-7945, extension 5442, or by email at MacmillanSpecialMarkets@macmillan.com.

First Edition: May 2019
First Trade Paperback Edition: April 2020

Printed in the United States of America

0  9  8  7  6  5  4  3

*For Shawn, who always knew that one day I would lead him to the Impossible City. Thank you for trusting me to find the way.*

# Failure

There is so much blood.

Roger didn't know there was this much blood in the human body. It seems impossible, ridiculous, a profligate waste of something that should be precious and rare—and most importantly, contained. This blood belongs inside the body where it began, and yet here it is, and here he is, and everything is going so wrong.

Dodger isn't dead yet, despite the blood, despite everything. Her chest rises and falls in tiny hitches, barely visible to the eye. Each breath is a clear struggle, but she keeps fighting for the next one. She's still breathing. She's still *bleeding*.

She's not going to bleed for long. She doesn't, no pun intended, have it in her. And when she stops breathing, so does he.

If Dodger were awake, she'd happily tell him exactly how much of her blood is on the floor. She'd look at the mess around them. She'd calculate the surface area and volume of the liquid as easily as taking a breath, and she'd turn it into a concrete number, something accurate to the quarter ounce. She'd think she was being comforting, even if the number she came up with meant "I'm leaving you." Even if it meant "there is no coming back from this."

Even if it meant goodbye.

Maybe it *would* be comforting, to her. The math would be true, and that's all she's ever asked from the world. He knows the words that apply to this situation—exsanguination, hypovolemia, hemorrhage—but they don't reassure him the way the numbers reassure her. They never have. Numbers are simple, obedient things, as long as you understand the rules they live by. Words are trickier. They twist and bite and require too much attention. He has to think to change the world. His sister just *does* it.

Not without consequences. That's how they wound up here, on the other side of the garden wall, at the end of the improbable road, at the end of everything. They never got to the Impossible City, and now they never will. The King of Cups wins again.

The King of Cups always wins. Anyone who tries to say he doesn't is lying.

The gunfire from outside is louder and less dramatic than he expected, like the sound of someone setting off firecrackers inside a tin can. Firecrackers never did this sort of damage. The walls are thin and getting thinner. The bullets are chewing the concrete away, and the people who followed them down the improbable road will be inside soon. Erin can't hold them off forever, no matter how hard she tries.

Dimly, he realizes he doesn't want her to hold them off forever. If this is where it ends for one of them, let this be where it ends for all of them. Let this be where it ends for good. No one—not even him—walks the improbable road alone.

He grasps Dodger's shoulder, feeling the solidity of her, the vital, concrete *reality* of her, and shakes as gently as he can. "Dodger. Hey, Dodge. Hey. I need you to wake up. I need you to help me stop the bleeding."

Her eyes stay closed. Her chest rises and falls, her breathing getting shallower all the time.

There's so much blood.

He knows the words. Shock; fatality; the brutally simple, brutally accurate *death*. She's leaving him again, forever this time. Going. Going. Gone.

"Don't do this to me." His own injuries aren't as bad as hers. He took a single bullet to the upper thigh early on in the battle. It was through and through, missing the major arteries, and Dodger was still alert enough to help him with the tourniquet. There's still a chance he could lose the leg if he doesn't get proper medical attention soon. Right now, that doesn't seem important. Maybe he's in shock too. Maybe he deserves to be. "You can't. You can't go. We've come too far. Are you listening? You can't go. I need you."

Her eyes are closed. There's so much blood.

There's one thing he can do. Maybe the only thing. Maybe it was always the only thing, and they've been building toward this the whole time. It feels like failure, like running back to the garden, and he doesn't care, because her chest is barely moving, and there's so much blood, there's *so much blood*, and it doesn't matter that he knows the words, all the words, for everything. The numbers are taking her away. He can't reach them without her.

"I can't do this alone. I'm sorry. I can't."

He leans in until his lips brush the seashell curve of her ear. There's blood in her hair, turning it tacky and clinging. It sticks to his skin, and he doesn't try to wipe it off.

"Dodger," he whispers. "Don't die. This is an order. This is a command. This is an adjuration. Do whatever you have to do, break whatever you have to break, but *don't you die*. This is an order. This is—"

This is her eyes opening, pupils reduced to black pinpricks against the gray of her irises, until she looks like she's suffered a massive opiate overdose. This is gold sparking in the gray, brief and bright, as the Impossible City tries to call her home. He feels the gold in his own bones respond, reaching for the gold in Dodger's, yearning to reunite.

This is the sound of gunfire going silent. Not tapering off; just *stopping*, like the world has been muted.

This is the world going white.

This is the end.

*We got it wrong we got it wrong we got it wrong we got it wrong we*

In the same ordinary town, on the same ordinary street, lived two ordinary children who had never quite managed to cross paths. This, too, was sadly ordinary, for the line that divided the students who went to the school on the *west* side of town from the students who went to school on the *east* side of town ran right down the middle of their block, an invisible barrier that had split them in two before they were old enough to notice. Every morning they got out of bed, put on their clothes, kissed their parents goodbye, and walked off down their ordinary street, through their ordinary town, in two ordinary, opposite directions.

The two children were very much alike and very different at the same time, as children so often are. One was named Hephzibah, because her parents had a languid and eccentric way of looking at the world. They called her "Zib," understanding that "Hephzibah" was more name than she had shadow. Every day they watched for signs that she was growing into her name, and every day they were disappointed.

"Soon," they promised each other. "Soon."

The other was named Avery, because his parents had a sharp and efficient way of looking at the world. They called him "Avery" when they were happy, and "Avery Alexander Grey" when they were mad, and gave him no nicknames. Nicknames were for people whose names didn't fit them properly, and they had measured him, every inch, before they named him.

"We did well," they reassured each other. "We did."

These are our two children: ordinary, average, wildly unique, as all children are. Our story begins on an ordinary, average day, a day which had never happened before, and would never, in all the length and breadth of time, happen again . . .

—From *Over the Woodward Wall,* by A. Deborah Baker

... the Doctrine of Ethos, as described by Pythagoras, held that certain musical instruments and modes could influence the balance between Logos (rational behavior) and Pathos (emotional thought). Later alchemists came to see this as the interaction between the two halves of the human heart, and more, as the balance between language and mathematics: the two methods through which Man has always been able to influence and even command Nature. The Doctrine must thus be viewed as the most dangerous and most desirable of alchemical incarnations. The people who are first able to seize control over the Doctrine shall command all things.

Ladies and gentlemen of the Alchemical Congress, you know what I am capable of. You have seen my masterwork, spoken to the proof of my mastery. I believe I am prepared to incarnate the Doctrine, if you are prepared to let me try.

—Address by Asphodel D. Baker to the American
Alchemical Congress, 1901

# The Beginning

Medicine rests upon four pillars—philosophy, astronomy, alchemy, and ethics.

—Paracelsus

Time is the substance from which I am made.

—Jorge Luis Borges

# Genesis

The air is heavy with the crackle of electricity, with the taste of ozone and mercury and the burning tang of alkahest, the universal solvent, which has a nasty tendency to consume everything in its path unless properly contained. Making it is a complicated process; destroying it is even more difficult. Still, a few drops of the thing can go a long way toward making the supposedly impossible happen. Even death, it seems, can be dissolved.

The woman who calls herself "Asphodel" walks a slow circle around the table, studying her handiwork for flaws. She finds none, but still she circles, restless as a shark, unwilling to commit to the final stages of her task until she's certain. Certainty is a requirement of her profession, a bone-deep, rock-solid certainty that her will is strong enough and her desires are clear enough to remake the world in her own image.

She isn't the greatest alchemist of her age yet, but she's going to be. There is absolutely no question in her mind of *that*. If she has to drag those fools in the Congress kicking and screaming into the bright and beautiful future she can see unfolding ahead of her, she'll do it, and she won't be sorry. If they didn't want to follow her, they should have had the sense to get the hell out of her way.

Asphodel Baker is twenty-one years old, thirteen years away from the publication of the book that will cement her legacy in the hearts and minds of children everywhere, twenty-three years away from her disappearance and "death," and she can no more conceive of failure than a butterfly can conceive of calculus. She's going to change the world, remake it in a better image than the one it's made in now, and no one's going to stop her. Not her parents and not her teachers and certainly not the Alchemical Congress.

She was a gifted student: no one who's met her, who's seen what she can do, would deny that. The denial of her mastery is nothing but shortsightedness and spite, the old guard refusing to see the brilliant and blazing future rushing up behind them like a steam engine roaring down its track. This is her time. This is her place.

This is her chance to show them all.

Asphodel stops circling and reaches for the bowl she has prepared, its contents glowing glittering gold and mercury bright. Dipping her fingers into it, she begins drawing runes down the chest of the flawless body that lies before her, skin naked to the air. He is a gorgeous man. Time and care and access to several morgues operated by hungry, unscrupulous vermin have seen to that. She has purchased each piece of him according to her precise specifications. Thanks to the alkahest, there aren't even any scars. A universal solvent has endless applications, when properly controlled.

When she is done, she steps back and considers her handiwork. So much of her plan depends on this piece being perfect. But what is perfection, really, if not the act of winning? So long as he can carry her to victory, he'll be perfect, no matter what his flaws.

"You will rise against me, my beautiful boy," she says, in a voice like honey and hemlock intertwined. "You will throw me down and swear you saw my bones. You will take my crown and my throne and carry my work into the new century, and you will never look back to see what follows in your wake. You will be my good right hand and my sinister left, and when you fall in finishing my design, you will die without complaint. You will do what I cannot, for your hand will never waver, and your mind will never sway. You will love me and you will hate me and you will prove me right. Above all else, you will prove me right."

She puts down the bowl and picks up a vial filled with liquid starlight, with mother-of-pearl that dances and shines against the glass. She raises it to his lips and pours a single drop between them.

The man she has assembled out of the dead gasps, opens his eyes, and stares at her with fearful wonder.

"Who are you?" he asks.

"Asphodel," she says. "I am your teacher."

"Who am I?" he asks.

She smiles. "Your name is James," she says. "You are the beginning of my greatest work. Welcome. We have so much to do."

He sits up, still staring at her. "But I don't know what the work is."

"Don't worry." Her smile is the first brick in what she will one day call the improbable road. Today, now, in this moment, they are beginning their voyage toward the Impossible City.

"I'll show you," she says, and the deed is done.

It's too late to turn back now.

Avery looked at Zib, and Zib looked at Avery, and neither of them knew quite what to do with what they saw.

Avery saw a girl his age, in a skirt with mended tears all the way around the hem. Some of them were sewn better than others. Some of them were on the verge of ripping open again. Her socks were mismatched and her blouse was patched, and her hair was so wild that if she had reached into it and produced a full set of silverware, a cheese sandwich, and a live frog, he would not have been surprised. She had mud under her nails and scabs on her knees, and was not at all the sort of person his mother liked him to associate with.

Zib saw a boy her age, in a shirt that was too white and pants that were too pressed. She could see her own reflection in his polished shoes, wide-eyed and goggling. His cuffs were buttoned and his jacket was pristine, making him look like a very small mortician who had somehow wandered into the wrong sort of neighborhood, one where there were too many living people and not nearly enough dead ones. He had carefully clipped nails and looked like he had never ridden a bike in his life, and was not at all the sort of person her father liked her to associate with.

"What are *you* doing here?" they asked in unison, and stopped, and stared at each other, and said nothing further.

—From *Over the Woodward Wall,* by A. Deborah Baker

BOOK I

# The Second Stage

Mathematical science shows what is. It is the language of unseen relations between things.

—Ada Lovelace

Sorrow is knowledge.

—Lord Byron

# One Hundred Years Later

TIMELINE: 23:58 CST, JULY 1, 1986.

For a man on a mission, a hundred years can pass in the blinking of an eye. Oh, it helps to have access to the philosopher's stone, to have the fruits of a thousand years of alchemical progress at one's fingertips, but really, it was always the mission that mattered. James Reed was born knowing his purpose, left his master in a shallow grave knowing his purpose, and fully intends to ascend to the heights of human knowledge with the fruits of his labors clutched firmly in hand. Damn anyone who dares to get in his way.

Damn them all.

He waits at the end of the hall for his moment, standing in the place where the light, by careful design, fails to reach. Asphodel taught him everything she could: he learned the delicate arts of alchemy and the blunter arts of the con side by side, drinking knowledge like mother's milk. This is all a show, and these men—these craven, prideful men, who think themselves kings of their corporate veldt—are his rubes, ready to be taken for everything they have.

(The Alchemical Congress does not approve of his dealings with the more mundane world, calling them risky and arrogant. The Alchemical Congress has no room to speak. Its members are arrogance personified, and their day of reckoning is coming sooner than they can possibly know or understand. Oh, yes. They'll learn soon enough that they should never have crossed Asphodel Baker, or by extension, her son, heir, and greatest creation.)

This is his sideshow of wonders, his collection of freaks, laid out for the edification and carnival-glass seduction not of the masses, but the chosen few:

The hall is wide enough to accommodate two stretchers side-by-side, lit by glass-screened bulbs too dim to show the color of the floor. They barely illuminate the walls, which could be white, or cream, or gray; the light is too diffuse to make their color clear. Rooms dot the hall. The bulbs inside them are brighter, illuminating the occupants behind the individual one-way mirrors, throwing them into a stark, clinical relief that carries them from "child" to "curiosity." They range in age from two to twelve. They wear colorful pajamas blazoned with cartoon bears, or spaceships, or comically friendly dinosaurs; they sleep under blankets decorated with more of the same; and yet, thanks to the light, they barely register as human.

One little girl has crammed herself into the corner of her room. She is a watchful, doe-eyed thing, sitting with her arms wrapped around her knees and her eyes fixed on the mirror, staring like she can somehow see the men outside. Her companion sleeps under a blanket covered with cartoon robots, his back to the rest of the room. According to the label outside their window, their names are Erin and Darren, and they are five years old, and there is nothing about them that has not been done by design.

But the focus of this day is outside the cells. It's on the men, three of them, soft, balding creatures in respectable business suits and sensible shoes. They would fit perfectly into a boardroom or stockholder's meeting. Here, in this precise, perilous place, they are as out of their element as a blizzard in a volcano. They cluster together, uneasy. This is their doing as much as anyone else's; they were the ones who dotted the i's and crossed the t's and signed the checks that made it all possible. They own this. They own every inch of it. And yet . . .

James Reed smiles as he watches them. Their unease is intentional, part of the balance of power. These investors may own everything they see, but he created it: here, he is God Almighty, capable of bringing life out of nothingness, able to command the forces of the universe. They would do well to remember that, these small men with their narrow minds and unstained hands. They would do very well indeed.

Behind the glass, a boy with eyes the color of concrete is rocking back and forth, looking at nothing. He has been humming for the last seven hours. Tiny microphones in his room—never "cell," this is not a prison, this is a breeding ground for the future, and language is incredibly important here—have recorded every second of his meandering tune. Nothing is wasted, ever. Nothing is allowed to slip away.

(Later, cryptographers will reduce his song to its mathematical components, eventually determining that he's been offering them a chemical formula, one atom at a time. The formula will yield a novel painkiller derived from several unexpected sources, nonaddictive and capable of offering relief to cases previously thought hopeless. Patenting and marketing the drug will take another twelve years, but the results will make billions for the shell company that handles the pharmaceutical side of things. Bit by bit, because of moments like this one, the lab becomes self-sustaining. It is already vast, and sprawling, and unspeakably expensive in the way of vast, sprawling things. And it must sustain itself, it *must*. If the Alchemical Congress paid a penny for its creation and upkeep, they would expect their investment to turn into ten times its weight in gold—and that cannot be allowed. Not now. Not with the Doctrine so close at hand.)

"Gentlemen." Reed times his speech carefully: it emerges from the shadows and he emerges on its heels. Each step he takes highlights the disparities between him and his investors. They wear cufflinks purchased by their wives, their balding pates polished to a mirror sheen. He dresses like a character from a Ray Bradbury story of the endless American twilight: tight black trousers, a buttoned-up shirt in sapphire blue, even a tailcoat with bands of strange glyphs embroidered around the cuffs and bottom hem. The embroidery is gold, a reminder of the promises that drew these men to his side, moths lured by the promise of an all-consuming flame.

Asphodel—master, mentor, martyr—taught him the value of showmanship. He was always an eager student, and he understands his audience. They must think him a distracted dandy, a character from a children's story, something to be tolerated and disdained. They must allow their arrogance to treat him as a synecdoche, using his little affectations to complete an inaccurate picture.

They forget, these pampered creatures of the corporate veldt, that always there are predators, and always there is prey. They think themselves lions when even a casual onlooker can see that they are zebras, weak and plentiful and ready for the kill.

His claws, draped in velvet and wrapped in affectation, are sharp enough to slaughter the world.

"Gentlemen," he says again, and his accent is all things and nothing at all. He has honed it over the span of a century, choosing plosives and sibilants to make him sound exotic and exciting without tipping over the line into "foreign." There is a reason the children on display in this hall are pale, made of milk and bone, rather than earth and stone and all the other things his subjects are rooted in. The white children seem almost like human beings to these greedy, grasping men, and here, in this cold, sterile hall bridging science and alchemy, reason and religion, appearances matter almost as much as words.

Children who seem human create guilt in the men who paid for them. Guilt opens wallets. It's simple racism and simple math, and it opens the chasm of his loathing even deeper, for who with any sense would reject any of the wonders the disassembled human race could have to offer?

"Dr. Reed," says one of the men, the self-appointed leader of this little cluster, elevated by self-importance and, more, by a lack of self-preservation. The other two fall back in what he will interpret as reverence, but which Reed sees as cowardice. "Why are we here? You told our offices you had some great breakthrough to show us, but we're seeing the same old things."

Reed's expression of shock would look almost comical on anyone else. Not on him. Never on him. Practice, as they say, makes perfect. "You're seeing subjects who can tap into the future, who shuffle probabilities like cards, whose cells regenerate at a pace we can't track on our equipment, and you call it 'the same old things'? Why, Mr. Smith. I'm ashamed at your shortsightedness."

The man—whose name is not Smith; he accepts the bland pseudonym as a necessity, as do they all. There are costs to doing business of this kind, hidden in the shadows and outside the boundaries of law—stands a little straighter, narrows his eyes a little more. He isn't being taken seriously. This must stop. "You've shown us wonders, but those wonders aren't marketable, Reed. We can't transform all the world's lead into gold without destroying the economy we're trying to control. What can you possibly have to offer us?"

"At last you're asking the right questions. Come." Reed stalks away, as fluid as the predator he is. The men in their flat-soled shoes have no choice but to follow or be left here, surrounded by the staring, unseeing eyes of the children they've paid to bring into the world.

Not one of them hesitates to go.

The hallway stretches like a band of taffy, passing more white-walled rooms, revealing more pajama-clad children. Some are older, moving into their teens; they sit at desks with their backs to the liars' mirror, aware that they could be under observation at any time. Others are younger, toddlers who play with brightly colored blocks or curl, innocently sleeping, under hand-stitched quilts. The people who care for them say it's better if their possessions are made by hand instead of by machine; something about the process of creation flavors the inanimate, and the children sleep better when surrounded by things with a less sterile past. Childrearing is difficult under the best of circumstances. What is being done here is so much more complicated than that.

The door at the end of the hall boasts three locks and a keypad. Reed undoes each in turn, making no effort to conceal the code as he punches it in. It will be different by morning. The security is for more than just show: it's a warning, making sure these men understand that the things he has to show them are to be taken seriously. If any of them attempt to challenge his sovereignty, there will be consequences.

The door opens. Reed allows the investors to enter first. When he follows them, the door slams behind him like a tomb being sealed, final and cold.

"The universe operates according to several basic principles," he says, without preamble or pause. "Gravity, of course; probability. Chaos and order. We're part of the universe, and so the things we embody are equal in divinity to the forces which act upon us from the outside. Gravity is important. No one wants to drift away because the bonds holding them to Earth have been carelessly shattered. But love, curiosity, leadership—those are equally important, or they wouldn't exist. Nature abhors a vacuum. Nothing without purpose has been made."

It is dark here, in this space that seems to have no exits; unless he unlocks the door again, there is no escape. None of the investors say a word. They are happy to exercise their power in small ways when there is no threat to them, but here and now, in this space, they are not in control. It vexes them. Reed can see that, and glories in it.

"As you're aware, our research has been focused on the creation of children attuned to these so-called 'natural forces.' Imagine a child who embodies transmutation so well that their touch alone is enough to transform base metal, or another who can bleed night into day. Success would put the most powerful weapons of all time in our hands. The power would be beyond description. Each of you was chosen to invest with us not only because of your financial resources, but because your emotional resources put you in good standing to help shepherd the world into this new era of enlightenment and understanding."

Every time he gives this speech, Reed worries he's shoveling it on too thick: that this will be the time one of their placid, milk-fed cattle finally remembers it was once a predator, too, and begins biting the hand that strives to feed it. Every time, he is relieved and disappointed in equal measure as they swallow his words, smiling and nodding in satisfaction. Yes, of course a new order will rise, and it's only natural that they should be at the forefront. They've earned it. They've *paid* for it, and by paying, they have made themselves entitled to every benefit, every opportunity. This is theirs, and no one else's.

Fools. But wealthy fools. Wealth has carried the project this far, away from the cowards of the Congress, to the point where they can become self-sustaining, where they can cut ties to businessmen who look at the miracle of the age and see only dollar signs. Not much longer now, and they can be free. Reed holds that thought firmly as he continues.

"Central to our efforts has been a force defined by the ancient Greeks: the Doctrine of Ethos. According to the Doctrine, music can influence individuals on an emotional, mental, and even physical level. Knowing as we do now that each individual is a microcosm for the creation, it seems obvious that something which can work on a single human could also work on the entire world. Alchemists have been striving to embody the Doctrine ever since."

Reed pauses, giving them time to absorb his words. Then, to his surprise, one of the investors speaks.

"I was here nine years ago, when you told us you'd succeeded at doing exactly that. Why are we going over old ground?"

"Because if you were here nine years ago, you understand that our initial success was, in many ways, a failure." Reed schools his expression with difficulty. How *dare* this man speak to him like that, as if he had any concept of the trials inherent in an undertaking of this nature? They are *changing the world*, and this man, and the men like him, only care about the color of the ink in their ledgers.

The investors are muttering amongst themselves now. He's losing them.

"Our first attempt to embody the Doctrine *was* a success," he says, before mutters can become outright revolt. "We forced a guiding principle of the universe into human flesh. There have been . . . complications, yes, but the theory remains sound."

Complications: a boy with so much of reality resonating in his head that he can't be bothered to interact with anything beyond what he sees behind his closed eyes. The child has never spoken. He stopped eating three years ago, and while he still lives, sustained by clever machinery and feeding tubes, he hasn't opened his eyes in eighteen months. The Doctrine is imprisoned within his shivering skin. There's no way to extract it, to make the world dance to their whim, save for giving it a new home and putting its old one in the ground.

"The difficulty of the Doctrine is its size. When placed inside the mind, there's no room for *humanity*. We believe that by splitting the Doctrine into its component parts—mathematics and language— we can create a gestalt of sorts. Two people who will embody the concepts we're attempting to harness, but whose abilities will be limited enough when separated that they will remain pliable and easy to control."

"How pliable?" asks an investor.

"Pliable enough. We've arranged for an upbringing that will both encourage their endangered humanity to flourish, and teach them that pleasing us is paramount. Once they're reunited, they'll do whatever we ask if they want to stay together—and they will. Their natures will leave them no choice, and we'll have them. We'll control their access to everything, including each other." What sweet torment it will be for them, these cuckoo children of the Doctrine, to be denied their other halves until he deems them worthy of reunion. "They won't be ordinary children—that is denied to them, and gloriously so—but they'll change everything."

"How long can we expect to wait before we know whether this is another failure?" asks Mr. Smith.

Reed grits his teeth. "That's what I've brought you here to see," he says. He snaps his fingers, and the wall rolls up, revealing three small white rooms. The first two are occupied, one by a pair of children coming on two years of age, the second by a pair of sleeping babies, no more than a year old. The third is empty, save for two isolated bassinets.

The investors gape and goggle at these children like creatures in a zoo. Reed allows himself to smirk.

"We've already succeeded," he says. The door at the back of the third room opens and two nurses step inside, each with a babe in arms. The newborns are placed reverently on their mattresses. The nurses slip away.

Three sets of children, representing three years of births. All were delivered by Cesarean section at the stroke of midnight, ripped from their mothers when the time was right, each pair divided by a single rotation around the sun. The original incarnate Doctrine will be gone by now, released from his earthly form as soon as the third pair of carefully tailored children drew their first unhappy breaths. All six of them are worthy hosts, and who owns the Doctrine now is anyone's guess.

Well. Not anyone's. No matter which of these pairs has drawn the concept home, they still belong to him.

"Gentlemen, I give you the Doctrine of Ethos," he says. "One of these pairs will embody everything we have been working toward, and when they do, the universe is ours."

*Ours, and not yours, you pompous, shortsighted fools,* he thinks. The investors crowd around the glass, fighting for a better view of their future.

The babies sleep on.

Later, when the investors have been ushered out, red-faced with excitement and buzzing about how the world is going to change, how *they* are going to change the world, Dr. Reed shrugs off his tailcoat and returns to the lab to check on his newest creations. The technicians and laboratory assistants whose shifts have kept them here this late into the night look up when the door swings open, paling before rushing to resume their duties. None of them want to catch his eye. Sometimes he has ideas about how things should be done. Sometimes those ideas are enforced in ways that leave scars.

Reed walks with shoulders back and head held high, content with the way things are progressing. Those fools in the Congress said it couldn't be done, said no man could blend science and alchemy without losing the best parts of both, drove Asphodel to lengths beyond imagining to prove them wrong, and now here he is, king of all he surveys, dragging the old ways into the new world one inch at a time. There have always been avatars, he argued when this began; all he seeks to do is bring them under proper control. Maybe Asphodel's ideas gave him his starting point, but by God, the rest has been his own.

(Summer kings and snow queens, Jacks in the green and corn Jennies; he knows the names, knows the secret stories whispered about them in the dark places of the world. He knows better than to try for the naturally incarnate concepts. That will come later. When he controls the Doctrine, when cause and consequence dance to his commands, then he'll be able to reach out and collect the other things that should be his by right. He'll hold the universe in his hands, and woe betide any who question what he chooses to do with it.)

"*There* you are." The voice is accompanied by a woman popping around a corner like a cork out of a bottle, his own personal djinn in blue jeans and flannel. Leigh is the finest alchemist he's had the misfortune of meeting since Asphodel's death, a whirlwind of motion with acid holes in her shirt and hair kept short to minimize the amount of time it spends on fire. She has a wide, honest face, freckles scattered like stars across the bridge of her nose. She looks like peaches and cream, like Saturday afternoons down by the frog pond, innocence and the American dream wrapped up in a single startlingly lovely package. It's a lie, all of it. He believes in exploiting the world for his own gains, but she'd happily ignite the entire thing, if only to roast marshmallows in its embers.

She is deeply flawed, and impossibly useful, and he'll enjoy the day when he's finally in a position to take her apart and reduce her to the components her originating alchemist used to make her. The old fool forgot the lessons of Blodeuwedd and Frankenstein: never create anything smarter, or more ruthless, than yourself.

Something about that thought bothers him—something about

Asphodel, who was many things, but was never a fool. He shoves the thought aside, focusing on Leigh. "How was the delivery?"

"Smooth. Fine. Butter. Whatever word you want. The excess material has been harvested and disposed of." She waves a hand carelessly. "Nothing out of the ordinary."

He knows when she says "excess material," she means more than just the afterbirth, which will possess strong alchemical properties of its own, thanks to the method of the manikins' creation. She means the woman who gestated them, unwitting surrogate to a pair of cuckoos. He doesn't know where Leigh found the surrogate, and he has enough humanity—if only barely so—not to ask. The cost of having his composite alchemist's brilliant mind at his beck and call is that she'll occasionally do things like this—and because of the woman's long proximity to the subjects, her body may be of alchemical interest. It's never possible to know in advance.

"The boy?"

"Dead. Waiting for you in your private lab. I know you wanted the honor of the dissection." Her lips draw back from her teeth in displeasure. When something needs to be taken apart, she prefers to do it herself.

Reed pays her unhappiness no mind. "And the subjects?"

"The male was removed from the womb first, which means he's likely the control; he's fine, healthy, and ready to ship to his adoptive family. The female was extracted less than two minutes later. She screamed for half an hour before she settled down."

"What calmed her?"

"The male. When we put them together, she doesn't cry." Leigh's mouth quirks. "Isn't the flight to her new home going to be fun?"

Reed nods. "And the others?"

"The adoptions have been arranged. We're cutting along the Humors. Two each to Fire and Water, one each to Earth and Air." For the first time, Leigh's veneer of confidence cracks. "Are you sure about sending them out? I mean, really sure? I'd be more comfortable keeping them here, under controlled conditions."

"The girl—"

"*All* of them." Leigh shakes her head. "These children are irreplaceable. There's never been anything like them in the world. They belong here, where they can be studied. Monitored. Managed. Putting them into the wild is *asking* for something to go wrong."

"The plan has been carefully designed to maximize the chances of success."

"You call this 'careful design'? Placing half of each pair with a civilian family, that's being careful? At least the other half will be with our people, but that's not good enough. This isn't how we control our investment."

Reed knows what they're doing: was the one who designed the protocol. Somehow, he manages not to scowl. "I was unaware that this was 'our' investment," he says.

Leigh waves a hand dismissively. "You know what I mean."

"Do I? Do I really? We've been over this. A certain amount of randomness must be introduced if we want the children to learn to access their abilities. We know strict lab conditions don't work." More, by raising them away from the lab, they avoid the risk of their subjects learning too much, too soon. Knowledge is power, for these cuckoos more than most. If he keeps them ignorant, he keeps them tractable—and oh, how he needs them to be tractable. Tractable things are so much easier to control.

"At least let us keep one of the pairs here. The newest. They're young, they won't know anything beyond what we show them. We can raise them in boxes, keep them apart, control everything they see and hear. We've tried absolute isolation together. We haven't tried it apart."

"Because it would break them."

She shrugs. "Some things need to be broken."

*Things like you,* he thinks, as aloud he says, "My will is law here, Leigh."

"But—"

"My will is *law*." His hand lashes out, grabbing her throat, slamming her back into the wall. Her eyes gleam with malicious delight.

This is what she wanted: the reminder that he is the superior predator, that he has earned his place at the top of their tiny pecking order. How he wearies of the violence. How he understands its necessity. "Do you understand?"

"Yes," she whispers.

"Yes, what?"

"Yes, sir."

"Good girl." He releases his hold on her throat, pulling his hand away and straightening his collar. "Believe in me, Leigh. That's all I ask. Believe in me, and I will lead you to the light."

"And the light will guide us," Leigh says, ducking her head until her chin almost brushes her sternum.

"We're following the correct path," says Reed, touching her shoulder.

As soon as his hand finds her flesh, the alarm begins to ring.

Both of them stiffen, heads snapping up, eyes scanning the lab for some sign of what's gone wrong. All around them, the technicians who have studiously ignored their disagreement are doing the same, checking their equipment, calling up chemical readouts. Reed is the first to move. He pulls his hand away from Leigh and runs for his private lab. The door is closed, but opens at the swipe of the card he wears on a lanyard around his neck.

Inside, an astrolabe, spinning endlessly, occupies half the space in the vast room. Reed freezes in the doorway. Leigh, sliding to a stop behind him, does the same, as both of them stare.

The dance of planets was calibrated by a master's hand, designed to mirror the heavens exactly. Asphodel poured years of her life into the spectacular machine, thinking it would be a key component of her legacy—and as her final, crowning touch, she knocked it outside of time, so that it could someday be used to chart the movement of the Doctrine. Reed has taken great pleasure in locking it away, using its mechanical horoscopes solely for his own gain. It *is* a wonder of technical alchemy. Only a great and terrible misuse of the forces of nature could damage this edifice of gold and copper and spinning jewels . . .

And it's running in reverse.

Slowly, Reed smiles.

"You see?" he says. "We don't need to wait to know if this is going to work. We've done it. All those old fools who thought they could control the world—Baker, Hamilton, Poe, Twain, even poor, damned Lovecraft—they failed, and we've succeeded. Two of those children, two of those six clever, clever children, have just reset their personal timeline. It works." He turns to her, beaming.

"We're going to control the world."

Leigh cocks her head, following his words to their logical conclusion. "Does that mean we don't need the bankers anymore?"

When keeping predators on a leash, it's important to give them room to run. Reed nods. "Yes," he says. "But make sure they understand why we're terminating our agreement. It's always better, when they understand."

Leigh's face splits in a smile as bright and wide as the gateway to the improbable road. In that moment, she is more terrible than she is beautiful, and Reed wonders how the alchemist who made her could ever have missed the warning signs.

"It will be done tonight," she says.

"Good. I have business with the Congress. Everything is proceeding exactly as it should." He tilts his face toward the window, his own smile smaller, and tamer, than Leigh's. "The Impossible City will be ours."

Behind him, Asphodel Baker's astrolabe continues to smoothly rewind, and all of this has happened before.

# The Improbable Road

The man whose name is not Mr. Smith wakes in a dark, silent room, with the feeling that something is terribly wrong. The shape of his wife is a familiar distortion in the blankets beside him. A strange, animal smell hangs in the air, coppery and thick.

He is not alone.

The thought has barely formed when a different shape looms over him, grinning widely enough to show every tooth in its head. They are even, white, and perfect, and yet he somehow can't stop himself from thinking there's something *wrong* with them, that they're mismatched, that this assortment of teeth was never meant to share a single jaw, a single terrible smile.

"Good evening, sir," says the shape. He recognizes it now. Reed's woman, the scowling piece of subservient arm candy who moves in and out of their meetings like she has a right to be there. Leigh. That's her name. He's never been this close to her before. Her eyes . . . something about her eyes is broken. Like her smile, they are perfect— and ineffably wrong.

"Don't try to move," says Leigh—and the man, who is not Mr. Smith, flinches in response, or tries to. The command does not carry to his limbs. He is frozen, and still, she is smiling.

"You men," she says. "You foolish, foolish men. You want to control the world, but you never stopped to ask yourselves what that *meant,* did you? What alchemy truly was, what it could do—you only cared about what it could give you. Congratulations. It gave you to me."

He recognizes the smell in the air now. He doesn't know how he could have missed it before, but maybe it was a matter of wanting: he didn't *want* to recognize the smell of blood, didn't *want* to ask himself where the blood had come from.

His wife is so still, and he is terribly afraid he knows.

"Reed gave you to me," says Leigh. "You see, we've reached the stage at which investors are no longer necessary. But I think you can make one last contribution, and that means I get to tell you a story. Words are power. You'll be worth more to us if you understand why you have to die. It's like . . . homeopathic medicine for the soul. Your flesh will retain the memory of everything I tell you, and that will make it easier to use. Are you comfortable?"

He can't speak. He can't answer her. He can only roll his eyes in terror. From the way her smile softens, she knew that before she asked.

"Good," she says. There's a knife in her hand. How is there a knife in her hand? He didn't even see her move. "This is the story of a woman who had too many ideas, and the man she made so she could make them all real. You've heard of A. Deborah Baker, haven't you? Everyone has heard of A. Deborah Baker."

The knife the knife *oh God the knife,* and he can't scream, he can't move, but when she lifts his arm, he feels his wife's blood, sticky on his skin. The pain is clear and bright, and the only mercy here is that he can't turn his face to see what she's writing, one slow cut at a time.

"She wrote a series of children's books about a place called the Up-and-Under. I know your kids read them. I saw them on the shelf when I went to visit Emily in her room."

He has never wanted to scream so much in his life.

"Fourteen books before she died. Six movies, four of them made after she was dust and ashes. Her cultural footprint spans the world. Everyone knows A. Deborah Baker, and her dear creations, sweet Avery and courageous Zib. But did you know that you became one of her acolytes when you wrote your first check?"

Her voice is calm, even soothing. It has a rhythm to it, like she's trying to whisper a small child into dreaming. If it weren't for the pain, for the body of his wife beside him and the bodies of his children lying in their rooms (all three of them, oh God, he knows she's killed all three of them, because a woman like this doesn't leave survivors, and *why can't he move*), it would almost be pleasant.

"Her real name was Asphodel. That's what the *A* stands for. She was the greatest of the American alchemists. Don't look so surprised. What better way to hide your teachings in plain view than to encode them in something that would be beloved of children the world over. She swayed generations to her way of thinking. She changed the way alchemy *works*. It's the middle ground between magic and science. It has repeatable results, but only if people truly believe it will work that way. Asphodel Baker rewrote the world by writing a new world into existence. She breathed life into a dying discipline, and the Congress hated her for it, because she was so much greater than they could ever hope to become. Petty fools. They still hate her, even though all they know of her now is what she left behind. They'll all pay. Soon enough, and forever."

The pain is so big it is eating the world. She is cutting pieces of him away, and he cannot fight, and he cannot defend himself, and he could not save his family.

"She made Reed by herself, proving she could create life one piece at a time. She made him and tasked him to do what she couldn't, to finish what she barely had the time to begin. And look—she's gone, and he remains. He asked me to thank you for your support, for helping him to come this far. But your services will no longer be needed. You have reached the end of the improbable road."

The knife moves, again and again the knife moves, until consciousness slips away from the man whose name was not Smith, and life follows shortly on its heels.

Leigh Barrow perches on the edge of the dead man's bed, bathed in blood. Then, smile fading, she bends forward. The real work begins. There is much to harvest, and only so many hours before dawn.

The improbable road spools onward, and outward, and the journey continues from here.

# The Impossible City

R eed hasn't felt this good in years.

Leigh is safely back at the compound, up to her elbows in small-minded fools who can, hopefully, be more use in death than they were in life; the three sets of cuckoos have been split up and whisked away to their new homes, to be raised by ordinary people in an ordinary world.

(The fact that three of those supposedly "ordinary" families belong to him, body and soul, is irrelevant. They are failed alchemists all, scholars who had the desire but not the skill to serve him more directly. They will play at being lovers—perhaps some of them will actually fall in love—and they will raise his experiments with dedication and care. They are scientists. They have been given a project to complete. Failure is not an option; it would result in their bodies being given over to Leigh's tender mercies, and no one who has met the woman would ever take such a risk. They are almost there. The Impossible City will be his.)

The car stops. Reed adjusts the collar of his shirt before he opens the door. Gone are the jewel tones and eye-catching runes, replaced by proper funereal black and a high-buttoned shirt that lends an almost parochial tone to his appearance. The Congress is not susceptible to the same showman's tricks as his erstwhile investors. They must be handled with a more . . . delicate hand.

(*Asphodel at the end: Asphodel the phoenix, on the verge of bursting into flames from the sheer force of her frustration. "They're so sure they know what's possible that they've limited themselves," she snarls, and he could listen to her rage forever, could help her tear down the foundations of the world if that's what she wants. She is his only love and his only superior and his only regret, for they both know what comes next in the story of their lives. They both know he'll have to be the one to hold the knife.*)

As he expected, they are waiting for him when he steps into the hall, his heels echoing in the stagnant air. The locals think this is a church, although none of them can name the denomination or remember anyone who comes to services here. Still, the shape of it is right, and when they drive by on a Sunday morning, there are always people standing on the green, dressed in modest suits, in sensible gowns. What else could it be?

Sometimes the easiest trick is hiding something in plain sight. That which can be found without looking can't possibly be dangerous, after all.

Reed regards the four men in front of him with a smile on his lips and murder in his heart. "I see you heard my news," he says. "I thought I was coming to inform Master Daniels of something that might surprise him. Where is he?"

"Master Daniels has better uses for his time than consorting with the likes of you," says one of the men, a pale whisper of a thing with barely visible eyebrows.

"I am a member of the Congress, am I not?" Reed continues to smile, and wonders whether the lack of facial hair is natural or the result of a laboratory accident. In either case, it could be resolved with simple cosmetics, and then the issue of the man's faintly alien appearance would be resolved. "I have as much of a right to appear before our principal as any of you."

"You tread dangerous ground," says the next man, stout and solid in his charcoal suit, his businessman's pose. "The Doctrine is not to be interfered with. Did the death of your master teach you nothing?"

Reed's smile doesn't flicker. "You have no right to speak of her, whose heart you broke, whose work you disdained yet do not shy away from using to your own advantage. Or have you retained your boyish figure through some mechanism other than her elixir of life?"

The man's cheeks redden; he turns his face away. Reed steps forward.

"I *will* speak with Master Daniels. I will inform him that I have embodied the Doctrine, and give this Congress one more chance to grant me the position and power my accomplishments deserve. If I am refused, I will be quit of you, and my eventual command of this world's defining forces will be your downfall. Do I make myself clear?"

"As always, you are nothing if not clear, James."

Reed turns.

Master Daniels was old when Asphodel Baker was young: all her accomplishments, while they have prolonged his life, have not been enough to turn back time. He is old now, old beyond measure, and he walks into the vestry of the church that is not a church with the ponderous slowness of a man whose hurrying days are far behind him. Unlike the others in their sensible suits, he wears the red robes of his office, timeless and antiquated in the same moment.

If there is anyone in the Congress who understands showmanship as Asphodel did, it is Arthur Daniels. Reed's smile as he beholds the man is genuine. They may stand on opposing sides of a divide, but at least Daniels stands with style.

(*Asphodel at the end: Asphodel the penitent, begging her own master to understand what she has been trying to accomplish all the days of her life, head bowed, hands clenched against the ground. Asphodel, her eyes full of tears, pleading with the old fool to listen to her, to see past her woman's form and her youthful face and hear her, for what is alchemy if not the use of all the myriad pieces of creation to forge a better whole? Refusing women their place in the upper reaches of the Congress only limits them, only lessens what they can do. And Daniels, the old fool, turns away.)*

"Is it true, then?" he asks, taking a careful step toward Reed. "Have you done it?"

"The Doctrine lives," Reed says. "It walks among us, prisoned in flesh, malleable, young, and foolish. I'll have my day. As your ally or as your enemy, I'll have it."

"Do you believe you can control it? A force great enough to remake *time*?"

"I believe I already have." The astrolabe, spinning, rewinding—oh, yes. He will control it.

The universe is his to command.

Daniels looks at him for a long, silent moment before inclining his head in acknowledgment. "Then it seems we must welcome you home, alchemist, for you have so much to teach us."

The other men look alarmed, unable to believe this is happening. Reed smiles, walking quickly across the vestry to kneel before the older alchemist. When Daniels's hand caresses his hair, it is like being touched by the fingers of a mummy: papery, ancient, and scented with the votive oils of the tomb.

"Believe in our works, and we will guide you to the light," says Daniels.

*(Asphodel at the end, bleeding her life out on the floor, a look of strange contentment on her face, like she always knew this would be the end of her; like she has been waiting. Like somehow, by losing, she's won. He rages at that expression, but it's too late. She's gone, she's gone, and if this was her victory, she's carried it with her to the grave.)*

"And the light shall guide me home," says Reed.

He is triumphant in his defeat.

By the time they realize why, he knows, it will be too late, and Asphodel, who would never have been forced to create him, her killer, if not for the small-minded fools who now surround him, will be avenged.

All he has to do is wait, and his cuckoos will spread their wings, and the universe will be his.

# The Astrolabe

Alone, Asphodel's astrolabe turns. The planets spin through their fixed and finite orbits; the jeweled stars move, charting a course as precise as the heavens themselves. Forward and back they go, revolving, twirling, avoiding collision by millimeters, so that it seems impossible that anything so intricate could possibly exist in physical space, unbound from the actuality of the cosmos. By looking into the mechanism, it is almost possible to see time itself modeled inch by inch and day by day, transcribed according to a human being's limited perceptions.

When it stops, even for a moment, creation trembles. When it spins, time resumes.

There are too many days between germination and growth to chart them all, and so the astrolabe spins on and on, faster and faster, until seven years have passed and the Doctrine—split between six bodies, six potential hosts, two by two and separated as far from one another as geography allows—is mature enough to make its presence known.

The Impossible City is at hand.

The girl was very pale, with waterweeds in her hair and tangled around her toes. Her feet were bare, and all of her glistened with a silvery sheen, like she had been dusted in glitter and set out into the world to see what could be seen.

"What *are* you?" asked Zib, forgetting her manners in the face of her awe. Avery stuck an elbow in her side, but it was too late: the question had been asked.

"My name is Niamh," said the girl. "I come from a city deep beneath the surface of a lake, in a place so cold that the ice only thaws once every hundred years."

"People don't live under lakes," said Avery. "There's no air. Only water. People don't breathe water."

"Oh, but you see, the people where I'm from don't breathe at all." Niamh smiled, showing teeth like pearls. "And only when the ice melts do we come up to the surface to see how other people live. But while I was on the shore gathering stones, a storm came, and the Page of Frozen Waters appeared, and snatched me up, and carried me to the King of Cups. He's a very cruel king, and he kept me so long that the ice froze solid again, and now I'm just a drowned girl with no city at all, until the next time the thaw comes."

"A hundred years is a very long while," said Avery. He couldn't let himself think too hard about the way her skin glistened, or her claims to come from a place where people didn't breathe. Surely she was kidding. "Won't you be too old then to swim?"

"Not at all. When I'm home, I don't breathe, and when I'm here, I don't age. That way, I can always make it back to the ice, if I'm clever."

Zib, though, had what felt like a more important question. "Who is the Page of Frozen Waters?"

Niamh sobered. "She is the worst of all the King's subjects, because she loves him and hates him at the same time, and she would do anything to please him. She commands the crows, and they do her bidding. For him, she gathers every strange thing that comes into the Up-and-Under. She'll gather you, if you're not careful."

Avery and Zib exchanged a glance and stepped closer together, suddenly afraid of this glittering girl, and of everything her presence might entail.

—From *Over the Woodward Wall,*
by A. Deborah Baker

# BOOK II

# The Doctrine Matures

Invention, it must be humbly admitted, does not consist of creating out of void, but out of chaos.

—Mary Shelley

Language is the most massive and inclusive art we know, a mountainous and anonymous work of unconscious generations.

—Edward Sapir

# Introduction

TIMELINE: 16:22 EST, APRIL 9, 1993
(SEVEN YEARS POST-EMBODIMENT).

Have you finished your homework?"

"No," says Roger, hiding his book under his desk before his mother sees. She likes the way he reads. She likes that he's smart. He's heard her bragging to her friends about her "little professor," and how he's going to change the world someday, just you wait. But she doesn't like the way he reads when he's supposed to be doing homework, and lately—after a few dismaying conversations with his teacher—she's started confiscating his books when she thinks he's using reading to get out of doing something else.

Which, technically, he is. This worksheet should have been done an hour ago. But he was at a good place in his book (*they're all good places*), and reading a little further seemed more important than multiplying a few stupid numbers. The numbers don't need him to give them meaning the way the words do. Words don't mean anything without someone to understand them. Numbers just *are*. He's extraneous to the process. "Extraneous" is one of his new words.

Roger Middleton is seven years old and so in love with language that there's no room in his world for anything else. He doesn't play sports or go on adventures in the nearby woods; he doesn't want a dog or to spend the weekend at a friend's house. He just wants to read, to *listen*, to expand his understanding of the syllables making up the universe around him.

(His mother isn't as bad as she could be. She takes his books when he neglects things like his math homework, but she gives them back, and she's never told him something was too advanced for him. Instead, she showers him with books, as many as he asks for, and seems to delight endlessly in how fast he learns. She's even given him some books written in other languages, like Spanish or German or Cantonese, and how she laughs when he reads her those stories! Even if she can't understand what he's saying, she still laughs. So he knows she's proud of him. She has to be.)

He looks at her and smiles hopefully, and she melts. She always does. "All right, mister," she says, mock-stern. "I'll be back to check your worksheet in fifteen minutes. You'd better have at least half the problems done, or I'm clearing all the books out of here for two days. Even the ones you have hidden in your drawers."

Roger gasps, horrified. "Yes, ma'am," he says, and bends over his paper, pencil scratching out answers as he sets himself to the serious work of keeping his reading privileges.

Ten minutes later, the short burst of productivity has burnt itself out, and he's once again staring at a sea of numbers and mathematical sigils, wondering whether he can risk pulling his book back from under the desk.

"The answer's sixteen," says a girl's voice. It is not, precisely, coming from the air next to him; it seems to be coming from the space he currently occupies. It is also not, precisely, one of the voices he sometimes hears in his head when he pretends to be a famous author, writing a new book, or a lauded teacher, explaining the definition of a newly discovered word to an eager audience. It's a *new* voice, an *outside* voice, and not his invention at all.

Roger stiffens. Voices from nowhere aren't a *good* thing. Being clever and quiet means hearing his mother brag about his cleverness to her friends. It also means hearing his teachers tell her how it worries them that he doesn't play with the other kids, that he prefers the company of books to the company of people. Maybe there's something . . . *wrong* with him. They only ever say that in a whisper, and never when they think he could be listening, but he hears them.

He doesn't want something to be *wrong* with him. So he says nothing. Most people go away if he doesn't talk to them.

The girl sighs, exasperated. "Did you hear me? It's sixteen, stupid. Write it down."

Automatically, Roger does. The answer looks correct, nestled under the eight and the two and the little "x" that means to multiply. Still, he doesn't say anything.

"I can do the rest for you. If you want."

"You can?" He claps his hand over his mouth, looking anxiously around in case his mother somehow crept into the room and heard him talking to the air. Lowering his voice, he asks, more softly, "You can?"

"Sure. I'm bored. Let me?"

"Um. Okay."

She rattles off answers as fast as he can write them down, sometimes skipping three or four problems ahead before doubling back. She never pauses to explain. He's not here to learn: he's here to do transcription, to let her scratch whatever strange itch would drive someone to do someone else's math homework. When they're finished, when the last math problem is complete—along with the four bonus problems at the bottom of the sheet, something he's never bothered to do before—he drops his pencil and stares at the graphite marks covering his paper.

"Wow."

"What? It's really basic stuff. Boring. We should do some calculus."

Roger can't take it anymore. "Who *are* you?" he asks. "Is this a trick?"

"No, silly, this is math. Math is never a trick. Math never plays tricks. Sometimes it makes problems, but they always have solutions. Not like stupid English." The girl's voice turns frustrated. "Frogs don't wear clothes and drive cars, and if you get sucked up by a tornado you wind up dead, not in someone else's country, and a road can't be improbable. It's all a big dumb lie for big dummy liars, but they still make us learn it. It's not *fair*."

Here is something Roger understands. "It's not a lie," he says, triumphant. "It's a metaphor." He pronounces the word with a long *e*, like "meet-a-for." Neither of them notices. (In later years, when mispronunciation has become one of his greatest fears, he'll look back on this moment and grimace, wondering how they could ever have become friends when he started their relationship with a mangled word.) "It's using a thing that's not true to talk about things that are."

"If something's not true, it's a lie."

"Not always." He doesn't have the vocabulary to explain why this is so: he just knows it is, that sometimes things are symbols for ideas bigger than they could ever be without help, that sometimes untruths are the truest thing of all. "I still don't know who you are."

"Dodger Cheswich." Her voice turns prim, and he recognizes that tone, because he's heard it from his own lips: it's the voice of the smartest kid in school being asked a senseless question. "We rhyme. *Ro*-ger and *Dod*-ger."

Roger goes very still. How does she know his name? She can't know his name unless she's really from inside his head, and if she's from inside his head, there's something wrong with him. He doesn't want there to be something wrong with him.

But she's still talking, the words quick and unrelenting, and it's easy to let the worry go. She's real. She has to be real. He could never imagine anyone like her. "Maybe us rhyming is why I can do your homework. Maybe all rhyming kids are like this. Do you have any more?"

"Names?"

"No, stupid. Homework."

"Not tonight," he says, and is dimly delighted to realize he's telling the truth: he, and the voice in his head, have completed all the problems on the worksheet. What's more, he did it all by himself, so the handwriting matches up. Then he frowns. "Is this cheating?"

"No."

"How do you know?"

"Because I argue with my teachers about whether I'm cheating a *lot,* and they never said 'a voice in your head that gives the answers is cheating.' So this can't be cheating."

The answer just raises more questions. Roger is beginning to feel like he's trying to run up the side of an avalanche. This Dodger girl—who isn't real, can't be real; voices in your head aren't *real*—is too exhausting to be a good imaginary friend. "I don't think we should do this."

"Come on. I'm *bored.*" She sounds frustrated. "Stupid Jessica Nelson hit me in the face with a red bounce ball during recess, and now I have to be in the nurse's office until my mom comes to take me home. I'm missing math *and* dance *and* I didn't get to eat my pudding cup."

None of this matches Roger's understanding of imaginary friends. It doesn't match what he knows about people who hear voices, either. He just knows she sounds so . . . so sad, and that she helped him with his homework. So he reaches for his pencil, and a clean sheet of paper, and says, "Let me teach you about metaphors."

When his mother looks in, sometime later, Roger is bent over the paper, mumbling to himself as he writes. She can see the finished worksheet off to one side, and she smiles.

Maybe he can be taught to follow instructions after all.

Midnight creeps into the room one second at a time. Roger is deep in a comforting dream—one about trains and teddy bears and that weird noise the pantry door makes—when a hand touches his shoulder. He sits bolt upright in bed, eyes already open, searching for the intruder.

There's no one there.

"Oh, good," says the voice from before. "You're awake. I was bored."

"Who's there?" He looks wildly around.

She sighs. "It's Dodger, hello? Why'd I have to have an imaginary friend who's a dumb boy who doesn't like math? I wanted something cool. Like an elephant."

Roger sinks back into the pillows, scowling at the ceiling. He's been in bed for more than three hours: the glow-in-the-dark stars have mostly lost their shine. A few still glimmer dimly, like he's looking at them through deep water. "I'm not an elephant."

"I know. Why were you asleep?"

"Because it's midnight."

"No it's not. It's nine. My dad says I have to be in bed so I'm not a butt in the morning." Dodger's tone shows how little she thinks of this advice. "It's not my fault I wake up before he's had his coffee. What are you doing?"

"*Sleeping*," hisses Roger. "I'm not your imaginary friend. I have school tomorrow."

"Me, too. And you have to be my imaginary friend."

"Why?"

"Because if you're not, I'm talking to myself." There's something familiar in her voice: fear. She's afraid of what it would mean if she started talking to herself. Roger lets himself thaw a little. None of this makes any sense at all, but maybe it's not such a bad thing. Maybe it would be good to have someone to talk to.

"How can you be talking to me?"

"I dunno." He feels her shrug. "I close my eyes and you're there. It's like picking up a phone. I can see the stuff you see, too, when I try. Like with the math. Do you have any more?"

"No. Hang on." He gets out of bed, limbs protesting all the way. His mind is awake, thanks to Dodger's cheerful refusal to be quiet, but his body knows it's supposed to be asleep. When he's sure he can walk without falling he shuffles out of his room and down the hall. The house is as close to silent as it ever gets. The clock downstairs in the kitchen ticks to itself; a branch scrapes against the hallway window; the wind whistles through the eaves. There's a dreamlike quality to everything, divorced from the waking world by the strangeness of it all.

(It has to happen now, he realizes, dimly aware that the things he's experiencing should seem impossible. Two years ago, he would have accepted voices in his head helping him with his homework as so natural that he'd have told everyone about it, cheerfully unaware that some things are best kept secret. Two years from now, he would think hearing voices meant he was going crazy and would claw himself to ribbons trying to make it stop. This is the perfect time. This is the one point on his timeline where contact can be made without trauma or damage. He doesn't know how he knows that, or why he's so sure that two years in either direction would change everything, but he's seven years old; he accepts his conclusion without questioning it.)

The door to his parents' room is closed. He's the only one awake. Well, him, and Dodger—but she doesn't count, does she? She's in a different house, a different place entirely. If she exists at all.

He trails a hand along the wall as he walks, feeling the worn places in the wallpaper. His fingers have sketched them, night after night. When he was small, he used to reach up to find the wall, letting his hand land at a level even with his ears. As he got taller, his hand dropped to shoulder height. Now it trails slightly above his waist, following the same track it always has. Sometimes in the morning he looks at that worn strip of wallpaper and thinks about what it means: how soon he'll need to reach down to keep running his fingers along the same patch of wall. How he's growing, a little more every day, and nothing stays the same forever.

Most of the kids he knows are rushing toward adulthood as fast as they can, hands stretched in front of them, grasping for the unknowable future. Roger wishes he knew how to dig in his heels and stop where he is. Just for a while; just long enough to get a better idea of what's ahead.

He finds the bathroom door, eases it open, eases it closed again behind him. He can hear Dodger's breathing in his head, the fast, excited inhale and exhale of a girl with no idea what's happening but no qualms about finding out. *She* won't slow down, he's sure; if anything, she'll run faster, aiming for the golden finish line, the moment where childhood ends and adulthood begins, land of anything-you-want.

"Cover your eyes," he says, and squints his own eyes before flicking on the light. It's bright enough to be biting even through his closed lids. He waits for the pain to recede before cautiously opening them and turning toward the mirror.

Roger Middleton is a skinny kid, tall for his age, with a shock of too-long brown hair that never seems to settle right, no matter how much his mother tells him to brush it. He's pale, both because he rarely goes outside and because of the sunscreen he gets doused in every time he inches toward a door. Sometimes he thinks about getting a sunburn, just for the experience. His features are symmetrical, regular, and ordinary. This is a boy who could disappear in any crowd, given the right clothing and the proper attitude.

His eyes are gray, and as he watches, they widen, although he hasn't ordered them to do so. Instead, he feels Dodger's surprise flooding through him, Dodger's amazement at what seemed—to him—like such a logical step.

"That's *you*?" she asks. He can see everything behind him, and now he knows she isn't there: he's alone in the bathroom, wearing his Bumble Bear pajamas with the tear in the right sleeve. His lips aren't moving.

At least not until he speaks. "That's me," he confirms. "This is me. Where are you?"

"I'm in bed. My parents are still awake. They'd notice if I got up." She sounds genuinely regretful, like she can't wait to pull this trick in reverse. "Your eyes look like mine. Where do you live?"

"Cambridge." He's not supposed to give his address to strangers, but a town isn't an address, and can a voice inside his head really be considered a stranger? If she's not real, she doesn't count, and if she is real (which isn't possible; there's no way she can be anything but a very vivid dream), then it's not like giving her the name of the city tells her how to find the house. "Where are you?"

"Palo Alto." Her parents must not be as good about teaching her stranger danger, because she continues blithely, "It's in California. That's why it's so much earlier here. Cambridge is in Massachusetts, isn't it? You're way far away. In a whole different time zone."

"What's a time zone?"

He can hear her perk up. "Did you ever drop an orange in a swimming pool?"

"Um. What?"

"It doesn't all get wet at the same time. No matter how fast you throw it, part of it will always hit the water firster than the rest of it." She sounds utterly matter-of-fact. All things can apparently be explained using citrus. "Light is like water that way, and the Earth is like an orange. The whole world doesn't get daytime at the same time. So it's a different time where you are than it is where I am. Otherwise, some people would have to get up in the middle of the night and pretend it was morning, and that wouldn't work."

In that moment, Roger is sure—absolutely certain—of two things: Dodger is real, and he wants her to be his friend. He grins and his reflection grins back, gap-toothed and excited, despite the lateness of the hour.

"That was almost a metaphor."

"What?" Dodger sounds horrified. He doesn't know what she looks like, but he can picture her expression all the same, dismayed and furious. "No it wasn't! You take that back!"

"It *was*. The Earth isn't an orange, and you can't throw a planet in the pool. You made a metaphor. It's not all lies."

"I—you—that's—" She stops talking and sputters for a few seconds, utterly indignant. Finally, she says, "You *tricked* me!"

Roger can't help it. He laughs, even knowing the sound could wake his parents. It's worth the risk. "You made a metaphor! You did it all by yourself!"

"Oh, why am I even talking to you? Go to *sleep*." And just like that, the feeling that he isn't alone in the bathroom is gone; he's a laughing boy in his pajamas, alone with his own reflection. He stops laughing. His smile fades.

"Dodger?"

There's no response.

"Hey, come on. I was only fooling."

Still there's no response. When his mother comes, bleary-eyed and irritated, to usher him back to bed, he goes willingly enough, too confused to fight her.

Come morning, he'll get up, get dressed, and go to school. He'll turn in his homework, including the finished math sheet. He'll get a perfect score for the first time since moving beyond addition and subtraction. But all that is in the future, on the other side of the ocean of night flowing silently by. Here and now, Roger Middleton sleeps.

# Addition

I was a little concerned about some of this material," says Miss Lewis, and she's the most beautiful woman in the world, so everyone is listening, even Marty Daniels, who would rather be reading comic books under his desk. Miss Lewis has dark brown skin and darker brown hair and eyes like the sky after the lights go out, so close to black that they could be any color in the world.

Roger is pretty much in love with her, but he doesn't think she'd mind if she knew, because someone as beautiful as Miss Lewis has to know that *everyone* is pretty much in love with her. She walks in a mist of love, smiling benevolently at everyone who passes through it. To do anything else would be cruel, and she's never cruel. She's the best second-grade teacher in the universe, and he's so lucky to have her. All the testing to get into advanced placement was worth it, because it got him Miss Lewis.

Then he sees what she's holding, and he cringes. Lunch only ended ten minutes ago. How did she already score their math sheets?

He's going to get in trouble. He's going to get in *trouble,* and he's not going to be allowed to read for a *week,* and—

And the paper she has put down in front of him has a *100%* written in sparkly ink at the very top, with a smiley face drawn beside it. A *smiley face.* The rarest of Miss Lewis's many treasures, granted only for exceptional improvement or even more exceptional work. He's seen smiley faces before, on his spelling papers and short essays, but never on a math paper. Never on *his* math paper.

"But you've surprised me," says Miss Lewis, and she's smiling *right at him* as she continues, "You've all done really, really well on this week's assignment. I think you may understand it better than I do!"

Some of the other kids giggle at the idea of understanding the work better than their teacher. Not Roger. He's not even looking at Miss Lewis anymore. His eyes are fixed on the score at the top of his paper, and it feels like a pit has opened in the bottom of his stomach.

He got a perfect score.

He got a perfect score because Dodger helped him.

He got a perfect score because Dodger helped him, and she's gone. Or, not gone. She's where she always was, somewhere in California, so far away that she might as well be on the stupid *moon.* He doesn't know her address or her phone number or what school she goes to or *anything.* He can't call her and say he's sorry for laughing. He can't tell her how much he wants to be her friend, or how much he needs her help with math. All he can do is stare at the perfect score on the top of his paper and feel like a cheater and a bad friend.

A drop of water hits the paper. He wipes his cheeks, only distantly aware that he's been crying, and puts his hand up.

Miss Lewis pauses and looks at him. "Yes, Roger?"

"Miss Lewis, may I, um." He pauses, cheeks burning. Asking never gets easier, especially not with the rest of the class turning to look at him and giggle, like *they* never have to use the restroom, like *their* bodies are above such things. He's watched the same boys trying to piss a fly out of the air above the urinals during recess, or arguing over who can fart the loudest. He supposes girls probably don't do that sort of thing. But maybe they do. They giggle the same as the boys. "May I go to the bathroom?"

"You may," says Miss Lewis, taking pity. Normally, she'd look at the clock, with its hands standing at fifteen past the hour, and remind him that some things were meant to be done during lunch, when they wouldn't disrupt class time. But Roger has always been a quiet boy, withdrawn from his peers, and he's never done well at math. If he needs time to absorb the reality of his score, she's going to give it to him. There isn't much she can do for the sensitive ones, and so she's happy to do what she can.

Roger slides out of his seat and half-walks, half-staggers to the door, trying to look like he isn't mortified by the eyes on him. He could wait, he knows; he could let the school day end and try this from the safety of his room, probably with a plate of fresh cookies to celebrate his unexpected mathematical victory. His mom bakes the *best* cookies, and for a second, the thought of them—sugary, chocolatey, warm from the oven—is enough to make him feel a little better.

But waiting would be wrong. He knows that too, even if he doesn't have all the words for it yet. "Procrastination" is one of them. So is "malingering." (He got that one from his father last summer, when his parents started using the biggest words they could in an effort to keep him from knowing what they were talking about. It didn't work the way they planned. Roger thinks that's the trouble with grown-ups. The more effort they put into deciding what kids are going to do or think or be, the more things go wrong for them.) He got a smiley face because Dodger helped with his math. Not helped—because Dodger *did* his math. And he laughed at her.

He needs to say sorry. He needs her to know he didn't mean to upset her. So he hurries down the hall, past the classrooms (some with open doors, where students turn to watch him pass and smirk at him for being too stupid to go during lunch, when no one would have said anything about it), past the restrooms, until he reaches the janitor's closet, with its inviting, unlocked door.

Kids aren't supposed to be in here. He knows that. But Mr. Paul ("*Mis*-ter *Paul* who *mops* the *hall!*" as he introduces himself to younger kids, with a quick, jazzy dance step to make them feel better about this hulking, tattooed mountain of a man sharing their space) doesn't mind, as long as Roger doesn't touch anything he shouldn't. Like Miss Lewis, Mr. Paul is aware of the places where Roger is delicate—more aware than Roger himself will be for many years. Mr. Paul knows what can happen to delicate children when adults don't step in to offer a little protection. Turning a blind eye to unauthorized use of the janitor's closet as a hidey-hole may not prevent bullying or bloody noses on the playground, but if there's a chance it'll make things easier, he's fine with it, as long as Roger doesn't start drinking bleach or something.

Roger slips inside, into the cool, citrus-scented air. It's time for Mr. Paul to mop the cafeteria; he won't be back for at least fifteen minutes, which is longer than Roger can stretch a bathroom break, even if he's willing to go back to the classroom and tell Miss Lewis he had to number-two. (The thought is horror incarnate, and the fact that he's willing to entertain it for even a moment makes him giddy with disgust. But he has to apologize, he *has* to.)

"Dodger?" Roger closes his eyes, dimly aware that this is what people do on his cartoons when they're trying to talk to someone who isn't there. That, or they fold their hands and pray, but that would be sacrilegious—one of his favorite words—and he doesn't want to get in trouble with Jesus while he's trying to apologize for being a bad friend. "Can you hear me?"

What happens next is a surprise and a relief. The world goes soft around the edges, and he finds himself looking at a spelling worksheet. There's a hand in his frame of view, clutching a yellow pencil. The fingers are slender, the nails bitten to the quick. The nails are unpolished, and there's no jewelry or adornment. Just freckles, scattered across pale skin like beads across the floor.

"Don't circle that one, it's wrong," he says, as the pencil starts to move. "You want number two. S-U-B-T-L-E."

The hand pauses. Moves down. Circles the correct answer. Dodger doesn't say anything—probably because she's still in her classroom— but her hand keeps moving as he rattles off the answers, circling and circling. Two of the words she circles are wrong. In both cases, it's a simple transposition of letters, and Roger realizes she must do even worse in spelling than he does in math: a perfect paper would get her in trouble for cheating. This way, it just looks like she studied extra hard.

"Gosh, you're smart," he says admiringly. "I never thought of that."

Dodger's hand goes up in the air, ramrod straight, even as she lowers her other shoulder to make her hand look even higher. The teacher, who is not as pretty as Miss Lewis, and doesn't look half so nice, sighs.

"Yes, Miss Cheswich?"

"I'm done with my worksheet may I be excused I have to go." Dodger rattles off the words without hesitation or any sign of embarrassment, even as some of the kids around her put their hands over their mouths to smother their laughter. Roger gapes, his own eyes still closed as he uses hers to watch the classroom. He can't imagine being so brave.

Dodger's teacher looks dubious. She crosses to Dodger's desk and picks up the worksheet. Her eyes go wide as she skims it. Finally, lowering the sheet, she looks at Dodger. "Very good, Miss Cheswich. I'm surprised."

"I studied really hard please can I go to the bathroom?" Dodger squirms to illustrate her point.

"You *may*," says the teacher. "Straight there and straight back. Do not dilly, do not dally, do not stop at the water fountain. I don't want to go through this again in fifteen minutes."

"Thank you Mrs. Butler," says Dodger, still speaking rapid-fire, like she has a personal vendetta against commas. She's out of her seat and out of the room before her teacher can change her mind, moving at a fast walk that doesn't quite break the rules by turning into a run.

Like Roger, she walks past the bathrooms. Unlike Roger, she doesn't stop at the janitor's closet, but keeps going until she comes to the library and lets herself inside. The librarian looks up, sees Dodger, and grimaces sympathetically. She doesn't say anything as the girl heads for the back of the room, where the air is cool and the smell of old books perfumes everything.

Dodger drops to the floor, hugs her knees to her chest, and tucks her head against them, creating a small, private space with the frame of her body. "What are you *doing*?" she demands. "I'm at *school*."

"I know that," he says, even though he hadn't been sure when he'd asked to be excused. "What time is it where you are?"

"Ten," she says. "I have almost the whole day ahead of me, and now I won't be able to go to the bathroom even once. Mrs. Butler is really, really strict about potty breaks." She sounds personally offended by this, like anyone else telling her when she can or can't pee is a crime against nature.

Roger is getting the feeling Dodger doesn't like being told what to do. "I'm sorry," he says. "I didn't know what time it was, and I wanted to say sorry."

There is a pause before Dodger asks carefully, "Sorry for what?"

"For laughing. I could tell it upset you, and I didn't want to upset you. So I'm sorry."

"You're sorry you laughed at me?" Now Dodger sounds puzzled. "Everyone laughs at me, all the time. No one ever says sorry."

"How many of them can talk in your head like this?" Roger grins. His mom always says people can hear it in your voice when you smile. He wants Dodger to hear him smiling. "If they could, I bet they'd say sorry."

"Maybe," she says. Her puzzlement is fading, replaced by caution. "You're really sorry? You won't laugh anymore?"

"I'm really sorry. I might laugh, I guess. Friends laugh at each other, right?"

"I don't know." She changes the subject: "Thanks for helping with my spelling words. I hate spelling. It's stupid and it doesn't make sense. But I have to do it."

"I like spelling," says Roger. "Sometimes whether a word is one thing or something else is all about what order one or two letters are in. I'll help as much as you want, if you'll help with my math."

"It's a deal," says Dodger.

"It was a good idea to get a few of the answers wrong. I didn't think to do that."

Dodger shrugs. "People don't believe things that are too perfect."

There's something important in that statement. Roger will find himself thinking about it later, turning it over and over again in his mind as he tries to find the flaws. For the moment, and knowing time is growing short for both of them, he pushes on, asking, "How did you know you could come talk to me?"

"My dad."

The answer makes no sense. Roger hesitates for a moment before he says, "I don't understand."

"He was having a fight with my mom about why don't I have more friends, is there something wrong with me, should they send me away so I can meet other 'gifted' kids—that's what they say when they don't want to say 'freak'—and she said I needed time, and he said 'that imaginary friend of hers was the only one who ever came for a sleepover.' So later, I asked him what he meant, and he sort of stuttered and stammered and finally said when I was little, I used to talk to this made-up boy called 'Roger' all the time, until one day I stopped. That's how I knew your name. I knew if Roger was real, and I could talk to him, and I could talk to you, that you had to be Roger."

She doesn't need to tell him the rest, because Roger is smart too, as smart as she is, and he can see the gaps in the story. They're . . . familiar. She's lonely. Her brashness is meant to cover that, like his shyness does, but she's lonely. He doesn't remember talking to her when he was littler—but he's accepted the idea of her fast, hasn't he? He was surprised, not frightened, when she started doing his home-work. Like he'd talked to her before, long enough ago that it seemed like something he'd made up, not so long ago that part of him wouldn't always know her as a friend.

She's lonely, and she's one of those kids for whom loneliness has become a sort of fearless propulsion, forcing her forward at an ever-accelerating pace, searching for a way to make the loneliness stop. When her father said she'd had an imaginary friend, one with a name, one she liked well enough to have talked to for a long time, she'd gone looking, just like he had when he'd needed to apologize. And she'd found him. Just like he'd found her.

"Dodger?"

Dodger lifts her head. Through her eyes Roger sees the librarian approaching. The woman is old, maybe even older than his mom, but she looks nice; she has worry-lines around her eyes, and her mouth is painted a soft shade of pink, keeping it from looking too cruel, even when she has to shush people for being loud in the library.

"Are you all right?"

Dodger nods mutely.

"Are you supposed to be in the bathroom?" The question is gentle. Dodger has done this before, then, running away and hiding for a few minutes in a place where no one will expect her to be brash, to be bold, to be anything other than small and frightened and seven years old.

Dodger nods again.

"They're going to think you're sick if you don't go back now, and when your teacher checks the bathroom, she won't find you. I don't want you to get in trouble." Still so gentle, still so careful. Roger guesses people all over the world must use the same tone when they talk to the smart kids, like they were bombs on the edge of going off, instead of children with brains too big for the people they're supposed to be.

"Okay." Dodger gets up, unfolding easily from what had seemed like such a crumpled position. "I'm sorry."

"Don't be sorry, just be all right. You'd tell me if you weren't all right, wouldn't you?"

Of course not. Roger has only known Dodger for a day—maybe longer, if her father is right, if they were friends before, only to lose hold of one another—but he already knows she doesn't tell people things when she doesn't feel she needs to. She keeps her secrets close to her chest. That's how she survives in a world where she's so much smarter than she should be, and so much more delicate than she seems.

"Yes, Ms. McNeil," says Dodger obediently.

"Good. Now get back to class, and if anyone asks, I never saw you."

The librarian smiles. Dodger smiles back, and then she's in motion, heading for her classroom at a brisk walk. Roger is pretty sure she never takes her time getting anywhere.

She pauses at the classroom door and says, in a loud whisper, "It's ten. I get out of school at three. You can call in six hours." Then she opens the door and walks, head high, into a classroom filled with bright, judging eyes.

This is her prison, not his. Roger lets go of his place in her head and falls back into his own, opening his eyes on the dim janitor's closet. He picks himself up, pins and needles shooting through his legs, brushes his jeans off so no one will be able to see where he has been, and lets himself out.

Six hours has never seemed like such a long time. Roger watches the clock, counting the minutes. Ten for her was one for him, and dinner is served at seven thirty; that means he has half an hour in his room before he'll have to go downstairs and tell his parents about his day. He's finished all his homework except the new math worksheet, which is even more complicated than the last one. Worse, because he did so well on one sheet, they're going to expect him to do well on the next one. Maybe not *as* well, but . . .

He knows the words. Cheating, plagiarism, lying, lying, liar. He's not sure plagiarism applies when it's math problems and not words, but he doesn't want to find out; doesn't want Miss Lewis looking at him with disappointment or—worse—revulsion. He needs to do better in math. He needs to keep that look at bay. That means he needs the far-away girl whose name rhymes with his, and he thinks she needs him too, to guide her through the strangeness of spelling and English. They can help each other. They can make each other better.

The clock ticks over to seven. Roger Middleton closes his eyes. "Dodger?" he says.

For a moment, there's no response. Somehow, that isn't a surprise: part of him has been waiting for this to end since the moment it started, and end badly, proving once and for all that there *is* something wrong with him, that his mother has been right to be concerned.

Then someone else's eyes open on someone else's room, and he's looking at a mirror, at a freckle-faced girl with eyes the same unassuming gray as his own. She's wearing a shirt with butterflies on the front, and she's grinning ear to ear, looking relieved and pleased and surprised, all at the same time.

Her hair is red. Her shirt is yellow. Both these things are surprising, and he stares, unable to believe how bright her world is.

"Ta-da!" says Dodger, and Roger is startled out of surprise into laughter, because she learned this trick from him. They're already teaching each other so much. "I thought you'd want to see me."

"Do you ever brush your hair?"

Dodger wrinkles her nose. "Not when I can help it. It's long because my dad says girls should have long hair until they stop looking like boys without it, but I don't like it. I'd cut it all off if they'd let me. It gets caught on things."

"Things?"

"Trees. Blackberry bushes. Other people's fingers." Her expression darkens like a cloud rolling in. Roger has learnt to go unnoticed to avoid the persecution of others. Roger isn't a girl with bright red hair— how is anything so *red*? He's never seen a red like that before—and a passion for math. Going unnoticed was never an option for her: he knows that down to his bones. She had to go in the opposite direction, becoming mercurial and never stopping long enough to be caught.

Still . . . "People pull your hair?" The thought is vaguely horrifying. Girls aren't supposed to have their hair pulled. There's nothing wrong with shoving them if they shove you first, but pulling hair is petty and mean, and it's not supposed to happen.

"If you were a girl, they'd pull your hair too," she says matter-of-factly. "Girl nerds are in even more trouble than boy nerds, because everybody says we don't exist, or if we do exist, it's because we're trying to get the boy nerds to like us. I don't *like* any of the boy nerds in my school. I'm smarter than all of them, so they're mean to me just like everybody else."

Roger nods solemnly, not thinking about the fact that his body is in Massachusetts while hers is in California; she won't see his agreement. But he's experienced what she's talking about. Smart kids get put on a pedestal by parents and teachers alike, and the rest of the class gathers around the base of it throwing rocks, trying to knock them down. People who say "sticks and stones may break my bones, but words will never hurt me" don't understand how words can *be* stones, hard and sharp-edged and dangerous and capable of doing so much more harm than anything physical. If someone chucks a real stone at you on the playground, it leaves a bruise. Bruises heal. Bruises get people in trouble, too; bruises end with detentions for the rock-throwers, with disapproving parents ushered into private offices for serious conversations about bullying and bad behavior.

Words almost never end that way. Words can be whispered bullet-quick when no one's looking, and words don't leave blood or bruises behind. Words disappear without a trace. That's what makes them so powerful. That's what makes them so important.

That's what makes them hurt so much.

Dodger turns away from the mirror, which hangs, he realizes, on the inside of her closet door; the first of the concrete differences between her room and his. The walls are painted a cheerful yellow, almost matching her shirt. His walls are white. They both have rugs on hardwood floors, but where his is plain gray, hers is a riot of butterflies and flowers in bright primary colors, until it almost hurts to look at. He's never seen most of these colors before. He'd be awake all night if he had a rug like that. He wouldn't be able to look away.

(It will be hours before he realizes how *many* of the colors in her room were new to him, or starts to wonder what that means.)

Where his walls are lined with bookshelves crammed with every scrap of paper he's been able to get hold of, hers are lined with taller, deeper shelves packed with plush toys, dolls, and other symbols of a carefree childhood. He wonders whether the adults in her life—she *must* have adults in her life, has mentioned parents, and parents usually come with a range of aunts and uncles and grandparents—have noticed how dusty her toys are, especially compared to the much more carefully stored bins of blocks and tinker toys and geometric wooden shapes. A tower stands in one corner of the room, bright blue blocks piled higher than he thought gravity would allow.

Dodger looks at the tower and smiles, smug. "I figured out how to position the bases for maximum stability," she says. "I think I can get another six or seven layers on before it falls down. I'm going to do it this weekend. I'll call when I'm done, so you can see."

"Okay," says Roger, awed. If he could do that . . . "Um. I got a perfect on my math paper."

"You told me."

"I don't want my teacher to think I cheated."

"You didn't cheat," says Dodger matter-of-factly. She walks to her bed and sits, one foot tucked under her body, the other dangling. Roger is a passenger, not a driver, but he's painfully aware of every move she makes, like someone is writing down every single gesture and reading them off to him, only slightly delayed. "There's nothing in the rules about a voice in your head telling you what the answers are supposed to be. I checked."

"I think the rules think any voices in your head will belong to you," says Roger.

Dodger shrugs. "It's not my fault the rules don't think of everything."

"I guess not." Roger pauses before he says, "If it's not cheating, can you keep helping with my math? Not just doing it. I mean. I like you doing it. But can you make me understand it? I need to be able to do it for myself, too."

"I already said I would, if you can help me with my reading. And my spelling." Dodger wrinkles her nose. "I hate spelling. It doesn't make sense."

"It does, once you know the rules," says Roger. He's almost giddy with relief. This will make everything so much easier, and if she's right—if this isn't cheating—then there's nothing wrong with doing things this way. They can help each other. They can shore up the broken places. He knows the words for this: cooperation, symbiosis, reciprocity. So many words, and he'll teach her all of them, if she'll just keep being his friend.

"Okay," says Dodger, sounding suddenly shy. "Let's do it."

"Okay," says Roger. Then: "I have to go. It's dinnertime. Talk to you later?"

"Okay," says Dodger, for the second time.

In his room in Massachusetts, Roger opens his eyes. His mother is calling him down to dinner. Grasping his math worksheet in one hand, he runs to tell her about his day.


D odger feels the moment Roger's presence leaves her mind the way she'd feel a cotton ball being pulled out of her ear: a sudden absence, creating a space for the world to rush into. She flops backward and closes her eyes, fighting the urge to call his name and push herself into his life the way he'd been riding along on hers. It's hard. In the end, she perseveres. If there's one thing Dodger has a lot of experience with, it's being alone.

Her parents would never call her lonely, if anyone thought to ask them. Sure, she's alone a lot of the time, but she has friends. They're sure of it. Absolutely sure. They'd be horrified if Dodger ever bothered to tell them how wrong they were.

Maybe if she'd been Roger, smart about books and words and spelling and stuff, she could have made friends. Book-smart is okay for girls, as much as any sort of smart is okay for girls. But math-smart isn't the same. Math-smart belongs to skinny boys with glasses and pocket protectors and heads full of science. That's what the books say. That's what the TV says. And that's what her classmates say in a thousand tiny ways, every time she finishes her math book ahead of the rest of them. Even the math-smart boys don't like her, because she's smarter than them, and some things are too much to be borne.

She's learnt to make it look like she doesn't care. She's not class clown—one-liners and comebacks aren't her forte—but she's brassy and loud and she talks like nothing matters. She's been to see the principal for squirming and shouting more than half the boys she knows, which has earned her a certain grudging respect, even though she still sits alone at lunch every day. Her teacher doesn't like her because she's a disruption. The school librarian loves her, though, and lets her hide in the cool dark when she needs to. She'll survive. She knows that. She'll survive, and she'll do it with a smile on her face, because Roger's back. Roger's real, and he's back, and she's not alone anymore.

Her bedroom door opens. She sits up, turning, and there's her mother, a sheet of paper clutched in her hand. She brandishes it. "You know what this is?"

Dodger stiffens. "That's mine," she says. "It was in my bag."

"You left it on the stairs again," says her mother. "I picked it up and this fell out. A ninety? Really?"

"I studied." The lie comes quick and easy. The necessary lies always do. (She'll try for years to explain her dislike of metaphor to Roger, even as they both learn how to pronounce the word correctly: to make him see why lies should be reserved for life-or-death situations, because anything else would make them weaker, and weak things can't save you. She'll always be a better liar than he is. He'll always have a better grasp of metaphor. Some things run too close to the bone to change, no matter how much you want to.)

"You studied? Are you sure?" Her mother's eyes scan her face. Dodger looks guilelessly back, confident her deceptions will go unseen. Sometimes she thinks being adopted is the best thing in the world, because it's made her a better liar where her parents are concerned. All the kids she knows think it's hard to lie to their parents, because their parents can say things like "you have your mother's eyes, and she always squints when she's lying," or "see, that blush means you're not telling me the truth." Dodger doesn't have anyone's eyes but her own, and maybe Roger's . . .

That's just wishful thinking. She doesn't have anyone's eyes but her own, and those eyes are wide and innocent, devoid of anything but childish delight at her own accomplishment.

Finally, her mother yields. Heather Cheswich's retail job is only part-time, starting after she puts Dodger on the school bus and ending early enough to let her beat her daughter home by almost half an hour, but it's still exhausting, and she doesn't have the energy to pursue this any further. "I told you that you could do it if you applied yourself. Didn't I tell you?"

"You told me," agrees Dodger solemnly. "You told me until I listened." She's not being sarcastic. Sarcasm will come later, after the world has kicked her more.

"Your father will be pleased."

Dodger perks up at that. "Is he coming home for dinner?"

Her mother looks at the hopeful expression on her little girl's face and feels herself wither a bit more inside, way down deep, where the light never reaches.

"I don't think he'll be home for dinner tonight, sweetheart; he has a class," Heather says, and Dodger's face falls. Heather forces a smile. "Now why don't you show me that spelling worksheet?"

Dodger does, and time marches on.

# Purple Stars

A re you sure California *has* February?" asks Roger. Dodger is slid-ing down the embankment on the sides of her feet, plunging into the bushes behind her house. She's shredding her shoes; she goes through them five times as fast as he goes through his, even though their parents buy the same brands. Up until a few months ago, they even wore the same size. She's hitting her growth spurts early and hard, and her mother is beginning to look thoughtfully at the shoes in the athletic section, which might stand half a chance of lasting for more than a month.

"The calendar says it does, and calendars don't lie," says Dodger. She grabs at branches as she descends, scraping the skin off her palms. Roger winces in sympathy, feeling the idea of her pain with-out feeling the pain itself. The brief moments of physical synchronic-ity they used to have, where he could feel her tap his shoulder, where she would know if he had a headache, have been fading. He's sort of grateful for that. Some things shouldn't be shared.

Dodger is paler than he is—neither of them goes out in the sun much, but she's turned avoiding it into a game, while he just sighs whenever it comes out from behind the clouds—and her bruises stand out brighter than his ever do. Sometimes she looks like a flower of a girl, drawn in white and purple and healing yellow, all the more striking because those colors only seem to exist in California. She laughs when he tells her to take better care of herself. No one else cares if she takes her skin off, so why should she?

He knows so many words, to describe so many things. His vocabulary has grown immeasurably, aided in a sideways manner by the girl whose head he currently occupies. Once his math scores started rising, his teachers became more understanding of his boredom. They knew how to handle a well-rounded genius in a way they'd never been able to handle a focused one. He's spent the last two years reading whatever he wants, providing he keeps the rest of his grades up. He's taking German, French, and Mandarin. He's learnt so many new concepts, and the words to pin them to the surface of his soul, perpetual and immutable. Without words, some things would slip away, impossible to describe and hence impossible to hold.

He doesn't know how to tell Dodger to take care of herself. She's his best friend, and she knows that, but he doesn't know how to make her understand that when she hurts herself, she's hurting him, too. He doesn't have the phrases to describe the shape of his fear, and so sometimes he doesn't say anything at all. Silence is not a natural state for either of them. It's especially unusual and unsustainable for him, who lives and dies by the word.

Dodger has reached the bottom of the gully. She shoves herself through a gap in the blackberry brambles that was easier to navigate a year ago, even six months ago, before her hips began spreading— not enough to be noticeable until she's trying to wiggle through a hole—and her shirt began taking on a different shape, enough so that Roger no longer watches when she's getting ready for bed, but turns his distant face away. He's always known she was a girl, and that if she lived in Massachusetts, there'd be questions about crushes and childhood puppy love. He doesn't feel that way about her, and she doesn't feel that way about him; he knows that as surely as he knows the color of her hair and the slope of his hands. Not feeling that way about someone doesn't make it right to look.

"You still with me?" she asks, even though she knows the answer. They've each become adept at sensing the presence of the other, and more, at sensing its absence. He stays awake until her bedtime almost every night, so they can fall asleep together, and she wakes when he does, both of them walking through their lives with the constant, immutable sense of *presence* at the back of their minds. Sometimes they have to work to turn it off, to split themselves apart. Still, sometimes she needs reassurance.

"I'm here," says Roger. His alarm is set: he's supposed to go downstairs in half an hour for game night with the family. They're playing Monopoly tonight. He'd crush them all if he let Dodger play, and so he doesn't, because that wouldn't be fair; having a tutor living in his head is one thing, but using her to beat his mother at a board game is something else entirely.

(Melinda Middleton takes her board games very seriously. She plays Candyland the way some people play poker, all close-held cards and thin-lipped frowns. Roger thinks it would be funny, if it wasn't sort of scary.)

"Cool," Dodger says, and sits cross-legged on the ground, backpack in her lap. She unzips it and pulls out her notebook, opening it and looking at the page like she's trying to read it. She's not: she's giving him a chance to see.

The paper is covered in squiggles, mathematical symbols, and a dismaying number of letters. There aren't many numbers. That's the thing with Dodger: she seems to think numbers are irrelevant to the process of doing *math*. What's scarier is she seems to be right. She still helps with his math, but hers has progressed to college level and beyond. Half her local library's reference section is stored under her bed in photocopies that swallow the bulk of her allowance every week. What feels like half *his* local library's reference section is there with it, copied by hand in California as he read it, uncomprehending, in Massachusetts.

"I don't know what that is," he says.

"That's okay. I didn't expect you to." Dodger taps the top of the page, where she's transcribed an equation. She's discovered gel pens recently. Her math papers are a rainbow explosion of figures, symbols, and confusing results. "This is a really famous problem by a man named Monroe. There's a reward for solving it. Like, a lot of money. People have been trying for sixty years, and no one's been able to figure it out."

"And you have?"

"I have." Dodger smiles. For the moment, she is still; for the moment, she's at peace. Roger sometimes feels like he's the only one who gets to see her that way, and he knows how lucky he is to have that, even as he wishes there was someone else she trusted this much. He's very far away. They may never meet. They may not even be in the same world—because once you say "I have a friend who talks in my head, and I'm pretty sure she's real, she knows things I don't know, and I guess that's what real looks like," it's not such a leap to say "I think she's in another dimension"—and if she ever gets really hurt, he's not going to be able to do anything to help her. He can imagine calling the police and trying to make them understand that his imaginary friend who isn't imaginary has fallen and broken her leg. He'd go to the nuthouse so fast that they'd probably leave his shoes behind like in a cartoon.

"Can you tell me the answer?"

"No." There's no rancor in her reply: she knows he wouldn't understand, like he knows she wouldn't understand if he started trying to explain the etymology of the words they're both using. They shore up one another's limits. That means knowing where those limits *are*. "But if I send this in, if I show my work and send this in . . ." Her fingers skitter across the page like water bugs across the surface of the pond, hesitant and proprietary all at once.

"They'd give you the money?"

Dodger's smile turns serene. He can feel it. "They'd have to. I did the work, and the rules say anyone can enter, anyone can do the work and enter. It's a *lot* of money, Roger."

"How much?"

"Ten thousand dollars."

For a moment, Roger is silent, staggered by the size of the figure. Ten thousand dollars is a lot of books, a lot of photocopies; it's the sort of money even adults only dream about. For Dodger, it could mean her own home computer, one of those fancy ones that does math faster than a calculator, even faster than her; it could mean the tools she's shown him in her scientific catalogs, the ones that would let her figure out the way the universe is made.

"I was thinking, if I send it in, and they give me the money . . . I could say you were my pen pal. That we met last year at chess camp. If you sent me a couple letters, it would be a way for me to have your address that wouldn't look weird, you know?" She sounds suddenly shy, like she can't believe she's saying this out loud. "Ten thousand dollars is a *lot* of money. I bet my parents would be okay with spending part of the prize on plane tickets, if it was so I could visit a friend. We could come to Cambridge. Me and my parents. Daddy says the East Coast has a lot of history he'd love to see, and Mom likes anything he likes, and I could meet you. You could meet me. For really real, not just like this."

Roger is silent. Roger is reeling. This is moving so fast, and what if he sends her a letter and it never gets there? They've talked about this before, about the possibility that they're in different dimensions, talking through some sort of wormhole or cosmic hiccup. About the chance that trying to make contact—because it would be easy to pass a phone number or an address along their mental link, it would be so *easy*—would sever that bond and leave them both on their own.

Roger has gotten better at making friends in the past two years. He knows the words they want to hear from him, and he's no longer so scared of rejection, because he knows Dodger will always be there; if the kids in his class say he's not worth their time, that won't render him eternally alone. He's not sure he could hold on to that confidence if he lost her. And Dodger . . .

He's not in her head *all* the time. She has class and baths and stuff, and so does he; sometimes they have to walk solo. But he's never dropped in to find her talking to anyone else about anything that feels like friendship, and when he's asked, she's never been willing to answer. It doesn't feel like she has any friends but him. That's a little scary.

"Roger?" she whispers.

"Are you sure?" He shakes his head. She can't hear it, but he needs to move. If he opens his eyes, he'll lose her. He's had a lot of practice at doing things with his eyes closed. "What if . . . Remember when we were talking about wormholes and stuff? What if that was true?"

"I don't think sending a letter could violate quantum entanglement," she says. "If you send it and it doesn't get here, we'll know we're not in the same dimension, and we don't have to try doing this again. But don't you want to meet me for real?"

He does not. What they have is strange and fragile and it's the best thing in his world, but it's also terrifying and weird. It's not *normal*. Dodger doesn't seem to care whether people think she's normal. Roger does. He likes it when people treat him like everybody else, like he's just a smart kid and not some sort of circus freak. What if meeting her makes their connection go away and suddenly he's a lopsided genius again, taking remedial math classes while he argues with college professors about verb tenses? Or what if it's like on *Star Trek*, where touching somebody who reads minds makes it worse, and they can never turn off the connection between their thoughts again?

He's been quiet too long. Dodger's hand flashes into her frame of vision as she reaches up and wipes her eyes; she's crying. He didn't answer when she asked if he wanted to meet her, and now she's crying. "Dodge—"

"Forget it." She slams the notebook, wrinkling the pages. There are glittering stars drawn on the cover, fidget-constellations marching from margin to margin in silver and purple ink. Somehow that little reminder that she *is* a person when he's not around, that she's *not* an imaginary friend he can take or leave at will, makes it worse. "It was a stupid idea, okay? I'll use the money to go to Disney World or something. Roller coasters are like math you can ride."

"I'm sorry."

"You should go now, Roger. It's family game night, isn't it?" She wipes her eyes again as she stands. "Maybe I can get Dad to play chess with me. You don't like watching that, anyway."

Roger doesn't say anything. He's learned to recognize Dodger's moods: there's no getting through to her when she's this upset, and maybe that's good, because it means he has time to figure out what to say to make her stop crying. It's not that he doesn't care about her— he loves her, the way he assumes he'd love a sister—but sometimes changing things isn't the right thing to do. Sometimes changing things means throwing the whole world out of alignment.

"Well?" she demands.

"I'll come back at bedtime," he says, and opens his eyes on his own bedroom ceiling. The California afternoon is gone, replaced by the snow outside his window and the gray-and-brown wallpaper he picked out for himself the last time his mother decided to redecorate.

Carefully, he sits up, checking his body for tingles and numbness. He's not *out* of his body when he's visiting Dodger, but he's less connected to it than a person is supposed to be. He can forget about it, if he's gone long enough. Sometimes he snaps back into his own skin and discovers he's been lying wrong on his arm for an hour, and then everything buzzes and stings while it's waking up. He's had to bite his lip more than once to keep from whimpering and attracting the attention of his parents. His mom has already expressed concerns that he might be narcoleptic. He's had to plead with her not to have him tested, claiming he just gets headaches sometimes.

(That's not entirely false: he *does* get headaches sometimes, and the school nurse has seen enough of them that she was happy to explain to his parents that no, there's nothing wrong with him, it's just that kids work their brains too hard and make them hurt sometimes. As long as it's nothing worse than the occasional nap in a dark room in the middle of the day, there's nothing for them to worry about. Roger doesn't like the way she looks at him—with pity, like he's halfway to becoming an invalid, like she's trying to protect what remains of his childhood by refusing to refer him to a doctor—but it's kept his parents from probing any deeper, so he supposes he's grateful.)

He's still sitting on the bed, rubbing his elbow with one hand, when the door swings open and his father is there, dressed in khaki slacks and a button-down white shirt, like he came home from the office five minutes ago. "Roger?" he says. "You feeling up to a little game, sport?"

"Yeah, Dad," he says, grinning ear to ear. He slides off the bed, his fight with Dodger already virtually forgotten. He'll remember it later, but sometimes it's best to let his brain work like this, puzzling over the problem in the background while he gets on with the business of living. It'll be okay. It always is. He and Dodger have fought before, and it's always been okay. So why should this time be any different?

Dodger sits at the kitchen table with her notebook in front of her, trying to make her parents understand. Her frustration is obvious in the red tips of her ears and the high, bright color in her cheeks; no matter how much she explains, there will always be concepts she doesn't have the words for, ideas she doesn't know how to express. She wishes Roger were here to feed her what she needs, and she hates herself for being weak enough to need him, and she hates him for being gone.

Her father picks up the notebook, frowning. He hasn't looked at any of her "independent study" in years; while he's happy to stick her schoolwork to the fridge like any proud parent, this isn't math anymore. This is poetry written in a language he doesn't know, and something about it makes him feel unnecessary and small, like she's gone on to decode the universe without him.

"You're sure you didn't copy this out of a book at the library?" he asks, for the third time. "We're not going to be angry. It's not like there's anything wrong with copying things for your own use. It's only wrong if you pretend you created them."

Dodger, thinking of the reams of copier paper beneath her bed, sits up straighter and shakes her head. "No, Daddy," she says. "I didn't copy it. Only the equation at the top, in the purple ink. That's the puzzle Mr. Monroe's institute has been trying to solve, and I solved it. It's my work, for real. I can come to the school and do it again while one of the math professors watches, if you want." She doesn't really understand the difference between teachers and professors, except that professors know so much more than teachers. Professors are like wizards: they create the universe. Having her work checked by one of *them* isn't insulting, like it is when Mr. Blackmore does it. He doesn't think girls are good at math. When he checks her work, it's because he knows, all the way to his toes, that she cheated. A professor wouldn't know that, wouldn't even *think* that. A professor would be neutral.

(And to be honest, somewhere deep, deep down, she harbors the fantasy that if a real professor saw her work, they'd gasp and cry, "This girl is a genius!" and pull her out of elementary school to put her in college, where she could do all the math she wanted, and no one would whisper about her behind their hands or throw things at her "accidentally" during lunch and recess, or make fun of her name, or tell her girls weren't supposed to be more interested in decimals than dolls. All she has to do is find a way into one of those classrooms, and her future can finally begin.)

"You say there's a monetary prize?" The idea of paid academic challenges is nothing new to Peter Cheswich, who has never left academia; he's seen manna from heaven a time or two, usually as a result of a translation project or the successful unraveling of an ancient riddle. He's never looked at the math side of things, but math isn't his forte. The scribbles in his daughter's notebook (in purple ink, no less!) might as well be cuneiform.

And yet.

And yet he knows enough to know she's smarter than he'll ever be, especially where things like this are concerned. They're comfortable—between his classes and Heather's work at the store, they don't want for money—but "comfortable" isn't the same as "wealthy," and this prize of hers could make a world of difference.

Dodger nods so vigorously that it looks like her head is in danger of popping clean off. "Ten thousand dollars," she says. Suddenly shy, she continues, "I was thinking maybe we could take a family trip to Cambridge."

"Why Cambridge?" asks Heather.

"My pen pal lives there," says Dodger. She's still the best liar in her household: she sounds utterly sincere. "It could be fun to go and meet him."

Heather and Peter exchange a look. Their nine-year-old daughter is talking about flying across the country to meet a boy, and somehow the only thing either of them can feel is relief. There's someone in the world Dodger wants to meet. Someone who isn't a famous mathematician or a children's science host. Although . . .

"How old is your pen pal?" asks Peter. They try to keep a tight leash on her activities, but she's slippery when she wants to be. She could easily have started writing to some retired mathematician outside of Harvard and be trying to trick her parents into taking her to meet him. Dodger is young enough that he doesn't worry about people trying to take advantage of her in the ways young girls are taken advantage of—although he's aware that she's a beautiful child, and the day will come when he has to add another layer of paranoia to his daily fears—but that doesn't mean he's all right with her corresponding with adults who haven't been approved.

"Nine," she says. "Same as me." She and Roger have the same birthday, even, like they have the same eyes. Mathematically, they were always meant to be friends, two halves of the same equation, designed to complement one another. She doesn't say that part. There's getting your own way and there's getting *in* your own way. She's better at the second than she is at the first, but she's learning, oh, yes. She's learning.

"*If* I can get one of my colleagues to look over your work, and *if* it qualifies for this prize, we can discuss it," says Peter finally. "Assuming you won this prize, most of it would need to go toward your college fund." Being his daughter, her tuition will be covered if she goes to Stanford. There are still other expenses to consider, books and papers and the like, and that assumes she's going to live at home, skipping housing costs. Raising a smart child is expensive in ways he could never have considered when he was a young man hoping for a family of his own.

But it comes with its own rewards. Dodger lights up, smiling like a sunrise. "I can meet with one of the professors to talk about math? I can really?"

"If I can set it up," says Peter. His mind is already racing, considering and rejecting names. He needs someone he can trust to take Dodger seriously, despite her age; someone who'll look at her work for what it is and not let their preconceptions of what a nine-year-old girl is capable of color their reactions. He closes her notebook. "May I take this?"

Dodger wants to tell him *no;* wants to explain that she needs it to sleep at night. All she does is bite her lip and nod.

Peter smiles. "I'm impressed, baby girl, even if you don't win this prize. Do you want to play a game of chess?"

"I'll set up the board," she says, and she's out of her chair and already running for the pieces, running for a future filled with professors and prizes, where she'll be able to finally meet Roger, and he'll understand that they were always meant to be best friends, forever.

That night she goes to bed and falls asleep almost immediately. She never hears Roger trying to make contact. She's already too far away.

# Isolation

It's nine-thirty in the morning. Dodger is supposed to be in school, but her father got her out with a note and an apology, and here she is walking alongside him, falling into another world. She feels awkward and small in her starched cotton dress and pale pink sweater. This isn't her: this isn't how she dresses, or how she stands, or anything. She's a creature of jeans and blouses with capped sleeves, sneakers and T-shirts and shredded knees. This is the sort of thing she wears when her grandparents come on Easter to take her to church, even down to the pinching patent leather shoes. It feels like a costume. It feels like she's being put on display.

In a weird way, she's grateful for the discomfort, because it blunts the force of her awe. Her father is leading her through the halls of Stanford, his hand grasping hers, and she's been here before—she's been visiting him at work since she was a baby—she knows these halls and this campus like it belongs to her, but she's never been here for *official business*. She's here to *show her work* to a real mathematician, which is even better than showing it to Batman. So, while she hates that she has to do it in a dress, hates that she can't look like herself while she's trying to prove she's as good as she thinks she is, she's also glad for the distraction. It's keeping her hands from shaking quite so hard.

"Now remember what we talked about, Dodger," says her father. "Answer any questions he asks, but only the questions he asks. Don't start babbling about things he doesn't care about."

"Yes, Daddy."

"He may ask you to do some math on his blackboard. If he does, it's all right for you to do it. He just wants to see that this isn't a trick."

If Professor Vernon asks her to do math on his real college blackboard, she thinks she'll probably die right on the spot. They'll bury her with a smile on her face, and maybe they'll be glad she got to go out that way. At least they'll know for sure she died happy. "Yes, Daddy."

"No backtalk, and don't ask about his own work unless he invites you to."

"Yes, Daddy," she says, and then they're there, they're really *there*, at the door of a classroom where a man who looks like her grandpa is waiting, smiling the tolerant smile of an adult who's about to see a child do a very impressive trick. Her feet suddenly feel like they're made out of lead, but she forces them to keep moving her forward, into the classroom, into the future.

W ell?" asks Peter.

Professor Vernon shakes his head. He is an aging ostrich of a man, tall and spindly, with limbs that seem too long for his body. He's seen many things in this classroom, geniuses and fools and people who don't care about math and people who love it like it's the only language in the world. He's done his best to teach them all, to offer each of them the support that they need. He's never seen anything like this.

"She's solving the problems correctly," he says. "She's not referencing a cheat sheet or getting tripped up by things she hasn't seen before. I think her answer to number three may be wrong, but I'll be honest: I'd have to pull out a textbook to be sure. If you say that's her work on the Monroe equation, I believe you. She's solved it." He shakes his head. "I never thought I'd see the day. You need to get this girl into advanced classes."

"She's already in advanced classes."

"Then you need to get her into *more* advanced classes. She needs tutors, access to books . . . She's a genius, Peter. A mind like hers comes along once a generation, if that. You say she found out about the prize money on her own?"

"She solved the problem before she told us about the prize," says Peter. "The only thing she wants to do with her share of the money is go to Cambridge to see a pen pal. I'm just relieved she isn't asking for a pony."

Professor Vernon is quiet for a moment before he asks, "Cambridge? Really?"

"Mmm-hmm. She says she met him last summer when we sent her to chess camp. We're inclined to say yes. Dodger doesn't make friends easily with children her own age. This could be good for her." What Peter doesn't say—doesn't need to say—is that any pen pal of hers is likely to have the same problems. There's little to be lost by bringing these children together, and there could be a great deal to be gained.

Dodger has finished the problems Professor Vernon left for her. She turns, chalk in hand, chalk dust on her nose, cheeks glowing with exertion and pride. "Do you wanna check my work?" she asks.

"I suppose I should," says Professor Vernon, and walks over to look at the figures she's written, perfectly mapping a small slice of eternity.

Later, after Peter and his daughter have left, Professor Vernon stands looking at the board. The girl's better than he'd expected her to be at this age. He's been waiting years for this call—for the announcement that Dodger has done something out of proportion with her supposed grade level—but he never thought it would be something this momentous, or this fortuitous. If Peter hadn't slipped and mentioned the pen pal . . .

No matter. The boy was mentioned. Because Professor Vernon doesn't need a name to know who Dodger has been corresponding with, or that no letters have ever passed between them. The Doctrine will seek itself. That's been true of every iteration, even the ones that failed and have been mercifully retired from the program. The Middleton boy and the Cheswich girl sought each other once before, and then, only the presence of a babysitter loyal to Reed had allowed them to intervene before it was too late.

The Congress is watching. The Congress is always watching. They know Reed's program is in the wind, loose and wild and evolving: they'll seize it for their own if given the chance. The children are too young to be entangling their lives in this way. They need to finish maturing. They need to learn how much they owe the man who made them.

The girl is committed, body and soul, to whatever course of action she chooses: she's not the weak link. He must admit that he doesn't want her to be. She has a remarkable mind. He wants to spend some time in the safe harbor of her good regard before Reed calls her back to the Impossible City to become a pet. He became an alchemist because he wanted power; he became a mathematician because of his love for the subject. The chance to study with the girl who will one day *be* the laws of mathematics is too tempting to be set aside. But the boy . . .

Anyone can learn to read the dictionary. At this stage, his half of the Doctrine is little more than an eidetic memory and a love for the written word. He can be leveraged. He can be used to stop this before it goes too far; before they come together on their own. Yes.

Professor Vernon is only protecting the Cheswich girl, really. Contact with the Middleton boy at this delicate stage of her development would only drag her down to his level. She needs the freedom to soar.

His course of action thus set and justified to himself, Professor Vernon tears his eyes away from the blackboard. It's time to make a phone call.

# Telephone Wire

I see," says Reed. "Yes, your loyalty is noted; yes, I will consider allowing you to tutor the girl. Thank you for your dedication."

He drops the phone back into the cradle without waiting for the man on the other end to finish babbling his gratitude and terror. Vernon had not expected Reed himself to answer the phone, had expected to deliver his terrible discovery to some apprentice, or better, to some technician. Moments like this are precisely *why* Reed makes it a point to be the one on the other end of the line whenever possible. Nothing terrifies an underling like being confronted with someone who can actually *hurt* them.

Rage pounds in his temples; fear, unwanted and unfamiliar, thunders in his chest. He grips the side of the desk, head bowed, waiting for the moment to pass.

There is a flicker of motion out of the corner of his eye. He looks up. A child stands there, older than his cuckoos, but not by much, no, not by much. One day, he'll be able to pass her off as their peer.

She is dressed in a shapeless gown of flowered cotton, and her hair is strawberry blonde, a color that belongs in a bottle, not on a body. She watches him with solemn, frightened eyes. He terrifies the child: he knows that. That, alone, is enough to clear his panic away, at least partially. He terrifies her and yet here she is, looking at him, waiting.

"What is it?" he asks.

"Something's broken," she says, in a voice like a wounded animal, all hurt and dismay. "Something's not right."

Of course. The girl is from Leigh's little project, a minor incarnation of a simple, controllable force. She's not the first to carry that mantle. He doubts she'll be the last. "What's broken, child?" he asks.

She raises a trembling hand and points to the wall. He frowns—and then freezes as understanding strikes.

The astrolabe is on the other side.

"It spins and spins and spins, but it never gets where it wants to go," she says. "It *hurts*. It isn't supposed to be like this."

"No, it isn't," he agrees. Then, carefully, he asks, "Do you know how to fix it?"

Her mouth opens. Closes again. Finally, she shakes her head, and says, "It's too big. I can't see where the break ends."

"But it *can* be fixed."

This time she nods.

Reed smiles. "Come here, girl." He holds out his hand.

Her fear is a beacon, a radiant light that almost hurts to behold, but she comes to him obediently enough, folding her fingers around his own. "Where are we going?" she asks.

"To see your maker. I have a task for her."

He leaves the lab and the girl walks silently by his side, her bare feet making no sound on the tile. She's a charming little thing, if half-feral—Leigh lacks the simple social graces necessary for childrearing, is too easily distracted by the latest bit of mastery or mayhem to catch her magpie eye. Perhaps it's time for him to take more of a role in the lives of these minor incarnations. Having the living personification of Order itself walking beside him could be pleasant when she's older, when her creator has finally come to the end of her usefulness.

There's something pleasant and poetic about the idea of Leigh engineering her own successor.

Yes. This is something to consider.

Leigh is in her own lab, measuring alkahest into a tungsten flask held by a sullen-looking dark-haired boy whose every motion seems to be the precursor to escape. The girl pulls her hand out of Reed's when she sees her counterpart, drifting across the room to stand quietly beside him, watching the precious, flesh-eating liquid transfer drop by drop from one vessel to another. Reed says nothing. There is a hierarchy to be observed, but alkahest cares little for who is or is not in charge. It will devour the worthy and the unworthy alike.

The only sign that Leigh has noticed his presence is a slight tensing of her shoulders. She finishes the task at hand, setting the container of alkahest gingerly back on the shelf before claiming the flask from the boy.

"Erin, Darren, both of you, run along," she says. Their names are an imperfect rhyme, ever so slightly out of true, and this, too, is intentional: Chaos could not tolerate perfection. She finally glances at Reed. "I have work to do, and children will just be in the way."

The girl—Erin—grabs her counterpart's hand, and they're off, running from the dangerous adults with every scrap of strength and self-preservation their tiny bodies can contain.

Reed lifts an eyebrow. "Keeping them from me?"

"They're not mature yet. Erin is useful, but Darren . . . he fights me. I can use him for tasks that could turn fatal, because he's afraid of leaving her. Anything else, he'll make a mess." Leigh sets the flask into its cradle. "Why are you here?"

The matter of the cuckoos is urgent. Still, he has another question. "They're paired but they're not linked, correct?"

"They're distinct embodiments. Order can survive without Chaos. It just won't be happy." Her eyes narrow. "Why?"

"Would the girl mature more quickly if the boy were removed?"

Leigh hesitates before she says, "Perhaps. Why?"

"I want her useful. Sooner rather than later."

"It will be done. Now. Why are you here?"

"The third set of cuckoos has made contact again." Reed raises a hand as Leigh opens her mouth to protest. "It's confirmed. Professor Vernon reported it, and he's been waiting years for the girl to start manifesting her potential. He wouldn't sound a false alarm."

Leigh scowls. "What do you want me to do?"

"Fix it. Before the Congress notices them entangling across a continent, and we lose this pair to meddling old fools who don't know when to keep their hands to themselves."

"You'll have to deal with them sooner or later."

Cuckoos or Congress, it doesn't matter: her words apply equally to both. "Yes, I will. But for now, I need you to break the contact. Break it thoroughly enough that they won't think to try again until we're ready for them."

"Can I break *them*?"

Splitting them apart may do precisely that. It's a risk Reed is prepared to take. "Only if you must. Start with the Middleton boy. His parents will make sure he toes the line, once they understand what's at stake. If that doesn't work, you can go to see the girl."

"Your will be done," says Leigh, bowing her head.

"When you get back, I want to discuss—Darren was his name?"

Her nod is a study in resentment.

"Excellent. He may be ready for retirement." The girl who can measure the motion of the astrolabe without laying eyes on it—he wants her ready.

He's going to have use for her.


There are ways to travel quickly, when one has power, and purpose, and the willingness to damage the world to achieve one's goals. Ohio to Massachusetts should be a longer journey, and yet when Roger comes home from school not two hours later, he finds his parents in the living room, *both* his parents, sitting with sorrowful expressions on their faces and coffee mugs cupped in their hands. The smell of coffee is almost overwhelming. (Later in life, when his own molars are coffee-stained and his hands feel empty without a mug in them, part of him will remember that this is where it started; this is where coffee became a symbol for adulthood and authority to be conquered and claimed as his own. But that is very far away from the timid, trembling *now*.)

The third person in the room is a stranger, a woman too pretty to be real, her hair styled short and swept back, so that she looks less like a kindly librarian and more like a school counselor, someone whose job it is to explain why you can't have what you think you want—that really, you didn't want it in the first place. She's wearing a sensible pantsuit and sensible pearls, and he has never been so afraid of someone he didn't know before.

"Roger." His mother half-rises, only to be pressed back down to the couch by his father's hand. Her face is pinched and drawn; she looks like she's been crying.

Roger's heart seizes in his chest. He's young: panic is a foreign thing to him. Fear, yes, but panic is supposed to be reserved for years from now, when he's lost his elasticity of thought. "Is it Grandpa?" he asks, voice trembling. "Did he have another stroke?" Roger loves his grandparents. They live in faraway Florida (but not the part with Disney World, which sort of seems like a waste of grandparents in Florida to him), and he only sees them twice a year, but he loves them with the sort of bright, single-focus love that could consume the world, if he let it.

"No, son," says his father, and gestures toward the one remaining chair in the room—*not* toward the remaining slice of couch, where Roger would be pressed against his mother's hip, safe from anything that might hope to harm him. "Sit down."

Roger's heart seizes again, leaving him dizzy. Maybe this is what dying feels like. Maybe he's the one having the stroke, and they'll be sorry they scared him so bad when he collapses and stops breathing and his lips turn blue and they realize they had a son, they had one, but now he's gone, and all because they scared him.

His legs are numb as he walks across the room and sits. He doesn't know what to do with his hands. They're suddenly awkward, taking up too much space at the ends of his arms. He finally folds them in his lap, looking from face to face, waiting for someone to tell him what's going on.

"Roger, this is Dr. Barrow," says his mother, glancing at the woman with the sensible hair. She grimaces, just a little. The doctor probably doesn't see it; the doctor doesn't know Melinda Middleton the way Roger does. He's made a lifelong study of his mother's face, and he can see that she's disgusted, even as he can see that she's afraid. "Dr. Barrow is here because she received a disturbing phone call from your school nurse. Our agreement with the adoption agency where we . . . where we got you means that any time there's a question about your situation, she gets to come discuss it with us."

"For your safety," says Dr. Barrow, in a voice like butter and cyanide. (He knows that voice *he knows it,* somewhere deep down, deeper than memory, and he's afraid.) She turns to Roger, smiling a small, concerned smile that doesn't come anywhere near her eyes. "Hello, Roger. It's nice to meet you."

"Hello," he says automatically, manners overriding confusion. He watches her warily, waiting for the other shoe to drop. His parents are terrified, he's sure of that now. His mother is brave. His father is the bravest man he knows. For them to be this scared something must be genuinely wrong.

"Roger, do you understand that you were adopted?"

"Yes."

"Did your parents ever talk to you about the circumstances of your adoption?"

"No."

"Please don't be concerned that I'm here to take you back to your birth mother—that's never going to happen. But when you were placed here, there were some conditions. One is that if we ever found evidence that your mental health was suffering, we'd have to remove you from the home and find you a new one." Dr. Barrow continues to look at him with false compassion, her own hands occupied with cupping her mug. His parents are pressed together, virtually shaking. "Roger, we received a very worrisome phone call. Your school nurse says you've been talking to yourself. Not playing pretend—all children do that—but really *talking* to yourself, like you were carrying on a conversation with someone who wasn't there. Do you want to tell me about it?"

Terror crashes down on him, hot and fast and utterly consuming. He doesn't want to be taken away, has never known this was something that could happen. He's happy here, with his family and his things and his familiar little world. If he lies, she'll be able to prove it: someone at school must have seen him talking to Dodger. A lie paints this woman as in the right, and puts his family in danger. The less appealing option is the only one that remains.

"I wasn't talking to myself," he says, and sees his father relax, just a little—enough to make him sure he's doing the right thing. He focuses on Dr. Barrow and says triumphantly, "I was talking to my friend Dodger. She lives in California, and we communicate via quantum entanglement. That's why I can talk inside her head and she can talk inside mine."

His mother gasps and buries her face against his father's shoulder. Dr. Barrow's expression becomes one of understanding and, more worryingly, pity.

"Oh, Roger, sweetie," she says. "I wish you'd said something sooner. I wish you'd told someone about this delusion. The adults in your life have only ever wanted to take care of you."

"Please," moans his mother, raising her head. "Please, we didn't know, he didn't show any signs, please. We'll get him the help he needs. We'll make sure this stops. Just don't take our little boy away from us, please."

"Mom?" says Roger. His voice is a squeak.

"There will have to be tests," says Dr. Barrow. "A brief hospitalization may be necessary. We'll want to avoid medicating him long-term if we possibly can; a brilliant mind like his shouldn't be subject to the sort of side effects that come with antipsychotic drugs."

There is another moan. Roger realizes, with surprise and dismay, that it came from his father.

"But if Roger is willing to work with us to recant his delusions, I don't believe removal from the home would be in the child's best interests." Dr. Barrow's eyes are sharp and glittering as she turns her attention back to Roger. "Well, Roger? Which is more important to you? A little girl who doesn't exist, or your family?"

"I don't want to go!" He will never remember moving, but he moves; he shoots across the room like an arrow, wedging himself between the bodies of his parents, clinging to them harder than he's ever clung to anything in his life. This is where he belongs, this is *home,* and yes, he loves Dodger, she's his best friend, but a best friend isn't worth a family. She'll see that. She'll understand. The numbers don't add up.

He turns a tear-streaked face to Dr. Barrow. "My family. My family is more important than anything in the world. Whatever you need me to do, I'll do. She's not real, she's just a g-game I play that got too big for me, I'm sorry, I'm sorry, I won't talk to her ever again, I'm sorry. Don't make me go."

Dr. Barrow smiles.

# Refuse Me

Reed is waiting when Leigh returns, still dressed in that ridiculous suit she put on to go and put the fear of God—the fear of him—into the Middleton boy. "Well?" he demands.

"It's done," she says. She stops in the middle of the hallway, looking at him. "He won't make contact again. He's too afraid. We should have pulled him from that household. Brought him back here. *Broken* him. They still have potential as a pair—so damn much potential, if they've figured out how to access the improbable road without us telling them how—but they need guidance. They need to be *controlled*."

"It sounds like you're questioning me, Leigh. You know what happens when you question me."

Leigh scowls, radiating frustration. "These are *children*, Reed. Messy. Unpredictable. They need to be brought to heel." She was never a child. The individual women who are her foundations were, but their childhoods are the filmy memories of ghosts, and carry little weight with the creature they have been combined to become. "You want to have sway over my children. Why can't I have some input on yours?"

"You have only what I allow you to have, Leigh. No more and no less." Reed's voice is cool. "Those children were never yours in anything but name."

"I—" Leigh takes a step back. She recognizes danger when she blunders into it. "My mistake. I misspoke."

"Good girl." He smiles, quick as a knife. "As to my cuckoos: right now, they're too real. We need them to cross the border into fiction. We need them to become more than they are. Only then will they find the improbable road and lead us to the Impossible City. Don't you want to go to the Impossible City?"

Leigh looks hurt. "Of course I do."

"The Impossible City will only become manifest if we restore Baker's definitions," says Reed. His tone is patient. His eyes are not. "She told this country what to be in alchemical terms when there was no one strong enough to argue with her, and she roused the whole damn Council against her. Baum, Lovecraft, Twain, they broke themselves against the tide to rewrite her definitions, but they did it. We can't go against that much belief. The world won't change unless we have a bigger lever."

"We could do this without—"

"No." The word is a wall. She runs against it and can go no further. Reed walks toward her. "We can't do this without the Impossible City. It is the key. We take it, we make it our own, or we take the country knowing there's a weakness in our defenses the size of a canyon. We *must* hold the City, or all this is for naught, and to take the City, we *must* change the rules. We need the Doctrine. Everything else we've done . . . we can be rich, we can be powerful, we can be immortal, but without the Impossible City, we can never be gods. Don't you want to be a god?"

Leigh Barrow—perhaps the last person in creation who should have a divinity's power, who should be allowed to set reality's rules—sighs. "Yes."

"Then leave them. Trust me."

"I need to hurt something."

Reed cocks his head. "Then hurt something."

Leigh smiles.

# Checkmate

It was supposed to be a big deal when the Academic Decathlon team got tickets to watch a bunch of grandmasters play chess. It was presented like a real treat, a sporting event for smart people, and skipping it was out of the question. Roger doesn't even *like* chess—too many numbers, too much focus on pattern-recognition—but he likes his teammates, and he *really* likes Alison O'Neil, who does science and plays chess and sometimes smiles at him out of one corner of her mouth with her eyes dipped low, like she has a secret. Alison has been excited about the exhibition since their advisor said they might get to go, and if Alison's excited about it, he supposes he can find a little enthusiasm.

Roger Middleton is fourteen years old—will be in two weeks, anyway, and that's basically the same thing—and sometime in the past eighteen months, girls have changed. Or maybe he's changed. He knows the words, puberty, hormones, metamorphosis, but the words can't contain the raw excitement he feels when Alison touches the back of his hand, or when he catches the scent of her shampoo. Everything is changing. He guesses he's okay with that.

Their seats are near the front, in an area set aside for local middle school and high school geniuses who might be inspired by watching a bunch of people push pieces around a chessboard for a couple of hours. It's a circular arena, like a football stadium but smaller, and the organizers have wisely put up four matches at a time, each with their own sector of the arena and their own announcers to explain the game. A game is wrapping up as they sit, an older Chinese man against a younger Latino boy. The man moves a piece. The announcer calls "checkmate," and the two shake hands before they vacate, leaving their board to be reset by the event attendants.

"Wow," says Roger. "Bad timing."

Alison wrinkles her nose at him. "Are you kidding? We get to see a whole new game. We're so *lucky*!"

Then she hugs his arm, and there's no way Roger would even dream of disagreeing.

The attendants prep the table before vanishing, clearing the way for the next set of players. One is a white man about the age of their teacher, gawky in his corduroy pants and red bow tie. Order of play must have been decided at the beginning of the event: he sits at the black side of the board.

His opponent is a teenage girl with skin the color of bone china, hair cut in a pageboy bob that frames her face without getting in her eyes. She looks like she hasn't seen the sun in a year. She wears what looks like the uniform of some unnamed private school: a gray pleated skirt, a white blouse, a short blue tie. Her shoes are patent leather, and squeak when she walks.

Roger is aware that he's staring, aware that he shouldn't be, but he can't stop himself. He knows her. He watches Dodger—the girl he turned his back on five years ago—take her seat on the white side of the board. She hits the clock and moves her first piece, and the match begins.

He knows Alison is talking, but for the first time since he realized she was beautiful, he doesn't hear a word she's saying. All his attention is on the girl, her hands moving too fast to follow whenever it's her turn. He'd be an inch or so taller than her if they were both standing (*when did that happen*, he thinks wildly, remembering a perspective that switched to a dizzying height when he looked at the world through her eyes; the thought is followed by another, despairing: *how much did I miss*), and his shoulders are broader than hers, but they still look surprisingly alike. They have the same eyes. He doesn't know much about chess, but he knows enough to see that she's good, she's genuinely good; this exhibition game is for masters, and she's playing a man more than twice her age into a corner, her pieces chasing his relentlessly across the board. She plays like her life depends on it, remorseless and cold, and her expression never changes. She never smiles, not even when she stops playing and starts winning.

Their game takes half the time of the other three. When Dodger's opponent cedes and stands to offer his hand, she takes it, shaking with her eyes still trained on the board, like she's looking for the mistakes she knows are there, the ones that will let her play the game faster, clearer, more flawlessly. She never looks at the audience.

Roger is suddenly aware of Alison's hand on his elbow. He glances toward her, and sees that she's staring at Dodger, cold venom in her eyes.

"Like the game?" she asks.

"Yeah," he says, and offers a smile, hoping it looks sincere enough to be believed, not sure what else he's supposed to do. Dodger isn't real. Dodger was never real. He knows that, just like he knows thinking anything else could ruin everything. "You want to teach me to play?"

And Alison is suddenly all smiles again, and everything is going to be all right.

When he glances back to the arena, Dodger is gone.

That's for the best, all things considered. It's time for him to get on with his life.

They had been walking for some time—long enough for Avery's shoes to become scuffed at the toes, and for Zib to have climbed and fallen out of three different trees—when Quartz waved them to a halt. The crystal man's formerly jocular face was set into a scowl.

"What," he asked, "do you think you're doing?"

"We're walking to the Impossible City, so the Queen of Wands will send us home," said Avery, and frowned, because that sentence should have made no sense at all.

"No, you're not," said Quartz. "To get to the Impossible City, you need to walk the improbable road."

"But we are!" protested Zib.

"You're *not*," said Quartz. "Everything you've done has been completely plain and probable. If you want to walk the improbable road, you need to find it."

Avery and Zib exchanged a look. This was going to be more difficult than they had expected . . .

—From *Over the Woodward Wall*,
by A. Deborah Baker

# BOOK VII

# The End of

*Yet this my comfort; when your words are done,*
*My woes end likewise with the evening sun.*
　　　　　—William Shakespeare, *The Comedy of Errors*

Chess is life.

　　　　　　　　　—Bobby Fischer

# Deed

There's so much blood.

Dodger hasn't moved in almost a minute, her hand outstretched like she's going to resume using her own blood to sketch numbers on the crumbling brick, an expression of quiet resignation on her face. She's breathing, but barely, and those breaths are slowing, weakening, becoming less reality and more hopeful thinking.

He should finish the equation she was writing when she fell, should show her work and bring it to a close, but he can't. She stopped explaining the math to him when they were nine years old, when he was convinced to give her up by hollow threats and lies that could never have become reality. He's a genius. He knows all the words—prodigy, polyglot, natural—but his genius and hers were never the same, and he can't understand the symbols that spiraled from her unmoving fingers.

They've lost. They didn't even know they were playing a game, and still, they've lost. They lost a childhood together, they lost the balance they could have provided one another, and now they're going to lose their lives, all because he doesn't know how to finish the figures surrounding them, red drying into brown as his sister's chest rises in shallower and shallower arcs, winding down toward eternity. He can't keep them on the improbable road. Not alone. Neither of them could ever have made this journey alone.

When she stops breathing, his own heart will follow hers into the dark. He knows that as surely as he's ever known anything, as surely as he knows the difference between myth and miracle, between legend and lie. It's almost over.

The gunfire continues outside, and it's not like it is in the movies, it's not loud and dramatic. It's a whisper in a thunderstorm, and that whisper is going to be enough to kill them. Erin's gun speaks periodically through the din, and either her silencer isn't as good or she's just not using one, because he hears every shot she fires.

He hears when her gunshots stop.

This is it, then: this is the end. They've lost, it's over. Erin is dead and Dodger is bleeding to death and he's never going to reach the Impossible City, and he's never going home. This is where they stop. He fumbles for his sister, gathers her in his arms, not caring how much damage he does in the process of pulling her as close as she always should have been. It's not like he can kill her. She's already dead. She just doesn't know it yet.

"Dodger. Hey, Dodge. I need you to wake up. I need you to help me stop the bleeding."

Her eyes stay closed. Only the shallow rise and fall of her chest betrays the fact that she's still with him.

There's so much blood.

"Come on, Dodge. Leaving isn't a competition. You don't have to get me back like this." His own injuries aren't as bad as hers. One bullet to the side of the head, taking out a chunk of his ear. It bled like nobody's business, but there were no arteries involved; if it weren't for the fact that he can feel her impending death looming over him like a shadow, he'd expect to recover. He won't. "You can't. You can't go. I just got you back again. Are you listening? You can't go. I need you."

Her eyes stay closed. There's so much blood.

*When you can't win the game, knock over the board.* He doesn't remember who said that. Maybe it was his first girlfriend, Alison, with her equal passions for chess and for picking fights over the smallest things. Maybe it was someone else. It doesn't matter, because they've been working toward this since the beginning. This is the only way. Her chest is barely moving, and there's so much blood, there's *so much blood,* and it doesn't matter that he knows the words. The words are what's going to take her away.

"I can't do this alone. I'm sorry. I can't."

He leans in until his lips almost touch the curve of her ear, exposed by the short sweep of her blood-soaked hair. He doesn't lean close enough to get her blood on his face. One of them should die as close to clean as possible.

"Dodger," he whispers. "Don't die. This is an order. This is a command. This is an adjuration. Do whatever you have to do, break whatever you have to break, but *don't you die.* This is an order. This is—"

This is her eyelids fluttering but not quite finding the strength to open, lashes matted to her cheeks by a gluey mixture of blood and tears.

This is the sound of gunfire going silent outside. Not tapering off; just *stopping,* like the world has been muted.

This is the world going white.

This is the end.

*We got it wrong we got it wrong we got it wrong we got it wrong we*

The owl looked at Avery and Zib. Avery and Zib looked at the owl. It was difficult not to notice how long the owl's talons were, or how sharp its beak was, or how wide and orange its eyes were. Looking directly at them was like trying to have a staring contest with the whole of Halloween.

Privately, Avery guessed that the owl did not give away licorice or candy apples on Halloween night. Dead stoats and stitches were much more likely.

"You are very loud," said the owl finally. "If you must spend the whole day fighting, could you do it under someone else's tree?" The owl had a soft and pleasant voice, like a nanny. Zib and Avery blinked in unison, bemused.

"I didn't know owls could talk," said Zib.

"Of course owls can talk," said the owl. "Everything can talk. It's simply a matter of learning how best to listen."

—From *Over the Woodward Wall,*
by A. Deborah Baker

BOOK II

# Reset

No physical theory of local hidden variables can ever repro-
duce all of the predictions of quantum mechanics.

—Bell's Theorem

The call was coming from inside the house.

—Urban legend (traditional)

# Checkmate

Dodger plays chess the way she used to slide down the gully behind her house: hard and fast and like she's afraid any loss of momentum could prove fatal. Every move is an attack. When she isn't touching the pieces, she sits frozen, barely seeming to breathe, a predatory halt that bears no resemblance to actual calm. She is a marble statue masquerading as a girl, coming alive only when the rules of the game allow.

Her opponent moves; she responds, swift and unflinching as a master debater arguing some unprovable point. The fact that they play for a crowd doesn't matter. (Neither does the fact that her coach has asked her—virtually *begged* her—to slow down, to draw out her moves and give the rubes something worth watching. "If they wanted to see something flashy, they should have gone to the aquarium" has been her reply every time the subject has come up. She's as unwavering in her answers as she is in her ruthless, results-based style of play. She'll never be a rock star, but at least she'll fade into obsolescence with a trophy in each hand. That's good enough for her.) Winning is the only thing that matters.

Winning is something she can do without anyone to help her.

The last piece is moved; her opponent tips over his king, signaling her victory. She finally lifts her eyes to his, holding out her hand for the ritual, perfunctory handshake. Someone in the crowd—the great, faceless beast of the crowd—shifts positions, and somehow, her attention is caught.

Training conquers distraction: she shakes her opponent's hand, fingers cool and nerveless, before she pulls away from him and does the unthinkable. Dodger Cheswich, who once did three games back to back while suffering from food poisoning so bad that she excused herself between moves to vomit, who has another game to prepare for, who has never, during the six long weeks of this tour, which he's heard her call "geniuses on parade" without a hint of irony in her voice, paid attention to anything but the board . . . Dodger Cheswich is walking away.

It's hardly more of a surprise when she breaks into a run. After all, she's already broken script; what's a little more deviation?

She runs, eyes fixed on a teenage boy with slightly too-long brown hair and a faint tan underscored with years upon years of freckles. His glasses are too large for his face; they make him look like a confused cartoon owl, someone trotted into the episode long enough to dispense wisdom before being carted off again. He's wearing a T-shirt with a Shakespeare quotation on it, blue jeans, and the possessive hand of the blonde girl next to him. Everything about the blonde screams "back off, he's mine," and if Dodger were the one who got the words, she'd find a way to explain that she doesn't want him, not like *that,* not ever. But she doesn't have the words, and she's never going to have the words. What she has is numbers, probabilities, a whole universe of potential in her head—and those probabilities tell her the odds are a million to one against her being right.

It's not him. *It's not him.* It's someone who *looks* like him, or like she thinks he'd look if she saw him now, five long years after he decided to stop answering when she tried to call. She knows it's not him, and still she doesn't slow until she hits the edge of the arena hard enough to knock the wind out of herself, fingers locking around the low bar that's supposed to keep kids from falling in and landing on the ice skaters, or circus acrobats, or whatever other show is on display *this* week. When it isn't chess, which she figures has to be most of the time.

He stands. He takes a step toward her.

She opens her mouth. She wants to say his name. She wants to scream it, to pack it with five years of sleepless nights, five years of struggling to be the best at everything, since it was her fault he went quiet. She can't make a sound. No matter how hard she tries, she can't even squeak. All she can do is stare, hoping he'll know her silence for the screaming it is.

"Dodger." He sounds half-strangled, like speech hurts him as much as silence is hurting her. He stands, the blonde still grasping his elbow, and when he shrugs her off, she goes without fighting, a slow and petulant frown growing on her face. Dodger doesn't know her, but she's met her all the same, the one smart girl in the classroom full of smart boys—and it's not that girls are less likely to be smart, no, it's that girls are more likely to be encouraged to *hide* it—who's as poorly socialized as the rest of them, and doesn't know how to handle another girl showing up on *her* territory. Dodger has met her a hundred times, and only the fact that she's never cared about who gets the boys has kept her from *becoming* that iconic girl. There's never been time. Math takes up too much of the world for that.

She clings to the railing, staring at the boy who said her name. *Of course he knows me,* she thinks, scolding herself in silence. *They* announced *me at the start of the match, they announce me at the start of every match, stupid, stupid*—

"Dodger," he says again, and steps into the aisle. His legs are shaking and his face is going white; he looks, in fact, like he's on the verge of fainting.

The rail is too high for Dodger to climb, but she tries, stretching onto the tips of her toes and grabbing for the top like she's going to haul herself into the bleachers. Her defeated opponent is still behind her, staring, and he's not alone anymore; several other players have joined him, all gaping at the spectacle of Dodger Cheswich, the Un-smiling Girl, hurting herself trying to get to an unprepossessing teen-age boy who looks like he's seen a ghost.

She's started to make a noise, a high, thin keening sound, like a coyote with its leg caught in a trap. It's enough to set teeth on edge. She doesn't seem to realize.

Roger realizes. "Dodger!" he finally shouts, and breaks into a run, his limbs moving in the sort of uncoordinated avalanche of bone that haunts boys between the ages of thirteen and thirty. Dodger is still trying to climb the arena's edge when he reaches her, leans over the rail, and grabs her hands in a motion so abrupt that there's no time for either of them to think better of it. He's just there, holding her fast, and she's staring up at him, eyes wide and stunned and filled with the sort of loneliness that should be criminal. *Is* criminal in the tribunals of the soul, where the innocent are punished alongside the guilty.

"It's you," she sighs, breaking the seal on her voice. Getting louder with each word, she continues, "It's *you*, Roger, it's *you* what are you *doing* here did you know it was me did you come to see me play I'm sorry whatever I did I'm sorry I didn't mean to I won't do it ever again if you'll just—"

"Stop," he says. His voice is sorrow and apology in equal measure, and she stops immediately, looking up at him with those big, sad eyes. She'll have bruises on her toes in the morning, from balancing on them for so long in shoes that were never intended for this sort of abuse. In the moment, she doesn't care. Nothing is going to make her care.

Roger laughs unsteadily. "Wow," he says. "You got really tall."

Dodger blinks. Then, somehow, somewhere, she finds a smile and offers it to him. "I think you're taller now," she says. "You finally caught up."

"That happens."

The blonde has recovered her shock and come trotting down the steps to appear at Roger's shoulder. She looks at Dodger, assess-ing. She's scoping out the competition. The fact that she has to hurts

Dodger's heart, as does the obliviousness on Roger's face. He doesn't see the signs girls pass between themselves, and that makes her wonder whether boys have a secret language of their own, something she's never seen and maybe never will.

*If it's a language, he'll learn it,* she thinks fiercely, and she's never had a truer thought in her life.

"Hi," says the blonde, interposing herself into the conversation. "I'm Alison. How do you and Roger know each other?" Her hand returns to his arm, resting lightly just above the wrist. If she's not his girlfriend already, she will be by tomorrow.

Dodger wants to be happy for her, and for him; Roger will enjoy having a girlfriend. She remembers him talking about girls in the confused tone of someone who craves something but can't even start to explain why he'd want it. She remembers how much that aggravated him; he liked having a definition for everything, even back then. At least now he knows he *wants* a girl, and here's a girl volunteering for the position. It may have taken another girl showing up—"the competition," despite the fact that Dodger is anything but—to make her see it, but that doesn't change the fact that she'll probably be good for him. Roger is too smart to like a girl who wouldn't be good for him.

"We were pen pals when we were kids," she says, and the lie is so easy that it might as well be the truth, because it's not like there's a word for what they were to one another. He was the voice in her head, the reason she learned to read for meaning as well as for superficial content, her best friend and the thing that kept her sane.

He was the first person who ever broke her heart, and that was an important lesson, too. It had taken Roger to teach her the world was cruel, and that was something she'd very much needed to learn.

"Yeah," says Roger, picking up her cue. He was always good at that. This is the first time she's seen it from the outside: the way his nostrils flare slightly as he decides which way he's going to jump, the particular set to his shoulders before he tells a lie. He's an open book, written in a language few people can read. She supposes she should feel privileged to be one of them. All she's really managing to feel is tired. "We, um, we were pen pals. For years. Until we just . . . lost touch, I guess."

She wants to scream at him, to remind him that he's the one who went silent, leaving her alone in a world that was too loud and too sharp and too unforgiving. She doesn't. She drops to the flats of her feet, the motion yanking her fingers away from his. There's no shock when their connection is broken, any more than there was a shock when it began. They were touching. Now they're not. Linear time may be many things, but it's not sympathetic about things like this.

"Did you come on purpose?" she asks. "To see me play?"

To her shame and delight (because why would she have thought that? Even for a second, why would she have thought that? But if he didn't come on purpose, she doesn't have to let her anger go: the math says she can keep it, if she still wants it), Roger shakes his head. "No. Our class got tickets, and they were good for extra credit, and Alison plays chess."

"Oh." Dodger shifts her attention to the blonde—to Alison—allowing herself, for one brutal, self-indulgent second, to look at the other girl the way the other girl is looking at her. As an opponent; as the competition in a game that society has been priming them for since they were born, no matter how little they want to play.

Alison will play a defensive game, she decides, loath to sacrifice pieces even when it would serve the greater good. Checkmate in ten moves or less. Not worth the time it would take to humiliate her. The thought is cold, and Dodger is ashamed of it even as it finishes forming.

She smiles, and she thinks it's as good a smile as any she's ever worn. She doesn't think too deeply about that; about why her false smiles and her real ones look the same. "Wow. I guess we just got lucky. It's nice to meet you, Alison."

"Nice to meet you, too," says Alison grudgingly, taking advantage of the introduction to slide her arm through Roger's, making her claim even more apparent. "I don't think I've ever met anybody named 'Dodger' before."

"My dad teaches American history," says Dodger, with the shrug she's perfected for moments like this, when people comment on her name and she has no idea what to say. That isn't where her name comes from: it was a condition of her adoption, lain down by a birth mother she's never known and rarely wonders about. The woman who gave her life also gave her up. As far as Dodger's concerned, that's something people are only allowed to do once.

And Roger's already done it.

She straightens, still smiling her false, practiced smile. "It was good to see you, Roger. I hope you enjoyed the game, and you both get lots of extra credit for coming. We're supposed to play again in an hour, so I'd better go get ready."

Roger watches helplessly as she turns and walks away, head held high and stiff. He's losing her again, he knows he is, and he doesn't know how to make her *stop*. Not without saying things in front of Alison that would make him sound crazy at best, and like some sort of weirdo ex-boyfriend at worst. He doesn't want either of those things.

He also doesn't want Dodger to go.

So he closes his eyes and fumbles in the dark behind them until he finds a door he hasn't looked for in years—a door he stopped looking for when his family was threatened. But he's fourteen now, not nine; he knows more about how the world works, he's read more books on adoption law and contracts, because it impacts his life, and he wanted to *understand*. No matter what contract his parents may have signed, there's no judge in the world who'd take him away from them for the crime of speaking to someone, especially not when she's standing *right there*. She's real, she's really and truly real, and that means he's not crazy to talk to her, and if he's not crazy, then there's nothing wrong with acknowledging her existence.

He "knocks." She doesn't open the door. She doesn't let him in. And so he shoves as hard as he can. He pushes his way through.

Maybe it's quantum entanglement and maybe it's not, but the door opens under the questing fingers of his mental hands, and the world appears in vivid color, showing him the arena from a floor-level view. The angle of Dodger's eyesight is wrong enough to be jarring. That makes him feel even worse. He'd be accustomed to her perspective if he hadn't broken contact, like he used to be accustomed to seeing the world from a higher point of view, when they were younger and their heights were reversed.

(He's also profoundly, disturbingly color-blind, something he didn't understand when he was younger and might never have noticed if not for the fact that she *isn't*: when he looks through her eyes, the world has a thousand shades that aren't normally there, and he resents her a little for getting colors when he doesn't, even as he hungrily matches them to names that were previously academic, ideas that had no anchor on the world.)

"Please don't go," he whispers, as softly as he can, and his voice in her mind is as loud and clear as it ever was.

Dodger stumbles. She doesn't fall: her shock is enough to short out her coordination, but not enough to kill it completely. She stops walking, back still to the audience, and asks, "Why not? You did. I think it's my turn."

"Because I'm sorry and I shouldn't have done it, and please. Don't go."

"I have to. I need to play another game. We're in the same time zone tonight; call me at nine." And she's walking again, moving faster now, like she's trying to get away from something that may or may not pursue.

Roger doesn't want to be the thing that chases her. He pulls back, opens his own eyes, and watches, from his familiar point of view, as she disappears through the door at the back of the arena. Alison is tugging on his arm. He turns, and the way she's looking at him makes him realize things have changed; introducing another girl into the mix made her start looking at him the way he's been looking at her for ages. Part of him wants to be overjoyed. The rest of him is muddled and confused, not sure how to cope with the speed at which everything is shifting around him.

"You want to get a soda?" he asks, and is rewarded by her smile blossoming like a flower, and maybe everything isn't so complicated after all.

\* \* \*

Dodger plays three more games that day, and she wins them all, although two of them are closer than she likes: after the third, when they're packing their things, the event organizer comes over to thank her for making things more interesting for the audience. Dodger, who can see the mathematical possibilities of the game spreading out in front of her with every move, who might as well have a map in hand every time she picks up a pawn, says nothing. She can't toy with her opponents the way they want her to, and she can't be distracted every time she sits down to play; neither would be fair, either to her or to the people she plays against. When she's at the table, she needs to know the people she's challenging will fight her with everything they have. Anything less would be cruel.

(This is her first chess tour. She signed up for the college credit, and because her father promised she could audit one of Professor Vernon's courses if she did something extracurricular this semester. She loves Professor Vernon. He's been a mentor to her, and she thinks losing Roger would have broken her even worse than it did if she hadn't been able to run to Professor Vernon for support. This is also her last chess tour. She could be a darling of the sort of people who enjoy these things, the little girl who never smiles as she annihilates her opponents, but there would be no joy in it for her, and without the joy, she doesn't understand the point. Chess is meant to be something sacred, not a party trick to be trotted out and used to entertain people who'd be just as happy to watch a seal balance a ball on the tip of its nose.)

That night, she returns to the hotel. As the youngest, she has a room of her own, with a connecting door to the room where the tour chaperone sleeps. For the first couple of stops, she'd been required to leave that door propped open, so the chaperone could see she was in her bed and not off getting into trouble. Pleading difficulty falling asleep and showing no inclination to leave her room after curfew has earned her a few privileges, chief among them a door that can actually be closed, giving her the privacy she needs.

Carefully, she removes her performance clothes and trades them for flannel pajama pants and a faded *Jurassic Park* T-shirt. Dinosaurs are okay, but in the grand scheme of things, she wears the shirt in honor of Dr. Ian Malcolm, fictional mathematician slash rock star and focus of more than a few confusing teenage dreams. She's worn this shirt so much that the seams are fraying. It's not attractive, not the sort of thing she should be wearing to invite a boy into her room, much less into her *head*. But it's comfortable. It's comforting. Right here, right now, that's what matters.

She wants to be angry. Wants to pull back and let him have it with both barrels, as her dad always says; wants him to understand how badly he hurt her, that she's not the sort of girl who forgives on a moment's notice. She can't do any of those things. As badly as he hurt her, as badly as she's still hurting, she missed him twice as much. She doesn't have the words for what she's feeling—and there was a time when, if she needed a word, she would have reached for Roger, trusting him to supply the missing piece. For the last five years, she's been muddling through this alone. So has he, but math is easier to avoid than words are. Words are everywhere. Words *hurt*.

Carefully, she stretches out on her bed, eyes closed, hands folded across her stomach. She feels like she's measuring herself for her own coffin. That should make her uncomfortable. Right here, right now, it's a set of simple parameters that makes everything better. Six feet by three feet by two feet; the dimensions of the world. Breathe in, breathe out, fill the world. Let everything else fall away. Let everything else go.

She's been lying there for a while (*seventeen minutes, thirty-one seconds*) when the world shifts, a new weight appearing behind her eyes.

"You're late," she says. It's not "hello," but it's the only thing she feels: he's late. He's seventeen minutes and five years late, and she's been alone too long.

"I had to say I had a headache to explain why I was going to bed early," says Roger. He sounds apologetic.

Dodger relaxes, and hates herself for doing it. She wants so badly to be angry with him, and all she can feel is that damned *relief,* like she's the lucky one because he chose to come back, after being the one who chose to go away in the first place. She wants to yell, to rage, to shut him out and see how he likes it. She doesn't do any of those things. They would all be bad math, creating equations her heart might not survive.

"I didn't just mean tonight," she says, and her voice is a whisper, her voice is a shadow of the anger she wants it to contain. She sounds small, and lost, and alone.

Roger sighs. "I'm sorry."

"Why did you leave me?"

"They said . . . this psychologist came to my house and said people at school had seen me talking to myself. She said if something was wrong with me, the contract my parents signed during my adoption meant she could take me away and place me with another family."

Dodger frowns. "You *believed* her? Roger, that's *stupid.* Adoption doesn't work like that. Why would they want to take the broken kids back? It's hard enough to find homes for the ones who *aren't* broken."

She hears him sigh again. When he speaks, he sounds beaten-down, and for the first time, she realizes she's not the only one who's been alone for the last five years. "I know that now. I read a lot of law books, and there's no way that sort of contract could be binding, even if it was real—which I don't know. My parents seemed to think it was. They were wrong, but I guess when you're a parent, sometimes impossible things can be scary anyway, and they were so scared of that woman, Dodge, and it was my fault; I was the reason she could come into our house and scare them like that. I was *nine.* I made the wrong choice. I'm sorry."

"I didn't sleep for three months."

The admission is so simple, so unornamented, that Roger stops, examining it, looking for the key to open it up and force it to make sense. The key isn't there. He's not accustomed to words not making sense. "What do you mean?"

"Just what I said. I didn't sleep for three months, because I was waiting for you to stop being mad and try to talk again, and I didn't want to miss you." Dodger's tone turns distant. "I couldn't be in bed or I'd start to drift off, so I'd sit at my desk with tacks to hit against my thumbs, so the pain would keep me up. My parents caught on after a month, when I started seeing things. They begged me to sleep. They finally took me to the doctor and got these pills that were supposed to knock me out. It took them another month to realize I was spitting the pills out, and a month after *that* for them to stop me from hurting myself to stay awake. I'd pretty much given up by then. I was just staying awake because I'd forgotten what it was like to sleep. Because I thought I had to have done something to make you go away. I thought I deserved it."

"Dodger, I'm sorry. That wasn't . . . I didn't . . . They threatened my *family*." Roger is out of the habit of speaking quietly to himself: it takes too much effort to keep his voice from peaking on the final word. "They said they'd take me away. You were my best friend. You're the best friend I've ever had. But you would have done the same thing if they'd come after your family. You would have had to."

"No, I wouldn't," she says. "I would have *lied*. I would have said 'oh, that was a game, I didn't know it was bothering anyone,' and I would have promised not to do it anymore, and I would have been more careful. I would have told them it was over, and I would have kept going, because you were important to me. I was supposed to be important to you, too. That's what you always said. So I would have lied for you, because that's better than leaving you alone."

Roger is silent.

"That's what you did, Roger. You left me alone. You left me with no one to . . . to explain things, or to tell me everything was going to be all right. You said we'd be friends forever and I believed you. I don't believe anyone about anything, but I believed *you,* and you left me alone. You decided *for* me that I didn't deserve to be your friend anymore. Maybe it's selfish to be mad at you, because you were scared about your family and we were little and you thought I was stronger than I was. I don't know. I don't care. You left me. I can't forgive you for that, no matter how much you want me to. No matter how much I want to do it."

Dodger stops talking. Tears burn her eyes, turning her vision blurry. What Roger can see of the room is smeared and out of focus, like a badly done watercolor painting. It seems so unreal. This began with a girl he used to think didn't really exist speaking inside his head; maybe it's right that it seems unreal now. Maybe this was always the way it had to be.

"I'm sorry," he says. "I don't have any words but those ones. I did what I thought I had to do. I know I was wrong. I can't get those years back. Time doesn't work that way."

Dodger has a vague idea that time *could* work that way, if she figured out how to twist the numbers. More and more, she's starting to feel like time is an intricate puzzle box, and she has the key hidden somewhere in the space between breath and heartbeat, as much a part of her body as blood and bone and marrow. She doesn't say anything. It's her turn to be silent, to see what Roger is going to say. She's made her speech, and she's exhausted. Words were never—will never be—her forte.

"But you weren't the only one who was hurting, and you're not the only one who got punished when I shut the door. I left you alone. I left me alone, too."

Dodger knows that isn't true, has seen the evidence: the girl with the possessive hand and dubious eyes, holding Roger's elbow like she might lose him if she loosened her grip. There's no point in saying that, though. It would look like self-pity if she admitted how there's never been anyone in the world who looked at her like that girl looked at him—if she tried to explain how much time she's spent by herself, trapped and trembling on the borders of her own life.

And it doesn't matter. He's said sorry. He's invoked the magic of apology. Dodger closes her eyes, leaving them both in blackness.

"Okay," she says. "But don't do it again."

On the other side of the city, Roger smiles.

"Cross my heart and hope to die," he says, and everything is going to be all right.

# Calibration

M aster Daniels. What a pleasant surprise."

This is not a pleasant surprise. This is a danger, a disaster, a calamity in all senses of the word. Reed holds himself perfectly straight, perfectly still, blocking as much of the entrance to the compound with his narrow frame as he possibly can. He has often wished that Asphodel had taken the time to build him a body with more heft: he is tall and slim and attractive to the eye, but none of these are things that get a man taken seriously in the presence of other men. If the alchemists accompanying Master Daniels wish to move him, he will be moved.

(Leigh could stop them. Leigh is small, swift, and utterly deadly when he needs her to be, striking like the scalpel her creator used in piecing her together. But Leigh is inside, deep in the lab, securing the experiments these men must not see, locking the doors they must not be allowed to open. They were never intended to come here. They were never meant to find this place.)

"Is it, James?" Master Daniels's voice is gentle, and weary. He dislikes being here, in this Ohio cornfield, surrounded by the emerald of the harvest, beneath the sapphire sky. He is a creature of sepia-toned rooms weighed down with the import of the things that have been done within them. "It seems to me you've been keeping secrets, out here in the hinterlands. It seems to me that we should have been keeping a closer eye. We have allowed you to do yourself harm, and for that, you have my sincere apologies. It was our responsibility to do better by you. We owed it to you, and to Asphodel."

"Master Baker."

For the first time, Master Daniels looks confused. "I'm sorry?"

"On your lips, in your mouth, her name was Master Baker. She was the greatest alchemist of her age. There has been no greater since."

The alchemists who have accompanied Master Daniels—Reed doesn't know their names, doesn't care to know them; they serve no purpose in his grand design—look first amused, and then offended. One of them steps forward.

"Remember your place," the man snaps. "We have allowed you back within our number, but that does not give you the right to lie."

"I tell no lies. I only speak the golden truth, which you have struggled for so long to transmute into basest lead." Reed looks at Daniels with murder in his eyes. "If you must speak of her, speak of her with the respect she deserves."

"She was never a master of our order, James," says Daniels gently.

"Because you forbade her that position. Because *you*, and the men like you, dismantled as much of her design as you could, all before you'd admit that a woman had bested you at your own ambition! Because you—"

"You killed her," says Daniels.

Reed stops.

"If we have any culpability in this matter, if we bear any blame for her death, it's that when she created you, we allowed it. Transmutation of the dead into the living has always come more easily to the female of the species. She proved nothing with your assembly, save that she was, in the end, exactly what we had always assumed her to be. Talented, yes. Gifted, there can be no doubt. But she was a dabbler. She never swam far enough from shore to understand the dangers of the depths." Daniels smiles. Perhaps he thinks he's being kind. Perhaps he considers this a form of absolution. *You killed your maker and your master, but see, you were always her superior. She could only have held you back.*

Reed grinds his teeth until his molars ache, and wonders what it will sound like when Daniels dies.

"You were the knife. She honed you with her own hand. A strangely elaborate form of suicide, but suicide all the same. A failing of her kind."

"And what kind would that be?" asks Reed, in a voice like a rusty saw being drawn across bone.

"The weak. The wanting." Master Daniels's eyes flash. "But we're not here to discuss *Miss* Baker, however much you try to bait us. We're here to talk about you. Have you been keeping secrets, Reed?"

"I told you I had embodied the Doctrine. We're merely waiting for it to mature."

"Yet you won't allow us to examine it. Why is that?"

"The conditions for proper maturation—"

"We understand delicate work. We're men of science, in our own way. We can be trusted around your experiment."

Master Daniels takes a step forward, the other two flanking him.

"Let us in, Reed. We are all on the same path to enlightenment."

But they're not, they're not. Reed left the path to enlightenment behind long ago. The improbable road is different. The Impossible City is not enlightenment, but something more, for the enlightened have no need for power, and the City is power incarnate. Whoever holds the City will hold the world.

"I did not invite you to my sanctum," he says. "Leave, and I will forgive this trespass."

"I cannot, child," says Master Daniels.

"Then I am sorry," says Reed, and raises his hand in a beckoning gesture. A boy steps out of the corn.

He is slim, skinny even, with dark hair and mistrustful eyes. His arms hang by his sides, loose and gangly. He is, perhaps, at most, nineteen years old.

"What is this?" asks Master Daniels, suspicious. "I wasn't informed you were taking an apprentice."

"Darren," says Reed calmly, "kill them all."

The boy nods, and lunges.

What follows would be comic, were it not so dreadfully serious. The first alchemist pulls something from inside his coat, a vial filled with a terrible smoke that writhes like a living thing. He throws it, but somehow the boy is no longer there, somehow the boy has stepped to the side and the vial is in his hand, ready to fling back at its maker with a terrible swiftness. The vial breaks when it strikes the man's chest, and the smoke is loose, the smoke is devouring the flesh from his bones as he screams and screams and—

The second alchemist looks in horror at his compatriot, who has fallen to his knees, hands clawing at his diminishing face. It is a pause that lasts only a few seconds. A few seconds is long enough. Darren is upon him, a knife suddenly in his hand, and the alchemist's throat is an open book, spread wide, spilling its contents onto the ground.

Reed has not moved. Master Daniels has not moved.

Darren pivots, launching himself at Master Daniels with knife held high, ready to end this. The old man produces a handful of dust from his pocket and flings it at the boy, catching him in the eyes. Darren cries out, falls back, collapses. He does not rise again.

"You shame me," says Master Daniels, turning back to Reed.

But Reed is gone.

There is time only for realization and resignation before the spike of hardened silver is shoved through the old man's heart from behind, before his wizened body goes limp and he falls, silent, to join the others. Reed alone remains standing, panting slightly, blood on his hands.

There is something like regret in his eyes as he looks at Darren. This was not intended. Apologies will have to be made to Leigh, excuses given to his counterpart. Still. The girl was ready for better things, and the boy was only ever made to be a killer.

"There are more in your order who are loyal to me than you could ever know," he tells the corpse of the man who would deny him his birthright. "The plane that would have carried you home will crash. Such a mystery. Such a shame. They'll never know where your body fell, and you will be forgotten."

There is no greater curse he can utter. Satisfied, he turns and walks to the shed which offers access to his domain. He enters, and descends.

The air is cooler beneath the ground, scented with cleaning products in place of corn. Reed relaxes. This is his Kingdom, this underground warren of labs and cells and strange alchemic altars. Here, he has already won.

"Well?" Leigh demands, emerging from a darkened doorway like a bad dream. "Is it done? I need Darren. Erin's having some sort of attack, and only he can calm her down."

Years of practice enable him to look at her without flinching. It's best never to show fear when dealing with someone like Leigh. She can sense it. She does not forgive it. She would consume him if she thought she could, a snake swallowing the sun. She is his own private Fenris, ready to bring about the end of the world, and he loves and fears her in equal measure.

He could never have come this far without her, and they both know it. Asphodel gave him the education and the map to follow, but he lacks the raw power of someone like Leigh Barrow, who was assembled to channel the strength of a star.

She looks at him and stills, face clouding over like the sky before a storm. "Where is he?"

"He was an excellent piece of work," he says. "You should be proud."

Her face darkens further. "You *broke* him," she accuses.

"He killed two apprentices nearing their mastery before Daniels took him down, and even in dying, he provided me with the opening I needed. Truly an impressive showing."

Leigh hesitates, anger over the misuse of her property warring with her pride. Finally, she scowls and says, "There's been a development with your cuckoos. Two sets on the same day. If that's not synergy, I don't know what is."

Reed's heart leaps. For the cuckoos to show progress on this day, when a barrier to his progress has fallen before him . . . "Which ones?"

"The middle pair, Seth and Beth; the youngest, Roger and Dodger." Her nose wrinkles as she says their names. Leigh has her idiosyncrasies: her hatred of the rhyming names assigned to the cuckoo children is the least of them.

"What happened to the middle subjects?"

"There was an accident." Her voice remains level, but her eyes are filled with silent fury. "Beth—the control—convinced her family to take a vacation to Disney World. It was a ruse, of course."

"Of course," agrees Reed. They were the Earth and Air children. Beth had been placed with a family in Saskatchewan; Seth had been placed with a family in Key West. If she'd convinced her adoptive parents to take her to Florida, it was because the two somehow made contact. They were trying to come together.

"It looks like it really *was* an accident. Her father was driving the rental car, he was overly tired from the flight, and he lost control of the vehicle. They spun out and smashed up not half a mile from the Happiest Place on Earth." Leigh smiles, a bitter grimace of an expression that shares as much with joy as it does with cold and righteous fury. "Beth was killed on impact. Seth had an aneurism in the middle of a presentation to his school's academic review board. They were accusing the poor kid of plagiarism. He was dead before he hit the floor."

"And the bodies?" The question is sharp enough that even Leigh notices, and calms herself.

"Already on their way here," she says, a bit more softly. "The girl is pretty messed up, but we should be able to get a decent amount of tissue for analysis. The boy is basically intact, except for the bleed in his brain. At least now we know for sure that if you kill half a pair, you stand a good chance of killing the other half. That'll make things a lot easier on our snipers in a few years." She pauses before adding,

"Erin's current condition makes more sense now. She wasn't as tightly linked to her counterpart. She'll likely survive."

"You said there was news about the youngest pair as well."

"Roger Middleton and Dodger Cheswich. Yes. They've restored contact."

Silence falls. It's not the soft, pleasant silence that stretches between friends, or even the wire-tight silence that stretches between enemies. This is a silence with teeth and claws, ready to strike and destroy its prey. This silence *hurts*.

Slowly, Reed asks, "What do you mean, they've restored contact?"

"The Cheswich girl has been doing that chess tournament thing. It had a stop in Boston. The Middleton boy wound up going to see her play. They were seen speaking after the game. She looked upset."

"And him?"

"He looked . . . You ever seen the look on a kid's face right after they've seen their puppy reduced to beef stew in the middle of the highway? Like they can't process what's happening, so they're going to be sort of shell-shocked and sad until someone tells them how they're supposed to feel? He looked like that. He looked just this side of busted." Leigh shakes her head. "He's their control, and he can't even handle a little accidental encounter with his imaginary friend. We should scrub them both and start over with something hardier. Something we raise under lab conditions. My subjects—"

"Are not under discussion," says Reed sharply. "Was that all? Did they arrange to meet again? Were they seen in one another's company?"

"No. The girl walked away. The boy left with another girl—pretty thing, completely natural, not tailored at all; we could modify her to suit our needs, if we started now—who didn't look happy about him speaking to Miss Cheswich. Teenage boys being what they are, the situation has probably already sorted itself out."

"You're talking about the only pair of nestmates to have established independent connection without physical contact," says Reed. "They found each other through sheer loneliness and need. Do you know what a huge leap forward that is?"

"I don't care what kind of leap forward it is," says Leigh. "It wasn't part of the project outline. It isn't safe, it isn't right, and it isn't necessary to the successful manifestation of the Doctrine. This isn't something we planned for. We don't control it. We should be treating them as rogues. We should be reacting to this encounter with full censure."

There's no question of what "full censure" would represent: with Leigh, there is never any chance of half-measures. She would take their child cuckoos apart if he allowed it, reducing them to component atoms, hunting the place where lead becomes gold, where flesh becomes cosmic principle of the universe. Reed looks at her coolly. He will not tell her *no*, not in so many words, because Leigh is rarely fully wrong; she understands the deep threads of the project as few others do, himself included. The scales of human mercy do not cloud her eyes.

He will also not accede to her requests. They've spent too much time already, devoted too many resources, to cut themselves short when they are so blissfully close to victory. Unless the project has become an active danger, it will continue. The road to the Impossible City has always welcomed accidental travelers. Sometimes he suspects that's the only way to truly get there at all.

"How are they embracing their aspects?"

Leigh looks at him with sullen hatred in her eyes, and does not speak.

Reed sighs. Sometimes it's sadly necessary to remind her of what she is, what he is, and why she is here. "You could be replaced, Leigh. It would be a dire loss, and I'd miss you, but you could be replaced."

"The boy speaks seven languages, and he's been asking for more lessons," says Leigh, eyes still burning hate. "His soft palate has remained flexible; there don't seem to be any sounds he can't make. He hasn't realized yet how unusual that is, or what a freak of nature it makes him. Maybe he never will. It depends on how long he remains operational. The girl plays chess at a grandmaster level. She could make a career of it, but she doesn't care enough; she'd rather be doing pure mathematics. Probably will, once her parents stop pushing her to have a normal life. As if that were ever going to be possible." There's a venom in Leigh's voice that can't be explained by any of the things she's said, something deep and cold and brutally cruel.

Reed says nothing. He looks at her, and he waits.

The wait is not a long one. "They're not good work," she finally explodes. "The boy could be a *king* by now—he can make anyone do anything by snapping his fingers and telling them what he wants, and what does he do? Academic decathlon, and a girlfriend, and reading up on linguistic dead ends. We're supposed to be making tools, not scholars afraid of their own shadows. And the girl! She's socially maladjusted, she's withdrawn and dysfunctional, and she hasn't laughed since we broke contact between the two of them. We need to scrub this generation and start over."

"It was your idea to sever that initial contact, Leigh. You were the one who used Galileo's planetary charts to prove that intersecting their orbits too early would be detrimental to their development. I listened to you, because you've been right before. Now you're telling me severing that contact may have damaged them, and that this justifies canceling their portion of the project. Which is it? Did we serve the Doctrine or do it irreparable harm when we untangled them from one another?"

"I said to keep them apart, not to send them out into the world. If we damaged the Doctrine's manifestation, it was because *they* weren't properly made," Leigh says. "If a vase shatters when you cool it, it's not because it wasn't meant to be cooled. You must cool what you bake. But sometimes there are flaws in the making, places where the clay fails to properly bond. It's not my fault if they're bad clay. It's not my fault if they can't hold when they're fired."

"Perhaps not, but I think you're too swift to dismiss them as poorly made," says Reed. He sees the reasons for her objection now, sees them more clearly than she ever will. Leigh relishes destruction, the point where one thing can be broken down to make way for the next, because her true devotion is to perfection, the line past which nothing can be improved. To her, their cuckoos have been a spiral of increasing elegance, but they are not yet perfect.

"I think you're too swift to embrace them as the ideal."

"What would you have me do?"

"Start again. We know more now; we have a better idea of the shapes we need, the angles we desire. We can make them better."

Her point is valid. There is a compromise to be reached. "I'll approve your creation of another generation of cuckoos to race for the manifestation, but you must agree to stop calling for the dissolution of this pair. I want to see what they can accomplish if left to their own devices. They're developing into something new. The Doctrine, when it manifests, will be something new." It will also be the oldest thing in the world, the note which, when sounded without obstruction or acoustic manipulation, creates reality. It's impossible to say whether this pair of cuckoos is on their way to manifesting, for these are uncharted waters. There's no map. There's no compass. There is only the project, stretching out ahead of them, unchanging, unchangeable.

This is alchemy of the type the masters could only dream of. Paracelsus, Pythagoras, Baker—not one of them has touched these vaunted heights, or come this close to finally fully realizing their dreams.

Leigh looks at him for a moment more before she bows her head and agrees, "I will leave them."

"Good." He leans forward, kisses her forehead, imagines he can hear the rustle of dead leaves and feathers inside the ivory cage of her skeleton. She is dangerous, this construct of dead women and living vermin. She is bright and brilliant, and she will kill him one day, if he isn't careful. If he allows it. "Remember the auguries. Have faith."

"I always have," she says.

"Now get your people. I want that mess upstairs gone before the plane takes off." He turns and walks away.


Patience is a virtue to Leigh Barrow. She was born in stillness; she will die in motion. Everything between those points is the tension of the coiled spring, the held breath, the knife in the process of being drawn. She holds herself patient and cold as Reed—her keeper, her lover, her master, and her rival, all bound in a single imperfect human skin—leaves her behind.

Only when he rounds the corner and is gone does she move, potential converting into action as she whips around, balancing on the balls of her feet, and runs, cat-light, down the darkened hallway. She doesn't bother turning the lights on. Even were her night vision poorer than it is, that wouldn't matter; she knows every curve of this hall. She's walked it every day for years. She needs no visual cues to tell her where she's going, and wouldn't know what to do with them if they were provided.

Leigh is aware of the contradiction inherent in her existence. She is a human being, a scientist; she remembers half a dozen PhD programs, and another half-dozen disciplines on top of those. Her bones were stolen from the graves and deathbeds of thirteen brilliant women—and if those deathbeds were made by a long-dead alchemist, rather than by natural selection, she has no sympathy for them. Without their deaths, her birth would have been impossible. She is a palimpsest girl, a denizen of the Up-and-Under called into the light and brightness of the modern world, and if the women who make her up didn't want to die, they should have been more careful. They should have barred their doors and locked their windows, not left them open for a shadow to slip through like a thief in the night, hands full of knives and heart full of larceny. They should have *known* that what they possessed, the bright, brilliant nature of their minds, was more precious than gold, more transmutable than lead. They should have realized precautions were required.

For her, life is the lab and the lab is life. The lab is where she awoke, confused, filled with the shrieking souls of countless dead. The wings of crows beat in her ribcage, prisoned in the fleshy confines of her heart; sometimes she feels their feathers brushing against her bones, which are a mixture of human, caprine, and whalebone scrimshaw, carved so beautifully that she sometimes thinks it a pity she needs skin. She would be so much more attractive as a walking specter of tendon and bone, exposing her creator's artwork to the world.

This portion of the lab is her territory before anyone else's; even

Reed is cautious about walking down her halls. There's never any way of knowing what terrible things she has cooking in her private rooms, or how they might react to someone exposing them to the light. Reed is her master: she won't directly disobey his orders. Those horrible cuckoo children, with their twee names and their calf's eyes, will be allowed to live their petty little lives, at least for now. At least until he sees the wisdom of doing things her way.

Someday he'll understand why she hates them so, all the members of their terrible generation, raised outside the lab and under the all-seeing eye of the unforgiving sun. Someday he'll see that she was right all along. Until then . . .

She opens the door to her private lab, revealing a white room with bright lights set into the ceiling. Erin is strapped to a chair, writhing and wailing, while several technicians stand around her with solemn faces, making notes.

"Outside," snaps Leigh. "Reed's made a mess by the door. Clean it up."

They go without complaint. They know their place.

Quickly, she crosses to the girl and kneels, reaching up to touch her face. Erin stills. Even in the face of a pain she can't understand, she knows when danger is at hand.

"Hello, sweetheart," says Leigh, and smiles. "It's time."

# Breakdown

Cambridge is beautiful in September. The weather isn't always accommodating—some years it seems to rain from the beginning of the month all the way to the end, or to trip over itself in its hurry to present the first iced-over sidewalks—but the city is glorious in the fall. Roger leans against an old maple tree at the edge of campus, smoking a cigarette and watching underclassmen stream through the doors, smirking at the chime of the warning bell. There are certain perks that come with being both a senior and one of the smartest kids in school. Among them is starting the day with a free study period. As long as he's on school property, he's neither truant nor tardy, and can do what he likes for the first hour of his day.

Most of the kids in his class chose the end of the day for their free period, wanting to get out of school as fast as they can. He understands that. But he has things to do with his morning—essential things, that can't be moved—and so he went with the beginning. Besides, Alison is in his seventh-period American History class, having chosen a full course load for her senior year, and he likes to have the excuse to spend the time with her. They're looking at different colleges, and both of them know their relationship, mutually satisfying as it has been, won't survive the end of high school. They're not in love. If they were once, it faded into friendship and physical attraction long ago. That's been more than enough for both of them.

Roger takes one more drag on his cigarette before dropping it to the dirt and grinding it beneath his heel. Then, calmly, he closes his eyes. 8:20 here is 5:20 in California, and Dodger will be getting out of bed in three . . . two . . .

"Good morning, asshole." She sounds groggy. She always does when she wakes up. Neither of them is *good* about going to bed at a reasonable hour, but he at least tries to get five hours a night, if only for the sake of his ability to conjugate irregular verb tenses. When last he checked, Dodger was running at three hours, tops. He's not sure how much longer she can do that. He's sure nothing he says is going to make her stop.

They fight more now than they did when they were kids. Part of it is that they're different people: more rigid, more adult, less willing to accept everything as inevitable and reasonable just because someone else says it's so. Part of it is that she's never really forgiven him for cutting off contact the way he did. She says she has, and he knows she's lying, and she knows he knows, and neither of them does anything about it, because neither of them is sure what there *is* to do. They have the kind of connection that looks good on paper, but it doesn't fix anything: they're not telepaths, he can't read her mind and figure out the exact right things to say to make her understand that he's sorry, he'll always be sorry, he'd change it if he could. She can't see his thoughts. All they can do is worm into one another's heads, like the world's least explicable telephone line.

(At least they can shut each other out now. They can bar the mental doors and throw the mental locks and have some sense of privacy. They couldn't do that when they were kids. It still doesn't work if they don't make an effort. It's not enough to be unreceptive. They have to be actively opposed, and that's exhausting. They don't feel each other the way they used to, either. He doesn't feel her exhaustion. She doesn't feel him nod. Something has been lost in the long gulf of their separation, and he doesn't know whether he wants it back or not.)

It would be different if they could spend some time in the same place. He's sure of that. She's still his best friend, and if they could sit in the same room, not talking, not doing anything but existing, they could get through this. He knows they could.

"Good morning," he replies. "Did we forget to sleep again?"

"I didn't *forget*, exactly," says Dodger. "I had other things to do."

"Other things like . . . ?"

"There was a Nightmare on Elm Street marathon on TV."

Roger sighs. "You say you don't read because you don't like being lied to by books. Why are you addicted to lousy horror movies? Are you trying to punish me for my sins?"

"Always," says Dodger. "Anyway, it's not like you can see my nightmares. How would you know if I were trying to punish you? Just be glad I like *something*."

"I have to put up with you when you're exhausted."

"Fair point." She yawns. "Who's in charge right now?"

"You are. I'm already at school."

"Lucky dick with your free period." She opens her eyes, giving Roger an unobstructed view of her ceiling. The cartoonish plastic stars from her childhood are gone, replaced by a solid field of dark blue, spattered liberally with glow-in-the-dark paint. She's charted the cosmos on her bedroom ceiling. It's lovely. Sometimes when he has trouble sleeping, he'll ask her to turn off her lights and let him count the painted stars. He's never gotten to the end before passing out.

"You could have had a free period too, if you hadn't decided to do a half-day at Stanford."

"Because you would totally have been able to pass that up if you had the option. Shadowing Professor Vernon while he teaches the geniuses of tomorrow? Heaven." Dodger's field of vision shifts as she slides off the bed and begins rooting around in the clothes littering her floor. "Although I guess that wouldn't tempt you."

"No, but the language offerings would. I know why you do what you do. I just wish you'd sleep more while you were doing it."

"You're one to talk, *Mom*." Over the years since they started speaking again—swearing never to cut contact for any reason short of coma, death, or intensive cramming—they've both gotten very good at dressing without looking at themselves. Neither has a mirror in their bedroom. Roger can see this becoming a problem when they hit college. Presumably the dorms will come with mirrors on the closet doors, or with roommates who want to be allowed to hang their own things on the walls. That's one more bridge to be crossed when they get to it. Assuming they both survive their last year of high school, which seems absolutely likely and utterly impossible at the same time.

To the cat that's lived in the shelter for half of its life, the box is the only reality. Adoption is unthinkable. Roger thinks high school is like that box. It's learning, yes, and he appreciates that, appreciates the time and effort and concern shown by the adults devoted to hammering knowledge into his thick skull. He knows it hasn't always been easy on them, especially with the range of required subjects they spread out in front of the student body every day. He'd be valedictorian if it weren't for physical education, which has damaged his GPA—not to the point of putting him completely underwater, but enough that two people were able to squeak past him in the student rankings. One of them is Alison, and that makes him more okay with it.

Dodger got off easier than he did. Her California curriculum included options like "aerobics" and "swimming" after freshman year, and she's been able to avoid the horrors of team sports and endurance running. She didn't do well on her Presidential Fitness Tests, but then, who does? Jocks and people whose native intelligence is in their bodies, not their minds. He can't be mad at those folks for blowing the bell curve—it's not like he doesn't do the same to half his classes. That doesn't mean he can't be a little bitter.

"Plans for the day?" Roger wants another cigarette. Dodger gets mad when he smokes while he's inside her head. She says it's rude to subject other people to his filthy habits, even if she can't actually smell or taste it. He can wait five minutes, until they've finished their morning call. This is normalcy. This is something that predates addiction, that will—he hopes—postdate it as well, remaining a normal part of life long after he's decided that nicotine has become a crutch and kicked it to the curb.

"School, more school, homework, and then playing chess at the Y," says Dodger. She leaves her room, heading down the short, familiar hall to the bathroom. Her parents are accustomed to hearing her mumble as she goes about her daily business; when they've asked, she's smiled blithely and told them she's trying to work out some snarly formulae. If pressed, she'll start spewing numbers and mathematical concepts until they back off. It's happened before. Roger has regretted his lack of popcorn every time. "I have a class of middle school kids who want to learn the game, and it looks good on my application forms."

"I thought you were going to go to Stanford."

She shrugs, face coming into view in the mirror above the sink as she reaches for her hairbrush. She still wears her hair in the bob she had when he saw her playing chess for the first time, short enough to be easily cared for, long enough to remind people that she's a girl. Not that she needs the reminder anymore: he'd never invade her privacy by looking on purpose, but she's an adult woman now, like he's an adult male. She can wear all the shapeless shirts and ripped-up jeans she likes. The essential facts of puberty won't change.

"If I go to Stanford, I'll always be Professor Cheswich's daughter," she says, brushing her hair with sharp, almost violent strokes. Roger winces in distant sympathy, aware of her pain without feeling it. "Not only that, but I'll always be the kid genius who didn't want to skip the back half of high school. They don't have much sympathy for that sort of thing around here, you know? No amount of 'my social development needs me to be around my peers' will make up for the fact that I could be more than halfway to my degree by now."

"Sorry," says Roger.

"Don't be." Dodger drops her hairbrush into the basket, picks up her toothbrush, covers it in minty paste. "Your parents wouldn't let you leave high school early, and I can't blame them. We both needed more time, and you would have missed Alison way too much if you'd broken up with her before you were finished being in love. Brushing my teeth now. Tell me your day."

She sticks the toothbrush in her mouth before he can argue that he's not done being in love with Alison, and even though it's his turn to talk, he doesn't start. Because she's right. He's not going to cry when he and Alison break up. A year ago, he would have. A year before that, it would have been the end of the world. Everything changes.

"Class," he says. "I shouldn't have much homework, and what I do have, I can finish by five. I'd *better* finish by five, since that's when Dad's coming to take me to the ballgame."

Dodger makes a muffled, inquisitive noise around her toothbrush. Roger smiles.

"Red Sox versus Giants," he says. "My hometown against yours. I guess we'll finally know conclusively which is better, huh, California girl? I'll be sure to send flowers to apologize when we stomp you into the dirt."

She spits, rinses her mouth, and says primly, "You'd have to know where I live to do that. Find something else to threaten me with."

Roger pauses. "Well, you could give me your address," he says finally.

"Nope," says Dodger. "Try again."

Since the chess tournament, it's been like their childhood positions have been reversed. Roger has offered his home address, his phone number, even a post office box rented with carefully hoarded lunch money, all to give her a means of contacting him that doesn't involve her voice whispering through his mind, her eyes seeing through his own. She's always refused. She's always refused, and more, she's declined to offer him any of the same things. He knows every inch of her house, from the latch that sticks on the back door to the loose baseboard in the computer room where she hides the things she doesn't want her parents to see—the razor blades she buys at the local pharmacy, the dirty magazines, the caffeine pills, the carefully rolled bag of what could be, but isn't, oregano—but he wouldn't know how to get there if he suddenly found himself in Palo Alto. When she's coming up the walkway and talking to him at the same time she keeps her eyes on the grass or the sky, anything but the landmarks that could lead him to her, everything but the address.

She's still avoiding him. That's more frightening than he has words for—and *that's* frightening, too, because he's supposed to have words for everything. Dodger is hiding something. What it is, he doesn't know. Doesn't think he can.

"If not Stanford, then where?" he asks.

"I don't know. Cambridge is excited to have me come for a visit. So is MIT. And there's always Yale. I know that shouldn't be anyone's fallback school—it's *Yale*—but their math department doesn't excite me. Maybe I'll tour Brown. Or surprise everybody and go to Oxford. I like British food. Most of it, you don't even have to chew." She smooths her hair, looking critically at her reflection. "Okay. That's as presentable as I'm going to get. Look, I need to run. Catch you tonight after your game?"

"Sure," says Roger. "Have a great day, okay?"

Her smile is barely a quirk of her lips, so faint that only years of familiarity allow him to see it for what it is. "Sure," she says. "Anything you say."

Roger opens his eyes. The sky is turning deeper gray; it's going to rain soon. That thought hurries him away from the tree and toward the front of the school, thoughts of distant friends and impossible connections quickly chased from his mind.

Later, he'll wonder how he missed the intonations she was using, the quiet finality of what should have been an ordinary conversation. Later, he'll blame himself, knowing this was all his fault. Later, he'll realize how broken she was. But that's all later. Time is a funny thing; it doesn't forgive the things we don't see. Here and now, he's running, racing against the rain, and he doesn't have time to worry about a girl on the other side of the country. He doesn't have time to consider how much they both have to lose. He's just running.

In a way, they both are.

\* \* \*

D odger closes her eyes when Roger's presence fades, waiting to be sure she's truly alone. Sometimes he comes back after she thinks he's gone, returning to remind her of something coming up, some appointment or occasion or sporting event he wants her to know about. It's adorable, the way he takes such care to keep her informed about his life. Like he thinks she can't survive without the constant lifeboat of his existence to support her. And why shouldn't he think that? She as much as told him it was true, when they fell back into contact with one another. She said she'd been lost without him. She said she'd been alone. Of course he worries that she's fragile. He knows she is.

What he doesn't know is how alone she still is. Having one friend who might as well have been imaginary had been fine when they were kids, but she'd learned her lesson when his reply to her proposing they meet was to cut her off completely. Roger says he's not as good a liar as she is—says he's telling the truth when he talks about the woman who threatened to take him away from his family, that he was only acting out of fear and desperation—but that's what a good liar would say, isn't it? She can't know. She can't know.

But she can see how happy he is, how much he enjoys his friends and the girlfriend he loves without being in love with. She can see how *well adjusted* he is, to steal the language of the adults who study her mental health, watching for signs that genius, like acid, has eaten away at the flesh of her soul. They think she's well adjusted too. Lonely, sure, but not broken.

Dodger is many things. Foremost among them: she is a very good liar.

She walks down the hall to the computer room, knowing her mother will be downstairs in the kitchen with a cup of coffee and the newspaper, listening to her daughter's footsteps overhead. Morning visits to the computer room are normal, tightly regulated to keep her from being late to school, but expected. No deviation from the pattern here. She's maintaining the same equation she's used for every school day so far this year. That's important.

The loose baseboard comes away from the wall easily, not making a sound. She's been planning this day for a while: she knows that, even as she spent more than a year trying to deny it to herself. Why else would she have taken so much care in sanding the edges of the baseboard, creating a perfect, soundless seal? She must have been planning this.

Dodger is so very, unbearably tired.

She wouldn't describe what she feels quite like that, but deep down, she knows "tired" is the right word: maybe the only word. She's *tired*. She's tired of being too smart to slow down and appreciate things that aren't performing at her level. She's tired of adults treating her like a circus sideshow and other kids treating her like a freak. (They're not the same, not quite: to the adults, she's the strongman, the fire-eater, the girl who dances on the trapeze without a net. To the kids, she's the bearded woman, the lobster-girl. The adults gape and whisper because of what she can do. The kids her own age do it because of what she *is*. They're both right and they're both wrong and she's exhausted from the effort of trying to make them understand.) She's tired of being lonely, and having Roger back in her life has made things worse when it should have made them better, because she always thought he was the same as she was, but he's not, he's *not*. He has friends. He has people. He has a life. And she has numbers, and figures, and math enough to redefine the sky.

The numbers would have been enough, if she'd never found the door at the back of her own mind, leading to a boy her own age—to the day—who couldn't finish his worksheet. They might even have been enough if he'd never slammed and locked the doors between them, shutting her out and giving him time to change the world he lived in. She could have adjusted to how much better he was at people than she was, if she'd watched it happen, if he'd boiled her like a frog. But he didn't do that. He closed her out, and while she was gone he raised the temperature of the water, and now that she's back, she can't take it.

The flaw, she knows, is hers. The weakness is hers. That's okay. She's the math girl. She's the one who appreciates the necessity of the inevitable equation. She can see where these numbers go.

One by one, she removes her prizes from the space behind the baseboard: the pack of razors, the bottle of painkillers stolen, one and two at a time, from unguarded medicine cabinets and un-watched purses, the topical numbing gel. She's worked her plan out so carefully. All the pieces need to be perfect. She's good at perfect.

She stuffs her prizes into her backpack, returns the baseboard to its place, and stands. Soon—so very soon—Roger won't have to worry about her anymore, and she won't have to worry about her loneliness driving him away. She won't have to worry about anything.

She only has to be perfect one more time, and she can be done. Re-lief outweighing her fear, she shoulders her pack and heads for the door. Time for breakfast. Time to say goodbye.

# Perfection

TIMELINE: 10:37 EST, SEPTEMBER 5, 2003
(SAME MORNING, SAME DAY, ALMOST TOO LATE).

Roger is in his AP English class, listening to his favorite teacher—Ms. Brown, who will never have his heart the way Miss Lewis did in the second grade, and that's okay, because he figures no one ever loves anyone the way they love their second-grade teacher—explain *King Lear* when the world goes white and everything drops away, leaving him suspended, screaming, in a terrible void. It isn't pain, exactly: pain would require nerves, skin, a body. It's an anti-pain, a pain born of absence, and because of that, it hurts more than anything.

The white turns gold around the edges, burning. The transition forces the edges to *exist*, transforming them into a frame around a place he's never seen. A skyline, writhed with flame; a road of rainbows, stretched like a soap bubble across the landscape.

A girl with red hair (he can see the color of her hair) lying sprawled in the dirt, her eyes half-closed, her own pain receding as blood loss wrings her dry. The blood is gray, gray as blood always is when Dodger isn't with him, but he knows it all the same, yes, he knows it. She's going. She's going. She's not gone yet.

*The Impossible City is burning,* he thinks incoherently, and opens his eyes.

He's sprawled on the classroom floor, surrounded by the stunned, staring faces of his classmates. The back of his head hurts. He slammed it against the tile at least once when he fell, and maybe more than once, because his hips and shoulders hurt too, like he's been thrashing, or seizing. The front of his jeans is wet. Normally, that realization would be followed by shame, or anger, or some combination of the two. Here, now, he can't muster more than a calm confusion. It feels like someone just ran a few thousand volts through his brain, scrambling everything.

Miss Lewis is kneeling over him, hair hanging to frame her face the way it always did in his dreams, eyes wide and terrified. "Roger, are you all right?" she asks. "Can you hear me?"

"I love you, Miss Lewis," he says dreamily, and she isn't Miss Lewis anymore: she's Ms. Brown, and this isn't second grade, and he's just had a seizure. It's the only thing that makes sense. It feels like his brain is struggling to reboot, to start making sense of a fall he doesn't remember and an impact he didn't feel. There's a moment of absolute terror—what if this was a stroke? What if he's had a stroke, and something essential has been lost, and will never come back? What if he's less now than he was at the beginning of the day? The fear passes quickly. He's fine. He knows he's fine, and he knows, with as much certainty as a heart can hold, that he *won't* be fine if he doesn't start moving. This is not a situation that allows for slowing down.

Ms. Brown doesn't have the reassurance of being in his body, of feeling what he feels. She looks petrified. "Roger, do you know where you are?"

"Classroom." His tongue is slow and clumsy. He tries to sit up, and is delighted to find that he can. Everything is reacting normally. If not for the wet patch on his jeans and the sore places where he slammed into the floor, he'd say he was in tip-top condition, no problems here, all systems go. He's *fine.*

"Roger, you need to lie still." Ms. Brown flutters her hands helplessly, motioning for him to lie back down. The rest of the students are watching in mute fear. The seizure must have been pretty impressive: normally he would have expected at least a few of them to be suppressing snickers over the fact that he wet his pants. "Please. I've called the office, they're going to get you an ambulance—"

Math is not his strong suit, but he does the math anyway, adding up travel times, test times, the amount of time hospital admissions will take, the possibility of sedation . . . all the things that stand between him and a phone call if he does as he's told. The figure he comes up with is brutal in its simplicity, and it says "too long." He can't listen to his teacher. If he does, Dodger is going to die.

*The Impossible City is burning,* he thinks again, and while he doesn't know what the words *mean,* he knows what they're trying to say. If Dodger dies, so does he.

"You're supposed to walk off a seizure if you can," he says glibly, and it may be the most convincing lie he's ever told. He climbs to his feet, proud of the fact that his knees barely shake, and bolts for the door before Ms. Brown can order him to stop. The last thing he sees as it swings shut is her face, white as whey, crowned with eyes gone huge and childlike in her fear. He feels bad about that, he really does, but as Dodger is so fond of saying, there isn't *time.*

There's a "no leaving campus without permission" rule in effect for all grade levels, but this is an emergency, and he's already going to be in trouble when Ms. Brown gets over her shock and tries to follow him, because he's not heading for the office. He's running, full-tilt, toward the street. The rain has stopped, for the moment, but it wouldn't matter if it were pouring. He's got to get to a phone. The seconds are ticking by, too fast to trace or catch, and the entire world seems to be oversaturated, too bright, too sharp, until the air irritates his skin.

*This is how Dodger sees time,* he thinks, feeling almost fevered. She's bleeding into him the same way she's bleeding into the dirt. Everything is fluid. Everything needs someplace to go. Time is running out. He knows that like he knows the shape of his own skin, like he knows the shadow lurking at the back of his mind, threatening another, worse seizure. There's no way he should be doing this in this condition. He shouldn't be doing anything but going to the hospital. But *there's no time, time is running out, there's no time* keeps running through his mind, a jumbled string of words that barely holds together as it tumbles end over end, and he knows the hospital won't save him. He couldn't say *how* he knows: just that he does.

Right now, he's accepting the fact that given a choice between running off by himself immediately after a seizure or going to the hospital, the right choice puts him on the street. If he goes to the hospital, they'll both die.

He hits the sidewalk at what feels like a hundred miles an hour, trying to relax into the motion, to level out his breathing, to find comfort in the act of running. He can't. Even the shape of his own skin is starting to feel wrong. It's too long, too lanky, stretched too tight across the bones. He doesn't want to think about what that might mean, and so he runs, as hard and as fast as he can.

The sky is a bruise, pulsing with clouds, heavy with the promise of more rain. The air is electric. This is a Frankenstein day, ready to strike out at any moment. He darts across the street without looking, hearing the horns blare behind him and not looking back. He can't look back. He's not one of the rich kids, whose parents will trust them with a phone, and he doesn't know any of them well enough to ask to borrow their phones, not when he's seizing for no apparent reason, not when he's running out of time. There's a payphone half a mile up the road, at Harvard Square. He has a handful of quarters in his pocket, intended for feeding into parking meters when he takes Alison out on Friday nights. She'll understand if he has to borrow a few dollars. She'll see that he was helping a friend.

(Or maybe she won't, because there's no way to explain this so normal people will understand: he barely knows how to explain it to *himself*, and he has the situation burning bright as tinder in his mind, illuminating the dark corners. *Here there be monsters,* he thinks, and knows if he survives this, if *they* survive this, there won't be any more Friday nights with Alison. She'll never understand why he ran off campus when he needed medical help, why he put himself in danger, why he risked breaking her heart like that. There are no words in their common language to explain why he's doing these things, and that's the final nail in the coffin they've been building between them, to bury love with honors.)

Roger reaches the corner of Massachusetts Avenue and JFK as the sky rips open and begins pelting down rain. He's a little bit grateful as he races for the ledge sheltering the payphone. No one knows you've wet your pants when you've been drenched by a September storm. The water is frigidly cold, but that's incidental; as long as he has enough feeling in his fingers to feed the quarters into the machine, he can—

If the first seizure was a flash of lightning, the second is a roll of thunder. He feels his knees buckle, feels his cheek hit the brick sidewalk hard enough to bruise the entire side of his face, and the world goes sapphire blue before it fades to black, and he feels nothing at all.

When Roger opens his eyes, the rain has stopped and the shadow at the back of his mind is almost gone. There are people walking by on the sidewalk, some with umbrellas still hoisted high, looking at him with the calm disregard of people who can't find anything more interesting on television. Sitting up is harder this time, more like it should be after a major medical event. The quarters are spilled all around him, gleaming silver under a veil of rainwater. Curiosity and caution appear to have fought each other to a draw, keeping him from being robbed blind. He fumbles for as many quarters as he can, hands shaking, knees aching from their second hard impact in under an hour.

He feels drunk as he staggers to his feet and reels toward the payphone. The distance is short, but it's enough to wind him; he stops, hand pressed against the rough brick wall, chin tucked toward his chest, trying to suck in enough air that he won't sound like a crazy man when he starts making calls. Everything is getting hazy and strange. There's a third seizure lurking, the granddaddy of them all, slinking closer like one of Dodger's horror-movie monsters. It'll have him soon, and then it's lights out forever. No more words.

This is the line past which words can't help him.

Or maybe they can. *"Dodger,"* he hisses, and for the first time in his life, he doesn't give one flat fuck who might hear him or judge him for speaking to his imaginary friend. He throws himself forward into the void, into the space they've always made between them, the one that lets him use her eyes as she uses his. "Dodger, *what did you do?"*

She doesn't reply in words; words were never her strong suit, and if they're slipping away from him, they must have abandoned her completely. Instead, her eyelids flicker open, and he has a glimpse of blackberry brambles, twisted and wild and cradling the last of their late-summer berries; California's growing season seems to go on forever, ending resentfully, resuming the second the weather allows. It's an alien world, or it might as well be, filled with creatures whose motivations are as incomprehensible as pi.

"Dodger. Talk to me."

She doesn't talk to him. They've almost never picked up feelings from each other, but maybe this feeling is a language all its own: deep contentment, mixed with a bitter apology that cuts to the bone, knocking the air out of him. She closes her eyes. Not fast enough. He sees the blood on her fingertips (red through her eyes, red, red, red), her outstretched arm the only part of her body that's in her view, and he knows she predicted this call, this frantic attempt to reach her; she has organized herself with a mathematician's precision, concealing anything that might tell him what she did, where she pressed the razor, how deeply she bore down. The fingertips were an accident. He knows that, too, and what they represent, how much blood she'd need to lose before she wouldn't understand that he'd see. He doesn't think she's asking to be saved.

He doesn't think she understands that she's taking him down with her—and at this point, he doesn't think she could do anything if he told her. She's too far gone.

"Fuck quantum entanglement," he mutters, and opens his eyes, and picks up the phone.

Getting the number for Stanford University is easy: the operator is happy to provide it, even happy to connect him for an extra quarter.

His vision is blurring around the edges, what little color he normally sees leeching out of the world, like Dodger's taking the rest of it with her on her way out the door. He closes his eyes, not to reach out, but to remove one more distraction from a world that seems increasingly full of them. He doesn't have the time to let himself lose the thread of the narrative now. It's too late it's too late the line has been crossed it's save her now (and save himself in the process) or save her never.

"Your princess is in another castle," he says, and laughs, and is still getting his laughter under control when the ringing stops.

"Stanford Administration, how may I help you?" asks a sharp female voice. It is the voice of someone with no time to waste on nonsense, who will hang up on him if given the slightest reason.

Roger opens his eyes. Looking at his increasingly blurry feet, he says, in as polite a tone as he can pull from his exhausted reserves of energy, "Hello, ma'am. I need to speak to Professor Cheswich, please."

"Professor Cheswich's office hours are eight to ten on weekdays. He's not currently available for student calls. I can put you through to his voicemail."

Damn. *Damn.* Those stupid time zones again. Voicemail will be too late; he knows that, would have known it even without the glimpse through Dodger's eyes, without the blood on Dodger's fingertips. Time is running down. "Ma'am, I'm sorry, but if there's any way to connect me now, this is important. I'm one of his daughter's classmates, and Dodger isn't at school."

"I don't believe this is a matter of sufficient importance—"

*"Please."*

Hundreds of miles away, on the other side of a continent that might as well be a world, Patsy Sinclair stops. The despair in the boy's voice is shockingly strong, but more, there's a command there, and part of her wants to answer it. Part of her wants to do whatever he's asking her to do. And it's a *loud* part. It seems like it's a part worth listening to.

Patsy Sinclair has been a secretary for thirty years. She's good at what she does; she knows how to winnow the wheat from the chaff, as it were, when making sure that cranks and weirdos don't get through to the faculty in her care. She's heard it all, from the honors students desperate not to be held accountable for plagiarism to the slackers praying for one more chance. This boy . . . this boy sounds like he's dying. Or like someone else is.

When she speaks again, her own voice is gentler, softer, designed to calm. "It's all right, son. What's going on?"

"Please. Dodger was talking about hurting herself, but we didn't think she'd do it, only she's not here, and I think she's done something terrible. Please, can you try his number?"

"All right," she says. There's a breathlessness to her tone, and Roger knows he has her. Maybe, in the absence of Dodger, he's a decent liar after all.

(Maybe it's something else. But whatever it is, this is not the time.)

The line clicks. The line rings. The blurriness keeps spreading across Roger's field of vision, creating a narrowing tunnel leading down, down, down into the dark. It's like a rabbit hole. Any moment now Dodger will appear, wearing the White Rabbit's waistcoat and watch, and tell him he's going to be late. It's all falling apart. It's all going to pieces.

*I'm not bleeding, but I'm suffering the effects of blood loss,* he thinks, and that third, final seizure noses a little closer, like a dog straining toward its master's hand. He isn't its master, but it doesn't know that. It will love him to death. *We weren't supposed to go to Wonderland,* he thinks, and the Impossible City is burning, and it will all be over soon.

The line rings, and then—miracle—someone answers. "Professor Cheswich's office, Professor Cheswich speaking."

"Sir, I'm a friend of your daughter's, and she's bleeding to death in the gully behind your house." He's too tired to lie anymore. He needs to frighten this man into immediate action. "She has a spot under the blackberries. She's been going there since she was a kid. It's not too late, but she's lost a lot of blood. You need to hurry."

"Who is this?" There's rage in Professor Cheswich's voice, yes, but there's also fear; enough fear that this may work after all.

"A friend. Please. I know you don't want to believe me, I know this sounds insane, but for Dodger's sake, you need to go home as fast as you can. You need to save her. You need to go home, and you need to save her."

Professor Cheswich is sputtering and demanding more details when Roger gently sets the receiver back in its cradle. That's all; he's done what he could do. He's tried. He has reached the end of his endurance, and he has tried.

"How many times we gonna do this, Dodge?" he mumbles. His words are soft around the edges, mushy, like they're crumbling away. She can't hear him. There's no sense of connection, nothing to indicate the door is even still there. That's okay. That's okay. He tried. He tried to . . . to . . .

The third seizure pushes forward, and it's bigger than the world. Everything else goes away, and then *he* goes away, and that's okay. That's okay. He tried.

He tried.

# Rescue

Peter Cheswich is not easily frightened. He never has been. He watches horror movies with his daughter, laughing at the rubber monsters and over-the-top violence; he reads the news with mounting disgust, but not with *fear*. Fear has always been for other people, not for him.

The flashing lights of the police cars parked outside his house when he comes racing around the corner are almost enough to stop his heart.

They have the driveway blocked, so he slams his car into the first open spot he sees, front wheel humping up onto the curb. He doesn't care. He's already out of the car, running for the front door, and when a police officer steps into his way, he howls, "I'm her *father*!" with such passionate despair that the man steps to the side, not arguing, not asking him to calm down.

It's bad. He knew it was bad when that boy with the New England accent hung up on him (he'll be tracking that boy down, oh yes he will, first to thank him and then to punch him so hard he cracks a tooth, because that boy knew, *he knew,* and he didn't call until it was already too late). He knew it was bad when he called home and Heather didn't know where Dodger was, only that she'd left for school early after kissing her mother goodbye, which wasn't something Dodger did anymore, was something she hadn't done since the eighth grade. Every single signpost on the road that started when his phone began to ring has told him it was bad, and he's believed them all.

He just didn't believe it was *this* bad. Not the kind of bad that has three police officers in his yard; not the kind of bad that has a conspicuous open spot where the ambulance must have been. How quickly did they remove her? Did they remove *her,* or did they remove a body, something empty and abandoned and useless? She's an organ donor. Has been since she was old enough to make choices about bodily autonomy. They'd want to get her to the hospital as fast as possible, whether she's alive or dead.

The thought of his daughter's heart beating in someone else's chest makes him stagger, catching himself against the doorframe while the officers look sympathetically on. Not one of them moves to help him. It's bad. It's so, so bad.

Heather has waited for him, rather than allowing herself to be bundled into the ambulance. She's in the kitchen, her hands empty, a coffee mug smashed on the floor. She's looking at it in dull puzzlement, like she can't understand how it got there; gravity should have been suspended, says her face, all the essential functions of the universe should have been turned *off* the second this began. The universe should have warned her. Somehow, somehow, the universe should have warned her.

There's another officer here. He holds the twin of Heather's broken mug, looking at the silent, shaking woman with the wary poise of a man who has seen grief do a lot of strange things. He'll be here as long as he needs to be, but he doesn't want to.

"Heather." Peter stops shy of the mess on the kitchen floor. His wife continues staring at it, seemingly deaf to the sound of his voice. "*Heather,*" he says again, louder.

She looks up. She had time to put her makeup on this morning before he called, screaming for her to go out back and find their daughter; her mascara has run down her cheeks in great muddy lines. She hasn't even tried to wipe them away. What would be the point?

"Is she alive?"

Still the blank stare, the mascara-streaked cheeks, the silence.

"Is Dodger alive?"

"Yes." Her voice is a cracked whisper. It seems to surprise her; she shies back, away from it. Then she repeats herself: "*Yes.*"

"Oh thank God." Peter is not a religious man, but he has to fight the urge to kneel. Instead, he turns to the officer, and asks, "Where did they take my little girl?"

"Mr. Cheswich?" asks the officer. Peter nods, and the officer puts his coffee mug down on the counter, safely away from the edge. "Your daughter sustained severe injuries, apparently self-inflicted. Has she been depressed lately? Has she said anything about fights at school or experienced any unexpected setbacks?"

"Not a word." But she *had* said something, hadn't she? To that boy who'd called the office. The one who might have saved her life.

The boy who'd never given his name.

"How sure are you that her injuries were self-inflicted?" he asks slowly, feeling his way through that minefield of a sentence like it might explode and kill them all.

The officer's expression sharpens. "Why do you ask?"

Haltingly, Peter explains the call he received, the one from the boy with the New England accent. The boy he'd never heard of before, but who seemed to know Dodger was in trouble, who was *so sure* of her location, even after he'd told Patty that he was at the school.

When he finishes, the officer's face is unreadable.

"Well?" he asks.

"I think it's time for me to drive both of you to the hospital," he says. "You should be there." He doesn't say why. That isn't his job. But he saw the Cheswich girl loaded into the ambulance, as pale as paper, with gauze dressings running from wrist to elbow on both arms. He hopes the father is right about the unknown boy attacking her and making a call, whether out of remorse or simply to gloat: he can't imagine such a delicate thing doing that much damage to herself, even though that's what all the evidence indicates. It would be better for her family if she'd been attacked. That way, there would be someone he could bring to justice, someone who could pay. If the girl did this to herself, well . . .

She'll be paying for years, assuming she lives. Failed suicides always pay. From what he saw of the EMTs as they prepped her for transport, that's far from guaranteed—and that, too, is not his job to explain. Let the folks at the hospital handle the grieving parents, the aftermath of this tragedy. He'll just get them where they need to be.

"All right," says Peter. He steps into the puddle of coffee and puts a comforting arm around his wife. At least, he intends it to comfort. She doesn't react to his presence. Not at all.

"Let's go," he says.

Dodger opens her eyes on a white ceiling in a dimly lit room, and her first thought is that death feels an awful lot like waking up after a bout of the stomach flu. Everything is a little distant and detached, like it isn't *real,* but some sort of clever movie set constructed by elves while she wasn't looking.

Her second thought is that if this is death, there shouldn't be so many things beeping at her. She tries to sit up, and finds she doesn't have the strength; her muscles seem to have been replaced with props alongside the rest of the world. There's a strange pressure in her right arm. She turns her head. Bandages cover almost all the skin from her shoulder to her wrist; an IV line disappears beneath them at the bend of her elbow. A moan escapes her lips, equal parts frustration and despair. She's never been the sort of person who dealt well with failure, and this failure? This isn't the sort of thing people bounce back from. She's going to stop being the weird genius and become the suicidal girl. The suicidal *failure.* Couldn't even do that right.

Dodger closes her eyes and wonders how much blood she lost. *Maybe if I lost enough, I'll have a heart attack from the shock of the transfusion,* she thinks, almost hopefully. She doesn't know if that's a thing that can actually happen, but it sounds good, and so she's going to go with it, at least for now. It'll help with the disappointment of being the sort of person who can't even die correctly.

"Dodger?" Her mother's voice is a broken thing.

Dodger opens her eyes again, turning her face toward the sound. "Mom?" she croaks.

"You're awake!" Her mother all but flies across the room, stopping just short of her bed, hands fluttering in front of her face like she doesn't know what to do with them. She's washed off her mascara, but her pallor remains; like mother, like daughter. Both of them seem to have been drained entirely of blood. "You're awake," she repeats.

"Yeah," whispers Dodger, closing her eyes. "I guess I am." She's so tired. She's not even sure this is happening, that this isn't just some terrible dream on her way down to the grave. She braces herself all the same. This is where the shouting begins.

Only it doesn't. "The police told us what happened. That boy from New England . . . they'll find him. Just give us his name, and I promise we'll find him."

Dodger's eyes snap open again. She stares at her mother. "What?"

"He called your father, you know. After he dragged you into that gully and hacked you open, he *called* your *father* at work and told him you were out there, bleeding to death. If I hadn't been home, why . . ." Heather Cheswich shudders. She can see that future with surprising clarity. It's a world gone gray. "You're so lucky, Dodger. We're so lucky. Just tell the police his name, and we'll catch him, and he'll never do anything like this again."

"Oh," whispers Dodger. This time, when she closes her eyes, she leaves them closed.

*So this is how you pay for leaving me alone; you save me when I don't want to be saved,* she thinks, and that's exactly right, that's full circle. He left her falling for a long time, but when she really needed him, he was there to catch her. He caught her. He's catching her right now.

"I don't know his name," she lies, and her mother believes her. So does her father, when he comes, because Dodger Cheswich is a very good liar; because her story is better than the truth, at least this time. At least right now. Maybe forever. The police don't believe her completely, but they write down her statement, and they say they'll keep an eye open. She's going to live. Their job is done.

It takes a week for her to be released from the hospital. She goes home with stitches running up the inside of both arms like equations she'll never solve, and when they come out, the scars they leave behind will be minimal, at least to the naked eye. She'll always know that they're there, but maybe that's all right. Maybe that's the reminder she needs that she can't jump, because someone will always catch her, whether or not she wants them to.

She hears Roger's voice, off and on, for almost a year. She never answers. The police are looking for the boy from New England, and she knows exactly where he is, and she never answers him. Eventually he stops calling. That, too, is exactly right; that, too, is full circle.

It will be five years before they meet again.

It won't be nearly long enough.

Zib hugged her knees to her chest, watching Avery pace back and forth along the rainbow sheen of the improbable road, his hands in his pockets and a scowl on his face.

"Are you done being angry with me yet?" she called.

"No," he replied, voice sullen. "You shouldn't have done that."

"We needed to give something to the Bumble Bear if we wanted it to let us pass. It couldn't be my slingshot, and it couldn't be your ruler. The shine from your shoes was something we could lose. It didn't hurt us."

"It hurt *me*," said Avery. He finally stopped pacing and turned to look at her.

Without their shine, his shoes were ordinary brown leather, like any kid might wear out on the playground. His shirt seemed just a little less starched without them reflecting it; his hair seemed just a little less combed. He looked like an ordinary boy.

Zib felt fear tickle her ribs. If they had to lose themselves to walk this road, would it ever really be able to lead them home?

—From *Over the Woodward Wall,*
by A. Deborah Baker

# Graduate

Chaos: When the present determines the future, but the approximate present does not approximately determine the future.

—Edward Lorenz

There is a time for many words, and there is also a time for sleep.

—Homer, *The Odyssey*

# Familial Visitation

TIMELINE: 0:00 PST, SEPTEMBER 6, 2003
(MIDNIGHT).

The man in the purple coat walks through the hospital by candle-light, and no one stops him, or asks him where he's going. No one even looks in his direction. He is invisible, or close enough as to make no difference, and all thanks to the wax-dipped hand he carries. Wicks sprout from beneath the fingernails, burning with a steady blue light.

Darren would be pleased to know that every part of him has been put to good use, or so Reed supposes. It was always difficult to tell, with that boy.

He walks on, heels clicking against the polished floor, until he reaches a private room. The door is closed. Good. He wants to see her. He hasn't seen any of them since they were born, and they came so close to losing this pair today.

Reed opens the door with a twist of his hand and slips inside, into the room where Dodger sleeps.

She looks so small, lost in the tangle of sheets, connected to the machines which monitor her fate. He thinks this may be the best way to see her: a hospital is much like a lab, after all, sterile and polished and perfect. *She* is perfect. With her eyes closed, red lashes resting against pale cheeks, she looks so much like Asphodel that even his wizened, hardened heart feels a pang of regret for what might have been, had he not killed his master and taken everything she'd ever loved.

Heredity is not only in blood. It is in the sympathetic vibration of the universe, in the places where atom becomes alchemy. Asphodel made him and he made this broken child: she is, in a very real sense, Asphodel's granddaughter, her Zib finally become flesh and laid out in a bed of white linen and gauze, waiting for his approval.

"Hello, child," he says, and runs the fingers of his free hand along the curve of Dodger's cheek.

The girl whimpers and twists in her sleep, but she does not wake. The Hand of Glory does its work, and does it well.

"You've presented me with a quandary," he says. "You tried to kill yourself. You nearly succeeded. Either you're weak, or you're a failure, and either way, I fear you may be unfit for the program you were designed for. Two of your siblings are already gone. Two more show no promise, only a plodding determination to survive. You have too much fire and not enough firmament. Why should I let you continue?"

Seth and Beth, dead and dust and dissected; Andy and Sandy, enduring and emotionless and uninspired. They'll be eliminated soon, failing some great and unexpected change. Dodger and Roger are the last hope of their generation, and as he looks at her, it's difficult to see where that hope could possibly bear fruit. Perhaps it's time to start over.

But the astrolabe began running backward when this pair drew their first breath. Their birth began the final part of his plan, and he *wants* it to be them, oh yes, he wants it to be them. Even if they lack the strength to lead him to the City, he wants them to draw the Doctrine fully down.

"Why?" he asks again, and his word has the power of command.

Dodger sighs in her sleep, small and sad. "The sky burns gold, and the road is so long," she says. "He can't get there without me."

"He?" Reed leans closer. "He who?"

"There's a tower," she says. "At the center of the city. A tower made of calculations. If I solve them, I'll know what the universe is made of. Please, may I solve them?"

Reed hesitates. She's math, not language; she could be speaking imprecisely. "Can you?" he asks.

Eyes still closed, breath still steady, she laughs. "I can, I can, I know I can, but I have to get there, may I? Please, please, may I?"

"Will you solve them for me?"

"I'll solve them for myself. I don't care what happens after."

She isn't Asphodel's after all, lacks the ambition of the grandmother she so impossibly resembles. She isn't even his, for all he's ever wanted is to know the secrets of the City, the lost words in the golden library, the hidden numbers in the diamond tower. She wants to uncover them for the sake of knowing it's been done, and then walk away.

She's perfect.

"For now, the road is yours," he says, and leans forward, and kisses her temple. "A gift for you, my daughter, to see you through the days ahead, while you recover: none of this was ever real. The boy was a dream. When you wake up, he'll be gone."

Dodger moans in her sleep, and is still.

In the morning, she will have a blister where he kissed her. It will burst in a week, remaining red and weeping for the better part of a year before it finally, resentfully heals. But no matter.

The morning finds her sleeping, alive and alone. Everything continues from there.

# Enrollment

Dodger hits the edge of campus like she has a grudge, hunched over the handlebars of her bike and pedaling hard. She knows she's late, three hundred and seven seconds, ticking over into three hundred and eight as she swerves to avoid a squirrel. Three hundred and nine when she rides over the curb, tires somehow finding purchase. She almost wishes they wouldn't. She won't hurt herself on purpose—the razor blades and nightmares and group therapy sessions for victims of violent crime are in the past, not the future—but showing up bruised and bloody might garner her a little sympathy, whereas "sorry, I was up until four in the morning arguing with mathematicians on the other side of the world" just makes her look like a flake.

(Sometimes she thinks the razor blades aren't that far behind her. She's transmuted her self-destructive impulses into "healthier" forms, like riding her bike into traffic and shorting herself on sleep until she starts seeing things, but that doesn't mean the impulses are gone. They're just harder for anyone else to see. She's learnt how to be a better liar than she ever thought she could be, even when she was convincing her parents she was fine. Healthy California lifestyle as metaphor for suicidal depression. Roger would have yelled at her for that, saying he didn't teach her about metaphors—*meet*-a-fors—so she could abuse them. But Roger doesn't matter. She's never going to see him again.)

Three hundred and seventeen seconds when she skids to a stop at the base of the library stairs, tires audibly shedding rubber on the poorly maintained slate walkway. The rest of her walkthrough group is already there of course, of course, waiting for her, the girl who has now been late one hundred percent of the time. She'll cut it to fifty percent when she's on time for their next outing, followed by thirty-three percent, twenty-five, dwindling down and down into meaninglessness, but that won't matter. Her first impression will always be of lateness. She's sorry for that, even as she plasters a smile across her face and hops off her bike, leaving it leaning against the base of the steps.

"Sorry," she says. "Lost track of time."

"Time, space, where you left your keys . . ." says one of the other incoming grad students, and laughs, a sound unnervingly like a kookaburra's mating cry. She's pretty, with dark skin, long black hair, and a sweatshirt patterned in geometric squares of orange, pink, and canary yellow. Maybe she's the other mathematician Dodger was promised when she signed up for this tour group. That would be nice. Female mathematicians *exist*, they're just rarer than she'd like, and most of them have no sense of humor.

There are six of them in total, counting the girl in the remarkable sweatshirt. A tall boy with a shaved head and eleven visible tattoos; a Chinese girl whose eyes haven't left her phone once, not even to mark the screeching of Dodger's tires; a plump, tan girl with pink and blonde hair and an expression of wonderment, like this campus is the most amazing thing she's ever seen; and a broad, brown-skinned man with a bushy beard and a T-shirt instructing people to ask him how to get to Sesame Street. They all look more awake than Dodger feels, but more importantly, they look like her peers. They have the air of amiable stress that she's come to associate with graduate students, and the calm resignation to the inevitable that she's come to associate with people she's unlikely to drive insane. Maybe they can be friends.

"We're waiting on one more," says the tattooed boy. His voice is surprisingly soft, with traces of a Nova Scotian accent. His leather jacket is a wonderland of badges, safety pins, and patches advertising punk bands she's never heard of. It's like looking at a time traveler from several decades and a few continents away. "So hey, you're not the last one here. I'm Snake."

"His parents didn't name him that," says the girl with her eyes on her phone.

"Your parents didn't name you 'Jessica,'" says Snake. There's no rancor in his tone: this is a conversation they've had before.

"No, they gave me a name white people can't pronounce. I'm tired of hearing it butchered, so everyone gets to call me Jessica, and we all feel good about how progressive we are." Jessica finally glances up. "You know what white people can pronounce? 'Tom.'"

"But I don't *look* like a Tom," protests Snake.

"You have limbs. You don't look like a Snake either."

Dodger snorts to keep herself from laughing and raises one hand to shoulder height, pulling their attention toward her. "My parents named me 'Dodger,' if that helps," she says.

"See, that's cool," says Snake. "That's a name I can get behind."

"Try going through middle school with me and see if you agree," she says mildly.

"Smita," says the girl in the remarkable sweatshirt, gesturing to herself with one hand.

"Dave," says the man with the beard.

"I'm, um, Lauren?" The girl with the pink and blonde hair has a Midwestern accent that peaks at the end of her sentence, turning her name into a question. "I'm in biochem."

"Cool," says Dodger. "We all STEM?"

"Chemistry," says Dave.

"Genetics," says Smita. "You need a biologically accurate velociraptor,

I'm not your girl. You want a terrifying hybrid of science gone wrong, give me a few years, I may be able to deliver."

"Cool," says Dodger again. She has the feeling she's going to be saying that a lot. She's okay with the idea. This is grad school. If it wasn't cool, she'd have to question her life choices. It's not like she *needs* the degree. She doesn't want to teach—can't imagine shutting herself in a classroom for her entire life like her father has—and with the prizes she's already won, the things she's already accomplished, she could have a comfortable career without further schooling. But she wants to learn. Knowledge is more addictive than anything she could put into her body, and she should know—she's tried everything there is and a few things there *aren't,* thanks to innovative chemistry majors. None of it has held a candle to learning.

(That's not true. She's never smoked. The smell makes her think of Cambridge, and thoughts of Cambridge are thoughts of something that was never real, something that almost got her killed when she was too young to know how to keep herself on an even keel. So she avoids cigarettes and things that might remind her of them. Besides, it's not like nicotine is an effective neural stimulant. It's the ritual that stimulates, and rituals she has in plenty.)

Jessica has looked up from her phone again and is studying Dodger with narrow-eyed suspicion. "Dodger," she says.

"Yes," says Dodger.

"Dodger *Cheswich.*"

"Yes."

"You solved the Monroe Equation when you were what? Nine?"

"Something like that," says Dodger.

"I've never believed that," says Jessica. "Who helped you?"

"No one," says Dodger. "Let me guess: math?"

Jessica nods. "Applied, but definitely something computational. You?"

"Still in flux between dynamical systems and probability, but I may stick around for an extra year and do both instead of blowing this Popsicle stand in four. What I really want to do is chaos and game

theory, at least right now. I don't know where I'll actually land."
Dodger shrugs broadly. "That's sort of the point of being here. There's
time to figure out what I want."

"Chaos theory, like the dude in *Jurassic Park*?" asks Snake.

"Sort of," says Dodger, and is privately grateful she didn't wear her
movie logo shirt. She's replaced it over and over throughout her lifetime; thank God for Hot Topic, which is more than happy to cater to
nostalgia. Other kids got Santa Claus and the Easter Bunny. She got
Ian Malcolm and a world where mathematicians could be rock stars.

"I still don't believe you did it," says Jessica.

Dodger shrugs again. "Suit yourself." She's used to this reaction:
it's lost most of its sting. There's a lot of rivalry within the mathematical community, a lot of racing to be the first to solve a puzzle that's
broken scholars for years. She's solved eight of those puzzles, and published the solutions to six. Some people think she's a liar, others think
she's a hoax, and one particularly verbal group thinks she's an actress
hired as a front for a revolutionary AI. She's not sure what that would
accomplish, but it's a charming thought, in its way.

"So where's our latecomer, anyway?" asks Dave. "I'm happy to do
campus tours and 'build connections within my incoming peer
group,' but not if it means I'm going to be late for everything else I
have going on. There's being social and then there's being stupid."

"I think we're going to be friends," Dodger informs him.

Dave grins.

The social patterns are beginning to emerge: who wants to be here,
who's been pressured into agreeing. Who feels like they're scoping out
the competition, and who genuinely wants someone to talk to on an
unfamiliar campus. Dodger has gotten better about reading the
underlying logic of moments like this one, mapping them like equations. It'll never be a perfect predictive tool—annoyingly, people are
not numbers—but she can run the probabilities. It's all part of being
a better liar. She'd finished high school in long-sleeved shirts, listening to people whisper about her "mystery attacker" when they thought
she couldn't hear them, and she'll always be aware of how narrowly
she avoided them whispering about the crazy genius girl who tried

to kill herself because she couldn't handle the pressure. Social isolation wasn't working anymore.

She'd started college a new woman. Smiling, laughing, engaging with the people around her, all while keeping copious notes on how and why they reacted the way they did. She'd approached the issue of social interaction like it was another puzzle to be solved, another prize to be won. She has friends now, people who swore they'd keep in touch via the Internet, since they aren't at the same school anymore. She has people who would notice if she disappeared.

She wishes that meant more, or that she actually cared about them the way they seem to care about her, but no one gets everything in this world. As long as she can feign connection believably enough that people will answer it in kind, that will be enough. That has to be enough.

Dave and Smita could be friends, if she takes the time to cultivate them. She thinks she will. Friends are useful things, and she gives as good as she gets, following the established rules of friendship. If she brings people soup when they're sick because the rules say she should and not out of empathy, what does that matter? They still get the soup. She still gets the contact. The math is good. Lauren is an unknown quantity. Snake would probably *like* to be friends, but he hasn't taken his eyes off her breasts in almost five minutes, and Dodger has moved out of the phase of her life where that would seem like a good thing. It was nice to have the boys noticing her for a little while, when she was trying to work out social interaction; boobs were like a cheat code for getting along. As her grasp of the math improved, she stopped wanting to cheat.

Jessica is going to be a problem. That's all right. She likes problems.

"Where did you do your undergrad?" asks Smita.

"Stanford," says Dodger. This is the most common question in her world right now, and she volleys it back without pause: "You?"

"Brown."

The others offer their own answers as the minutes move, until Dodger's late arrival is completely overshadowed by their tour guide, who is going for the record.

"If this guy weren't showing us around campus, I'd suggest ditching him," says Snake. Everyone murmurs agreement, even Dodger and Jessica, who might never agree on anything again. (Not that this is a bad thing. Rivalry inspires good work. Not peaceful work, but since when does peace have anything to do with the march of scientific progress?)

"Maybe we should ditch him anyway?" Lauren ducks her head like she's ashamed of her own question. "We could all get lost together? It might be fun?"

The way the girl sounds as if she's constantly questioning things is going to get old soon. But they're not in the same discipline, so it's not like they're going to share advisors, and besides, this is Amiable Dodger time, Friendly Dodger time, Dodger-who-gives-a-damn time. Dodger slaps a smile on her face and says, "I think I saw a Starbucks just off campus."

"I know I did!" says a new voice. The group turns to see a tall, rail-thin man walking toward them. His brown hair is long enough to be pulled into a ponytail; his glasses are wire-framed and as stylish as mud. The cup in his hand bears the familiar green mermaid, complementing his blue-and-gold UC Berkeley sweatshirt. He looks like a campus tour guide out of a student handbook, and he puts Dodger's teeth instantly on edge. Something about him is familiar enough to hurt. She's learned, over time, to fear the overly familiar.

"Are you our guide?" asks Smita. "Because you're late. There was almost a mutiny."

"Wouldn't be my first," says the man. "Something about my face inspires people to rebel against me. Even when my face isn't there, they rebel against me. I'm Roger Middleton, and I'm going to be your gateway to the wonders of the UC Berkeley campus. Please watch your step, forgive my tardiness, and don't feed the squirrels, as they have been known to mug people for their—Miss? Where are you going?"

The group turns again, this time to look at Dodger, who has grabbed her bike and is in the process of swinging her leg over the seat, hands already tight on the handlebars. She blanches when she sees them—when she sees *him*—staring at her.

Then she slaps her smile back into place like it was never gone. "Sorry, just realized I didn't feed the cat before I left. I'll see you guys around, right?" The cat came with her apartment, and he's already been fed, and that doesn't matter. What's one more lie in the face of the lies she's already told, the ones she's telling every time she smiles like she means it, or doesn't open her mouth and scream? Lies are nothing. They're the currency she uses to pay for the rest of her life.

They're not going to be enough. Roger went pale the second she spoke, and how could he not? He can't see the color of her hair, her most recognizable feature, with his own eyes, but her voice had been echoing through his head for such long stretches of their childhood. They grew up in one another's pockets, hand and glove switching positions whenever the need arose, and he knows what she sounds like better than anyone else in the world—better than her, even, because he'd heard what she sounded like to her own ears as well as to his own. There's no way she can hide from him. She never could. And she shouldn't have to, because he's not real, he's not real, he's *not real*.

He's just a dream that almost killed her, and she can't fall asleep again. Not when she's come so far. She doesn't give him time to speak. Just waves, and kicks off, and she's away, she's away, she's pedaling as fast as she can, and it's never, never going to be fast enough.

Roger stands frozen in front of the library, entire body numb, staring at Dodger's swift-receding back. *Of course she's here,* he thinks, half-nonsensically. He's been waiting for her to fall back into his life since the day he woke, drenched and bleeding, on the sidewalk in Harvard Square. He'd seized, over and over, his body fighting to live while Dodger's fought to die. In the end, he was able to hold on, and they both survived. He knew that, because the "mysterious attack" on a "California math prodigy" by an unidentified teenage boy had made the papers all the way to Massachusetts. The local angle didn't hurt, since that was all the authorities had to go on: the boy, whoever he was, had a New England accent.

It took a shamefully long time for Roger to realize they were looking for *him*, that Dodger had convinced them *he* was the one who'd
attacked her. In his defense, he had problems of his own to worry
about. Ms. Brown called the office to find out how he was, only to
learn he'd never shown up. When they discovered he was no longer
on campus, they contacted his parents, and a brief manhunt had en-
sued before they found him sitting next to the payphone, back to the
wall, holding a wadded-up handkerchief—Alison's, stuffed carelessly
into his pocket at some point, forgotten until it proved useful—against
his still-bleeding nose.

There was screaming. There were lectures. There were a series of
X-rays and MRIs, and the discovery that somehow, he'd been bleeding
into his brain; a small bleed, but enough to cause the complications
he'd experienced. He didn't know the applicable words back then.
He knows them now: aneurism, hematoma, ecchymosis. At the time,
all he was worried about was brain damage, losing the thin, indefin-
able edge that made him who he was. Then, once it was clear that no
such thing had happened, he started worrying about Dodger, calling
out to her, waiting for a response.

He'd always known she wasn't dead. But she never answered, until
he began to wonder if that was what had been lost: not natural ability, but preternatural. Their quantum entanglement had been severed
by whatever she'd done to herself, and while he'd managed to save her,
he hadn't been able to keep them together.

He'd been in the hospital for a week before Alison came to see him,
carrying a box that contained everything he'd left at her house over
the duration of their relationship. She didn't need to break up with
him after that; he looked at the box, and he knew exactly what it was.
To her credit, she didn't yell. To his credit, he didn't try to explain. She
just placed the box gently beside his bed, turned, and walked away.

Now it's five years later and he's surrounded by shiny new grad students, coming in from schools around the country if not the world,
all watching him watch Dodger riding away. He could try to call
her back, close his eyes and say her name and hope she hears him,
but that would be a great way to cement himself as a stalker or ob-

sessed ex-boyfriend in the eyes of his peers. Plus she's on her bike. Even if they can still make contact the way they used to, the shock of hearing him in her head might cause her to lose her balance and crash. Not a good way to renew an acquaintance that has been . . . troubled, at best.

Roger takes a long drink of his coffee before turning to the remaining members of his tour group and saying, "I didn't think we'd lose one of you so soon. If anyone else is going to run out on me, could you do it now, so my ego takes all its blows at once? It would be a big favor. Anyone? No? In that case, let's try this again: my name is Roger Middleton, and I'm going to be your gateway to the wonders of campus. How many of you have been here before? Show of hands."

They show their hands. All of them have been here before, touring the place in the company of their fellow applicants while trying to settle on which campus they were going to grace with their brilliance.

Roger has been here for five years, combining undergrad and graduate work in one smooth sweep that doesn't require winnowing his shit for the move back to Massachusetts a second before he absolutely has to. Even moving from dorm to dorm to off-campus apartment has been enough to make him give serious thought to staying in California. There aren't real seasons here—California still doesn't know how to do Februarys right—and people put avocado on everything, but staying would mean not needing to figure out how to part with or pack five years' worth of carefully curated books. That might be worth it.

"All right, so that's all of you," he says. "How many of you want the facilities and library tour, and how many of you want me to take you down to Telegraph and introduce you to the food options that will be keeping body and soul together for however long you're here?"

As expected, all of them choose burritos over blackboards. Roger keeps smiling as he leads them toward the edge of campus. That's really all he can do right now. Just keep smiling.

* * *

Dodger is sharing an off-campus apartment with two other grad students: Candace, who's studying child development and leaves wooden blocks scattered around the entryway, and Erin, who's studying theology, keeps odd hours, and has only been seen twice since the three of them moved in. Both her roommates are out when she gets home. That's good. That's very, very good. She needs to think.

Propping her bike against the wall, Dodger walks down the bookshelf-lined hallway to her room: a small white box with a bed and a desk both situated well away from the glistening walls. The first thing she did upon moving in was get permission to paint the room with high-gloss paint, effectively turning the whole thing into one giant whiteboard. Her clothing is stored in the closet, and her books are on the communal shelves outside. This is the room where she lives. She can't live where she can't work.

Uncapping a marker, she turns to the nearest wall, and begins.

It's a horror movie cliché: the unstable genius who spends all their time writing on the walls, chasing an equation that might as well be a dream. Dodger knows that. But the horror movie geniuses never take the time to buy special paint and never erase their work; she does both. The advent of cellphone cameras has made it easier to capture things in a more lasting medium. She works big, photographs small, transcribes into her computer, and continues virtual, moving the numbers and equations in a space where size doesn't matter, where ink never smears and chalk never wears away. As long as this is just a ritual to calm herself down, she doesn't see the harm.

She's still writing when the front door opens and Candace calls, "Hello, the house!"

"Hi, Candy," Dodger calls back, and keeps writing. She's removed her sweatshirt. The scars running from her wrists to her elbows are visible, thin white lines that tell their terrible story to anyone who cares to look. What she finds interesting is the way the story is interpreted. Some people see the scars, see her face, and flash directly onto the newspaper articles identifying her as the victim of a vicious attack. Others see the scars and understand them, even if they saw the same articles. Those are usually the people with scars of their own, she's found; people who have reason to know them for what they are. People who have no reason to judge.

Footsteps pad down the hall—Candace is one of those crunchy granola "shoes are for the outdoors, not the house" people—and Candace herself appears in the doorway, short and softly rounded, the kind of woman made for blue jeans and cable-knit sweaters. Her hair is a sensible brown only a few shades darker than her eyes. She likes to say she's a survivor of the diet industry still learning how to be fat and happy, but she seems more comfortable in her own skin than Dodger's ever been.

Candace's eyes go to the walls. Two of them are already covered in numbers; Dodger is well along the way to filling the third. "Do I even need to ask how the tour went, or should I back away slowly and hope you don't decide to start covering *me* with algebra?"

"If this looks like algebra to you, it's time to add some remedial math classes to your course load," says Dodger. She puts the cap back on her marker. "This is all bad math. I'm trying to solve something that doesn't want to be solved, and I fucked up somewhere back there"—she waves a hand vaguely toward the first wall, the snarl of incomprehensible symbols scrawled in black on white—"so now I need to start it over."

"If you know you screwed up, why are you still going?"

Dodger shrugs. "Even a wrong answer can be interesting. I'll keep solving as long as solution is possible, and when it stops being possible, I'll figure out what I did wrong. It's soothing. It gives me things to play with. Don't you study child development because you like *toys*?"

"Yes, toys, not numbers on a wall and risking our security deposit," says Candace. "You didn't answer my first question. How was the tour?"

"I didn't go." The lie comes light and easy. She's gotten so *good* at this. "I was up all night talking to some computational mathematicians in Australia. They're working on a set of proofs that's going to blow everyone else out of the water, me included, and they wanted to gloat. By the time I realized I should be getting some sleep, my alarm was going off. It seemed better to meet my new classmates when I wasn't a sleep-deprived nightmare."

Candace cocks her head. "You don't seem like a sleep-deprived nightmare right now."

"I had a nap. And a two-liter of Mountain Dew. I'm basically good to go. Who schedules a grad-student walking tour at eight-thirty in the morning anyway? Don't they know most of us are nocturnal at this stage in our careers?"

"People who are no longer nocturnal, and resent the fact that they need sleep," says Candace. Her tone is light but her eyes are sharp, narrowing as she looks at Dodger.

Not for the first time, Dodger thinks she may have made a tactical error in agreeing to room with someone whose discipline includes developmental psychology. She smiles as brightly as she can, trying to force the memory of Roger's startled face even further toward the back of her mind. He's the reason she messed up her math, because she can't *focus*.

She was never supposed to see him again. She's never really seen him before. He's not *real*. He's not real, because if he were real, she would have hurt him, by slamming the door between them. He can't be real, because if he's real, she's a monster for what she did to him.

He can't be real.

"I guess I just wasn't up for it," she says finally.

Candace's eyes dart to the scar on Dodger's left arm, and Dodger has to swallow the urge to put her hand over it. Candace is one of the people who knew what it was the first time she saw it, and knew the newspaper articles for a childish—if eagerly accepted—attempt at a cover-up.

"You want some tea?" Candace asks. "It might make you feel better. I know it always helps me when I'm not feeling good."

"That would be great," says Dodger, and smiles, and Candace smiles back before she turns and disappears, leaving Dodger alone in her room of flawed equations, numbers that don't add up, marching ever onward into the future, never finding their solution, never really being solved.

# Reunion

Roger never knew there were so many ways to be a math major. The field is enormously divided and subdivided, a fractal web of specializations chasing its own tail into the depths of the course catalog. It's like peering through the gates of hell. Infinite math classes packed with infinite mathematicians, all of whom would be delighted to explain in great and painful detail exactly why the fact that he gave up as soon as he fulfilled his general math credit requirements was a mistake.

But Dodger Cheswich is famous in mathematical circles: Dodger Cheswich is the girl who solved the Monroe Equation. (The memory of her shyly showing him her work, written in gel pen on wide-lined paper, hurts less than it used to, because he's going to see her again, he's going to *see* her and tell her he was wrong to run away but so was she, and she's the mathematician—can't she see that this makes them equal? Can't she see that the time for running is over?) Getting her to come to Berkeley for grad school was an accomplishment. Not a big accomplishment, like netting a real celebrity or someone whose parents could afford to endow a new library, but an accomplishment all the same. Someone has to have bragged about getting her for their specific specialty.

Someone has. He finds a reference buried in one of the chess club newsletters to "incoming student D. Cheswich, joining our esteemed Mathematics department as she pursues her degree in game theory." Armed with a name, description, birth date, and area of study, it was a small thing to find her advisor, and an even smaller thing to present himself as her brother hoping to surprise her. It's a lie, but a believable one: they look alike enough to pass as siblings. They have the same eyes. They were born on the same day and adopted by families on opposite sides of the continent. And once upon a time, impossible as it is to believe when nothing like it has ever happened again, they were able to talk to each other by closing their eyes.

People usually give him what he asks, when he takes the time to do his research and understand his own requests. It's been three days since the campus tour that went off-campus after she ran out on it, and now here he is, standing on her doorstep with a chessboard tucked under his arm, trying to find the courage to knock.

"Hey."

He looks up. There's a woman on the balcony above him. Short, curvy, pretty in an all-American way: she'd look perfectly at home at a baseball game, or wearing cut-off shorts and sitting in the bed of a pickup truck. His romantic life has been a succession of Norman Rockwell paintings, and this girl would slot into place without disrupting the line. Her hair is ashen and her eyes are pale and she's looking at him like he's an interesting new species of insect, something meant to be placed in a jar and studied for as long as possible.

"Hello," he says.

Her gaze sharpens. "You're not here for me, because I don't know you. You're not here for Candy, because she has a boyfriend, and he's built like a Sherman tank. There's no way you could be here for Dodger. She doesn't date. I'm not sure she understands why humans have anything other than a waste exhaust port in their pants."

He lifts his eyebrows. "How long have you been living here?"

"A week, but I pay attention. I know stuff." The woman leans further out over the rail, taking a drag off her cigarette and blowing the smoke in his direction. When she taps the ash over the rail it falls perfectly into the bushes below her, practice making perfect. "That a chessboard?"

"Yes," he says, trying not to sniff the air like a starving dog. His last cigarette was eight days ago. A personal best, which is something to be proud of, but doesn't currently feel like it. It feels like he's torturing himself for no good reason.

"So you're here for Dodger, then."

"Yes."

"Why?" The woman's gaze is sharp enough to nail his feet to the porch. "She's not interested in making friends. She says she is, but she's lying. She's a good liar."

"So how do you know she's not just nervous?"

"Because I pay attention." The woman takes another drag on her cigarette, still watching him closely. "What's your name?"

"Roger."

"Your names rhyme. That's cute. If you were related, you'd have grounds to sue your parents." She blows smoke out through her nose. "Last chance, *Roger*. If you don't knock, you could walk away clean. I'm pretty sure she doesn't want to see you. She's been acting spooked for days. You could get out of here and probably never see her again."

"Thanks for the advice . . . ?" He leaves the question dangling, waiting.

Her lips twist in what might charitably be called a smile. "Erin," she says. "Don't say I didn't warn you." She drops her cigarette, grinds it under her heel, and goes inside.

Roger rings the bell.

Dodger's class schedule has been designed to give her long blocks of uninterrupted free time, followed by long blocks of time spent teaching classes for professors with better things to do, grading papers, and trying not to be too mean to undergrads. It's not their fault that they're at a different point in their studies than she is, and maybe if she reminds herself of that often enough, she'll stop feeling the need to throw things at them. It's frustrating enough that when she's teaching, she's expected to dress like a grownup, or at least wear something other than pajamas. Dress codes are the bane of her existence.

(Several people have looked at her schedule and told her it doesn't make sense, it doesn't *work,* she can't possibly have that much time to herself. She doesn't understand why they're making such a fuss. All she had to do was rotate the numbers until they slotted together the way she wanted them to. It's not like it was *hard.*)

The doorbell rings. She looks up from her computer. Neither of her roommates is home, and she's pretty sure she'd remember if she'd ordered a pizza, since that would have meant noticing and accepting that she was hungry. Awareness of her own body's needs is not and has never been her strong suit. Conclusion: it's not pizza.

There aren't that many other things it could, or should, be. They live off-campus for a reason. No one has their address, and with as little time as they've lived here, every knock on the front door is an adventure. She's met three neighbors, a door-to-door pot brownie vendor, and a teenage girl with a box of kittens and a harried expression. Who knows what today will bring? Carefully, she saves her work and stands, ready for a new surprise.

Dodger is smiling when she opens the door. That's the first thing Roger notices. Whoever she's become in the last five years, it's still someone who can smile. Her face freezes when she sees him, smile turning into something crystalline and sharp. He could cut himself on that expression.

"Please don't close the door," he says.

Her crystal smile vanishes completely. It's almost a miracle he doesn't hear it shatter on the floor. "You're not real."

Roger blinks. "That's a new one."

"You're not real. You're my imaginary friend and I dreamed you, and if I dreamed you you're not real, and if you're not real, you can't be here. What are you doing here?"

"Can I come in?" He hopes he doesn't sound as nervous as he feels. Although maybe it would be better if he did: it would be harder for her to pretend this isn't hurting him as much as it's hurting her. He forces a smile of his own, trying to look harmless and hopeful at the same time. Trying to look like he's not a threat. "I mean, we can do this with me on the porch if you want—this is Berkeley, we have people running around pretending to be vampires every Sunday night, no one's going to care about a couple of Midwich cuckoos—but it might be easier if I come inside."

"The Midwich cuckoos were blonde," says Dodger. Her voice hasn't changed much. It's a little deeper, but puberty was basically finished with her long before they'd stopped speaking. "You have brown hair. I'm a redhead. We're not the children of sexist bucolic aliens. Also you don't exist."

"And let's be grateful for that, because they were trying for breeding pairs—the aliens part, not the 'I don't exist' part," he says. "How do you know that, anyway?"

"Even math geniuses have to do book reports. We don't get to skip English because we think it's *silly*." Her voice almost breaks.

His heart feels like it cracks a little. "Please. Dodger. Can I come inside?"

She doesn't want to let him in: that much is clear in the way she looks past him to the street, scanning for anyone who might give her an excuse to say no. It both hurts and offends him that she'd feel the need to do that. No matter what lies she may have told the police, he's never laid a hand on her—was on the other side of the continent when she decided to lay a hand on herself. All he's ever done is try to save her, except when he had to leave her behind to save himself.

Sacrifice. That's what they've each done, at least once: they've sacrificed the other for their own protection. Maybe that's the key. "I brought a chessboard," he says, holding it up. "I couldn't find any pieces, but I figured you'd probably have something we could use."

Now a corner of her mouth quirks, like she's about to smile again. It seems more genuine this time. He's already figuring out a few things about Dodger's smiles, piecing them together from what he remembers of her as a child, what he remembers from the one time they ever met face-to-face: when she's lying, she smiles with her whole face. When she's actually happy, she only smiles with the left, like she's trying to make sure she can control who sees it.

"Did you think I *wouldn't* have a chessboard?" she asks, and she doesn't sound angry, she doesn't sound frightened, or tired, or any of those other things. She sounds like *Dodger*. She sounds like his best friend.

He knows the words: relief, alleviation, contentment. None of them encompass the feeling of weightlessness, like all the troubles in the world have been lifted from his shoulders. He guesses this feeling is probably a cliché, but the people who like to put those labels on things don't always remember that things become clichés because they keep happening, over and over, all around the world.

"Not really," he says. "So can I exist again, and come inside?"

"Third time's the charm, I guess," she says, and holds the door open wider so he can get by. She presses her back against the wall, avoiding even accidental physical contact.

Roger regrets that, a little. He was the one who'd first introduced the idea that their quantum entanglement—or whatever it was—might be enhanced by physical contact, and it appears to have stuck with both of them. He doesn't *want* to touch her. He just wishes she didn't look so scared that he would.

Once the door is closed, he clears his throat and asks, "Berkeley?"

"You have a good math department," she says, flipping the deadbolt with her thumb. "I wanted to work with Professor Kong. Her research in game theory is revolutionary. And there's the Mathematical Sciences Research Institute, of course. Talk about a kid in a candy store. The kitchen's this way." She turns her back on him—a show of trust or a show of dominance, he doesn't quite know—and heads down the hall, apparently trusting him to follow.

He does, studying his surroundings as they walk, looking for the vocabulary of the woman she's become. If he can read her, he can start to understand her. The trouble is figuring out which of the things around him belong to her and not to her roommates. That she has roommates is obvious: the place is too big for her to afford on her own, and the Dodger he knew would never have brought a complete set of the Up-and-Under books with her to college. The math texts are probably hers. The books on chess. He's not sure about the books on social engineering and finding your better self, but something about the way she walks—shoulders back, neck elongated, like she's practiced this—makes him suspect they might be hers.

The girl on the balcony said Dodger wasn't interested in making friends, just in having people believe she was, and Roger suspects that she was right. It would fit with who Dodger was when they lost contact.

The kitchen at the end of the hall is small but bright, with windows taking up most of one wall. There's a concrete patio out back, no more than six feet deep, and every bit of it that can be packed with planter boxes has been. They bristle with dozens of succulents in a dozen varieties, a dozen different shades of gray. There's a cat sitting on the fence, a scarred orange tom with one green eye. The cat looks at Roger. Roger looks at the cat.

"That's old Bill," says Dodger, clearing an armload of newspapers off the folding card table crammed into the breakfast nook. "He comes with the apartment. The landlady asked us to feed him when we remembered, and to call her if he got hit by a car or anything like that. He's pretty sweet. Only tries to convince us to let him in when it starts raining. So I wasn't necessarily lying when I said I had to feed the cat, even if he's not actually mine."

"What a good kitty," says Roger dutifully. He likes cats. They have their own agenda, and he respects that. "Is there anything I can do to help?"

"I'd rather you didn't." Dodger continues clearing the table, head down, hair shielding her face. He knows it's red, even if he can't see the color right now, red as sunset, red as a warning. It's as if that, of everything about her, was designed to attract attention, and he knows she doesn't like people staring at her.

"Did you ever think about dyeing your hair?" he blurts, and instantly regrets it. He's supposed to be the one who's good with words, and here he is saying things he should know will upset her. It's like everything gets scrambled when they're in the same room, like the fundamental laws of nature have been twisted twenty degrees to the left.

(He knows he can never tell anyone about this feeling, because he knows what they'd say: "you're in love" and "bang the girl, get it out of your system." But he's not in love with Dodger. He loves her, has loved her since the moment he admitted she was a real person and not an imaginary friend, but that's not being *in* love. It's just that when they're together, it feels like the world is finally complete, and if he can keep it in one piece for long enough, he'll learn what the rules actually *are*.)

Dodger turns her head, enough that the hair falls away from her eyes and he can see her looking at him. "Do you think I should?" she asks, with honest curiosity. She's looking at him like she *sees* him, now, like he actually exists.

He wishes he weren't so grateful for that. "No," he says. "I mean, I remember how pretty it is. I just know you don't like it when people stare."

She raises a hand to touch the side of her head, briefly confused. "What do you mean, you remember?" Her eyes widen. "Oh! The color-blindness thing!"

"Yeah," he says, feeling a strange relief wash over him. If she knows he's color-blind, it's because she remembers looking through his eyes, seeing the ways the world differed from her expectations. She's remembering that it wasn't all some weird childhood hallucination. "I mean, I know it's red, it's just not . . . it doesn't look red to me, you know?"

"I know." She lowers her hand. "I've thought about it. Especially after . . . after. I didn't like how easy it was for people to spot me. But I could never go through with it. I don't know why. It just seemed . . . wrong."

"You wouldn't be able to draw fire like you're supposed to," says

Roger without thinking, and stops dead, staring at her as she stares at him. His words are true: he knows that, without knowing *how* he knows it. (And hasn't that always been the way? A lifetime studded with facts he knows beyond the shadow of the doubt, never with any proof to back them up. It's not scientific. It's not scholarly. It's just the way things *are*.)

Dodger shakes her head, visibly unnerved. "I think you're right," she says, in a small voice. She sounds scared, and Roger hates himself a little for making her sound like that. Dodger isn't supposed to be scared. She's supposed to be the brave one. It's the compensation for her also being the breakable one.

Silence spools out between them. If they let it go on for too long, they're never going to break free. Roger does the first thing he can think of: he drops his chessboard onto the clear spot Dodger has formed on the table, and asks, "You want to go get some pieces?"

She laughs, and everything is going to be okay. At least for now, everything is going to be okay.

"No, but I'll go get a chess set," she says. "The whole thing. This is amateur hour. I mean, *really*, Roger." She breezes past him, twisting her body at the last moment to keep their shoulders from touching. He wonders how long it will be before they feel comfortable with physical contact. He wonders whether they'll be able to be in one another's presence for that long. The last thing he wants to do is drive her away again, or drive her to do something she can't take back. She's wearing a short-sleeved shirt. He saw the scars on her arms.

It's difficult not to think he had something to do with putting them there. He knows he didn't. That doesn't change anything. The mind is an imperfect engine, and it does what it will with the information it receives. He failed to see how lonely she was; she felt he didn't need her; events followed their natural course. It wasn't his fault. It could never have been his fault. But he didn't see it coming, and he should have. Somehow, he should have.

When Dodger returns she finds him outside the sliding glass door, crouching on the concrete step that serves as their "porch," scratching old Bill behind the ears. The ragged battle-axe of a tomcat is purring so loud she can hear it from three feet away, almost tumbling over himself in his effort to get closer to Roger's practiced fingers.

"You have a cat?" she asks, putting the chess set she carries down on the table.

"Not right now," he says. "Student housing wasn't so good for pet ownership, and I just moved off-campus. My most recent ex-girlfriend had one, though. She got a note from her psychiatrist calling it a necessary therapy animal, and we mostly spent time in her room."

"Oh," says Dodger. "What was her name?"

"Zucchini."

Dodger blinks.

Roger looks over his shoulder, sees her expression, and bursts out laughing. "Oh, man, your face—not the *girlfriend*, Dodge, the *cat*. The cat was named Zucchini. The fact that I gave you the cat's name first explains why we broke up. We were both exhausted all the time, and I'd go to her place to pet the cat and try to ease my nerves. Eventually, Kelly decided she wanted to find a boyfriend who'd pet the Kelly instead of the kitty, and we parted ways. Amiably."

He's good at that: parting amiably. Every relationship he's ever been in has ended amiably. Even his relationship with Alison, which had had the most potential to go horribly wrong, ended with the two of them being perfectly civil to each other when they passed in the halls or met in class. Parting amiably is one of his great skills.

Except with Dodger. Every time they've parted has been incredibly traumatic, for both of them. He gives the cat one last scratch and stands, stepping back into the apartment and closing the glass door before old Bill can follow. The big tom tries anyway, stepping right up to the glass and meowing. His eyes are locked on Roger.

"You're doomed," says Dodger, laying out the chess set. Her movements are quick, practiced, precise; she barely looks at the pieces before putting them on the board. If it were possible for someone to feel the difference in color between two otherwise identical pawns, she'd be doing it. "That cat knows a sucker when he sees one, and now you're doomed. It's been nice knowing you."

"Now, you and I both know that hasn't always been true," he says. Dodger pauses for an instant before she resumes setting out the pieces, hands moving too fast to be acting on anything but autopilot. "Maybe not, but it's polite to pretend," she says. She sets out the last piece, puts the shoebox she was taking them out of aside, and sits, taking the chair farthest from where he's standing. This puts her on the black side of the board. Normally, they'd agree to the sides they were playing, he knows that. He isn't going to object. If she's choosing her color based on whether it keeps her away from him, he's not going to pursue.

He sits. Then he frowns, squinting at the set, and leans forward to pick up a bishop, rolling it over in his hand. "Isn't this the set you used to keep down in the gully?" he asks. "I remember when you thought you'd lost your bishop. You were inconsolable for *days*. And then it rained, and washed the mud away so you could find the missing piece, and you started keeping everything in your room, because an incomplete chess set wasn't any good."

"You kept saying that even if the piece was lost forever, I could find a new one. You said you'd look in every Goodwill in Massachusetts if you had to."

"I was really hoping I wouldn't have to," he says. "I hate seeing you cry, but I had no idea how I was going to explain to my parents that I needed to buy just one chess piece and mail it to a girl in California."

"At least then you would have let me give you my address."

"I don't think I could have found a way to avoid it."

"Maybe it would have been better for both of us if the bishop had stayed lost." She finally looks up. They really do have the same eyes. He wears glasses and she doesn't, but their irises are the same. It's like finding someone who shares his fingerprints. "I would have had a return address. I could've written you letters. Made you talk to me."

"Dodger, we were *nine*."

"Nine-year-olds are still people and can still feel pain. That's a scientific fact." She drops her eyes back to the chessboard. "Your move, Roger."

So he moves, and she moves, and for a few minutes, all is silence:

their focus is on the game. He takes his time with his choices, shifting the pieces in a defensive pattern he's hoping will keep him on the board for at least a while.

Dodger doesn't play defensively. Dodger plays so offensively that it's almost profane, and it's almost poetry, and there's no contradiction in those things—no contradiction at all. She was good when she was a teenager, playing masters and grandmasters all over the country in her black and white schoolgirl outfits, but she also played like a teenager; she understood the game innately enough to be a workman. She hadn't been possessed of the kind of experience that would make her an artist. She has that experience now. Her every move is ruthless, designed to end the game as quickly as possible. They're not just playing different sides: they're playing different *games,* him to last, her to end.

"You're good," he says.

"I always was," she says.

Roger pauses in the act of reaching for a pawn, hesitates, and pulls his hand back, letting it rest in his lap. He waits.

As he'd expected, Dodger is still not built for patience: stillness is anathema to her. She can stop when she has to, can transmute physical motion into mental; anyone who's ever seen her doing math knows she can go without moving for *hours* if she has the right kind of problem to occupy her mind. But this is not a problem she can solve. This is an interaction, one person answering the other, and he is refusing to give her the satisfaction of progress.

Seconds tick by, forming minutes, until she can't take it anymore. Her head comes up, her eyes narrowing. Blood is rising in her cheeks, and for the first time since their game began, she is present: she is *engaged.* "I know you're not this bad," she says. "Move your piece."

"What if I don't want to?"

"Then forfeit, and call the game in my favor."

"What if I don't want to do that either?" Roger shows her his empty hands before letting them rest on the table. "I want to talk to you. I came here because I wanted to talk to you."

"So talk."

"I tried that. You didn't answer me. I'm not leaving until you talk to me, Dodger. I saved your life. You owe me at least a conversation."

Dodger blinks, the blood draining out of her face a drop at a time, until she's as pale as ever, a wax figure of a mathematician. Then, with a shake of her head, she laughs. "Really?" she asks, syllables distorted by her amusement but comprehensible for all of that. "That's what you're going to go with? 'I saved your life'? I didn't ask you to, Roger. I went out of my way to make sure I'd be able to go down to the gully and do what needed to be done while you weren't looking. You were never supposed to *know*."

"If you hadn't been so damn determined to shut me out, you'd be asking yourself *how* I knew." Roger glares. He's been trying to keep himself from getting angry, but there's only so much he can take before enough is enough. "Quantum entanglement, remember? That whole 'I say it and you hear it on the other side of the country' gig? Turns out it's good for more than just giving you the answers on a pop quiz."

Dodger frowns at him. Unlike her smiles, her frowns engage her whole mouth, making her look utterly perplexed. "What do you mean? You felt me cut myself? You never felt anything I did to myself before."

(Thank God for that. Both of them had been terrified, after they restored contact, that the other would somehow pick up on certain things. Certain *personal* things. Roger *liked* girls, but the idea of a girl—any girl, but especially *this* girl—coming along for the ride when he was alone under the covers was enough to darken even the teenage libido. Experiments and trials had followed, until they were both satisfied that only their thoughts could cross the void between them. Feelings, emotional or otherwise, were not capable of making the jump. Except that her feelings had, when she was almost at the end. Trauma could work miracles.)

"I mean that when *your* heart started getting fucked up because it didn't have enough blood to beat, so did mine," he says grimly. "I had a seizure in class. I blacked out and hit my head on the floor, and when I woke up, I knew you'd done something to yourself. I knew you'd hurt yourself, and I was thousands of miles away, and I couldn't do a damn thing to help. I called for you. I screamed. You didn't answer."

Dodger turns away, refusing to look at him. Too bad. The floodgates are open: the story is coming out now, whether he wants it to or not. He's spent too many years unable to be mad at her, because she was too far away, because she wasn't speaking to him, because he honestly wasn't sure she was still alive. Well, she's alive now; she's here now, sitting on the other side of a table, shying away from the touch of his hand like he had been the one to hold the razor blade.

Maybe he has some culpability here. Maybe he missed the signs; maybe he helped to create an essential weakness in her foundations when he cut off contact at nine years old. Maybe no one is an island. But in the end, he's not the one who fed her a bottle of painkillers and opened her wrists. He missed the signs. He was seventeen years old. There's a point where blaming himself has to end, and he's finally reached it.

"I had three seizures while your brain tried like hell to take me down with it. *Three.* The third one hit right after I called your dad. I passed out in the middle of Harvard Square, in the rain, by myself. It's a miracle I didn't wake up in jail on a public drunkenness charge." It's a miracle he woke up at all. He's thought, more than once, about how easy it would have been for him to have rolled over during one of his seizures, leaving him to drown in the heavy September rain. As ironic ways to go went, that one was pretty high on the list.

Dodger is staring at him in undisguised horror. "I didn't know," she whispers, and he doesn't doubt her, and it doesn't matter.

"Didn't know all that happened, or didn't know all that *would* happen?" he asks.

"Either. Both. I swear, Roger, I didn't know I could hurt you by hurting myself. I would never—"

"Yeah, you would," he says gently. She goes still. "Dodge, you're my best friend. Always. Even when we're not talking—and I sort of feel like we've spent more time not talking than we have talking, at this point—you're my best friend. Hell, I would have flunked second grade if not for you. Did you really think it wouldn't hurt me to lose you?

Like, honestly and truly? Fuck, just *almost* losing you hurt like hell. And then you shut me out so hard that I started thinking you were dead after all, or that you'd gone without oxygen for so long that you'd managed to damage yourself and couldn't hear me anymore."

"I heard you," she whispers, chin dipping toward the table again. "I always hear you."

"So why the hell didn't you *answer*?"

"I was mad," she says. "I woke up in the hospital, and they were saying some boy from New England called my dad at work to brag about how he'd cut me up and left me for dead, and I knew it had to be you. I knew they were wrong about why you'd called—I knew you wouldn't have called because you were *glad* I was dying—but I knew you'd called and ruined everything, again. So I was mad. And I was grateful, because once I wasn't dead, I didn't want to be. I wanted to have died. I didn't want to be dead. I told myself you were a dream, a bad dream that wouldn't go away, and somehow, I . . . I believed it."

There's so much she can't figure out how to say in words. How her mother cried, and how it hurt to know *she* was the reason for that expression on her mother's face, that utter and total despair. How her father raged for days, losing his temper at the slightest thing, calling the police over and over to shout at them about how they weren't doing their jobs if they couldn't find the boy who'd hurt his daughter. How the police had known from the start that it was a suicide attempt, and just humored her parents. How she found them sitting on the couch, holding each other and sobbing when they thought she wouldn't hear them. Removing herself from the equation had seemed like the easiest solution when she had decided to do it. She hadn't realized just how many sub-formulae depended on her until it was almost too late.

"I didn't want to be grateful to you, you know," she continues, voice still soft and level. "I was so *mad* at you, all the time."

"Because I stopped talking to you when we were kids? I thought we had—I mean, I thought you had accepted my apology."

"Of course I accepted your apology. What else was I supposed to do?" She shakes her head. "If someone says 'sorry' and you don't say 'it's okay, I'm not mad anymore,' you're a bad person. Especially if you're a girl. And I missed you so bad, I thought it would be okay. I thought I could say 'we're okay' and make it be true. But the numbers didn't add up. I couldn't understand how you could mean so much to me and I could mean so little to you."

"You never meant anything less than the world to me, Dodger," says Roger. "It's just that my family needed me more than you did. When we were kids, you were always the one running ahead. You never looked to see if you were going to fall. I figured you'd do better without me than I would without you."

"I only ran like that because I knew you'd always be there to catch me," she says. "You were my safety net. You meant I couldn't hurt myself too badly."

"I caught you and you left me," he says. "What does that mean?"

"That I'm really stupid for a smart person?" A tear rolls down her cheek. She swipes it away with the back of her hand. "I thought you'd be as messed-up as I was when I saw you again, and you were fine. You had friends, you had a girlfriend, and I had this big notebook filled with apologies that might be good enough to make you love me again. I didn't know how to deal. So I ran the numbers, and figured you'd be better off without me."

"I never was, Dodge," he says.

She sniffles, and that's it, that's *it*: he can handle a lot of things, but he can't stand seeing Dodger cry. He's up before he has time to consider the ramifications of his action, moving to kneel next to the chair where she sits, and put his arms around her, and let her bury her face against his shoulder. There's no way to keep skin from touching skin in this position, and that's all right; if that means their quantum entanglement gets worse, well, it's not like she didn't already almost kill him. Maybe a little more severity would have meant he could feel her picking up the razor, and things would never have gone that far.

"Alison dumped me for running off campus after I had my first seizure. She couldn't be with someone who'd do something like that to himself, or to her. I didn't blame her then and I don't blame her now. It was a pretty amiable breakup."

"It had to be," mumbles Dodger, her voice muffled by his shoulder. She's not lifting her head. She's not loosening her grip either; she's holding on like she suspects this all of being a dream that's about to end and leave her falling. "If you'd stayed together, she would have told the police they were looking for you, eventually. She would have gotten scared."

Roger doesn't ask how she knows that: her words are accompanied by a strong sense of déjà vu, or maybe déjà entendu, like she's describing something he witnessed once, long ago, and never wants to see again. *We've been here before,* he thinks, almost deliriously, and then: *We got it wrong.*

Dodger slackens her grip and pulls back, eyes wide and shiny with tears. She looks more confused than frightened. That's a good thing, because Roger is terrified, and one of them needs to not be scared.

"Why do I know that?" she asks. "Because I *do* know that. It's not a guess and it's not a suspicion, I *know.*"

"I don't know," he says. "But Dodger, please. Please don't ever think I'm better off without you. Do you have any idea how many makeup exams I had to take to finish math my senior year? I was nearly the first person in my school's history with an early admission to Berkeley who couldn't graduate with his class."

She giggles, the sound small and thick with snot, before wiping her nose with the back of her hand and saying, "My teachers took pity on me, since I was clearly traumatized, and let me switch my English and History classes to pass/fail. I passed by the skin of my teeth, but I passed, and it wasn't like Stanford was going to keep me out. Not with Daddy teaching there and my face in all the papers."

"See, if you'd been speaking to me, you could have passed without needing to look pathetic."

"I didn't look pathetic, I . . . Okay, I looked pathetic. It worked, don't knock it." Dodger grins, the left side of her mouth twisting sharply upward while the right side remains where it is. Then, with no warning but that, she flings her arms around Roger, hugging him tightly. "I missed you so much."

"I missed you too," he says, and stays where he is, just holding her, just being held, until the sound of the front door slamming jerks them both out of the moment. Roger pulls away. Dodger turns to blink at the door, eyes first wide, then narrowing.

"Candace?" she calls. "Is that you?"

There's no sound from the hallway, no footsteps or hint of breath.

"I think it was your other roommate going out," says Roger.

Dodger blinks at him. "What, Erin? She's not here."

"No, because she just went out," he says. "She was here when I got here. Out on the balcony, having a cigarette. This is a two-story apartment?"

"Only on a technicality," says Dodger. "Upstairs is Erin's bedroom, the master bathroom, and the balcony. She got the upstairs bedroom because it's the smallest and she's a smoker. She said giving up a little personal space was worth it if she could go outside to smoke in the middle of the night. Since our security deposit says no smoking inside, this seemed like the best way to arrange things. And I didn't want to deal with stairs every time I went to bed. But she's never home."

"She was home today," says Roger. "She told me you weren't interested in making friends, and that if I left without knocking, I'd never need to see you again. Then, when I said I was going to knock anyway, she told me not to say she didn't warn me. You have interesting taste in roommates, Dodge."

"Yeah, but she was right, so it's not like I can be mad," she says. "I'm not really interested in making friends."

Roger raises an eyebrow. "What do you call me?" he asks.

"Roger," she says. Her smile is radiant. "I call you Roger. Now come on. Let's finish that chess game. I think you've gone too long without me whooping your ass."

He laughs, and she laughs, and he moves back to his side of the table, and while things are not entirely okay between them—won't be for a while yet—things are getting better. The world is getting back to true.

# Experimentation

Rebuilding old friendships is never easy. Doing it during the first month of grad school, when there are new things to learn and new duties lurking around every corner, is virtually impossible. Roger's advisor keeps him occupied for two solid weeks with campus tours, reminding him over and over again that his volunteering unlocks certain privileges within the library system. A little wasted time is worth it, for the ability to take his reference materials home without worrying about whether they're restricted. As for Dodger, she's finding her way around campus, learning where she can safely chain her bike, and discovering the local food options—although she seems content with pizza, which is fast, cheap, and nutritionally complete, as long as they add extra artichokes.

Still, they steal the time they can, meeting up at the Starbucks just off campus, or in front of the library, or on the quad. They avoid touching as much as they can. They get less anxious, less poised for something terrible to happen. They don't talk about how much he smokes, how thin he is. They don't talk about her scars, how fast she rides her bike. For the first time, it feels like they have secrets between them, and it aches a little, but it's comforting, too. Secrets mean that all of this is really happening.

Two weeks pass before Roger appears on the doorstep again, ringing the bell this time. It has a thin, buzzy quality to it, like a hive of wasps sounding a greeting from inside the wall.

A woman he doesn't recognize answers the door, short and plump and beautifully proportioned, with expertly feathered brown hair. She frowns. "Can I help you?"

"Candace, I presume," he says. "Is Dodger home?"

The frown takes on a puzzled quality. He's clearly not a mathematician: he doesn't have any of the visible characteristics, the calculators, the geeky T-shirts with their math puns. Some of the underclassmen even carry antique slide rules, just to make sure they can be spotted by their own kind. It's a fascinating form of collegiate tribalism. Kelly— the ex-girlfriend with the cat—has written papers about it, documenting student clique behavior at both high school and college levels.

"Did someone sign her up for the new student social?" she asks. "Because if you're here to serve as her escort, I want you to wait right here while I get my phone. I want pictures of the colors she turns while she's yelling at you."

"Not a date," he says. "Best friend."

"Dodger doesn't have friends," says Candace.

"Brother," says Dodger, coming up behind Candace. There shouldn't be room for her to get around the other woman, but she manages. It's a surprisingly elegant movement. Turning to face Candace, she puts a possessive hand on Roger's shoulder, and says, "We're going to see a lot of him, since this is the first time he and I have been at the same school. Be kind. Or at least, don't be horrible."

"That's Erin's job," says Candace. "I didn't know you had a brother."

"I am a font of mysteries," says Dodger gravely.

Candace shakes her head, says, "Nice to meet you," and retreats down the hall.

Roger shoots Dodger an amused look. "A font of mysteries?" he asks. "I thought words were supposed to be my thing."

"Can you make change for a dollar?"

"Yes . . ."

"Then I can occasionally come up with a witty one-liner. If I want something translated from the original Greek, I promise, I'll come to you. What's the plan?"

"Hanging out on campus is great and all, but I was hoping we could sit and talk for a while? In semi-privacy?" Roger looks over his shoulder at the street before returning his attention to Dodger. "That means letting me inside."

"Ah, but you see, I have two roommates in residence, so . . . how much do you trust me?"

It's a simple question. After everything they've been through, it doesn't have a simple answer. But there's only one answer he can give. "Completely."

Dodger grins. "Good. Follow me." She turns and heads down the hall. Roger follows, closing the door behind himself. Dodger may not care if he leaves it open, but he's willing to bet her roommates would, and he has no desire to inspire their wrath.

Candace's door is closed—at least, he presumes it's Candace's door; the other door they pass is open, showing a room with equations scrawled on the walls and a bed situated in the middle of the floor. If that's not Dodger's, he'll be genuinely shocked. Dodger doesn't stop to point out features of the apartment; she's heading for the back door, where old Bill is once again perched on the fence, waiting for someone to come along and pay attention to him.

"I don't think there's enough room out here for us to sit comfortably," says Roger.

"That's because we're not going to," says Dodger. "Close the door so Bill can't get in." She drags a collapsible ladder from the fence to the wall. Roger does as he's been told, and watches with growing trepidation as she unfolds the ladder and props it against the side of the building. It doesn't reach the top. It *does* reach the bottom of a rusty old fire escape–style ladder that appears to have been bolted to the roof.

"Come on," she says, and starts climbing.

Dodger has always been the risk-taker of the pair. Watching her bike accidents and tumbles told Roger what *not* to do when his own time for those stunts arrived. She's also better at risk assessment. When she says a thing is safe, it generally is, because she's already tested and rejected all the really dangerous options. With a sigh, he follows her up the ladder.

It's not the most stable thing he's ever climbed. It's *far* from the most stable thing he's ever watched *her* climb, and he pauses a few rungs up to watch the way she makes the transfer to the bolted-on ladder, checking her grip and the angle of her transfer. She scrambles past the lip of the roof, disappearing. Then her head pops back over the edge, a bright smile on her face.

"Well?" she asks. "You coming?"

Roger hesitates. Roger takes a step back down the ladder. "Not yet," he says.

Dodger's face falls, excitement becoming confusion. Sometimes he feels like they're still children in one another's presence. He's a grown man, needs his coffee and longs for cigarettes during the brief periods—like this one—when he manages to put them down; he's progressed from high school girlfriends and eager over-the-shirt petting to having lovers who appreciate his facility for active listening and his practiced linguist's tongue. But put him near Dodger and it's all board games and climbing ladders to the roof. Things children do.

(They were supposed to grow up together: he knows that, on a deep, almost primal level, below the surface of conscious thought. They were supposed to grow up with their hands in each other's pockets, compensating for one another's weaknesses, encouraging one another's strengths. That didn't happen. For whatever reason, it didn't happen, and now, when they're together, it's like they're trying to accelerate through those lost years, using the cheat codes to get the experience without actually playing the game. He doesn't like this sort of knowledge, which bubbles up from a source he can't find; he doesn't like not knowing his own mind. But more and more, he also knows this is the only thing that's going to save them. He just wishes he could know from what.)

"It's time for us to try," he says. "Can you go to the far side of the roof?"

Her smile doesn't return. Instead, her face goes blank, falling into the perfectly neutral expression he saw her direct at her opponent in that long-ago chess game. It gives nothing away; it might as well be the face of a porcelain doll.

"Are you sure?" she asks. "We just found each other, and—"

"We found each other two weeks ago. It's time. If it's over, it's over, but we need to know," he says. "Isn't it better to find out under controlled circumstances than to have me roll my car and start screaming in your head during one of your classes?"

"I guess," she says. Her face remains blank. "If it doesn't work, you come up, okay?"

"Okay," he says. She withdraws, head vanishing. He moves to the corner of the garden farthest from the ladder and sits on the brick retaining wall keeping the thin strip of potting soil and succulents contained. Bill hops down from the fence and strolls over to strop against Roger's ankles, purring loudly, as if to make sure the human understands what he wants.

"I like self-petting kitties," says Roger, and takes a few seconds to pet the cat, giving Dodger time to get to the far corner of the roof. Then he closes his eyes.

Skills can atrophy: he knows this, has observed this in himself. He can drive a car, but he'd be a disaster on a bike, and the last time he strapped on a pair of roller skates, he damn near broke his neck. If a thing isn't used, it withers and turns inward, becoming difficult to coax out. So he's not expecting the click to come instantly. He's also not sure what this sort of proximity will mean. He's closer to her—still—than he was on the day they physically met for the first time, and he's touched her, which could have increased their quantum entanglement. The outlines of the experiment are outside of his control.

"Dodger, can you hear me?" he asks. "Are you there?"

There's no response. It feels like he's doing exactly what he's doing: sitting with his eyes closed in someone else's yard, stroking a cat and feeling increasingly ridiculous.

Maybe that's the problem. This never felt ridiculous before. Even when it felt impossible, it didn't feel *silly*: it felt like the world was working the way it had always been intended to work, running smoothly on all cylinders for the very first time. He reaches for the memory of that feeling, settling deeper into his stillness, letting go of everything, even the darkness behind his closed eyelids.

"Hey, Dodge," he says.

There's a snap. It feels almost like that second seizure back in high school, the one that knocked the world out of true for a single, painless second. It's like getting struck by lightning and it's like blacking out and it's not like either of those things; it's like his mind is a broken bone that's been forcefully shoved back into position.

His eyes are still closed, but he can see light, and blurry blotches of color. Dodger blinks several times, and with each blink the world comes more into focus, until he's seeing Derby Street from above, from a perspective he hasn't shared in years. The world is recast in sudden, vivid color, and the edges of things are a little softer; Dodger doesn't quite *need* glasses, at least not yet, but she doesn't have the clarity of distance vision that would come with corrective lenses.

She lifts her hand, holding it up so she—and by extension, he—can see it. "Hi, Roger," she says, and he hears her voice the way *she* hears it, distorted by bone conduction, and it's exactly right; it's like coming home.

He's winded. He shouldn't be, but he is. "Hi," he says. He's also grinning like a fool. He hadn't been sure they could still do this. "I can see your hand."

"I know." She raises it, flexes the fingers, and then starts moving them, flashing a quick series of signs. "How many fingers?"

"Three, five, two, four, three, one—that's not very nice, you know. If anyone sees you doing that, they're going to throw something at you."

"If people throw things for that in Massachusetts, I'm never going back there."

"We're polite on the East Coast."

"You're a liar, and I just wanted to check," she says, and closes her own eyes.

Roger knows what's coming: he takes a breath, opens his eyes, and says, "See, this is what the cat looks like when you're color-blind." Bill obligingly butts his head into Roger's knee.

"Huh," says Dodger, and she might as well be leaning over his shoulder, not speaking in the space behind his ears. "Look at that. You going to come up to the roof now? I don't want one of my roommates deciding there's something wrong with you and calling the police."

"Is that really a risk?"

"Search me. I've never done this before."

Roger shakes his head. "I don't think anyone has."

Dodger doesn't say anything. Dodger has, through whatever odd mental mechanism they both understand and can't explain, shut the door; the conversation is over, at least until he comes up to the roof. Roger smiles a little at that. She always did like to have the last word.

Bill follows him to the ladder, meowing plaintively when Roger begins to climb. Roger pauses to look back at the cat.

"If you honestly expect me to believe you can't get up to the roof whenever you feel like it, you must think I'm one stupid human," he says.

The cat meows again.

"Okay, you think all humans are stupid," says Roger. "Come up if you feel like it." He resumes his climb.

The folding ladder is stable; the bolted-on portion dangling from the roof is less so. It shifts when he moves his weight to it, just enough to remind him that gravity exists. It would hurt to fall from this height, even if it's not high enough to kill him. He grits his teeth and keeps them ground together until he pulls himself over the edge of the roof, back onto a reassuringly solid surface. Then he stops, still half-crouched, and blinks at the scene in front of him.

Dodger and her roommates have been busy. She kept her eyes on the street while he was looking through them, presumably so his first look at the rooftop proper would be from his own perspective, allowing her to watch. She's smirking at him from a folding chair perched on the roof's edge. It's the most temporary-looking of the furniture, which includes a full patio set with a vast canvas umbrella, and a dozen potted plants. There's a chessboard on the table, paused mid-game.

"How . . . ?"

"Candace has friends in the engineering department," says Dodger. "They spend a lot of time here, so they were happy to figure out how to get some furniture onto the roof. It was a fun challenge. I did a few calculations for them, helped them figure out the angles and everything. One of them tried to pick me up—in the metaphorical sense, not the physical sense. Candace kept that from getting ugly."

"So you're not, uh, seeing someone right now?"

Dodger's look of alarm is comical. Roger bursts out laughing, and only laughs harder when her alarm morphs into irritation.

"I'm sorry, I'm sorry," he says, putting his hands out to ward her off, still laughing harder than is strictly good for him. "You looked *horrified*. I've had girls make a lot of faces when they thought I was asking them out, but that's the first time I've managed outright horror. I was not asking you out. I will not be asking you out. I'm in a comfortable lull between girlfriends right now, and I'm enjoying it. Also, I love you, but I don't love you like *that*. You're more like my sister."

"Statistically speaking, that's not as unreasonable as it sounds," she says.

Roger blinks. "Come again?"

"Oh, come on, like you haven't thought it? We have the same birthday, we have weird closed adoptions where our parents don't know *anything* about our biological parents, we have the same eyes, and while quantum entanglement is a fairly extreme manifestation of the phenomenon, the closest thing I've found to the way we can talk to each other is in unsubstantiated reports of twins who always knew what the other was thinking, even when they were miles apart." Dodger shrugs. "We'd need a blood test or something to prove it, but I'd be willing to lay money on us being related."

"Do you . . . do you want to get a blood test?" Roger moves to the nearest chair and sinks into it, unsurprised when Bill appears and leaps up into his lap. Dodger's not saying anything he hasn't thought, but hearing it out loud, from someone else, makes it difficult to ignore.

"No."

"Why not?"

"Because what if the results say we're not related? I don't have a better way of coping with . . . whatever the hell it is we have going on between us. If I think of us as a really extreme form of twinning, we're not freaks. We're just a natural phenomenon turned up to eleven. And what if . . ." She pauses. "It's silly, because we've both been in the hospital at least once. They'd know if there was something wrong with us. But they weren't checking our blood for alien proteins or weird machines or anything like that when they were trying to keep us breathing. They were just fixing us. So what if there's something about us that's not *right*? We could go in for tests and open a whole world of badness."

"You've thought about this a lot."

Dodger shrugs. "I had a lot of time on my hands."

"So you didn't stay with chess?"

"No." She shakes her head. "I could have, but it was never . . . There were people I played against who'd spent their whole lives trying to get good enough for those games. They measured their self-worth against how well they could move the pieces. I just know where the pieces need to go. It felt like cheating. Like when I used to help you play Monopoly, and then you'd get mad because it wasn't fair to your family."

"You say 'help,' I say 'shouted in my head like a steamroller because it was taking too long.'"

Dodger shrugs again, this time smiling almost sheepishly. "I'm the most impatient patient person that you'll ever meet."

"That's probably true," says Roger. The conversation has meandered. There's a reason for that: neither he nor Dodger is comfortable with the idea that whatever it is that lets them speak to each other the way they do has endured into adulthood. It would have been *easier*, really, if she hadn't replied; if she'd let him sit in silence in the back garden and allowed this part of their shared past to die.

But quantum entanglement—or whatever this is—has never been that easy to dismiss. They were always going to wind up here, no matter how far they traveled, no matter how fast they ran. He can see that now, just like he can see the temporary animation draining from her face, leaving her watching him again, patient as only a truly impatient person can be. She's a predator in her own way, capable of absolute stillness when she thinks she needs it, capable of equally absolute momentum.

For her part, Dodger is watching to see whether he's about to turn and run, measuring every twitch and shift in his balance against a checklist built from observing other people—people who aren't him, aren't her quantum-entangled maybe-twin, and hence aren't the exemplar for whom the list was made. His constant state of low-grade animation is perplexing to her, as someone who lives her life in fits and starts, stops and goes. He could run her to the ground just by continuing to press forward after her sprint has been exhausted.

They balance each other. They always have.

"So no blood tests," says Roger. "I don't think we're alien robots or anything, but I guess it's not the weirdest of the possible options."

"The weirdest of the possible options involves the phrase 'Midwich cuckoos,'" says Dodger.

"I don't think the book was part of an elaborate cover-up. It seems excessive."

"No, 'excessive' was the remake of the movie. The book is very dry."

"Still not much of a reader, huh?"

Dodger smiles. "Fiction's not my thing. You want a nice epigram on spirals, and I'm your girl. Still reading everything you can get your hands on?"

"Books are made of words." Roger pauses, feeling like he's just unlocked something important. Dodger's start-and-stop, his steady forward movement, it's related to their fields of specialization. He can almost feel it. He just can't quite get his hands to lock around the idea, and so it slips away, leaving him saying, "I'm glad you're here. I missed you. Promise we won't do this again?"

"Do what?" she asks.

"Split up."

Her smile is quick and bright and almost overwhelming. "I think we're past that part of the equation, don't you?"

That night, after Roger is gone, Dodger stands in her room with a dry eraser in her hand, wiping the latest equations off her walls. She's still chasing the error she made on the day she ran into Roger, trying to figure out how the math diverged from its original track. There's something important in the twist of numbers and symbols: she knows that, just like she knows that if she tries to sleep in here with wrong answers scrawled on the walls around her, she'll have nightmares until morning and be useless in the game theory class she's TAing. The point of being here is to learn. She can learn a lot sleep-deprived, but like everything else in her life, that's a delicate equation, one unlocked with trial and error and a few fainting spells. Tonight is the night she sleeps.

There's a rapping behind her. The door is standing open; a house rule, after Candace found her curled in a corner, light-headed and disoriented from cleaning fumes.

"I have proper ventilation, Candy," she says.

"It's not Candy," says Erin.

Dodger turns. Blinks.

This is Erin: five-foot-seven, Midwestern farmer's daughter tan with a smattering of freckles across the nose (next to her, Dodger looks like the victim of a paintball war), strawberry blonde hair, eyes the color of South American morpho butterflies, down to the black ring around the outside of the irises, which is thick enough to seem unnatural. Blue jeans and a white tank top and the kind of body that seems to have been engineered to satisfy a focus group at one of the girly magazines, the ones where clothing is optional and everyone's name includes at least one $i$. She doesn't look like anyone's idea of a theology grad student; if anything, she looks like she'll be leading tent revivals one day, all mascara and thanking the Lord for His good gifts.

Dodger doesn't dislike her, exactly, but she doesn't trust her. Something about the woman puts her teeth on edge, some distant feeling of familiarity, like they've met before and mutually agreed to forget about it.

"What's up, Erin?" she asks. She doesn't realize she's raised the pitch of her voice and slowed her words, like she's speaking to a small child or a dangerous animal.

Erin realizes. Erin realizes more than anyone understands, and she likes it that way; likes the fact that, by and large, she's able to move through the world without attracting attention she's not prepared to deal with. (Oh, she gets stared at. She's attractive and living on a college campus, surrounded by people who are combining freedom and the last lingering storms of teenage hormones. She gets *noticed*. But being noticed is not the same thing as being paid attention to: being noticed is something that can be used, and being paid attention to is something that can get you killed. The difference is subtle. Roger would understand; Roger was designed to understand subtle differences of meaning. Roger doesn't *need* it, not like she does. Damned cuckoos, too privileged to understand how lucky they are.)

"Who was your friend?" she asks, leaning against the doorframe, effectively trapping Dodger in the room. The redhead would have to touch her to get out, and Erin knows she won't do that. Dodger isn't a touchy-feely person. "He stayed for *hours*. I didn't know there was anyone whose company you could stand for that long."

This is it: this is the point where an answer must be given, where things must be put into words and framed for someone else to understand. Dodger hesitates. Erin narrows her eyes, waiting. One cuckoo is dangerous. Two of them together is just shy of the end of the world as everyone knows it. If they're still in denial . . .

"My brother, Roger," says Dodger. "We haven't seen each other in a while, and we needed to catch up."

Erin lifts an eyebrow. "I didn't know you had a brother."

"It's . . . complicated," says Dodger. "We didn't grow up together."

Except for the brief periods where they had. Too brief, broken up by silence and mistrust and misunderstanding. They should have been longer. They should have been *always*.

"Huh. And you both decided to go to Berkeley? Why? Family reunion? You should've gotten an apartment together, spare the rest of us your pre-coffee crankiness."

"He's worse than I am in the mornings."

"Now I *know* the two of you should have gotten a place together." Erin continues to watch her closely, measuring her replies. "Who's older?"

"Roger." A quick answer: no time taken to think about it. If she'd taken the time to think, she would have agonized over which was the correct response, or whether a response mattered at all. The first answer is almost always the correct one, with Dodger. Instinctive math doesn't lie to you.

"Huh. He talks funny. Where's he from?"

"Cambridge." Dodger realizes with a twinge that anyone who remembers her "assault" might find it strange that she's spending time with someone from the Boston area. The past is never really past. It's always lurking, ready to attack the present.

"Wow. When your parents split up, they really split up." Erin stays where she is, watching Dodger intently. "He seeing anyone?"

"A few girls." She doesn't want Erin dating Roger. It's not possessiveness, quite: she isn't bothered by the idea of Roger dating, not the way she was when they were teenagers and she was still trying to work through her own complicated ideas on the subject. (Her main objection to Alison, and to the idea of girls like Alison, had been the thought that Roger might find someone he liked better, someone who came with physical, rather than quantum, entanglement. But that was a long time ago, and she's better now.)

"Aw, too bad. Well, if he's going to be around here pretty often, maybe I can convince him I should be one of them." Erin pushes away from the doorway, eyes seeming to darken. She looks at Dodger, and Dodger does her best not to squirm under that black-and-blue gaze.

"Yes?" she finally snaps.

"Be careful," says Erin, and she sounds serious for the first time: she sounds utterly and unquestionably serious. "I know it's nice to re-build bridges, but you need to remember why you're here. For your education. To arm yourself for the future. It's coming, and when it gets here, it's not going to care how often you and your brother braided each other's hair, or how much time you spent laughing. It's going to care whether you have the weapons you need. So be *careful*. Now, if you'll excuse me, I'm going to do the dishes. You people live like ani-mals." Then she turns, and walks away, leaving Dodger blinking after her, bemused.

After a moment, Dodger goes back to wiping the marks off the walls.

# Report

"Master Daniels tolerated your foolishness, but I am not he, and this has gone on long enough," spits the new High Priest of the Alchemical Congress—a useless title. The religious aspects of what they do have faded long since, replaced by skepticism and stoic scientific method. "What you say you would attempt—"

"I attempt nothing," says Reed, voice smooth and calm. "I appeared before Master Daniels to tell him it was done, and to ask for readmission to your number, that you might all share in the glory to come. I did this to honor Asphodel's memory, and not out of any obligation. I am here, now, to tell you as I told him that I *have* embodied the Doctrine of Ethos, that I *have* changed the mechanism which controls the universe. I will do what none has done since Asphodel. I will unlock the doors of the Impossible City, and I will bring magic back into the world."

"You're a construct, a—a *thing*," objects one of the lesser alchemists, a man whose name he has never bothered to learn nor cared to know.

"You can't have achieved what better alchemists have lived and died failing to do."

"Magic never left the world," objects another. "Magic is a natural law, like gravity. It endures."

It is the second, less-insulting alchemist who Reed chooses to address. "Magic *has* been lessened. The age of miracles has been ground to a powder by the twinned stones of caution and rationality. We pulled back too far. We allowed belief to turn against us. This will change."

The High Priest shakes his head. "Have sense, Reed. People aren't ready."

"People are sheep. They'll do as they're told, once they see that the world is not as they always assumed it was." Reed smiles. "The Impossible City will open. The world will change."

They glare at each other, these two men divided by an impossible ideological gulf, and the Congress holds its breath, frozen and enthralled.

The Impossible City. It wasn't always called that. It was Olympus once, Avalon, the Isles of the Dead, the alchemical apex which waited at the peak of all human knowledge and potential. The city that is dreamed of but never claimed or controlled. The place whose streets were paved in gold, whose rivers ran with alkahest, whose trees flowered with panacea. Over time, it had drifted further and further from the known, from the true, until all roads were severed, and there was no way back. It was Asphodel Baker, again, who turned enough of the world's attention toward that distant ideal to reopen a single narrow path. The improbable road, which could lead the questing home.

"The Impossible City is a myth," says the High Priest finally.

"We shall see," Reed replies. "Have I broken any compacts? Violated any laws? I seek to open the Impossible City for us all, in memory of Master Daniels, of Asphodel. The children I've created are built from my blood and bone, and hence my property. I walk in the light for this endeavor."

The High Priest narrows his eyes. "If the City is achieved . . ."

"It will be shared, as my agreement with Master Daniels promised."

Reed lies. Reed always lies. But if he can keep the Congress at bay just a little longer, it will be too late for them to stop him. It may already be too late. What a wonderful thought, that it may already be too late. He may already rule the world.

There is nothing they can charge him with, nothing they can do; he has been too careful. Even the deaths of Master Daniels and his associates have been well concealed. When the session ends, he walks away a free man, glorying in the scope of his success.

Leigh is waiting for him outside the Congress doors. She looks like a schoolteacher standing in front of the principal's desk, waiting to hear that her problem students will finally be well and truly punished.

He favors her with a smile. "The day has been going so well. I trust you're not here to spoil it?"

"They've made contact."

Reed knows from experience that Leigh won't let whatever she's talking about go until she's satisfied, and that for her, satisfaction may mean that someone else starts bleeding. "Walk with me," he says, and continues down the hall, away from the doors, away from prying ears.

They are less safe here than they would be in their own territory, but sometimes making nice with one's peers is essential to keeping up the masquerade that one is still interested in their fellowship. One day, he'll bring all this nonsense crashing down, and he'll laugh, because this was never necessary. Only will, and the willingness to do what needed to be done.

When they are far enough away to trip no alarms, he removes a coin from his pocket and plays it between his fingers, eye flashing over pyramid flashing over eye. So long as it remains in motion, they will not be overheard. "Who's made contact?"

"The last chicks from your failed rookery," spits Leigh. "The Middleton boy and the Cheswich girl. They're attending the same college, and they ran into each other as soon as they were both on campus."

"I thought you had minders assigned to them." Reed's tone is mild, but the accusation it harbors is clear: if his cuckoos have made contact, it's because Leigh has failed to do her job. She's failed to keep them apart, distracted, maturing in their separate shells. They put a country between these children, and yet the children have come together over and over again, as if to spite their creators.

"The Middleton boy's minder had to be . . . removed . . . from the program due to a failure to hold his attention," says Leigh, with a surprising degree of delicacy, at least for her. "I thought you had convinced the girl that her 'brother' was a fantasy."

"Compulsions never stand up to confrontation with reality," says Reed, dismissing the idea of his culpability with a wave of his hand. "What of the Cheswich girl's minder?"

"Doing her best, but she's limited. They're inherently chaotic creatures, and she channels the opposing force. Once they came together, she was overwhelmed."

Reed narrows his eyes. "How?"

Leigh shakes her head. "They met by accident, but Middleton tracked Cheswich down after he realized she was on campus. He seemed very invested in getting her to talk to him."

"Are they still capable of communicating non-verbally?"

"I don't know." The admission clearly pains her. "After the amount of time they spent apart, the ability should have atrophied—but we didn't expect them to be so tightly bonded that the Cheswich girl could call for help after she opened her damn wrists." She makes no effort to hide her disappointment. A cuckoo that attempted to kill itself was weak, as far as Leigh was concerned: it had no business in the program. Had things been allowed to progress to their natural conclusion, the Cheswich girl would have bled out, the Middleton boy would have died of shock, and that entire generation of cuckoos would have been excised. She could have closed the book on a failed experiment, not been forced to devote time and resources to continuing to monitor their progress.

For Leigh, there is nothing more terrible than a waste of time. Time is the most precious commodity of all.

"Tell your remaining minder to find out. We need all the information we can acquire on how they interact . . . and tell her not to interfere." Reed folds his hands behind his back, coin still dancing from knuckle to knuckle. "I want to see how they'll mature without roadblocks. They should be old enough to have fully distinct senses of self; that will keep them from blending into each other to such a degree that they become useless."

"Sir—"

"Leigh." He looks at her. This time, there's no mercy in his eyes. "Have I not been right up until now? Have I not fed you, clothed you, kept you, given you the materials for your own experiments, and covered up the signs of your less . . . savory interests? I could have discarded you as a failed Eve when I found you in that lab, but I took you as my own, testified to your stability before the Congress. I took *responsibility* for you, and all I've ever asked in return is that you obey me without question. Trust me. Believe in me, and I will lead you into the light."

"I'm sorry." She ducks her head, that old, not-quite-human motion that presses her chin to her sternum and reveals the extra vertebrae tucked into her neck. "I'll tell my girl to watch without interfering."

"Good. Very good. How is your generation?"

Suddenly Leigh is all smiles again. "Good," she echoes. "Very good. Two of them have abandoned the idea of individual bodies. They treat themselves as a single thought-form entity with four hands and four feet that sometimes needs to be fed. Two more committed a ritualized form of murder-suicide without even needing to be asked. They're all coming along nicely."

Reed doesn't remind her that she's just described losing two of her subjects as "coming along nicely." Instead, he looks at her, and says, "I thought you had three pairs. Multiples of three are ritually important." Roger and Dodger started as one pair out of three, and have outlived their fellows by a matter of years. Of the pairs he created after them, two remain, neither showing their early promise, neither showing their early problems.

"I wish you'd been willing to sign off on twelve," she says. She shakes her head. "My third pair is good around the lab. They pull their own weight, don't complain about the chores they're given. The boy is language, and he's been translating some of my old workbooks for me—but not for fun. He has to *work*. He does it dutifully, without complaint, but there's no joy in it. The girl is math, and she's the same when I set her jobs that involve measurement or calculation. Her work is always perfect. It's not inspired. I think they didn't bake properly."

"You can recycle them if you like."

This is a rare treat, the opportunity to dismantle something living without needing to justify herself. To his surprise, Leigh says, "Not yet, unless that's an order. As long as my first pair is around, you won't authorize a new batch, and they make an interesting control group. One set has become so entangled as to be ritually useless, even if they're a fascinating puzzle, and a second set has managed to avoid the Doctrine almost entirely. I want to understand why. I'm going to give them another six months, and if they haven't produced useful results by then, I'm going to set them against each other and see who survives. It will be interesting to see what happens to either set if one of them is killed. I have theories."

"You always do," Reed says. "Middleton and Cheswich are the closest we've come to the controllable manifest Doctrine. Even her attempts at self-harm have served us; they'll make him protective, which makes her a lever that can be used. Keep them under watch. If they show signs of entangling further, we may have to intervene. For the time being, we can let them alone. See what they'll do, given the chance to exist together without external conflicts."

Leigh frowns. Just a little. More than she usually allows in the presence of her owner and employer. Like all failed experiments, she's far too aware of what it could mean if she incurs her keeper's wrath. "All right." She doesn't sound pleased. Reed will not punish her for that; flashes of empathy are rare enough from her that he feels inclined to encourage them. Perhaps a bit more empathy would make her a bit less vicious. No less gifted, but . . . less inclined to "accidents" in the lab. "I'll call Erin with her updated instructions."

"Very good," he says. They walk together through the halls of the Congress, away from the old fools who dream of an Impossible City they will never see, and the improbable road has never been more achievable, or closer to hand.

# Bucolic

When are your parents expecting you?" Dodger is at the far wall, a dry-erase marker in her hand, adding numbers to the columns already there. Her handwriting is surprisingly precise, more like a font processed through a human hand than anything natural; every digit fits into the same amount of space, perfectly matched to its neighbors on either side.

Roger wouldn't expect anything less. He's cross-legged on her bed, elbows on his knees. The way she has the room arranged offers no back support; the mystery of her morning yoga classes has been answered. Without them, he's fairly sure she'd pull a muscle trying to deal with her homework every morning, much less handle the rest of her day. The air smells of marker fumes and cleaning fluid; the single open window can't clear it all out. Old Bill is on the sill outside, showing with his presence that he *could* come in if he wanted to, he's just *choosing* not to. The sky is gray, and the air tastes of rain, and the world has never been so perfect.

"My flight leaves Sunday morning," he says patiently. She already has this information: she helped him find the tickets, working some sort of mathematical wizardry to find the best deal for a holiday flight between Berkeley and Cambridge. (Well, San Francisco and Boston: she may be a math wizard, but conjuring airports out of nothing is outside both her skill set and her overall interests. Where would they *put* it?) "I'll be gone six days, returning the Saturday after Thanksgiving. You're still welcome to come, if you want to."

"And get murdered by my own parents for being an ungrateful child? No, thank you." She adds another row of figures. "I'll go home to Palo Alto, and have my father's deep-fried turkey, and like it. Really. He's good at things that involve borderline ridiculous amounts of fire. Remember the time zone: I don't get out of bed before nine, which'll be noon for you."

"I remember when you habitually got up at five."

"Yeah, because you were up and active and eager at eight, and because I had people enforcing a tyrannical and unreasonable bedtime on my growing mind." She smiles over her shoulder. "I keep different hours now."

He lifts his head and smiles back. They're falling more and more into sync lately; not enough that she's worried the quantum entanglement is getting worse, but enough that she once again truly believes he'd be there to catch her if she fell. (Quantum entanglement is still their best way to describe the situation, despite carefully asked questions directed at the physicists they know. What they're experiencing is, if not unique in the annals of human history, at the least unusual and bizarre. This has also made them cautious when it comes to looking for additional information. Exploring a strange phenomenon from the comfort of their respective apartments is one thing. Doing it from someone else's lab is something else altogether.)

"And I've learned how to read a clock," he says. "I won't wake you up. Although I may scold you if you're still awake when I'm going to bed. You have to sleep sometime, Dodge. Not sleeping is not good for you."

"Says the man who stayed awake for three days reading and analyzing a bunch of books in ancient Sumerian. For fun."

"It *was* fun," he says, turning on the bed to face her. "I had a question for you, if you've got a second."

"Is this 'got a second' in the 'you can keep working' sense, or in the 'please cap your pen and give me your full attention, this is important' sense?" Dodger keeps writing. She's running out of room at eye level; soon, she'll have to kneel, and eventually lie flat on her belly, numbers and figures unspooling from her pen, Scheherazade of the mathematical world. Roger rarely knows what she's working on. The few times she's tried to explain, he hasn't been able to follow beyond the superficial level. He's stopped asking. It's worth it to see how happy it makes her.

"The latter, if you don't mind."

Dodger pauses. "Let me get this down," she says, and writes double-speed until she reaches the end of the line. Then she caps her pen and turns, sinking to the floor as she does. It's like watching a crane fold itself into its nest, an impossible amount of material compacting into something equally impossibly small. She cocks her head to the side, and asks, "Are you about to ask me to move in with you? Because I think it's a bad idea. I've been doing some research—not into the physics, just into the math—and I have concerns—"

"Many of which keep me awake at night, believe me," says Roger. "I don't want to get a place together for a lot of reasons. That's one of them. Trying to explain you to any girls I happen to bring home is another."

"Most people on campus believe I'm your sister. Not that it matters. Any girl worth dating would listen when we both told her nothing like that was going on between us."

"I agree with you. But twenty years of romantic comedies do not agree with you, and they sort of make things complicated when, say, I bring a girl home and you're just getting out of the shower, so the first thing she's confronted with in my swinging bachelor pad is my wet, half-naked, redheaded sister."

"Everyone knows redheads are insatiable sex machines," says Dodger blandly. "With our freckles and our math and our eschewing dating because it takes up so much time that could be spent on doing other things."

"Not everyone skips out on the dating part of their college experience."

"Not everyone enjoys having free time."

Roger shrugs. "We all prioritize what we enjoy. Can we get back on the topic?"

"I wasn't aware we'd left the topic. I don't know what the topic *is*."

"You interrupted me before I could get there," he protests. "It's about my parents."

Dodger goes still. Roger settles in to wait. He's seen her do this a few times before: he understands what's happening. Words aren't her forte, exactly. She can carry on a conversation easily enough, and she isn't *stupid,* but sometimes the subtler meanings of language escape her. When that happens, and she knows it's important, she shuts herself down, blocking out all extraneous input, and digs straight into the issue. *What is he really asking? Why is he really asking it? What will happen when she replies?*

(He does something similar when he has to do math more complex than making change. Kelly used to joke about "tipping fugue," when he'd stop responding for up to five minutes as he tried to calculate the appropriate amount to leave on a check. What he finds truly interesting about this phenomenon—what he wasn't able to consider when it was just him, and Dodger was a phantom from his past who might never show her face again—is the fact that when she shuts down, he feels a faint tingling at the back of his mind, like he's struggling to recall something he's forgotten. It's not quite déjà vu—call it jamais vu, the feeling of knowing something he knows he's never seen before. Dodger worries more about the quantum entanglement than he does, in a quiet reversal of their childhood positions on the subject. He doesn't want to scare her by bringing this up. Eventually, he's going to have to.)

Finally, she cocks her head and asks, "What are you hoping to achieve?"

"I want to tell them about you. Maybe something in my adoption paperwork mentions a sister." It would be easier than a blood test. It wouldn't involve anyone new.

Dodger's frown is slow but deep. "I really thought you were going to ask about, I don't know, asking Erin on a date or something."

"Uh, no. Dating Erin would be sort of like dating a blender. Sure, it makes great smoothies, but one day you're going to be minding your own business and it's going to switch on and remove your hand."

Dodger raises an eyebrow. "Okay, one, your metaphors have gotten weirder, and two, you are not allowed to borrow horror movies from my collection anymore. Your girlfriends may be a vague, amorphous mass to me, but that doesn't make them kitchen appliances."

"You know what I mean, though," says Roger. "It seemed sort of cliché to compare her to a wild animal, which would have been the easier choice."

"Heaven forbid you do anything *cliché*, Mr. English-Professor-in-Training," says Dodger. "You might find a single cliché is a gateway drug to tweed jackets and khaki slacks, and the next thing you know, you're teaching Kerouac and making eyes at that cute undergrad in the front row who makes you think about fucking all of Middle America in one triumphant go."

Roger blinks.

"How long have you been saving that one up?" he asks.

"About a week," Dodger admits.

"Feel better?"

"Little bit." She still grins like she did when she was nine years old, on the rare occasions when she's relaxed enough to grin at all. Even when she smiles with her whole face, one side of her mouth is a little higher, making it obvious that her real smile is buried in the mix. Then the smile fades. "I don't mind if you want to tell your parents about me. Just . . . be careful."

"I will be," he says. "I always am."

"Not always," she says.

Roger catches his breath and holds it, studying her. She doesn't look upset. If anything, she looks . . . calm. Like she's finally moving past their separation. He exhales.

"You're a pretty cool sister, you know that?"

"I'd be a lot cooler if we'd grown up together."

He pauses. "You rethinking that blood test?"

"Considering it," she admits. "If we could prove we were related, I could take you to meet my parents. Maybe someday you could take me to meet yours. It would be a lot harder to split us up again, if our entire support structure was conjoined."

Her father probably wouldn't take well to having her show up with the boy from Boston; it's been years, but Roger has absolute faith that Professor Cheswich would recognize his voice. How could he not? There are things that can't be forgotten, and the voice of the boy who called to say your daughter was bleeding to death has got to be at the top of that list. On the other hand, if they had proof they were related . . .

"What if the blood test comes back and says we're wrong?" he asks. "What then?"

"That seems less likely with every data point," says Dodger. "We have the same eyes. We have a similar bone structure. Same birthdate—same birth *hour*. If you can find your birth certificate while you're at home, see if you can't get a birth state. Mine's Ohio. That can all be falsified, but when you add it to the rest of the data, it becomes pretty conclusive. We know we have the same blood type. Red and brown hair are frequently found in the same family."

"This is important to you, isn't it?" asks Roger.

"Yes."

"Why?"

"Because if we're related, they can't ever tell you to give me up again." Dodger is calm, precise: she's done the math. "You don't get to run away from family."

She's talking about herself as much as she's talking about him; more, even. He left her for a little while. She tried to leave him forever. Still. "And if we're not related?"

"You're still my brother. Quantum entanglement is thicker than blood."

"You know, the original quote—"

"Is irrelevant, and I have access to things I can throw, so don't get pedantic," she says pleasantly. "If we're not biologically related, that removes one data point from the list of causes for our entanglement. If we are, then maybe we can start looking for other cases and find out what the possible consequences might be. I'm not going to hurt myself again, but what happens if one of us is in an accident? We already know that a near-death experience for one of us is a near-death experience for both of us, but is it possible for you to survive my death, or vice versa? We need to know how much we're risking each other every time we do something dangerous."

"Then what? Wrap ourselves in cotton wool? I can't ask you to stop living your life just because it might endanger mine." Or vice versa, but he knows she'd never ask him to do that: her response every time the pressure has gotten unbearable has proven that. Finding proof that all injury could potentially transfer won't make her careful. It will make her paranoid, locking her door and never letting anyone inside.

"I don't *know*." She makes no effort to conceal her frustration. "This is uncharted ground, and it's not like we have a physicist to help us figure it out. Maybe if we know the base situation, we can go and find one. Convince them we need help without turning us into a science project. It all starts with a blood test. So can we get a blood test?"

"Sure," says Roger.

Dodger allows her shoulders to slump, showing her relief. "When?" she asks.

"Maybe after Thanksgiving . . ."

The rest of the evening passes like that, topic flowing into topic, all of them light, many of them easy. It's *nice* to sit and talk; both of them think, more than once, that this is how things should have been all along. That this is what the world was supposed to contain. There's tension, yes, but it's the tension of minds meeting, the conflict of differing core interests, not the tension of a world about to become terribly complicated.

It won't last, of course. But neither of them knows that consciously, and even if they did, it wouldn't change the moment, the comfort it contains, or the fixed point it represents on the tangled structure of

their lives. This is one of the moments around which all else will rotate, even when the world starts falling down.

This is one of the moments that will shine.

Roger leaves at eleven on school nights. They mostly meet at Dodger's place, due to her propensity for writing on the walls; he can
keep her in butcher paper, but there's always the chance she'll relax
so much that she'll forget *he* doesn't have whiteboard paint on everything. He likes his security deposit. He especially likes the way he's
going to get it back when he moves, allowing him to use it again on a
new apartment. The competition for grad student housing gets vicious
in the fall, when the incoming scholars fight the established ones for
the places nearest to campus, or better yet, nearest to the Derby food
court. He likes his current apartment, but he has his eye on a place
above Amoeba Records which is supposed to come open over the
summer. So protecting his security deposit is of the utmost importance, at least for now.

He also likes the walk from her place to his, especially late at night,
when the city is quiet and cool and the air smells of that curious
wooded-concrete blend the campus pumps off. It reminds him of
home. Most of California has its own weird scent profile, a combination of eucalyptus and oleander and desert heat masquerading
as human paradise. Berkeley, though. Berkeley smells like the college town it is, and while it isn't quite Cambridge—nothing is quite
Cambridge—it sometimes manages to come close, at least in the
middle of the night.

(His being the one who needs to walk home also means Dodger
isn't riding her bike at midnight. She's good with that thing, handles
it like she's been on it all her life, but accidents happen, and until they
know exactly how their entanglement works, he'd rather she didn't
get hit. He'd rather she didn't get hit *after* they know how their entanglement works, either—he'd rather she stay healthy and present
for their entire lives—it's just that right now, he doesn't know what

would happen. He might not admit it out loud, but that scares him. That scares him a lot.)

Now that he's alone, he can admit to himself how excited he is by the idea of beginning the testing process. It starts with blood: he and Dodger came to that conclusion independently, and it feels right. It feels *accurate*, even, which doesn't mean the same thing, and has just as much importance here. Dodger's math doesn't work if she doesn't take the steps in the right sequence, following the correct path through the equation. The question of their quantum entanglement feels similar. They need to find the right sequence to make their way through this, take the steps in the right order, or it could all fall down. And he doesn't *want* it to fall down.

Dodger's issues may be more visible—and that makes sense; she's always worn her heart on her sleeve, a bright banner to attract the world's snipers, like a bird feigning a broken wing to draw predators away from the nest—but that doesn't mean she's the only one who has them. Roger has spent his life trying to balance being the smartest person in the room with a genuine desire to be liked. He wants to talk about phonemes and the number of sounds the human body can produce and baseball and how hard it is to get a decent cup of chowder in this town, and he wants to do them all at the same time, and he *can't*. Half the smart people he meets are so hung up on the idea of being smart—the idea that all they *can* be is smart, defined by the discipline that calls them—that as soon as he mentions baseball, they jump in to tell him how boring they find it. How plebian. How beneath them.

He knows the words: balance, equilibrium, parity. He's always thought they were a pretty dream, something to be pursued but never caught. Now, for the first time in years, he's starting to feel as if they might describe something possible. All they need to do is figure out what they are, what they *mean*, and they can begin moving forward.

He's sunk deeply enough into his own thoughts that he doesn't notice the person falling into step beside him. Their footsteps are soft, and they're dressed entirely in gray, blending with the moonlit city streets. It's not until he catches a glimpse of pale hair out of the corner of his eye that he realizes anyone is there at all, and not until he turns that he realizes it's Erin.

"Uh," he says. "Hi?"

"You have an odd sense of direction," she says. "We should have turned two blocks ago if you were trying to get home in a timely manner."

"I'm enjoying the walk," he says, flustered. Dodger's roommates are both strange in their own ways. He finds Candace's brusque, often paint-covered strangeness endearing; he finds Erin's strangeness, which is feline and fluid and cold, off-putting. There's something about her that doesn't quite synchronize with the rest of the world, like she's been spliced in from a different story. She pays the rent on time and is almost never home, so Dodger doesn't mind her, but since that first encounter on the balcony, he's been doing his best to keep her at a safe remove. Something about her is *wrong*.

"You were," she says, and she's right, so he doesn't argue, no matter how polite it would have been to try.

They walk in silence for a short while, Erin pacing soundlessly beside him, Roger choosing the more economical turns, the ones that will get him home and end this game—whatever it is—that much sooner.

Finally, Erin asks, "If I gave you advice, would you take it? Or would you just go 'oh, that's Dodger's weirdo roommate, that's the one who never shows her face, I can ignore her without worrying about the consequences'?"

"I would consider what you said to me, try to assess it fairly on its own merits, and worry about the consequences endlessly, because I'm me, and that's the sort of bullshit thing my brain likes to do," says Roger. His tone is light. His expression is grim. Erin has always seemed off, but here, tonight, the strangeness of her is magnified: here, tonight, she's a wound in the fabric of the world, and she's bleeding, oh, how she's bleeding.

"Don't come back from Boston."

Roger stops walking.

Erin continues, momentum carrying her forward another several feet before she stops, and turns, and looks at him. "Stay home," she says. "There are schools there that would take you. Plead illness. Get your ass off this improbable road before you go too far, because the Impossible City is just ahead, Jackdaw, and it's waiting for you. It knows you're coming. Once it sees you round the bend, it's going to be too late."

Roger stares at her. "Uh, Erin? It's none of my business what you do in your spare time, but are you high? I'm not running away from school because you have some sort of weird Up-and-Under thing going on. And if I'm Jack Daw, what does that make you? The Corn Jenny?"

"I should be so lucky," she says, and there's such a terrible, painful *reasonableness* in her tone that he takes a step backward, away from her, away from the future she represents. "I don't walk the improbable road, Jackdaw; I don't go to meet the Queen of Wands. I've already *been* to see the King of Cups, and the Page of Frozen Waters made sure I knew I'd crossed the line. Hurt yourself if you want to, but think about Dodger. She's breakable right now. Her kind always are. Crow Girls and Jack Daws have a lot in common, but where you burn, she'll soak up all the water in the world and drown under the weight of her own lungs. You're the control. She's just the trigger mechanism. Stop this now before it's too late for both of you."

"Now you're talking crazy," says Roger patiently. "I was willing to tolerate a lot of weird, because you're Dodger's roommate and I don't know what you've had to smoke tonight, but you've crossed a few lines, and one of them is the line of reason. Go home, Erin. Sleep whatever this is off. I'll see you after Thanksgiving."

"I can *see* the fixed points in your timeline. I can't alter them or move between them the way you people can, but I can *see* them, and you've just passed one. Don't you get it? You're heading through the temperaments and into the center, and once you get there, I can't save you. Once you get there, *no one* can save you. The King of Cups will see you now. The King sees all the cuckoos when they come home to roost."

"Go home, Erin." Roger starts walking again, faster this time, quickly passing her. She doesn't move to follow him. He's grateful for that, but he doesn't slow down.

"When the time comes for you to see the King, don't say I didn't warn you," she calls after him. "Don't say I didn't try!"

"Go *home,* Erin," he says, and turns the corner, and is gone.

Erin stays where she is, counting down from one hundred, giving him time to come back. He might. It could happen. Some people, when warned about impending doom, come back to ask for more details. Most don't. Most would rather pretend the warning never came, that they had no idea of what might be coming for them.

Roger doesn't come back. Somehow, she's not surprised. She called him a Jackdaw, a Jack Daw, because that's what he is, according to Baker's formulae—that old bitch, with her carefully coded instructions for a generation of alchemists to emulate. But really, everyone who walks the improbable road to enlightenment is an Avery, a Zib, and Roger is no different. He and his sister only have one iron shoe apiece. That doesn't matter. As long as they walk together, they'll still walk all the way, and then . . .

"We'll see what we'll see," she says quietly, and turns, and disappears into the night.

# Home Again

The house smells like Thanksgiving, that complicated mix of turkey and stuffing and cranberry sauce and mashed potato and pie that shouldn't work but somehow does. It smells like holiday. It smells like *home*. When he was a kid, Roger thought Thanksgiving was the best possible holiday. It didn't involve lies or home invasion like Christmas; it didn't cram him into an itchy suit and tight shoes like Easter; even Halloween had its issues, with the masks and the monsters. But Thanksgiving . . . Thanksgiving was about food and family and spending time with the people you loved. Thanksgiving was *perfect*.

Now that he's grown, Thanksgiving still seems perfect. Sure, Mom cooks a smaller turkey, since he no longer has a teenage boy's appetite to see them through the leftovers, and sure, Grandma never taught anyone how to make her cranberry cheesecake, so when she died, the recipe died with her, but the feeling around the table is the same. Thanksgiving is the safest holiday, the one that encourages lowering walls and filling stomachs and enjoying the one place in the world that will always, always be safe.

The house seems smaller and bigger than it used to at the same time. Living in a cramped off-campus apartment means a four-bedroom single-family home with a backyard is basically the Promised Land: this is what half the people in his classes dream about at night. Having *space*. Space to collect things, space for clutter, space to lose yourself in. But the worn patch on the wallpaper where he used to rest his hand is impossibly low. He can't ever really have been that short. That contrast is everywhere he turns. Doorknobs that should dwarf his hand fit snugly into his palm. Windows that should be too high to reach are situated at eye level. He even got the blender from the top of the fridge for his mother when she was whipping the cream; for the first time ever, he's the tallest person in the house.

His old room has been redecorated. Still his, but adult-him, not child-him. There are a few shelves of beloved toys and souvenirs from his childhood—the rock he found the first time he went to the beach with his grandparents; the mouse ears from his first trip to Disney World—but the wallpaper is new, untorn, untattered, undefaced by crayons or markers. Looking at it makes him think of Dodger and her white walls covered with numbers; it makes his fingers itch to commit similar graffiti, scrawling verb tenses and lines of classic poetry over that unnerving newness. But he doesn't. This is his parents' house. For the first time in his life, he's a guest here. You really can't go home again. Not all the way. No matter how hard you try.

"Roger!" His mother's voice comes up the stairs the way it always has, bouncing off the walls, a distinct echo that calls all the way back to when he was a toddler clinging to the bannisters and wailing at the steepness of the stairs. "Dinner's about to be on the table!"

"Coming, Ma!" he calls back, and stands, leaving the too-new bed behind. He looks to the open door. Then, on a whim, he walks to the closet, kneels, presses his hands against the floor. It creaks. The loose panel where he used to store his childhood treasures is still here.

It was a silly idea, stolen from a hundred movies: pry up a board in the closet floor, sand the nails so it won't completely latch down again, and use the space between the floor and the downstairs ceiling as a secret compartment. Maybe it worked *because* it was so silly, because no one could believe a kid as smart as he was would try something so elementary. Whatever the reason, when they renovated the room, they didn't find his treasures.

"Roger!" The voice belongs to his father this time, louder, more strident. "Come help your mother set the table!"

"Coming!" he calls. The mysteries of childhood will be there later, ready to be explored at his leisure. Dusting his hands against his legs, Roger walks to the door, and out.

Dinner is delicious. That's no surprise; Melinda Middleton has always been an excellent cook, and having her boy home for Thanksgiving has motivated her to even greater heights than normal. The turkey is perfect. The pie is better. By the time the last dish is cleared away, Roger feels like he's run a marathon of calories. He could sleep for a year, snuggled under his childhood comforter, surrounded by the walls he grew up in. His father is leaning back in his own chair, sipping a cup of coffee, looking utterly content with the world. His mother is across from him, picking at one last piece of pie.

Maybe it's the comfort, and maybe it's the comfort food, but this feels like the perfect time to ask. He takes a breath and says, "I'd like to talk to you about something, if that's okay."

"Why wouldn't it be okay, son?" asks his father. There's gray in his hair that wasn't there when Roger went away for college, marching forward every day, slowly conquering the territory from scalp downward. (*At least he still has his hair* is the automatic thought, followed by the dull flush of shame; what does it matter if Colin Middleton still has his hair or not? It's not like Roger has any of his genes. Roger's future is a mystery.) The sight carries its own brand of dull shock. When did he get so *old*? When did they both get so *old*?

Blissfully unaware of the thoughts filling his son's head, Colin continues, "We've always been happy to talk with you."

"Unless you've managed to get some girl pregnant," says Melinda. "That's between you and her, and we're not going to give you any advice beyond 'think about your future' and 'think about *her* future.'"

"*Mom,*" says Roger, scandalized. "Do you really think I'd do that?"

"Accidents happen," says Melinda. "Not to us, of course. You were perfectly planned, every inch of you."

Relief replaces shock. Roger sits up straighter in his chair, trying to look like the adult he is and not the child he always feels like in this house, where the walls are full of remembered bogeymen and the attic creaks with childhood's ghosts. "That's actually what I wanted to talk to you about."

He'd have to be stupid to miss the glance that passes between his parents. It's quick, but it's so laden with dread and dismay that it falls into the convivial atmosphere of a family Thanksgiving like a rock into a quiet pond.

His mother recovers first. "What do you mean, dear?" she asks, and her voice is honey and sugar and dread. He analyzes her words—he can't help himself—and finds them packed with fear. Even the cadence is off, tension turning a question he's heard a thousand times before into a tripwire primed to catch him off-balance.

*They're worried I want to make contact with my birth parents,* he thinks, and it's a reasonable explanation for an unreasonable response: it works, it fits the facts without distorting them. It's the explanation that leaves his parents in the right, no matter what comes next, because what adoptive parent wouldn't worry about their child someday finding someone to love more? He could try to explain that they're irreplaceable, that they were so perfect for him that he might as well have chosen them—his bookstore-owning father, his stay-at-home, intellectually flexible mother—but for once, he doesn't feel like he has the words. The only way out is onward.

"We've never talked about my adoption," he says. "I've always known I *was* adopted, and I know my birth mother didn't want any contact with me after the adoption was finished. I've seen the paperwork. Before we go any further, I want to say I love you—both of you—very much, and you're the only parents I'll ever want or need. I'm not looking to find the woman who gave me up. Whether that was her mistake or her looking out for me, it gave me the best family anybody's ever had, and I'm grateful, but I'm not indebted to her."

His parents relax a little, his mother's hands unclenching until the color begins flooding back, his father's shoulders slumping.

"There's this girl."

The tension returns. It's an instant, unmistakable thing: his parents may as well have been replaced by statues that look exactly like them. They barely even seem to be breathing.

"Her name's Dodger, and she was adopted the same day I was. Born the same day I was, in the same state. She got her name from her birth parents. Keeping it was a condition of her adoption." Roger looks between them, waiting for them to say something, to *do* something, to show, in some small way, that they're still present. "She's nice. I think you'd like her, if you met her."

"Are you . . . dating this girl?" his mother asks, in a strangled voice. She looks almost like she's going to throw up, like she can't stomach the idea of him and Dodger together.

Something about that is wrong. Something about that is screaming for him to be careful. He forces his way on, saying, "No, Mom, jeez, no. Dodger's not my type. I mean, she's a girl, and she's smart, and she has boobs, so I guess technically she *is* my type, but she's not, because I think she's my sister. I mean, functionally, I *know* she's my sister, but I'm talking about biologically. When you adopted me, did the agency say anything about a second child? Was I a twin?"

"Go to your room," says his father, in a soft voice.

"What?" Roger turns to look at him quizzically. "Dad, I don't—"

"*Go* to your *room*," his father repeats, and this time, the stresses on his words are impossible to ignore. Colin Middleton is terrified. More than that: there's a layer of resignation to his terror, like this is the moment he's been waiting for since the day they brought Roger home. This was, somehow, the inevitable outcome.

Roger rises slowly, waiting for his mother to say something, waiting for one of them to start making sense. Neither of them moves. He pushes back his chair, steps away from the table, and climbs the stairs, all while waiting for them to say something.

Neither of them speaks.

The stairs haven't seemed this long since he was a child, being sent to his room for one infraction of the rules or another. This time, he knows, there won't be a book conveniently hidden under his pillow; his mother won't be coming by with cocoa or chocolate milk to tell him that all boys are rambunctious sometimes, they understand, they always understand, but if he could just try to be a little *quieter*, they would appreciate it so, so much. A little neater. A little tidier. *Read your book, Roger; finish your homework.*

This is the first time it's occurred to him that perhaps their reactions to his childhood misbehavior were unusual. Did other kids get antique dictionaries and glossaries of dead languages from their fathers when they were bad? Did they find themselves rewarded with the thing they loved most when they broke a plate or said a swear word? He always assumed they did, and so he never talked to anyone else about it. Maybe he should have.

Something is very wrong. Something that started with the silence his parents made between them when he mentioned his adoption.

Roger closes his bedroom door, walks to the bed, and sits. He'll explore the treasure trove in his closet later; right now, he needs reassurance that he didn't somehow violate some essential agreement between adopted child and adoptive parents. Closing his eyes, he reaches into the dark behind them, and says, almost meekly, "Dodge? You there?"

"Roger!" There's a blink, and the world is cast in startling color. Dodger's in the backyard of her parents' house in Palo Alto, sitting near the high, whitewashed fence between grass and gully. They must have rebuilt the fence after her . . . accident, making it higher, closing the gap she used to wiggle through. He recognizes the birdbath, and the climbing roses Heather Cheswich used to spend so much time tending. He always liked it when Dodger sat on the porch and looked at her mother's roses, which had so many more colors than the ones in Boston.

(He didn't know much about colorblindness back then, or that he couldn't see the delicacies of shade in the roses in his own neighborhood; he just knew California was supersaturated, more brightly colored than any real place could possibly be, colored like a fairy tale, colored like the Up-and-Under.)

"Shouldn't you be downstairs eating pie?" Dodger is stretched out on a plastic beach chair, dragged to the side of the backyard where her father—and the barbecue—aren't. He can't feel through her skin, but he knows the sun will be warm, and the air will be gentle, and he's never missed California like he does right now. He never knew Cambridge could be so cold.

"Shit's weird here," he says—understatement of the night—and forces himself to smile, so she'll hear it in his voice. He doesn't want her to worry. "How's your Thanksgiving going?"

"Oh, gangbusters. Mom made cranberry pie, which set itself on fire somehow, and Erin made roast root vegetables with garlic and rosemary, which *didn't* set itself on fire, and Dad set the turkey on fire twice. He's about to start barbecuing the corn, and . . . Roger? What's wrong?"

Sometimes he forgets how sensitive their connection is to sound. He hadn't even considered that his sharply indrawn breath might transmit, or that she might be able to tell it from a yawn. "Like I said, shit's weird. Erin's having Thanksgiving dinner with you guys?"

"I know, it's bizarre, right? Her flight home got canceled due to weather, and I couldn't leave her alone in the apartment to eat ramen and look gloomily out the window at old Bill. My folks think she's pretty cool. She's really useful in the kitchen, too. Not like me. My talents begin and end with pancakes, and that's a job for tomorrow morning, not for tonight."

"Has she said anything to you?"

"Anything like what?" Dodger sounds honestly curious, and honestly confused. For once, he's the one whose world is falling apart, while hers is continuing on a normal keel.

For the first time, he understands why she didn't tell him how unhappy she was, all those years and all that bloodshed ago. Being in someone's head like this, it's . . . intimate in a way nothing else in his life has ever been. Barging in on her and telling her how scared he was by the silence and stillness of his parents seems unfair, like an intrusion she didn't ask for and can't avoid. He wants to protect her. He wants to let her have her holiday. He can tell her later, with words spoken in the air and not in the space they make between them, about his concerns.

"It doesn't matter."

"It does." Dodger shifts in her chair. Across the lawn, her father waves. She waves back, smiling through her teeth as she hisses, "Remember what happened *last time* one of us decided to keep secrets? Now give. What's going on?"

"I just . . . Erin?"

"Yeah, Erin. What's going on with your *parents*?"

"I don't know." Quickly, he describes what happened at the dinner table. He wants to edit, to cast them in a better light. He doesn't. Dodger appreciates facts, says math is impossible if you don't know your starting figures. She won't judge them based on a single meal. She'll understand.

When he finishes, she's quiet. Too quiet, for too long. He's growing concerned when she says, "Their response to the idea of you and me dating was disproportionate."

"What?"

"Everything else could be written off as an exaggerated reaction to a conversation they've been worried about for twenty years. My folks don't like to talk about the adoption either. Not quite that viciously, but they get twitchy when I bring it up. I could make comforting noises and pretend everything about this was normal, except for that response. Your mother looked disgusted. You said I existed, you set a group of parameters that could apply to dozens of girls, you never said we were romantically involved, and yet she looked like she was going to throw up. That's not a proportionate response. They know about me. They knew before you brought me up."

"I don't think . . ."

"Do the math," she says, and it's a kind statement, a gentle statement, especially for her, who considers math the only true underpinning of the universe: she's trying, in her own sledgehammer way, to nudge him along. "Parents of adult adoptees are sometimes sensitive to the idea that their children might go looking for their biological parents; there's no 'right way' to respond. You get helpful parents, parents who've been in secret correspondence with the bio parents for years, and you get parents who'll lie to your face and say the bio parents are dead when they aren't. Humans are complicated. Humans make decisions based on the data at hand. So yeah, it's weird that they got twitchy, but if you've never tried to talk about it with them before, it's not outside the numbers."

"I guess."

"It's the rest of it." Dodger sits up fully, draping her arms across her knees. "They shouldn't have jumped straight from 'there's a girl' to 'are you dating her.' If they did, they shouldn't have been *disgusted*. Not unless they already knew there was a girl out there for you to find, a girl you shouldn't be romantically involved with. It doesn't add up."

"What should I do? Should I go talk to them?"

"No. Wait for them to come and talk to you." Dodger pauses. "And . . . be careful."

"I will," he promises, and opens his eyes. The feeling of isolation is immediate, stronger than the norm; usually, he and Dodger pop in and out of each other's heads a few times a day, checking in, asking questions, and exiting again, as comfortable solo as they are together. Here and now, however, the fact of his singularity is almost upsetting, almost too profound to be real.

He slides off the bed, aware of the irony of feeling like the *absence* of telepathic connection across a continent is the unrealistic part of this evening. His parents are moving downstairs; he can hear their footsteps, hear the occasional spike of raised voices. They're not quite arguing, but their conversation has definitely taken on a strained tone. He can't make out words with his door closed. Under the circumstances, he's not sure he wants to.

Carefully, he crosses to the closet. This time, when his questing fingers find the loose board, he pulls it up, revealing the treasures beneath. A few books that had been too grown-up for him, once upon a time; a dictionary of profanity purchased at the used bookstore down by Harvard Square, hiding it inside his coat and rushing home with it, red-faced and glancing around constantly, sure someone knew he was smuggling something he shouldn't have into the house. Other boys his age hoarded dirty pictures and copies of *Penthouse*. He hid books about the origins of words he wasn't supposed to know.

There is a layer of the more common detritus of boyhood. A bird's nest, almost disintegrated with time. A rock-hard bar of Hershey's chocolate. A few interesting rocks. Some shells, a bone—he doesn't know what from—a slingshot, a handful of comic books. Ordinary things, from an ordinary childhood. A few of them seem old-fashioned now, but so what? He loved them once, enough to hide them here, where he wouldn't need to worry about them being accidentally swept up and thrown away by an adult who didn't understand their significance.

Under the spindrift remains of his childhood is a folder, yellowed with age, curling at the edges. Carefully, Roger works it loose and opens it. Inside are a few papers his younger self was particularly proud of—an essay about seeing the Red Sox win a game, a spelling worksheet where *he* had corrected the *teacher*—and a small pile of crayon drawings. The first, labeled ROGER M., AGE 4 in his already meticulous handwriting, shows a boy he assumes is meant to be him standing in a field, holding hands with a girl. They're both smiling.

In the next picture, the girl is gone. It's just the boy, standing in the same field, a frown on his face. Around him, over and over, Roger has written a single sentence:

*How many times?*
*How many times?*
*How many times?*

The words fill the sky and cover the field, covering everything but the sad little boy. Roger looks at the two pictures, trying to reconcile them with what he remembers of his childhood. He doesn't remember drawing them. That's not unusual—how many people re-member the things they drew when they were four?—but they must have been important to him, for him to have hidden them away. For him to have transferred them into this cache. More, he must have known about Dodger, on some level, to have been drawing her. There's no doubt it's her in that first picture. Her features are crude as only a crayon figure in a child's art can be, but the smile goes up higher on the left than on the right and her hair is the dingy reddish brown that red crayon always looked like to him, and he *knows*. And he knows that, based on the date, he drew this picture three years before the day Dodger had a headache and said hello to the boy on the other side of her mind. He knew.

"Roger?" His mother's voice is sweet, almost saccharine as she shouts up the stairs. "Can you come down here, sweetheart? Your father and I have something to show you."

"In a minute, Ma!" he shouts back, and starts to put the pictures back in the hole in the floor, alongside his other treasures.

His phone rings.

He's almost forgotten it: it's an artifact of the present, not the past that drapes around this house like a shroud. He pulls it from his pocket and blinks. Dodger's number is on the screen. He doesn't know why she'd call him when she could as easily close her eyes and ask for his attention; maybe she's assuming he's with his parents by now, and wouldn't be able to answer her. No matter. He presses Answer, raises the phone to his ear.

"You need to call Dodger right now," says Erin. There's no greet-ing, no pause to find out who she's talking to: she knows who's on the other end of the line, and she doesn't have time for pleasantries. She never has. "You need to say the following: 'take us back to the last fixed point.' Tell her it is an order. Tell her it is an adjuration. Tell her it is a command. And do it fast, Jack Daw, because the whole damn Im-possible City is about to fall on your head."

"Erin? What are you doing with Dodger's phone? Does she know you're calling me?"

"No, and I don't have time to explain it to you, and I'm not *going* to have time, because you're about to wipe the last week off the board. This is a bad equation, dumbass; this is a sonnet that doesn't rhyme. Take whatever metaphor you need, but call her and end this, fast."

"*Roger!*" His father sounds angry, cancelling out his mother's sweetness. "Get down here this instant!"

Roger crouches forward, cups his hand around the phone, like that would make any difference in the world. "Look, Erin, I want you to give Dodger her phone back and cut this shit out right now, or so help me—"

"You found something."

He stops dead.

"I don't know what it was, because I'm not that attuned to you, but it was something you know shouldn't exist. A story you wrote about having a sister, maybe, or a photo, or a drawing. You found something that didn't happen in this timeline, hidden with the things that *did* happen. That's because we've been here before. Not exactly here, not this precise point, but close enough for government work. We've done this often enough for me to start remembering, and you need to call Dodger, and you need to repeat what I told you to say *right now.*"

"Or what?"

"Or this might turn out to be the last timeline. You're too old for chemical resets and therapy. You're old enough to be a failure. You listened to me last time."

"How do you know that?"

Erin's chuckle is grim. "We're still here, aren't we? Get the fuck off the improbable road, or you're a dead man, and you're taking Dodger down with you."

The line goes dead. Roger lowers his phone, staring at it. This makes no sense. This can't be true. But the picture in his hand is real, and there are footsteps on the stairs, and those things don't make sense either; those things are somehow terrible in their senselessness.

He closes his eyes. "Dodger?"

The backyard, a world in flowering color. Dodger's perspective shifts as she sits up again. "Roger? You okay?"

"You need to take us back to the last fixed point." There are footsteps on the landing now. They're trying to be quiet, but they don't know the creaks and groans of the floor the way he does. They didn't grow up here.

"I don't understand. What do you want me to do?"

"Take us back," he repeats. There's supposed to be more to it than that. Haltingly, he says, "This is an order."

"Roger—"

The doorknob is turning.

"This is an adjuration."

His father is pushing the door open, tread heavy enough to identify him. "What are you doing, boy? Open your eyes."

"This is a command."

Roger's eyes stay closed as his father grabs his arm and yanks him away from the hole in the closet floor. He doesn't have time to open them before Dodger's vision goes white, the flash traveling from her optic nerves to his, white taking black, upsetting the whole chessboard.

*We got it wrong,* he thinks, and everything is gone.

The girl had landed in a crouch, more like a wild thing than a child. Slowly she straightened, until she was standing a little taller than Avery, a little shorter than Zib, slotting into the space they made between them like it had been measured out to her specifications.

She had black hair and yellow eyes, and a dress made of black feathers that ended just above her knees. Her feet were bare and her nails were long and raggedy, like no one had ever trimmed them, but let them grow until they could be used to climb the walls of the world.

"Who *are* you?" asked Zib, all awe.

Avery had to swallow the urge to pull her away. She would stay there forever if he let her, of that much he was sure: she would never realize when she was in danger, and without her, he would never be able to go home.

"I'm a Crow Girl," said the stranger. She cocked her head. "Who are you?"

"I'm Avery, and this is Zib," said Avery. "Please, do you know where we are?"

"Why, this is the Up-and-Under, of course," said the Crow Girl. She cocked her head in the opposite direction. "You must not be very clever, if you don't even know where you are. I blame the shoes."

"Shoes?" asked Zib.

"Shoes." The Crow Girl held up her bare left foot and waggled her toes extravagantly. "If you can't feel where you're going, how will you ever know where you've been? Skies for wings and roads for feet, that's what the world is made of."

"How can something be up *and* under?" asked Avery.

"Up a tree's still under the sky," said the Crow Girl. "Here in the Up-and-Under, we're both things at once, always, and we're never anything in-between . . ."

—From *Over the Woodward Wall,* by A. Deborah Baker

BOOK IV

# Complicate

I think you are wrong to want a heart. It makes most people unhappy. If you only knew it, you are in luck not to have a heart.

—L. Frank Baum, *The Wonderful Wizard of Oz*

They were only pencil sketches, all the fantasies we chased;
Step right up if you can see me, I'm the one who got erased.

—Michelle "Vixy" Dockrey, "Erased"

# Phlegmatic

W hen are your parents expecting you?" Dodger is at the far wall, a marker in her hand, adding numbers in a swift, steady stream to the columns already there. She pauses after she asks the question, turning, a perplexed expression on her face. "Or did I already ask you that?"

Roger is cross-legged on the bed, looking equally perplexed. "Yes," he says, and then, "No," and then, "I don't know. I don't think so? Maybe you thought it really loud, and I picked it up."

"With my eyes open?" she asks dubiously. "If we're starting to communicate with our eyes open and our mouths shut, the entanglement is getting worse. We should probably be concerned about that."

"Or not," says Roger. "Maybe we're going through . . . I don't know, psychic puberty. That usually means more stability."

"Yeah, when it's *over*," says Dodger. "I don't know about you, but when I was in the middle of physical puberty, I spent an evening in the kitchen smashing plates and crying for no good reason. Mom didn't even get mad, because she'd done something similar with a hammer and a bunch of *her* mom's wedding china. Do you want to know what kind of damage we'd do during psychic puberty? Because I don't want to know that. I don't want to know that *at all*."

"The Midwich cuckoos have nothing on us," says Roger.

"They changed the title to *The Village of the Damned* when they made the movie," says Dodger. "Anyway, those kids weren't good planners. We would be the end of days."

"Probably less oddly sexist, though."

"Ever notice how our last names make the word 'Midwich' if you cut them in half?" asks Dodger. "Middleton gives us 'mid,' and Cheswich gives us 'wich.' Midwich. It's like a lousy word puzzle."

Roger straightens, looking down the length of his nose at her. "Did you seriously just ask me whether I had noticed a word puzzle? Even a bad one?"

"Yes."

"Have you been inhaling marker fumes again?"

"Yes." Dodger widens her eyes, giving him her best sappy smile. "They make my head all bubbly."

Roger picks up a pillow, weighs it carefully in his hands, and flings it at her. She dodges, laughing, and for a moment he can almost forget the crushing sense of déjà vu hanging over the room. *We're diverging from the original script,* he thinks, and that makes no sense, but it soothes his nerves all the same. Divergence is good. *We got it wrong,* he thinks, and that makes even less sense, and does nothing for his nerves. If anything, it sets them back on edge.

"Well?" says Dodger. He looks back to her. She's put the cap on her marker and is looking at him expectantly, clearly waiting for something.

Roger hastily reviews their conversation, backtracking to the point where everything went strange. His answer should be easy. It's not. "I don't think I'm going to go," he says, and the feeling of disoriented doom recedes. He can breathe again. "It's not a good time to fly to Boston. The tickets are refundable, I can say I have to stay on campus for some reason . . . Could I come to Thanksgiving dinner at your place? It's cool if I can't, I'm happy to roast a chicken and lecture it for not being a turkey."

"Charming as I find the image of you yelling at your dinner, of course you can come home with me," says Dodger, expectant look melting into a frown. She drops her marker on the floor. That's standard behavior: she leaves them scattered around the room like breadcrumbs, waiting for her to pick them up and begin another mathematical journey into mystery. She walks over to the bed, perches, birdlike, on the edge, looking at him gravely. "What's wrong? You were so excited about seeing your parents."

"I just don't think this is a good time." He can see how things will play out, like watching a flickering home movie projected on a makeshift screen. Each piece leads inevitably to the next, from his mother's cornbread to the footsteps on the stairs. The images are already starting to fray around the edges, and he's glad of that, in a way: these aren't thoughts he wants to have about his parents. These aren't memories he wants to keep.

He's also terrified. *How many times?* The question echoes. It has no good answer.

Dodger frowns. "You're sure?"

"I'm sure."

"My family's a little much sometimes."

"I could do with a little much." He manages to smile. He does it for her, and is rewarded when some of the tension leaves her shoulders. She trusts him not to lie to her. She's the better liar of the two of them, and sometimes she forgets that doesn't make him incapable of deception: he's good too, in his own way. "Hey, speaking of family, have you thought more about getting our blood tested?"

She blinks before her whole face lights up. "I have!" she says. "I've been thinking about it a lot, actually. I think we should do it. I want to know whether the quantum entanglement has a basis in biology, or whether we were just in the wrong place at the right time and somehow blundered into a cosmic anomaly—"

She keeps talking, and he keeps listening, clinging as he does to the thin line that reminds him, over and over, how something has gone wrong; how something is out of true. He responds when necessary, letting her carry the bulk of the conversation. *We got it wrong,* he thinks, and he doesn't know what "it" is, and the not knowing is like a splinter in his mind. He wants to talk to her about it. He doesn't know how.

By the end of the evening, he's confirmed for Thanksgiving in Palo Alto, and they've agreed to talk to Smita about performing a blood test after the holiday. She'll probably consider it beneath her, but at least they both know her, and they trust her to jab them with a needle. He leaves promptly at eleven. It's a school night, after all.

Dodger walks him to the door, all smiles, and shuts it firmly behind him. Only then does she let her knees buckle, sinking to the hallway floor. Candace is already in bed and she hasn't seen Erin in days; she's not concerned about her roommates walking in on her, thank God. Everything is spinning, everything has *been* spinning since she asked Roger when he was leaving. It's like the world has transformed into a carnival ride, constantly in motion, never growing still. She's experienced this before, but it's never been this *bad*. When Roger was talking, it was all she could do to keep smiling, to keep from running out of the room to vomit.

He'd think there was something wrong with her if he knew. He'd think she was broken, or that their quantum entanglement was overloading her synapses. To be honest, she's not sure that's not what's happening. There was a click earlier in the evening, like a metal rod being shoved into a battery pack, and everything went white for a heartbeat. It's happened before. Not often, of course, but often enough that the sensation was familiar. She almost welcomes those electric-shock moments when they come, because those memories will always remain sharp and crisp and easy to revisit, preserved in time like amber.

(The day she opened her wrists in the gully is one of those frozen moments. It's not a pleasant memory, not by a long shot. She's still grateful to have it trapped in her mind the way it is. Every time she starts to feel like the world is getting narrow, like she needs to open herself to let the blackness out, she goes to that memory. She remembers the way it felt: that it wasn't better, it wasn't an answer, it solved nothing, but it nearly took everything away. Sometimes perfect recall is a blessing that can be used to counterbalance all the curses in the world.)

Not here; not now. She starts to cry, big, wracking sobs that shake her entire body and make her eyes burn. She's getting snot down her front—she's probably getting snot in her *hair*—and that doesn't matter, because the world is still spinning, the worst carousel the world has ever known, bobbing and weaving around her. She doesn't know how to make it stop. She doesn't know how to make it *stop*. There is no exit from this funhouse.

Eventually, the tears run out. She curls herself into a tight ball on the hallway floor and waits in silence for the world to stop spinning.

Roger knows none of this, because she doesn't call for him, because he doesn't like to walk with his eyes closed. He's halfway home when he hears the footsteps. This time, he knows who they belong to. He stops walking and turns, waiting for Erin to catch up. She looks . . . satisfied, somehow, like things are going according to some complicated plan that she hasn't felt the need to share with anyone else. He hates her for having that smug look on her face. He hates himself for putting it there.

"What did you do to me?" he demands.

Erin's smile doesn't falter. "I have no idea," she says. "I'm not you, Jackdaw. When I see the Impossible City, I forget it afterward, unless you order otherwise. I guess this time you didn't care to retain the information."

"You're not making any sense."

"No, I'm not," she says. "That's the fun part. Because see, come morning, all this is going to seem like a funky dream—even this conversation, which wouldn't have happened if not for the things that came before it. Your mind is going to edit out the pieces that don't make sense. It's going to lie to you, and you're going to let it. The world's more comfortable that way. The world hangs together better that way. And you need a lot more foundation stones before you can start building this tower."

"Do you speak entirely in metaphor with everyone, or am I lucky somehow?"

Erin's eyes seem to darken. "Oh, you're luckier than you know. You're lucky I'm the one they chose to watch over you. You're lucky they hurt me. And you're lucky your sister is one of the tenacious ones. The guns are fragile. They need their triggers to keep them in check. The other pairs they separated didn't make it. You did. *They* want to know why. They want to understand you."

"They who?" asks Roger.

"The guards at the Impossible City. The Page of Frozen Waters. But the King of Cups most of all. You could be what he's been looking for his entire life—and he's not the sort of man you want paying attention to you. He's not a humbug, like some other wizard figures I could name. This isn't that kind of story. He's the real deal."

Roger scowls at her. "Do you know what happened to me tonight or what?"

"You remember I had something to do with it," says Erin. "That's fascinating. That means we've been here before more than once. Time is like skin: it can scar if you cut it enough times. Your sister, she knows how to cut it, but she isn't allowed to pick up the knife unless she's given permission. You gave her permission, and she cut time." She tilts her head, looking at him calmly. "You did this to yourself."

"You told me to." He's not sure why he's so certain of that—it's a feeling more than a fact, something snarled in the rapidly fraying cobweb of memory carried over from a timeline that never happened. "You said I had to."

"Is that so? Well, if I said something like that, I probably had a damn good reason." Erin sobers, the dark levity draining from her face, and looks at him. "I speak in metaphor because you're a Jackdaw, you're *Jack Daw,* and they didn't stuff you with feathers, they stuffed you with words. Things that make too much sense will drop right through you. Metaphors snag and stay. You need things that will stay with you. You need to figure this out. I can't help you."

"You're helping me now."

"No, I'm planting seeds in your subconscious, because I know that come tomorrow morning, you'll think this was all a dream." Erin takes a step closer. "I wouldn't even be doing this much if we weren't in the immediate lee of a timeline reset. When you cuckoos break the laws of reality, it creates a soft spot before it scars. The world is out of order. It wants to get back into order, and that gives me more flexibility than I'd normally have. I am *all* about taking advantage of flexibility. That's what I was designed to do. I'm like you, Jackdaw; we come from the same lab. I'm just not as important, or at least that's what the people who made us like to think. You and me and that crazy sister of yours, we're going to change the world, but only if I can keep you alive and innocuous-looking long enough for you to figure out *how*. You're not going home for Thanksgiving?"

Roger shakes his head before he stops to think about it. "No," he says.

"Good. Your parents aren't to be trusted, not anymore. They were safe enough when you were a kid—never really *safe*, but safe enough. They're not safe now. They'll turn you in and take your replacement in the same afternoon. If you can stay here for Christmas, too, that would probably be for the best." Erin's smile is entirely devoid of pleasure. "You're the word boy. Find an excuse that they'll believe."

"What are you even *talking* about? If you know so much, why aren't you helping us?"

"But I *am* helping you," she says, and for once, there's nothing mocking or strange in her tone: she's telling the truth as she understands it. "You're not ready to hatch yet, let alone stand up and fight. If you attract attention now, you're dead, both of you. So I need to keep you safe and kicking until you break that shell and start claiming what's yours. You can't skip to the end of the story just because you're tired of being in the middle. You'd never survive."

Roger looks at her for a long moment, puzzling through her latest words, comparing them to the ones she started with. Finally, he asks, "Are you saying that because we've already tried?"

She smiles, quick and sharp as a knife's edge. "Now you're getting it. Go home. Go to sleep. Forget all this, but remember to tell your parents that you're not coming. That's the only thing you have to hold on to."

"Erin—"

She turns on her heel. "See you at the Impossible City, Jackdaw," she says, and then she's gone, slipping into the maze of Berkeley's streets and leaving him alone.

Roger stares at the place where she was for a moment. Then he starts to walk again, slowly at first, but with increasing speed, until he's running, taking the last two blocks between Dodger's place and his at a dead sprint. He has to try three times to fit his key into the lock.

There's always a blank book next to his bed. He tries to remember to write down his dreams, but all too often, his mornings are a haze of need-coffee, need-cigarette, need-pants because class starts in five minutes. He grabs the book, grabs the nearest pencil, and drops to the mattress, starting to write with fevered speed. He writes until his wrist aches and his hand feels tight and hot, like it's grown three sizes, even though it looks the same to the naked eye. When he's done— when he's written down every scrap he can remember, every feeling, every impression, and every word that Erin said—he stares at it for a moment. Then he slumps over sideways, exhausted.

He's asleep before his head hits the pillow.

Morning announces itself with its usual lack of tact: by sending sunlight flooding in through his bedroom window, where the curtains he failed to close last night do nothing to protect him. Roger groans and rolls over, burying his face in his pillow. The zipper of his jeans digs into his skin, and he realizes with bemusement that he's fully clothed. He's even wearing his shoes. His head aches like he's hungover, but he was at Dodger's last night, and Dodger doesn't drink.

Pot and the occasional recreational hallucinogen, sure. Alcohol, though, that's not her style. She doesn't like being sloppy, and when he's with her, he usually doesn't either. Dodger is merciless when she feels like she has an advantage.

Still groggy, he sits up. His dream book is askew; he must have woken at some point in the night. He picks it up, opens it, and peers at the scribbled notes inside. None of them make any sense. It's like he's written the outline of some dystopian nightmare about *Over the Woodward Wall,* all mixed up with familiar faces.

"Golly, Zib, I don't know what I'd do without you," he mutters, and chuckles dryly, a sound that turns into a cough as the crud that's settled in his lungs overnight shifts and cracks. Smoking's going to be the death of him one day. The thought makes him realize how much he needs a cigarette. He stands, leaving the book behind, and heads off to start the morning.

It will be much, much later before he realizes that this was the moment when he decided which part he was going to play. By then, it will be a thousand miles too late.

# Variation

The doorbell rings. Dodger tears herself away from an ecstasy of Thanksgiving garlands, shouts, "I'll get it!" and races for the door, leaving her craft supplies scattered across the table.

In the kitchen, Heather Cheswich laughs and slides the yams into the oven. It feels like she's been waiting years for Dodger to invite people to Thanksgiving dinner. She loves her daughter more than anything, but a mother worries. A mother worries a lot. Dodger has never made friends easily or seemed to mind spending most of her time alone with her math books and her chessboard. Even chess, which initially seemed like a way to get the girl to socialize—hard to play a two-person game by yourself—yielded none of the social benefits Heather was hoping for. After less than two years of competitive play, Dodger retired, claiming it wasn't fair.

She'll never admit it, but Heather was starting to fear that her brilliant, beautiful little girl would be alone for her entire life, never realizing there was any other option. So naturally, when she wanted to bring her classmates home for a real family meal, both Heather and

Peter were delighted to agree. Buying a slightly larger turkey was a small price to pay for knowing Dodger is finally making friends.

The sound of laughter from the hall is like music. She knows Dodger's voice, high and perpetually excited, spiking on every other word, like she's afraid a failure to show her delight might bring the conversation crashing to a halt. The male voice beneath it is unfamiliar; tenor, light enough to provide a counterpart to Dodger's heavier stresses, like a soothing ribbon of reason. A third voice comes in intermittently, female, deeper than Dodger's, with a flat bottom note that speaks of a calm deadpan, a rational approach to the world. The fourth voice is also female, higher and sweeter than the others. Together, they make a choral blend Heather has been waiting to hear since the day she brought her daughter home from the airport. This is what it sounds like when your little girl is living in the world.

She steps into the kitchen doorway, unashamed of the cranberry sauce on her apron and flour on her hands. She's not worried about embarrassing Dodger in front of her friends; not on Thanksgiving. They're grad students. All they're going to care about is the food. "Hello," she says, beaming beatifically before she sees them. That's a good thing: it makes it possible for her smile to freeze.

The first female voice must belong to the short, curvaceous girl in the jeans and green sweatshirt. Her hair is strawberry blonde, and for some reason it makes Heather think of the color she gets when she tries to wash blood out of cotton, a color that isn't pink and isn't red, but is its own unique, nameless shade, the aftermath of carnage. Her eyes are blue and cold, irises rimmed in startling black. There's no denying her prettiness, but she looks at Heather the way a snake looks at a mouse, and for a moment—only a moment—Heather is very aware of the beating of her heart, the feeling of the muscle expanding and contracting, and how easily that process could be disrupted.

Heather assigns the second female voice to the slender Indian girl. Her skin is brown, her hair is black, and she is lovely, dressed in a slightly-too-formal yellow sundress too thin to keep her warm almost anywhere else in the country. California's eternal springtime must seem like a blessing. She, too, looks like a predator in her own way, but a hawk rather than a tiger, safer and more distant, assessing the world and belonging to it at the same time.

Oddly, though, the predator girls are not the problem. Heather has met Dodger's classmates before, students from her Gifted and Talented courses, child geniuses all too aware that everything they did was weighed and measured against the presumption of their brilliance. They are a predatory race by nature, these children of the golden mean, terrified of their edges being dulled by the world, measuring the love of their parents against the number of perfect scores they can achieve. Heather always tried to be kind to them, hoping they'd warm to her awkward, sensitive daughter, who approached her own brilliance more as a game than a calling. They might have been good for each other. But always and inevitably, Dodger was a better mathematician, or a worse abstract thinker, and would either be fled from as competition or discarded as deadweight. No; the predatory ones are not Heather's concern.

It's the boy.

Dodger is tall for a girl and he's short for a boy; they present an almost matched set when standing side by side. His hair is brown, but his eyes are the same clear gray as hers, shading toward white around the pupils, until it seems he must be blind; no one with eyes that light can possibly be able to see.

Their builds are similar, with the necessary allowances for gender: his shoulders are broader, his hips narrower; her face is rounder, but the structure of the skull beneath is so alike that it makes Heather's breath catch in her throat. And their faces . . .

Heather Cheswich has waited twenty years for the doorbell to ring and a red-haired woman with freckles on her nose to appear on her stoop, saying politely that she made a mistake, she wants her daughter back, and she hopes they'll understand. She prepared herself for legal challenges, for teenage tantrums ending with shouts of "you're not my real mother." She got none of those things. She has almost stopped waiting for the other shoe to drop, and now here it is, in the form of a politely smiling young man who looks so much like her daughter that it physically hurts.

*Do you even know how much he looks like you?* she wonders, and forces herself to speak. "Hello," she says, dusting her floury hand against her hip before she offers it in greeting. "I'm Heather, Dodger's mother."

"Erin," says the first girl, taking the offered hand and shaking it with perfunctory quickness. "You have a lovely home."

"Thank you," says Heather.

"Smita," says the second girl. "I appreciate the invitation. I didn't want to sit alone."

"Nonsense; it's our pleasure," says Heather. "The more the merrier."

It's the boy's turn. He takes her hand, shakes, smiles. "I'm Roger," he says. "I know I was a last-minute addition. I really appreciate your having me."

He has a New England accent, thick as pancake batter, oozing over every word. Heather freezes again, this time in fear. It's been years since Dodger was attacked, years since her recovery was complete, but the boy who hurt her was never found . . . and that boy spoke with a New England accent. (The papers reported it as Boston. That was easier. That was the simpler route.)

Roger looks at her with evident sympathy. It's like he knows what she must be thinking, somehow understands the words she's too frozen and afraid to say. Dodger's smile is fading, slipping away by inches.

There are questions here, questions that should be asked, but Heather's not going to be the one who ruins this day. She refuses. So she smiles again, more sincerely, and turns to her daughter as she says, "Daddy's out back prepping the turkey, and I've got things under control in the kitchen. Why don't you grab something to drink and take your friends out to the patio?"

"Okay, Mom," says Dodger, relief flooding her features. She bounces over to kiss her mother's cheek before turning to her friends and asking, "Coffee, lemonade, or root beer?"

"Root beer," says Erin.

"Lemonade," says Smita.

"Coffee," says Roger, with the sort of reverence most people reserve for the names of celebrities, saints, or vacation destinations. This time,

Heather's smile is sincere. They're so at ease with one another; there's no way Roger had anything to do with what happened to her little girl.

There's just no way.

The Cheswich home isn't large enough to be considered palatial, but it's huge, especially for a home presumably maintained on a professor's salary. Roger looks at the living room with its cathedral ceiling and the hallway with its hardwood floors, and feels like he's made a mistake. Thanksgiving belongs in an old English colonial house with repairs visible to the baseboards and the ceiling, if you know where to look. There should be signs of wear and tear on the wallpaper, not this pristine showroom shine.

Dodger glances at him, grimaces sympathetically, and says, "My folks were afraid we might have to sell and move when I was a kid. Daddy had tenure, but there were budget cuts, and tenure doesn't keep you employed if your department goes away. They inherited the house from Mom's grandparents. I never met them, but Great-Grandpa was some sort of apple baron or something, and they had a lot of money back in the day. So I always knew if I wanted to make a mess, I should either make it in my room or go outside and make it there."

Roger thinks of blood sinking into the ground, of messes made in ways and in places that can never be cleaned. He doesn't say anything. It wouldn't change anything. The past is set in stone, and he's not a sculptor; he doesn't get to go back and make something like that not happen.

Something about that thought nags at him, like a mosquito buzzing around his head. It's such a strange way to frame things. *He's* not a sculptor. But that opens the possibility that someone else could be; that such sculptors could exist in this world.

Clearly he needs more coffee. He gulps it as Dodger burbles about renovations, about how some of the prize money from the various mathematical puzzles she's solved over the years has gone back into the house, always with her consent, sometimes with her insistence, shoring up the foundations that kept her safe. There's a door at the end of the hallway; she opens it, and they're looking out on the backyard, and the roses, *he sees the roses,* the ones she showed him when they were children, the ones that always seemed so bright and beautiful to him, like roses grown in the Up-and-Under.

Their colors are as faded as any other roses. He sighs. Dodger glances at him and he closes his eyes, hiding the gesture behind a yawn as he looks through her eyes, looks out and sees the roses, as bright and as beautiful as ever.

He wonders what she gets when she looks through his eyes that she doesn't see through her own.

"Did you not sleep last night?" asks Erin.

He opens his eyes, but not before Dodger looks in her direction and he sees her through a different perspective: sees that her hair is strawberry blonde, not ashy, as he'd always assumed; sees her cheeks are flushed, even though it's not that warm, even though they haven't been doing anything to leave her in that state. It's strange. It's attractive, even. She's still dangerous, but it's a pretty sort of danger, the kind he could get used to.

Then his eyes are open, and the color is gone, one more layer of meaning removed from the world. "Not enough," he says, with a smile and a shrug. "I was excited about the idea of eating a real meal for a change. Sue me if there's something wrong with that."

"If grad students wanting to eat properly is something worth litigating, we're doomed," says Dodger, and drags him into the backyard. There's her father, standing near the fence—so much higher and sturdier than it was when they were kids, when Dodger's fascination with the gully was safe, and not the disaster it became—and fiddling with the barbecue, where he's grilling asparagus and corn to go with the turkey. He raises a hand in a wave. All four of them wave back but don't approach. It's better to let the people who enjoy playing with fire to finish before getting too close, at least if the goal is continuing to have hair that's not burning.

There's a table set up on the patio where they'll be eating dinner, and a pair of sliding glass doors lead into the kitchen where Heather is working. They must have taken the long way through the house to avoid disturbing her. It's an easy conclusion to reach, and is reinforced when Dodger steers them to a smaller table off to one side and says, brightly, "I'll be right back."

She's gone before any of them can object. Roger exchanges a look with Erin and says, "We're about to get *covered* in glitter."

"Craft herpes can strike anyone at any time," she says dryly.

"Practice safe crafts," says Smita. Erin laughs. She's still laughing when Dodger returns with a laundry basket full of supplies, dropping it onto the table and beaming at them.

"I was set up inside, but Mom said I should move out here once you arrived, since four of us is more than she could reasonably be expected to bear," she says blithely, and begins unpacking the basket. "Who wants to string popcorn?"

"Is there another option?" asks Roger.

"We need to make more paper chains," says Dodger.

"Maybe you should have invited Candace to this thing," says Erin, looking dubiously at the bowl of cranberries. "She's the one with an interest in early childhood development. This is probably like taking a final exam for her."

"Candace flew back to Portland yesterday," says Dodger. She waves a hand at the sky, like she's indicating the arc of Candace's flight. "Besides, she's a vegetarian. I don't think she'd appreciate the carnage that is my family Thanksgiving."

"Well, on behalf of the world's meat-eaters, I want to thank you in advance for the carnage," says Roger dryly. "I'll string popcorn for you, Dodge. How hard can it be?"

It can be quite hard. The popcorn is crumbly and the cranberries are slick, trying to shoot away when he holds them too tightly, rolling out of the path of the needle when he doesn't hold them tightly enough. There's a trick to this, and while he may have known it as a child, the skill seems to have left him. Only Erin seems to have the knack: for her, the craft supplies behave perfectly, the needle finding its angle every time. Silence falls, punctuated by the *snick* of scissors slicing through construction paper, the occasional soft curse word, and the distant sound of Dodger's father swearing amiably at the barbecue.

The first Roger knows of Peter Cheswich's approach is when a male voice—a voice he's heard countless times through Dodger's ears, but only once through his own—says behind him, "It's nice to see a normal-looking garland. When Dodger does them, she always winds up using the popcorn to make a Fibonacci sequence, with the cranberries as markers between the numbers we're supposed to pay attention to."

"Why is this not surprising?" asks Smita.

"You thought it was cute when I was four, Daddy," says Dodger, looking up from her latest paper chain. She wrinkles her nose, scrunching up the lower half of her face like a much younger girl. It's both endearing and a little weird. Roger has only ever seen her guard this low when they were alone together in her room, her holding a marker, him staying out of her way.

"It's still cute," says Peter. "Aren't you going to introduce me to your friends?"

Erin and Smita have been through this process before, often enough to know the expected steps. They turn, smiles on their faces. Roger does the same. In his case, the smile feels like it's cemented in place, so tight and heavy that it might crack and fall off at any moment. Dodger's mother was an easy bar to clear compared to this.

*I might have been better off going home,* he thinks, and feels his skin tighten, becoming two sizes too small. No. He would not have been better off going home. He doesn't know how he knows that, but he does, oh, how he does. Going home would have been the end of all things.

This may not be much better. "This is Erin, one of my housemates, Smita, from the biology department, and Roger, my best friend and most tolerant companion," says Dodger.

"It's a pleasure to meet you, Mr. Cheswich," says Erin, holding out her hand.

Peter, laughing, shows her his own grease-stained fingers. "I'm normally all in favor of normal social ritual, but right now, I think it's better if I leave you in the condition I found you in," he says. "I'll shake later, after I've had time to wash up."

"Good plan," says Erin.

"Hello, sir," says Smita.

Peter's attention shifts to Roger, taking his measure. Even if Roger didn't know that Dodger had never bothered to date during high school—it took time away from more important things, like homework—he'd be able to tell from the look on her father's face. He's been the first boy a few girls ever brought home. All of their fathers looked at him like that, with a mixture of hope and suspicion, like he could either rescue or ruin their daughters.

*Aren't you going to be surprised,* he thinks, and keeps smiling his forced smile, and says, "It's a pleasure to meet you, sir."

Like Heather before him, Peter goes still, the blood draining from his face, leaving him a silent, staring statue of a man.

"Can you show me where the bathroom is?" Erin asks abruptly, looking at Dodger.

"But—" She wants to help. It's written all through her voice, in the desperation of that single, unsteady syllable. She wants to *fix* this. Roger saved her life, and her father is her father, and she needs them to get along, because she can't imagine a world without either one of them. They're essential to the future as she sees it, a future made up of careful equations and perfectly arranged consequences.

"I really have to go," says Erin, all clenched teeth and tight syllables.

"I would enjoy knowing the bathroom's location as well," says Smita.

Dodger sighs. She knows her duty as a hostess, even if she doesn't want to do it. "I'll be right back," she says to Roger and her father, neither of whom are listening. She stands, beckoning for the other girls to follow, and together, the three disappear back into the house.

Roger doesn't move. He's looking at Peter, waiting for the explosion he knows is coming. He could try to talk his way out of this—he's persuasive when he wants to be, always has been—but he doesn't say a word. Trying to change the way this plays out will do him no good, and may do him a great deal of harm. He knows that. He *knows,* and still he has to bite his tongue to keep the words prisoned inside, where they can't get out and make things worse.

Finally, Peter asks, in an almost conversational tone, like he's re-marking on the weather, "Did you think I wouldn't know your voice? That you could come into my home, my place, and sit here with my daughter, and I wouldn't remember you?"

"No, sir," says Roger. "I almost didn't come, because I knew you would, and I didn't want to ruin your Thanksgiving. But I was going to have to meet you eventually. There was no way to avoid it. This seemed like the best way to do it without you calling the police the second I opened my mouth."

"What makes you think I won't?"

"Dodger would be crushed." The words are simple, small, and ab-solutely true. They represent the thing both men want most to avoid, and so they aren't questioned, even as they change the shape of the conversation. Roger remains seated. Standing might seem like a chal-lenge, even though he's fairly sure Peter Cheswich is taller than he is. "She brought me home to meet her family because you're important to her, and she wants us to get along."

Peter's eyes are steel. "What you did to her . . ."

"I saved her life, sir. That's all I did." Roger shakes his head. "I was in Cambridge when I called. I know you know that, because you're a smart man, and you would have checked the university call logs as soon as the police got involved. You *know* the call came from Massa-chusetts." From a payphone, no less. (It's not there anymore. The last time Roger took the T into Boston, he'd passed Harvard Square and seen that the payphones, all of them, had been removed. He'd felt an obscure sense of loss, like something essential and hence eternal was inexplicably gone. Time marches on. Only the dead are left behind.)

Peter has known for years that Dodger's wounds were self-inflicted; that the boy from Boston was a polite fiction. Still . . . "How did you know, if you weren't there?"

"Because I was her best friend," Roger says, and that's true; that's always been true. Even when they weren't in contact, even when he had other people to fill the void her absence left, he has always, always been her best friend. She was happier to live with the hole than she would have been trying to plug it with someone who wasn't right, and sometimes he wishes he were that single-minded, or that strong. "I knew something was wrong. Whether you want to believe me or not, it's the truth. I'd never hurt her. If anything, I'd hurt myself trying to keep her safe."

Peter hesitates. The things he's wanted to say for five years are difficult to swallow. The evidence of his eyes is harder to deny. "She seems . . . happy."

"We've been having a good time."

Peter's expression changes again, making it clear how he's interpreting that. It's all Roger can do not to laugh out loud.

"Nothing like that, I promise," he says. "We've mostly been arguing about the language used to describe math. She's pretty vehement when it comes to getting things right."

"That's my girl," says Peter, and he's smiling, and maybe things are going to be okay.

When Erin emerges from the bathroom—canary yellow and cream, with pictures of whales on the walls and scented seashells on the windowsill; it couldn't scream "Californian" any louder if it tried—and lets Smita push past her, she finds Dodger in the hall. She stops, raising an eyebrow.

"Yes?" she asks.

"Do you think my dad's going to kill Roger?" Dodger blurts the sentence out as a single breath, like she's been holding it clasped between her teeth as long as she's been waiting.

"Probably not," says Erin. "I mean, I guess he could, but it would be hard to get rid of the body, and it would probably mean dinner would be served late. Best not to risk it."

Dodger looks alarmed. That can be amusing—when Dodger blows her stack, she tends to do it in a huge, theatrical way, which is better entertainment than most of what's on television. At the same time, Erin really does want to eat on time and isn't interested in fomenting conflict today. There's enough conflict to come. No need to start things before their time arrives.

"I'm sure it's fine," she says. "I know there was some stuff with a boy from Boston—don't look so shocked, I know how to use a search engine, and there was no way I was moving in with you without looking you up—but I also know Roger wasn't here when it happened. He and your dad will glare at each other and things will be fine. It's patriarchal bullshit and we should hate it as feminists, but we should also find it endearing, because they're so cute when they puff their feathers out and try to show off for one another."

Dodger blinks before she asks, "Do you think my dad thinks I'm dating Roger?"

Privately, Erin doesn't think anyone who watches the two of them together for more than thirty seconds could see them as anything other than adult siblings. "Why would he? Roger's your brother, remember?"

The look of guilt on Dodger's face is almost comic. "Um. About that . . ."

"It's okay. I know the two of you were adopted. Your father doesn't know, does he?"

"No," says Dodger, shaking her head. "We haven't had a chance to tell him."

Erin smiles. "Won't this be a fun dinner?"

Her smile endures until Smita emerges from the bathroom. Erin turns and heads for the back door, slowly enough to encourage Dodger to trail along behind her like a duckling following its mother. She doesn't want to shake the girl more than she already has been. Fun as it is to see Dodger off-kilter and unsure of her next move, there's such a thing as taking it too far. If she pushes Dodger past her limits, there's a chance she'll snap, and the consequences could be dire. The timeline can't handle another reset this close on the heels of the last one. Worse, a timeline reset might result in Roger going to Boston, and that would be *bad*.

In the backyard, Roger is still stringing popcorn and cranberries, while Peter is back at the grill. Erin steps aside to let Dodger see, and watches the other girl sag in relief.

"Oh," she says. "No blood."

"See?" says Erin. "I told you. They just needed to sort things out. Come on."

The three of them reclaim their seats. Roger doesn't look up, but slides a cranberry onto the needle and says piously, "I'm not going to forget that the two of you took Dodger and left me alone. You may not understand the import of what you've done, but I assure you, you have made an enemy this day."

"I shall make a note in my day planner," says Smita. "I'm sure I'll rue the day."

"Isn't it cute, how he thinks he knows how to sound scary?" asks Erin. She picks up a strip of construction paper. "Somebody give me some glue."

"I thought you were terrifying," says Dodger, passing a glue stick to Erin.

"Thank you," says Roger. He glances up long enough to flash her a smile. "It's all good. We just needed to talk a few things out. No one got punched, and I think he's cool with me being here now. Or well, maybe he's not *cool,* but he's not asking me to leave, so I'll take it."

"Cool," says Dodger, and smiles back, and for a while, the only sound is the rustle of construction paper, the *snick* of scissors, and the occasional soft curse when Roger jabs the needle into his finger instead of into the popcorn. It's actually a surprise when the glass door slides open and Heather steps outside.

"All right, you lot," she says. "Time to get decorating. Roger, you're the tallest, and Dodger, you know where things go. Erin, Smita, can you help me with the dishes?"

"Of course, Mrs. Cheswich," says Erin, suddenly all sugary politeness. She gets up and follows Heather inside, leaving the others to blink after her.

"*That* was terrifying," says Dodger.

"That was my cue," says Smita, and trots after Erin.

"I didn't know Erin did 'friendly,'" says Roger. He holds up his popcorn-and-cranberry garland. "Where do I hang this?"

"I'll show you," says Dodger, and stands. He follows.

The next few minutes are the sort of thing people never truly outgrow, even as they try to convince themselves that they've moved past childish things and don't miss the simple rituals of their past. Dodger points and Roger hangs, paper chains and popcorn strings. Heather, Smita, and Erin move behind them, setting dishes on the table; plates and flatware at first, then moving on to serving trays, baskets of rolls, platters of corn. Absorbed as they are in the process of getting everything exactly right, Roger and Dodger don't even seem to notice.

Peter walks over with the turkey, holding the massive bird like an offering, and stops, blinking. Somehow, they've managed to string an elementary school's worth of paper chains from the roof of the covered porch, their ends tangled festively around the support beams. Dodger is atop the stepladder, Roger holding her hips to steady her, as she ties the last of the garlands. There's something about the scene that's so profoundly, simply *accurate* that for a moment, he knows in his bones that both of them grew up in this house: that he's been watching his daughter and her brother decorate for Thanksgiving since they were big enough to work a pair of safety scissors without cutting themselves.

The moment passes. Peter Cheswich says the only thing he can think of: "When were you two going to tell us you were related?"

Dodger jumps. It would end in disaster if not for Roger: his hands won't let her fall, not even when she twists, grimacing apologetically, and says, "We're not absolutely sure, Daddy. We still have to get tested. Smita's going to do that when we get back to school."

"That's a formality," says Peter. "You know it, or you wouldn't have brought him home."

"I'm not related to anyone here," says Erin. "Neither is Smita."

"You're different," says Peter. "We've had classmates before. Never for a major holiday, or even for a dinner, but it's not like we kept Dodger locked in a tower. She's never brought home a boy, and she's definitely never brought home a boy who looks like her."

"We don't look *that* much alike," protests Dodger.

"Yes, you do," says Heather, stepping up next to her husband. "Maybe not if you're used to looking at yourself in the mirror, but for the rest of us? You look so much alike that it hurts."

Erin leans back in her seat, watching with interest to see how this plays out. They're off-balance, both of them, rendered uncomfortable by scrutiny and parental attention. She can learn a lot from their reactions.

Part of her role is to watch them. Part of her role is to protect them. And part of her role is being prepared to take them down: finding their weaknesses, however small, and knowing how to exploit them. They're fine in an academic setting, presenting a united front against whatever challenges the school can throw at them. Their early connection must have allowed them to survive their undergrad experience with a minimum of tears; based on the pairs that didn't connect before high school, without the time they'd spent together as children, they would have been hopeless at the subjects that weren't innately theirs. Dodger was never going to be a linguist, any more than Roger was going to be a mathematician, but they could cope, which was more than some of their fellows ever learned. They balance each other.

That doesn't mean they're equipped to face their parents—although if they must face a pair of parental figures, better hers than his. At least hers want what's best for her, and not for the experiment.

Smita emerges from the kitchen. For the moment, she's silent, observing; taking it in.

"Were you adopted?" Peter asks, looking at Roger.

There's a wealth of information in that question. Roger unpacks it without thinking, finding the nuance, finding the things Peter wouldn't be able to say without a few beers and a lot of time to dwell. First and foremost, however, is the thing that must be addressed before it becomes the elephant in the room: the question that defines everything.

"Yes, sir, I was," says Roger. "Dodger and I have compared adoptions. We were born on the same day, both placed with sealed records. I've had no contact with my birth family, and honestly, I haven't

been tempted to go looking for it. I love my folks. It's just, well . . ."
He looks to Dodger and shrugs.

She picks up the thread. Still the better liar, even if she's not as pre-
ternaturally convincing as he is; sometimes it's not the words, it's the
way they're used. "We met at chess camp. Remember?"

Heather's eyes widen. "The pen pal you wanted us to go to Cambridge to meet. Dodger, honey, why didn't you say anything?"

"Because I told her not to come," says Roger. "I was a kid. I was
scared. Here was this girl saying she thought we might have the same
birth parents, and the kids at school used to make fun of me because
I wasn't wanted. But I *was* wanted. Being adopted meant I knew my
parents loved me more than anything. They'd chosen me out of all
the kids in the world. I was afraid if I saw Dodger again and she really
*was* my sister, like she said, that things would change. Our birth parents would appear out of nowhere and take us away from the people
who loved us."

Erin says nothing. This isn't her conversation, and he's closer to the
truth than he knows, whether by chance or because he harbors vague
memories of other, older timelines where that exact thing had happened. If the cuckoos came together too early, they were separated.
The pattern never varied. Its echoes still hang over them all.

"I thought if he was really my brother, like I'd thought he was, he'd
love me too much to tell me to stay away," says Dodger, picking up
the thread of the lie with ease. They would have been terrifying if they
had actually grown up together. They're more than a little terrifying
now. "So I didn't talk about it. We met again when I did that chess
tour, the one that went to Massachusetts. We lost touch after I . . . hurt
myself."

She looks down, cheeks burning red, as if the patio floor can ab-
solve her of the sins of her past. She doesn't say anything about lying
when she allowed them to think that Roger had been the one to hold
the knife; she doesn't need to. The confession is in her silence.

Peter and Heather exchange a look. When they turn back to the
trio, they're both smiling, her sadly, him seeming somewhat strained.

"Thanksgiving is for family," she says. "Let's eat."

*  *  *

That night, with Erin and Smita on the floor of Dodger's room and Roger in the guest room, Heather turns toward her husband in the bed and asks, "Do you really think she just happened to turn around and stumble over her twin brother?"

The word "twin" has entered the conversation without fanfare. It makes too much sense to be omitted: they were born on the same day. They have the same eyes, the same underlying bone structure, the same tense, uncompromising posture. Dodger shows it in the tightly wound way she stands, the way she reacts to the slightest sound. Roger seems more relaxed, but he's just as aware; he simply masks it better.

"It looks that way," says Peter.

Heather shakes her head. "And then there's the *names*. Thank God those poor children didn't grow up together. Can you imagine?"

"I wonder if his parents got the same 'you can't change your child's name' rider on their adoption," says Peter.

"Some people shouldn't be allowed to name their own children."

"No," he agrees.

Heather is quiet for a time before she says, "I suppose I should feel tricked, like she snuck him past the borders to make sure we couldn't push him away. But really, I'm relieved. She has a brother. She has someone her own age who understands the way her mind works. How can that be anything but good for her?"

"It can't," says Peter, and kisses his wife goodnight.

Down the hall, Dodger lies awake, staring at the slowly dimming constellations on her ceiling. The glow-in-the-dark paint still holds a charge, even after all these years; she can tell the time by the half-life of her artificial sky. She wants to talk to Roger. She wants to ask him what he thought of the meal, of her parents, of the overall situation. She can't. Smita is asleep, but Erin is right there, close enough that she'd notice if Dodger started talking to herself.

*We should have worked harder at that whole "silent communication" thing*, she thinks, and counts the stars, and tries to sleep.

Erin listens as Dodger's breathing levels out, turning deep and slow as the other girl sinks into unconsciousness. When she's sure Dodger is well and truly gone she opens her eyes, brushing the hair out of her face with one hand, and counts silently to ten in ancient Sumerian. There's no movement from the mathematician. She's not fully manifest yet; there will come a time when someone so much as thinking of numbers in her presence will catch the corner of her attention, risking her full regard. Erin won't take risks like this then, assuming they're still together, assuming they're still alive.

Carefully, she sits up, watching for any signs of motion. When they don't come, she stands, and pads toward the door.

The air in the house is still. Roger is asleep in his room, she's sure; put them this close together and the cuckoos will either be continually on guard, sleeping in shifts, watching one another's backs, or they'll be utterly relaxed, synchronizing in ways even they haven't started to figure out yet. Erin can't wait to see the looks on their faces when they discover how deep their entanglement goes.

This is not a house built for war. Everything in it speaks of peace, of indolence; no one who thinks in terms of a battle coming would choose cream carpets, or pastel accents in their wallpaper. Erin pauses at a picture of the Cheswich family in front of Sleeping Beauty's castle at Disney World. Dodger, who looks all of twelve years old, is wearing mouse ears and grinning the broad, bright grin of a child whose greatest trials have involved an imaginary friend who stopped talking to her and a series of math teachers who don't understand. Her parents glow with love and satisfaction. It's things like this that make these cuckoos so dangerous; there are bricks in their road to the Impossible City that are neither wind nor stardust but simple red stone, forged in the real world, where alchemy is a fantasy and immortality an impossibility.

"You made them too normal, and that's where you fucked up," she murmurs, touching the frame. Then she resumes walking, heading for the back door, and out into the green California evening.

Erin left the lab for New York City after Darren died, sent to a foster family as dedicated to the cause as the Middletons, to learn the things she'd need to know for her coming mission. Her "mother" taught her to wield civility like a weapon, to put on eyeliner and lipstick and a smile she didn't mean, one sharp enough to slice through skin, bone, and social barriers alike. Her "father" taught her to break down a rifle, wipe it clean, and reassemble it in under a minute, putting her through the kind of hard, unrelenting drills that would have made a military academy proud. They'd been working for the glory of the cause, working for citizenship in the Impossible City, and they had made her the kind of weapon that could be used to change the world.

The trouble with weapons is that they can be aimed in any direction. She sits on a lawn chair near the fence (the same chair Dodger, in another timeline, reclined in while Roger's life fell apart; the chair where she ordered a reset of the universe to save him from the consequences of his parents' choices) and pulls out her phone. The number she dials is found in no directory, listed in no database; even the phone company would have difficulty determining who owns it.

*Dodger, I'm sorry,* she thinks, and raises the phone to her ear, and waits.

There is a click. "Report," says a voice.

"Cheswich's parents recognized Middleton as a biological relative as soon as he entered the home," she says. "They asked whether the subjects were aware of their relation. The subjects replied in the affirmative. The subjects are growing closer but have not started showing any signs of second-stage reaction. They remain distinct individuals and do not appear to require separation. How do you want me to proceed?"

*Please don't ask me to kill her parents,* she thinks. Dodger is not her favorite person—Dodger is more a useful *thing* to her, and needs to stay that way, if her plan is to succeed—but that doesn't mean Erin wants to make her an orphan. The stability of the Rooks has always been questionable. They are violent reactions adrift in a world filled with things for them to clash with, and they require the Jack Daws to keep them from exploding. Killing Dodger's parents now might drive her away from Roger, and the consequences of that would be dire.

"Continue to observe," says the voice. "We'll provide you with further instructions." The line clicks again as the call terminates.

Erin leans back in the chair and closes her eyes. One more hurdle has been cleared.

This is going to get harder before it gets easier.

# Biology

Roger and Dodger lie on their respective chairs, staring up at off-white ceiling tiles speckled with small, seemingly irregular holes.

"How many?" asks Roger. He's studiously not looking at the woman beside him, holding the needle that's jammed into his arm. He asked for this, he *knows* he asked for this, but that doesn't make the actual process any more pleasant.

"Tiles or holes?" asks Dodger. Her blood has already been taken. She has a piece of tape holding a cotton ball to the bend of her elbow, and a juice box with a bendy straw. Oh, how he covets that juice box. He hasn't wanted someone else's treat so badly since grade school, when Miss Lewis (he will always remember Miss Lewis) would let them bring juice boxes from home for Friday story time.

"Tiles."

"Sixty-four."

"Holes."

Dodger's eyes dart for an instant, tracing the outlines of four separate tiles before she smiles serenely, sips her juice, and says, "Six thousand, two hundred and eight."

"Cool." Roger closes his eyes. His perspective shifts and he's looking at the ceiling through Dodger. There's no color to appreciate here; just the cream, and the metal struts holding the tiles in place. "Did Smita tell you why we needed to come back in, or was this a mystery to you, too?"

"Everything's a mystery." Dodger turns her face toward him.

Seeing his own body from the outside is always disorienting. The change in focal perspective alone explains so much about why others react to his appearance the ways they do. The woman beside him is pulling out the needle, and his blood is so *red*, so violently, brilliantly *red*, that he isn't sure whether he should be fascinated or disturbed.

"Smita will be right with you," says the woman, and heads for the door before either of them can ask her anything further.

They are, temporarily, alone. "Hey, Dodge. You know how I'm color-blind?"

"Only because you keep making me look at stuff for you."

"I like having colors to go with the words for them," he says. "I was just wondering . . . is there anything funky about your eyes?"

Dodger blinks. "You mean you never noticed?"

"No . . ."

"How far away from me are you right now? Based on what you remember of the room when we arrived, not on visual cues." She shuts her eyes, taking visual cues out of the equation.

"Okay, I'll play," says Roger. He reviews his mental floorplan of the room, and finally says, "About three feet, maybe? Maybe slightly more."

"Got it." Dodger opens her eyes, still looking at him. "Now tell me how far."

Roger watches his body frown. "I . . . I can't tell."

"I have poor depth perception," says Dodger. "It's why I run my bike into things so damn often. Once I know how big a space is, I'm fine, and I can do all my calculations on the fly. I used to pitch for the school baseball team, and I struck a lot of people out, because I knew the dimensions of the field. In a new space, without someone to feed me the numbers, I need to calculate them manually. It's the one place where the numbers fail me."

"Huh," says Roger.

The door opens before he can say anything else. Smita steps inside, wearing a lab coat and carrying a clipboard. Roger opens his own eyes, leaving Dodger's perspective behind, and both sit up straighter in their chairs, giving her their full attention.

"You two are more trouble than you're worth," says Smita. She doesn't bother with a preamble or a salutation: both would be a waste of her time and theirs. Thawing slightly, she adds, "Thank you for coming in again. I do appreciate it."

"It's not a problem," says Roger. "Though we don't quite understand the reasons. Did something go wrong with our original samples?" Giving blood isn't the most fun way to spend an afternoon, but blood tests require far less in the way of volume. The juice boxes are almost a formality. Which reminds him . . . "Also, where's my juice box?"

"I am the only adult on this campus," says Smita. She opens a small fridge, extracts a juice box, and tosses it to Roger, who catches it one-handed. "There was nothing *wrong* with your original samples, exactly. We had a bit of confusion when we thought we'd cross-contaminated them. I want to review a few things with you."

"Do we have some sort of fatal disease?" asks Dodger. "If it's sexually transmitted, only Roger has it, and I should be free to go."

"I love you too," says Roger, and punches the straw into his juice box. He takes a swig. Artificial grape: yum.

"You do not have a fatal disease, sexually transmitted or otherwise," says Smita, after a pause to scowl at them. "What you *have* is a virtually identical antigen footprint, lacking the distinctive methylations we'd expect to find in . . . Not a single word I've just said made any sense to the pair of you at all, did it?"

"Nope," says Roger amiably. He's lying. He knows all the words, if not the ways she's putting them together. He also knows Dodger doesn't. It's easier this way.

"Are we biologically related or not?" asks Dodger. She needs science to confirm the answer she already knows. Once science says it, it will become immutable fact, and right now, Smita is science. Smita holds their future in her hands.

Smita laughs. It's a strained sound: the laughter of a woman confronted with a question that can't be answered in any simple way. "Dodger, if you told me you were identical twins, I might be inclined to believe you."

"We're not identical," says Roger. "There are certain physiological differences that have absolutely taken that off the table."

"I'm aware," says Smita. "And yes, when we did the DNA analysis, we found that you are, in fact, biologically different genders, and you display the markers we'd expect to find given your general appearance. You understand that a DNA test is different from 'getting a blood test,' yes? Blood tests can rule *out* relation, but a DNA test is used to rule it *in*. We've been looking at the basic building blocks of what makes the two of you so goddamn annoying. I think I may be able to isolate the gene for 'smartass' based on your DNA. I'll win the Nobel Prize."

"Remember to thank us in your acceptance speech," says Roger, and takes another drink.

"Oh, believe me, you'll get *all* the credit you deserve," says Smita.

"We know what a DNA test is," says Dodger. "Did we mention how grateful we are that you agreed to do this? Because we're supergrateful. So grateful that clearly Roger can't even put it into words, which is sort of comic, if you stop to think about it."

Roger rolls his eyes and keeps drinking juice. For once, his input isn't needed. It's almost pleasant. He can just recline, wait for his blood sugar to recover, and listen to Dodger and Smita snipe at each other over someone else's field of science. This is the sort of activity he could enjoy on a regular basis.

"He's refreshingly silent," says Smita. "Let's go back to your earlier samples: I don't think anything happened to them. Based on the results, I think they were exactly what they were supposed to be. Some of the other students who helped me with the DNA tests wanted to be sure, so we needed more blood. More blood lets us run more tests.

More tests lets us figure out whether you're actually humans, or whether you're Martians doing a very good job of impersonating humanity. My bet's on 'Martians,' in case you wondered."

"We always assumed Midwich cuckoo," says Roger.

"We come in peace," adds Dodger dryly.

"I wish I could believe you," says Smita. She leans against the counter, looking at them. Her expression is grave, but there's interest in her eyes; she has a mystery. She has something to *learn*. Few things are more dangerous than a scientist with something to learn. "You asked me to perform a blood test because you wanted to know whether or not you were related. Out of the goodness of my heart, I refused, because it wouldn't do any good, and agreed to run a series of DNA and antigen tests instead. You agreed to let me use your results in my research."

Finally, Roger lowers his juice box, eyes narrowing. "Why are you recapping for us?"

"Because I want you to remember that you've consented to my using your test results in my research," says Smita. The brightness in her eyes is increasing. She has the topic in her teeth now: prying it away from her might be impossible. "You asked if you were related. The answer is yes: yes, you are related. You're close enough to biologically identical that your DNA may be able to tell us more about human development than I ever hoped to have at my fingertips."

Dodger sits up in her chair, quivering like a bird dog that's scented prey. Roger is more relaxed, but there's a sharpness to him now, a tightening of his posture and his expression that speaks to the potential for movement. Both of them are on edge.

Smita is blissfully oblivious to the tension she's creating. This is her field, this is her passion, and she's going to ride it to the end. "The two known forms of twinning are identical and fraternal. There's a school of thought which holds that in some cases identical twins may, due to chromosomal defects or other environmental conditions, wind up following divergent developmental paths, which could manifest as anything from different hair colors to different genders. We don't have many subjects, but as a research point—"

"You mean we could be some kind of weird mutants?" Roger's voice is dangerously level.

"Potentially," says Smita.

"So we're related," says Dodger.

"Unquestionably," says Smita. "You should really talk to the school paper. 'Adopted siblings find each other on campus' would make a great human-interest story. And we'd appreciate more blood in a month or so, of course."

"Right," says Roger. He still sounds too calm for the situation; calm enough that anyone sensible would be worried about it. He stands, leaving his juice box behind, and offers his hand to Dodger. "A few people owe us money."

"Yeah," she says, taking his hand and letting him pull her to her feet. Unlike Roger, she sounds dazed: this is the logical outcome of the math she's been doing, this is the only equation that makes sense, but the real world doesn't always listen to the math, no matter how right the math technically is. The real world doesn't care if she shows her work. "We can go for coffee."

"Smita, thank you," says Roger. She's been watching them sharply, and he can't help wondering if she suspects, on some level, that things with the two of them aren't quite *right*. Their blood told her more than he'd expected; she clearly speaks the language of plasma and platelet, which is one of the few languages truly alien to him. When he let her put a needle in his arm, he was hoping she'd be able to set Dodger's mind at ease, no matter what the answer was. This is more precise, and more definite, than he could have guessed.

"Don't thank me," says Smita. Her smile is packed with too many teeth. "I'm going to be coming to you for blood for the rest of our time here."

"And I'll be happy to give it," says Roger. "Just keep the juice boxes coming."

"Don't worry," says Smita. "After this, I'll let you pick the flavors."

She stands and watches as the two of them leave, Dodger still holding Roger's hand, like sisters have held on to their brothers since the beginning of time. It's hard not to see them as a lifelong unit, when she sees them this way; it's hard to believe that they ever questioned their relationship to one another. Anyone with eyes could see it.

She's so wrapped up in watching them go that she never glances toward the window; she doesn't realize that they're not alone. That's a pity. It might have saved her life.

Smita and the other genetics grad students have space in the Life Sciences Annex, shoved off to the side, while the biologists and zoologists and their ilk occupy the main Life Sciences Building. There are other disciplines packed in here, taking lab space where they can get it: geologists in the basement, chemists on the third floor. Getting out of the building involves walking past a fossil pterodactyl, hanging from the ceiling with its hinged jaw gaping in an eternal, silent scream. Its fleshless wings are spread wide, like it's about to swoop down on them, carry one of them away. Normally, Dodger likes to pause and acknowledge this piece of the deep past, which carries a thousand mathematical formulae in the petrified structure of its bones. Math takes something living, strips it down to its essentials, and then rolls forward into the future, not asking the thing what it wants. Math doesn't care.

Today, neither does Dodger. She lets Roger lead her down the hall and out into the cool afternoon. It's early enough that the sky is light, but there are dark spots around the edges: sunset is coming. California Decembers aren't long on light. They aren't long on dry, either; there's a storm hovering at the horizon, clouds rolling in almost at a pace with nightfall.

There are people on the steps, students she doesn't know, talking to each other like the world is the same now as it was an hour ago, as it will be in an hour. She could try to explain how wrong they are. Even if they were willing to listen, she doesn't have the words. All she can find are numbers, and they don't speak to most people the way they speak to her. So she keeps her mouth shut, and lets Roger lead her, down the stairs, across the quad, into the green of the trees that grow tall around the creek that flows through the middle of the campus.

Whatever long-gone architect was responsible for the design of the UC Berkeley campus, whoever was put in charge of the seemingly impossible task of creating a school that would embrace its students and honor the land it was built on, they understood that people were people, and people would sometimes need to run and hide from one another. They grasped *privacy* in a way that's honestly impressive, given how broad and open and institutional the campus sometimes seems. Together, Roger and Dodger walk under the trees, out onto a wooden path, and around a curve to a half-hidden bench. It will be wet for days after tonight's rain, deluged by water first falling through and later trapped by the leaves above. For now, however, it's the perfect place to stop.

Dodger lets go of Roger's hand first. It's a small thing. It's also the first time she's been the one to move away without running. Normally, she's the one who holds still while he goes, or the one heading for the horizon as fast as her legs can carry her. Here, now, she's calm. Serene.

Roger knows the words—shock, surprise, epiphany—but he doesn't know how to put them in an order his sister (his *sister*, he has a *sister*, not just a weird quantum entanglement with a girl on the other side of the country, but a *sister*, someone whose blood knows his almost as well as his heart does) will be able to hear and understand. He supposes she's stunned. He *knows* he's stunned. The impulse to close his eyes and retreat into the space that exists between them is strong. He forces it aside. This is a real thing; this needs to be a real thing. He didn't realize until this moment how badly he needs it to be a real thing, something spoken in the open air, something honest and concrete that he can put down between them, look at from all angles, and know for the truth. Real things are too important to entrust to quantum entanglement.

The creek chuckles a few feet away, bound by the banks it will burst as soon as the rain arrives. A crow calls overhead and is answered by one of its cousins. The campus crows are all related. *Just like we are,* thinks Roger, and is stunned anew by how dizzying the idea is.

Dodger sits on the bench, resting much of her weight on her fingers, curled tight around the wood and keeping her rocked forward, again like someone much younger. Roger's mind is racing, looking for words that can apply to the situation (and, once they are found, rejecting them and looking for something else, something better, something big enough). She, on the other hand, seems to be sliding back and forth along her own timeline, seeking the mental age where she'll best be able to handle the reality of the situation.

Finally, in a small voice, she says, "I was right."

"You were," he agrees.

"We're related."

"Yes."

"We're not . . . right. We're different. Something about us was made, not born."

"Yes," he says again. Letting her be the one to fumble her way through the words seems exactly right. He would be too accurate, and right now, that could kill them both.

"All this time . . . we were looking for each other, because they weren't supposed to split us up. Whoever arranged our adoption wasn't supposed to split us up." A note of anger seeps into her voice. How *dare* they? How dare some long-ago bureaucrats decide making two families whole was more important than preserving a unit that already existed, something sealed in blood and bone and the water of the womb? Both of them loved—and will always love—their adoptive families, and she can no more imagine giving hers up than she could ask Roger to desert his, but just because a thing is loved, that doesn't mean the thing should have been made. They wouldn't have loved those people if they hadn't been given to them. One of their families could have found another child to love and treasure and care for, and the two of them could have grown up together, the way they were meant to all along.

"Probably not," says Roger. He's done his share of reading on adoption law and the psychology of adoption. He thinks it's one of the most selfless things a parent can do, giving their children up for someone else to raise and care for. He's never regretted not knowing his birth mother. She loved him enough to give him to people who'd love him even more. Right now, however, he wishes he could ask her a few questions. Like whether she'd been aware that she was having two babies, not just one.

Like whether she'd approved of breaking up the set. Like whether it had been her idea, whether she'd thought "if I can't have this family, neither can you" when she looked at two purple-faced, screaming newborns, and willingly signed the papers that would send them to opposite sides of a continent.

He's not sure he wants to hear the answers.

"We're really related."

"Yes." He can tell Dodger will be circling this for a while: she's like this sometimes, incapable of moving on until she's cracked her latest obsession open to get to the soft parts hidden inside. This was her idea, this was her hope, and yet she's the one who's stunned when it proves to be true; she's the one who couldn't conceive of her math being as real as she always wants it to be.

But maybe it's not the relation that's the shock. Maybe it's the underlying strangeness, the confirmation that their quantum entanglement is somehow biological in nature. They're twins, and they aren't, and they're something more. It should be terrifying. Maybe it will be, when the shock wears off.

Roger sits on the bench next to her, his own weight shifted back, creating as much space between them as he can. He has a good view of her face from this angle. He can see the tension in her cheeks shifting upward a split second before her neutral bemusement turns into a smile, before her chin tilts down and her eyes slant up and everything is different.

"I guess you can't get rid of me now, huh?" she asks, and her tone is something like laughter and something like tears and something that isn't either, something deep and primal and pure. He's been waiting to hear that note in her voice for his entire life, even though five minutes ago he didn't know it was possible, and five hours ago he didn't know he needed her with him as badly as he does, and time is a concept invented by men who didn't want everything to keep happening at once. Time is irrelevant.

"Nope," he says, and moves closer, eliminating the space between them. She puts her head against his shoulder, and nothing has ever fit there this perfectly; nothing has ever been this intended to happen.

Everything is perfect.

Everything is doomed.

# Consequences

The rain has come. Berkeley is being washed clean of its sins, buried in a deluge of water so heavy it looks like a moving silver curtain, like fish should swim past the window at any moment, blissfully suspended in the storm. The storm has turned the ordinary world into something out of a children's book, a silvery slice of the Up-and-Under.

Smita gives the weather little attention; it's bigger than she is and doesn't care what she does, and besides, she's indoors. She's alone in the lab. She likes it that way; likes the silence, the hollow echo of her own footsteps, the comfort of knowing no one is watching her. She can leave her research spread out across the counters without concern that someone will see it—not another student, maybe, but an eager professor or greedy researcher—and claim it as their own. It's never happened to her. That doesn't change the stories that circulate through the department, tales of stolen effort and unreceived credit. Smita plans to change the world someday. She can't do that if the foundations she's been building wind up given to someone else.

There's a sound behind her, soft, like a candle being lit. It's an odd image, not like her at all, but the thought is foremost in her mind as she turns. Then she freezes, thought fading.

The woman behind her holds a novelty candle, one of those taste-less Halloween souvenirs. It's shaped like a severed hand, and who-ever designed the wax injections did a fabulous job; Smita would swear it's the real thing, if not for the ridiculousness of the idea. Who would use a human hand like that? The wicks protrude from the tips of the slightly curled fingers, each burning with a greenish flame. That, more than anything, convinces her this is some sort of prank, probably or-chestrated by the chemistry department. Fire doesn't burn like that unless you've done something to make it.

The woman looks vaguely familiar, someone Smita has seen in passing, in the time between classes maybe, or elsewhere in the build-ing. She's neither friend nor foe, and that makes her a problem to be dealt with quickly and efficiently. Smita folds her arms, shifting her weight onto one hip, and glares.

"What are you doing here?" she demands. "You're not supposed to be here."

The woman says nothing.

"I'm going to call security. They'll be happy to explain why tres-passing is not allowed."

The woman says nothing.

Something about her flat, affectless stare is beginning to make the hair on the back of Smita's neck stand on end. For the first time, she finds herself wishing she were more social; that other students were here to back her up.

"You need to leave," Smita says. "Take your creepy prop and get out."

The woman speaks for the first time. "This isn't a creepy prop," she says. "This is a real Hand of Glory. They're not easy to make, and they're not pleasant to use, but you shouldn't call it a 'prop.' Someone died to assure this item of its provenance."

"Erin?" breathes Smita. Familiarity and recognition rush in with the other woman's voice, making her presence even more of a betrayal.

Why hadn't she recognized her? The urge to take a step back, away from Erin and her "Hand of Glory," whatever that is, is almost unbearable. "What are you talking about? Why are you here? I very much want you to go."

"To make a Hand of Glory, you need the hand of someone who's been murdered," says the woman—says *Erin*. "Lots of people *seem* like they've been murdered, but the alchemy is specific. It doesn't work nearly as well with a victim of manslaughter, for example. The intent is embedded in the flesh. Murder-suicide is also a complicating factor. Someone who *wanted* to die creates an inferior light. You need a genuine victim of intentional and intended murder, the more brutal, the better. Violence also seems to embed itself in the flesh. It's funny, the homeopathic ingredients required to violate the laws of nature."

Smita's lips draw back from her teeth in an involuntary expression of disgust. "That's horrible. Why would you even say such a thing?"

"I didn't just say it. I killed this man. He was a guitar player. You might remember him. Used to sit down by Amoeba Records, playing bad acoustic covers of pop songs. I said I'd cook him dinner, and then I took him apart. I'm not much of an alchemist, but I'm an *excellent* killer." Erin sets her burning hand primly on the edge of the nearest table. The flame doesn't so much as flicker. "It doesn't matter that I'm not that good at alchemy, because this is one of the simpler recipes. If you're willing to commit a murder, that is. And if you're willing to work with the rest of the ingredients required. Some people get a little squirrelly when you ask them to play with rendered baby fat. I know there's been research dedicated to updating the recipe, but they haven't found anything yet. Sadly, some things are just inescapable."

Smita finally gives in to instinct and takes a step backward. Erin stops, cocks her head, and smiles. There's sorrow in her expression, like she doesn't want to be here, saying these things, doing whatever it is she's come to do. Smita finds she doesn't care. Dimly, with horror, she realizes her surprise and anger have transmuted into fear.

Smita is terrified. Erin is supposed to be her friend, they ate Thanksgiving dinner together, and she's *terrified*.

"Why are you here?" she asks. Her voice is a thread, thin and tight and easily snapped.

The look of sorrow on Erin's face deepens. "Because you opened a book that wasn't meant for you, and you read what was written inside," she says. "Please believe me, I'd avoid this if I could—and I think I have, at least once. There are scars in the air around this moment. But they need to know what they are to one another if I'm ever going to be able to bring them back together, and that means your part is already written. It's funny. They think they understand finally, and they don't understand anything at all."

No one has ever accused Smita Mehta of being slow. She's been at the top of every class she's ever deigned to join, all the way back to her elementary school years, when the other students made fun of her for everything they could find. The way her parents talked; the way her lunches smelled; even the way she braided her hair. They mocked her from kindergarten all the way to her senior year of high school, and she's never wavered, not once, from the prize of academic excellence. She was going to show them. She was going to show them all.

But now she's alone in her lab, and Erin is looking at her with such deep and abiding pity in her eyes, and Smita is afraid.

"Please leave," she whispers. "I haven't done anything to you."

"I know." Erin takes a step toward her. "I kind of wish you had. Like, if you'd pushed me in the hall or insulted my shoes, I might feel better about this. I wish there were another way. There's not. That book you opened, it belongs to people who *really* don't like sharing their secrets. Baker already gave too much away. So right now, I need you to tell me: where are the DNA test results for Dodger Cheswich and Roger Middleton? How many copies have you made? Who has seen your research?"

Smita stares at her. Erin calmly returns her gaze: she's holding nothing back. She's making no effort to conceal her intent, or hide her face. And Smita knows she's going to die.

It's a simple realization, quiet and resigned and oddly anticlimactic. She's always expected the awareness of her onrushing death to be a violent thing, ripping and tearing, leaving panic in its wake. Instead, it walks to the center of her mind and stops, expanding to fill all the available space. She, Smita Mehta, is going to die; when the morning comes, she will no longer exist. Depending on the actual endurance of the human soul, she may leave nothing behind but her work. She hasn't been alive long enough. She hasn't created a wide enough record.

"Why should I tell you?" she asks. Her voice doesn't shake. She's proud of that.

"Because I'm not the one who decided this had to happen, but I'm the one who gets to decide *how* it happens," says Erin. "I'm very good at what I do. I can make this as easy or as hard as you want it to be. I can chase you through this building all night long, I can give you your own personal horror movie, and I can cut you down with your hand on the doorknob and freedom only inches away. I can take you apart one centimeter at a time. Or I can pierce your heart so fast and so clean that you barely feel it when you stop. It's your choice. If you tell me what I need to know, then you're choosing wisely."

Smita's phone is only a few feet away, on top of the binder that holds most of her research. Her eyes dart toward it despite her efforts to remain outwardly calm.

Erin follows Smita's gaze and shakes her head. "You still don't get it," she says. "I guess that's okay. It's not like I'm saying things plainly. That's how you know I don't want to do this. I can order a hamburger in eight seconds, but it takes me an hour to decide I'm going to make mashed cauliflower. If you want your phone, you can have it."

Smita looks at her suspiciously. Erin nods.

"Please," she says. "I can tell you don't understand the situation. This will help. Get your phone."

It's like something has snapped, some dark compulsion that was forbidding her to move or defend herself. Smita lunges for the plastic rectangle of her phone, feeling relief wash through her as she snatches it off the counter. This is safety. This is rescue. This is—

This is the sudden, crushing realization that she has no service. But that can't be right. She always has service in the lab; has joked with the chemistry majors, who work two floors down, that they should have gone into genetics to be closer to the cell tower. This is where other students come when they want to make a phone call. And still she has no service; still the little bars that should be gleaming solid and strong are hollow lines, forbidding her contact with the outside world.

"The Hand of Glory has a lot of different uses. Funny thing: which one you'll get is determined by how the Hand was made, and what order you light the candles. Some people use them for invisibility, or to open all barriers before them. Others use them to lock the doors. You could smash the window and scream so loud you hurt yourself, and no one would hear you. You're a ghost, Smita. As far as the world outside this room is concerned, you may as well already be dead." Erin moves her hand, and there's a knife, long and sharp and matte black, the kind of blade that has no purpose in this world past killing.

Smita looks at the knife and cannot breathe. The air stops in her throat; her lungs are cold weights in her chest. This is her end, right in front of her, swallowing the light.

"This is where you start deciding how you'll die," says Erin. "Where's the research?"

There's still a chance. Erin—who was supposed to be her *friend*, not the instrument of her destruction—has a knife, but this is Smita's lab, and it's Smita's life on the line. The phone may be dead, but she is not. Not yet. So she flings her phone at Erin as hard as she can, not looking to see if it hits its mark before she turns on her heel and sprints for the door, running as fast as terror and adrenaline will carry her.

The phone bounces harmlessly off Erin's shoulder, falling to the floor. She sighs as she watches Smita go.

"I hoped this would be easier," she says. Knife still in her dominant hand, she picks up the Hand of Glory and pursues.

S mita has never been much for horror movies. They've always seemed like a waste of both time and fear: in the end, the monster will be defeated, the survivors will walk into the sunrise, and the only catharsis will be the knowledge of the inevitable sequel. Here and now, she finds herself wishing she'd paid more attention to that endless stream of virginal heroines and rubber monsters. Horror movies are not a substitute for experience, but at least they might have told her where she could be safe.

The elevator at the end of the hall is a tempting trap. Once inside, she'd have no chance of getting away: all Erin would need to do is descend to the next floor and wait. The stairs are safer; the stairs will let her see what's coming. So she hits the door to the stairwell without slowing, slamming it open and stumbling on the first step. She almost falls before catching herself on the rail and beginning to descend, as fast as she can, down into the building.

It's late enough that the floor below her should be empty, but the chemistry students are always here: the chemistry students would *live* in the Annex if they could. They have a shower in their lab, which almost makes up for the lack of cellphone service, and they're experts when it comes to cooking hot food in sterile glassware without poisoning themselves. (They keep a separate set of beakers and dishes for culinary purposes, and regularly upset visitors by eating out of them.) She should be able to find at least one person there who can help her.

As she runs, she hears footsteps behind her. They aren't hurried; they don't need to be.

The stairwell door is always unlocked this late at night. She bursts out into a hall identical to the one she just left, still running. There's a lab door ahead of her. It's open, and she can hear voices coming from inside. Smita finds speed where she would have sworn none existed, racing down the hall and grabbing the doorframe of the lab, hanging there, shuddering and panting, taking a moment to catch her breath and remember how to form words.

There are three chemistry students inside. Two of them are seated, eating pizza out of the box; the third is making margaritas in one of the lab blenders. None of them turns to look at her.

Smita pulls in a vast, sucking breath, and wheezes, "Please help me."

Not one of them stops what they are doing to turn around. The pizza-eaters keep eating, one laughing as the other draws a line of melted cheese from her lip all the way to the box. The margarita-maker continues to mix, calling something unintelligible to the others.

"*Please!*" Smita's voice is a shout this time; it echoes in the confines of the lab, inescapable, impossible to overlook.

And not one of them turns around.

A hand lands on her shoulder, squeezing until she feels her clavicle bend under the pressure. Like the chemistry students she still watches with helpless, hopeless eyes, Smita does not turn around.

Erin's lips brush her ear as she says, in a conversational tone, "I warned you. I told you that you were already a ghost. You could have stayed upstairs, and never realized how much I meant that. Now you get to make a choice."

"Please let me go," Smita whispers.

"It's too late for that. It's far, far too late for that. But if I kill you here, they'll see the blood. I can't sterilize their whole lab while they're in it, not even with the Hand of Glory protecting me. If I kill you here, I have to kill them too. Do you want that?"

*Yes*, thinks Smita fiercely, looking at the chemistry majors as they laugh, flicking pizza toppings at each other, unaware that the laws of science are being violated only feet away. What's happening is impossible. But she feels Erin's fingers grinding on her shoulder, and she knows no amount of denial will change the reality of her situation. She's going to die here. All that's left to her is to remember how to die with dignity.

Dignity means not condemning three innocent bystanders simply because she can't stand the idea that they will continue after she has stopped. "Please don't hurt them," she says.

"Good girl," says Erin. "Let's go back to your lab. We can take the elevator this time. You must be tired."

Smita doesn't protest, doesn't argue; she's already run once, and it got her no farther than a room full of people who couldn't hear when she begged for help. She isn't broken yet, but she's breaking, and when Erin pulls her away from the doorway, she goes willingly, allowing herself to be led back to the elevator. It is somehow utterly reasonable that the woman is carrying the burning hand again. That's the reason for the isolation, she knows it, and yet she also knows she can't get the hand away before the knife makes another appearance.

The elevator comes at the press of a button. The sorcery that's wiped them from the eyes of the world doesn't affect everything. There should be an escape route hidden in that fact. Smita can't see it. She's tired and afraid, and her lungs are burning. There are no escapes left.

Erin guides her into the elevator and presses the button for the top floor. The doors close. They start to move. "I really am sorry about this," she says, once it's clear that Smita isn't going to break the silence. "I like you a lot. You're good people. If I had another option, I'd take it."

"Don't kill me."

"That's not on the table this time around, I'm afraid. This is how it ends. The only question left is how badly it's going to hurt." There's a tightness in Erin's voice. Smita glances toward her. She looks pained, like this is the last thing she wants to do. "Please, don't make me hurt you more than I have to. Just tell me what I need to know, and I can make this as painless as possible."

"This is about Roger and Dodger?"

A slight nod, as the elevator doors open and Erin pushes Smita into the hall. "I understand why you agreed when they came to you and asked for help. Who wouldn't have been willing to help a friend? And Roger can be very persuasive when he wants to be. He doesn't realize just how persuasive yet. He hasn't matured fully in this timeline. I only remember snips from the ones where he has—usually because he's ordered me to remember something before he's hit the big redhead button—but hoo, boy. I can't blame *anyone* for doing what he asks. You didn't have a chance once he got the idea in his head."

"Dodger asked me," says Smita hopelessly. She's not sure why she's trying to argue with Erin, with this impossible woman who has somehow isolated her from the world, who pulls knives out of the air. "She said they needed to know whether they were biologically related before they tried to have their adoption records unsealed. I was just trying . . . I was just trying to help a friend. That was all."

Erin looks at her with sympathetic eyes as she guides Smita, almost gently, back to the lab. She looks sad. She looks like she doesn't want to be doing this, and somehow that's the worst part of the whole situation: Smita is going to die, and it's not even going to *matter*. She's going to cease, and the person who kills her won't be doing it out of passion, or anger, or anything other than a vague, inexplicable regret.

"A lot of us are trying to help our friends," she says. "Some of us are trying to change the world. Where's the research?"

Wordless, Smita points to her computer, to her notebooks.

Erin nods. "Have you posted it anywhere? Are there any backups outside this lab?"

"No," says Smita. Then, without heat or expectation: "Please."

"You know better," says Erin. She puts the Hand of Glory on the nearest table before she grips Smita by the shoulder, hard, with her free hand, twisting her around until they are facing away from one another. The pain of that unexpected clutch is enough that Smita gasps, taken by surprise.

Then Erin lets her go and steps back, and both her hands are empty; the knife is gone. Smita looks down, and the knife is found, slipped between her ribs with a magician's skill, so tidy that for a moment, it looks less like a murder weapon and more like some strange accessory. The hilt has made a seal against her skin. There's no blood. She knows enough about anatomy to know that this can't last. Seals break. Blood escapes. She's not going to die; she's already dead. The anomaly is her refusal to fall down.

"Thank you," says Erin, and reaches for her knife.

Smita thinks, too late, to step away, to run; maybe she's not a ghost anymore, now that she's been stabbed, now that the seal is broken. She could scream for help, and help might come. She might find salvation in the students three floors down, or in campus security, well-meaning and bumbling as they sometimes are. She might get away. But she doesn't think in time, and so Erin's fingers find the hilt, and the knife slips free, and the blood follows, red and hot and so, so plentiful. Smita knows how much blood is in the human body, the volume and the purpose of it, but she's never *seen* it. Not like this, flowing bright and precious and irretrievable.

The blade pierced her lung. When she tries to speak, there's no sound, only the soft whistle of the wind, distant, almost mocking her. She moves her lips anyway, silently cursing Erin, the false friend, the fiend who's taken everything. She curses Roger and Dodger. Whatever they are, whatever they do or don't know about themselves, this was their fault. This is on their heads.

Then she falls. Her last thought is of her mother, who was so proud of her for getting into graduate school, for becoming a scientist, for saving lives. "My Smita is going to save lives" was what she always said, chest puffed out and eyes crinkled at the edges, and Smita's never going to see her mother smile like that again; Smita is never going to see her mother do anything again. Smita is over. Smita is done.

Her eyes close of their own volition, and her blood spills across the floor, and her part in the story ends.

E rin waits until Smita stops breathing before she sighs, straightens, and picks up the Hand of Glory. Assignments like this are the worst. She should be home, watching TV and ignoring the homework that won't be graded anyway. (She's a theology student because they have people in the Theology department, loyal people, people who fear Reed as much as they adore him. She could show up for class naked and singing Queen songs, and they'd use her as an example of modern Dionysian behavior. Her supposed graduate career is just a cover for the life she's not openly allowed to lead.) Instead she's here, in this sterile, brightly lit place, watching a woman's blood—a *friend's* blood—spread across the tile floor like a benediction.

"I really am sorry about this," she says.

Smita doesn't answer.

The computer where the test results are stored—not by name, but the numeric codes are easy enough to decode, if you know what you're looking for, and Erin knows what she's looking for—is unlocked, and offers her the data she requests with mechanical joy, holding nothing back. Computers are orderly things. They want to please her. She combs through Smita's email, looking for signs the woman lied. It seems unlikely; terror and hope are uncomfortable bedfellows, and when they lie down together, frivolities like lies tend to fade away. Still, she was made to be diligent, and so diligent she will be.

The Hand still burns. No one comes to disturb her while she's looking at the pieces of a dead woman's life, and when she's done, she feels she can say with certainty that Smita was keeping the mystery of the antigens in Roger and Dodger's blood to herself: it was a toy she wasn't ready to share. Other students helped with the testing, and they'll have accidents of their own over the next few weeks, brakes that don't work, faulty electrical wiring in their dorm rooms, whatever's required to get the job done, but they're not a high priority. They won't have enough of the pieces to do any damage.

The scarring around this moment is less severe than it was before Smita died. She's probably demanded a reset here more than once, but not much more: two times, maybe three. Little flickering candle flames of alternate chances. They can't have led to good endings, though, or she wouldn't be here now. That's the trouble with playing Choose Your Own Adventure with reality: when they go back to the beginning of the book, none of them remember. Roger and Dodger don't know yet what she is to them, or them to her. They don't even know Darren's name.

Her fingers stumble on the keyboard, which has gone blurry. She blinks her tears away, trying to keep her composure. She shouldn't have thought of him. It's that simple. Darren is in the past, and until they find a clear path through this maze, they can't go back to get him. Each revision has corrected some prior mistake, like Dodger backtracking through her equations and fixing the numbers, but correcting prior mistakes creates the opportunities for new ones.

This would be so much easier if the two of them could reach the point of becoming fully manifest and able to *remember*. Erin pushes herself away from the computer. Deleting the data would leave a hole.

Anything that's destroyed leaves a hole. The only way around it is to create something instead.

Outside, the rain has stopped. The Hand of Glory sees her through her final bloody errands and out of the building, back into the world. The Hand of Glory keeps anyone from noticing when she lights the match. The fire doesn't want to catch, resisting in the face of sodden wood and weather-treated stone, but there are ways. There are always ways, if you want something bad enough, and eventually, like a phoenix, the flame rises.

The Hand of Glory keeps her hidden as she stands at a safe distance and watches the building burn. The chemistry students don't make it out. She's sorry about that.

By the time campus security shows up, with the scream of fire engines not far behind, there's nothing left to save.

# Blame

Someone hammering on the door drags Roger from a sound sleep. He was dreaming of his parents, sitting with them around the kitchen table, trying to explain how he has a sister, and that while she doesn't need to be a part of their family, she's always been a part of his. In fact, Dodger haunted all his dreams last night, calling his name, trying to get his attention when something else always seemed more pressing.

The hammering on the door hasn't stopped. He rolls out of bed, wiping the grit from his eyes, and bellows, "Hold your water!" The hammering doesn't lessen. If anything, it increases, like the person trying for his attention has been rewarded by the proof that he's home.

"I'm going to fucking murder someone," he says pleasantly, as he grabs yesterday's jeans off the floor. He doesn't bother hunting for a shirt. Whoever it is can cope with the sight of his bare chest, and if that's too much for their delicate sensibilities, too bad for them. He wasn't planning to be out of bed before nine. He certainly wasn't planning on this bullshit.

Then he opens the door and Dodger's there, also wearing yesterday's clothes, her hair snarled like she hasn't bothered to run a brush through it. She wails something incoherent, more sound and agony than words, and flings herself at him, eyes closed before she hits his chest. When she speaks, her words echo both inside and outside of his skull, like reverb applied to the real world.

"She's *dead* there was a fire last night and now she's *dead* the Life Sciences Annex is *gone* and she's *dead* and they called to say classes were canceled because you can't have a class without a classroom and she's *dead* and is this our fault? Did we do this?" She doesn't pause for air so much as she stops to suck it in, filling lungs that must have been deflated like balloons. She pushes back, opening her eyes, and this time when she speaks, her voice comes only from outside. For that moment, she sounds like a stranger.

"Roger, Smita's dead, and so are six other people. We made her look at our weird DNA. We made her start trying to figure out what we were. Is this our fault?"

Two things occur to Roger simultaneously: first that she's serious, her eyes wide and brimming with terrified tears. Second that they're standing at the threshold of his apartment, with door wide open and their conversation being broadcast to the world. It would be nice if their quantum entanglement came with silent communication, but it never has, and this doesn't seem like the time or place to try.

The comprehension of what she is saying comes third, and that almost grudgingly, like his mind has no interest in accepting her words. It would reject them if it could, and when he refuses it that right, it responds by dropping them, thuddingly, into the forefront of his awareness, where he must deal with them unsupported.

Roger's eyes widen. "Come on, Dodge," he says. "Let's get inside. I'll see if there's some coffee left in the pot from last night." Her love of stale coffee borders on the surreal. He's seen her drink the stuff when it was six days old and capable of supporting life. If anything's going to lure her, this should be it.

She isn't lured. "Smita's *dead*," she says again, louder. "What are we going to *do*?"

Curtains twitch in nearby windows. A trick of the light, perhaps, a manifestation of a mind that's guilty but shouldn't be—or maybe the neighbors are waking up, and things are about to turn awkward. Roger grimaces as he puts his arm around Dodger's shoulders and half-guides, half-pulls her into the apartment. "We're going to have coffee, and you're going to let me wake up, and then you're going to try this again, slower and with more words, until I understand you."

Dodger doesn't resist. If anything, Dodger seems relieved to be pulled, to let someone else take responsibility for what she does next. She's trembling, a movement so slight and so comprehensive that at first he doesn't notice. There's no part of her that isn't shaking. She's an earthquake forced into the shape of a girl, and as the door swings shut behind them, he wonders whether the fault lines at the heart of her are about to give way completely.

The hall runs from his bedroom to the front door, with the bathroom, kitchen, and small living room branching off at various points. He leads her to the kitchen, their footsteps muffled by the worn brown carpet, and seats her at the folding card table that serves as his dining room and study nook. (It's also where he plays poker with some other members of the English department. None of them are any good, and sometimes he thinks about bringing Dodger along, just to see the looks on their faces when she takes them for everything they have.)

Dodger won't stop shaking. He wants to hug her and tell her everything is going to be all right, and he doesn't want to lie to her. He knows she'd believe him; that's why he can't do it. Instead, he fills two mugs with coffee, reheating them in the microwave. His is taken black, with two sugars. Hers, with milk and six sugars. Hummingbird girl, running on caffeine and borrowed energy. He's seen what happens when that energy runs out. He never wants to see it again.

"Here you go," he says, setting the mug in front of her.

She picks it up; wraps her hands around it; doesn't drink. She seems content to hold it, letting the warmth seep through the ceramic and into her skin. Eyes on the liquid, she says, "The phone rang. I have tutoring sessions in the Life Sciences Annex. Had. I had tutoring sessions in the Life Sciences Annex. I don't anymore; they're canceled. The building burned down last night, sometime after the rain stopped. It was . . . They think it was some sort of wiring fault that managed to catch fire. Once it reached the chemistry labs, it found all the accelerants it needed to beat the weather. Those labs aren't even supposed to *be* there. They were going back to their own building as soon as their plumbing was repaired. A freak accident. People are going to call it a freak accident. Maybe it was. I don't know. Maybe it was. But. But."

"But what?" he asks gently. He already knows—she was clear when she showed up on his doorstep, even if she didn't give many details—but he doesn't want to accept it. Not yet. Maybe if he asks the question the right way, he'll get a different answer.

"But Smita was in her lab," whispers Dodger, bringing his hopes crashing down around him. "They found . . . they found her body when they went looking for survivors."

Something occurs to him. "How do you know all this?"

"The Dean's office called to say my tutoring sessions were canceled. I guess they're contacting everyone who's supposed to have been in there today, to try to keep us from showing up at a smoking ruin." She looks up. There are tears in her eyes. Still or again, it doesn't really matter. "Erin was already up. She said she'd been out when the police arrived last night, and heard them talking. She didn't wake me when she got home, because she knew I was going to find out eventually. She didn't want to be the one who told me."

Privately, Roger thinks Erin made the right call. He wouldn't have wanted to be the one to put this expression on Dodger's face, and he knows from past experience that he's the one person who will always be forgiven. He could destroy the world, and she'd love him on the other side of the rubble. That's what it means to be entangled like they are. That's what it means to be family.

"Smita probably collapsed from smoke inhalation before she could get to the stairwell," continues Dodger. "She was fighting all the way to the end. She died before the fire reached her. I guess that's a good thing. Burning alive isn't a good way to go." She says it with such conviction that for a moment, Roger could almost believe she knows from experience.

(The thought is followed by another: he could almost believe *he* knows from experience. He remembers—although of course it's not a memory; better to say he *imagines*—flames closing in on them in an underground corridor ringed with broken windows like blinded eyes. They never looked out on anything real. He imagines remembering putting his arms around her as the flames drew closer, all avenues of escape long since closed; imagines remembering her laughter, thin and brittle and bitter, as she said, "Well, at least this time's not bullets." Then, the fire, and his final plea for another chance, before the inferno took them both.)

Roger shudders. Sometimes a vivid imagination is closer to a curse than a blessing. "God, Dodge, that's awful. She was really great. I hope they do something for her family."

"What if this is our fault?" Dodger can be like a dog with a bone sometimes. A good attribute for a mathematician, but not the easiest one for a sister, especially not for a sister looking at him with such bemusement and guilt in her eyes. "She was looking at our DNA. What if . . . what if we were split up because there's something *wrong* with us, and they thought they could make it better by putting us on opposite sides of the country, like keeping bleach and chlorine apart? We're not normal. We've never been normal. What if Smita died because she got too close to figuring out what's not normal about us?"

It's a huge jump from "she looked at our DNA" to "she was killed to keep us secret"; Roger is opening his mouth to tell Dodger to stop being silly. Then he hesitates. For once, words have failed him. Yes, it's a jump, and yes, it's ridiculous on the face of things, but can anything *really* be ridiculous when your starting point is "we're secret twins who found each other across a continent through quantum entanglement, which is slightly more useful than a telephone, without being as good as telepathy"? Everything about them is ridiculous. It always has been. So what's one more thing added to the heap?

Haltingly, he says, "I don't know whether this is about us or not. It could be a freak accident. I hate to say it, but every time we've had a fire on campus, it's been the chemistry kids. Their lab was two floors below hers. They could have knocked something over at the wrong time, and when the wiring sparked . . . I don't know. I want to say you're wrong, that there's no possible way this could be connected to us, but I can't. I just . . . I don't know."

Dodger looks at him for a long moment. Then she wipes her eyes with the back of her hand, puts her mug down on the table, and stands.

"We have to find out," she says, and it's so simple, and so impossibly difficult, that he can't argue with her.

"Let me get dressed," he says.

Campus security has cordoned off the Life Sciences Annex. Caution tape blocks the usual approaches, orange as a Halloween jack-o'-lantern, ends snapping in the breeze. The air smells of char and flame retardants, all the hallmarks of a terrible fire. Even the sky looks ashy, although that could be a trick of the weather; the rain is threatening to fall again.

Students queue up along the tape, whispering to each other as they cup their hands over their eyes and squint at the ruins of the building, trying to pick out every ghoulish detail, every unrevealed sliver of information. A few are sobbing, burying their faces against the shoulders of friends. At least six students died in the blaze—maybe more, depending on what the firefighters found, depending on whether someone had fallen asleep in an empty classroom or gone looking for a private place to sit and study—and each of them had friends, family, a whole world of their own. Those worlds are over now. The world keeps ending, every minute of every day, and nothing is going to make that stop. Nothing can ever, ever make that stop.

Dodger has borrowed one of Roger's hooded sweatshirts, a baggy gray thing that fits her almost perfectly, her narrower shoulders balanced by her larger chest. With the hood covering her hair and her hands shoved into her pockets, she moves through the crowd like a ghost, and Roger moves in the space behind her, letting her forge the way. This is her part of campus, not his; she knows the shortcuts and the shape of things.

There are people everywhere. There is no clear approach. "We need to get closer or back off," says Roger, frustrated. "Those are the options. Dodge? Can you get us closer?"

She stops, cocking her head hard, like she's running some complex set of internal numbers. Then, with a quick nod, she says, "Yes," and turns, heading away from the building at a fast clip. Roger has to rush to keep up with her. She doesn't look back, doesn't slow down: she just keeps moving.

She just keeps moving.

Her steps are light and her eyes shift constantly from side to side, assessing, recalibrating, looking for a better angle. Most people will never see the world the way Dodger Cheswich sees it, and that's a good thing: the way she sees the world would drive most people mad. Her lack of depth perception makes it hard to estimate distances, to know for sure where one thing ends and the next begins, but once she paces something out, learns the dimensions, she never forgets. The numbers, the angles, the equations, those are the constants, the stars she steers by and the gospels she keeps closest to her heart. She doesn't run. She doesn't need to run. Math, done right, is a calm and steady thing, swift, but not hurried. Never that.

Roger has given her a problem defined by geography, which is another form of geometry, and she's going to solve it. Come hell or high water, she's going to solve it. She leads them down a trail mostly used by joggers and maintenance staff, around the shed at the trail's far end, into a copse of trees. The cordons keeping the students away from the burnt-out building don't extend into the trees. That would be silly.

There's an old trail tucked deep inside, one Roger has never seen before, one he doubts *Dodger* has ever seen before, because this isn't the sort of place where she tends to go exploring. It leads them to a narrow alley, mostly blocked by a concrete planter intended to dissuade students from grinding their skateboards along the brick edges of the flowerbeds. Once they've squeezed past the planter, they find themselves between the smoking ruin of the Life Sciences Annex and the nearby Life Sciences Building. The fire didn't jump the gap, possibly because of the weather, possibly because sometimes, bad luck runs out before everything falls down. The main building is smoke-stained but otherwise untouched, standing strong and inviolate. It could be open within the week, students stealing glances out its windows at the devastation next door. This, too, is normal.

At the end of the alley is a doorway. The wood is scorched and warped; the frame has bent. The three shallow stone steps leading up to it remain intact, not broken, only stained by the fire. The glass window at the center of the door has melted, running out of its frame like thick, twisted honey. There are holes in the wall to either side, blasted chunks of masonry and insulation showing through the bones of the building. It looks less like the aftermath of a fire and more like the aftermath of a war. There is no caution tape here, no campus security or gaping students. They're alone.

Dodger stops dead, the odd, focused look fading from her eyes as she turns to Roger and stands, perfectly silent, watching him.

"Good job," says Roger, bemused. "You okay?"

She shakes her head—the motion of a wet dog trying to become dry—and the strangeness is gone, replaced by her former worried, uncertain expression. "I'm fine. Just worried. This door isn't usually locked."

Roger nods. Then he hesitates, and asks, "Are you sure we should be going in here? There's just been a fire. The building could be structurally unsound."

"So we don't try to go up to the lab," says Dodger, dog with a bone again. "Architecture is chaos theory in sheetrock and two-by-fours. I can figure out where the weak spots are."

"Math isn't a superpower."

"Says *you*," says Dodger, and cracks her first smile since the day began.

That smile is the best thing Roger could have seen. It means that however upset she is, she isn't shattered: she's just taking some time to bounce back. With as long as it can take her to let people in, rather than keeping them at an eternal arm's length, it makes sense that she'd be so shaken. He smiles back, quickly, before he reaches for the door-knob.

The metal is stuck, or perhaps fused from the inside. It refuses to turn.

"Roger . . . ?"

"I'm sure it's just jammed," he says. Letting the doorknob go, he pulls the sleeve of his sweatshirt over his hand and wraps it tight around his fingers. This time he grasps it as hard as he can, willing it to yield; this time he twists until the knob abandons its resistance and the latch clicks open, allowing him to pull the door outward, away from its twisted frame.

On the other side of the door, water and flame-retardant foam have pooled in puddles and patches on the smoke-stained floor, creating a swampy patchwork of dangers. The walls—what remains of them; many of the interior walls are completely gone, torn down by fire or rescue personnel—are riddled with holes. The building seems cancerous, diseased, a thousand years old.

There's a hole in the floor, leading to the basement. The bolt that held the pterodactyl to the ceiling remains, but the fossil beast is gone, fallen below or consumed by flames. Dodger stops and looks at the place where it hung, a look of childish gravity on her face. Something that endured for millions of years is gone; something that should have outlasted them both is over. Somehow, that's the worst thing yet about this tiring, terrible day.

Then she turns away, looking at Roger, and says, "We need to look for answers."

They're standing in a burnt-out building; they'll be arrested, or worse, expelled, if someone catches them here. They're not arson in-vestigators, or investigators at all. Neither of them is equipped to be here. Neither of them has a clue what they're doing.

But Dodger needs this if she's going to accept that it isn't their fault that Smita's gone. She needs to walk the floor and try to figure out why this is happening, and if that's what she needs, then Roger's going to give it to her. It's a small thing. It's all he can do.

"Wood burns at—"

"Four hundred and fifty-one degrees Fahrenheit," says Dodger, without missing a beat.

Roger nods. "So we have a starting point."

"Absolute zero," she says.

"Exactly."

They walk the floor like tightrope performers, placing each foot gingerly in front of the other, testing for weaknesses, waiting for the moment when the whole thing gives way. Occasionally, one of them will say something: a word, a number. The other will answer, a number, a word, completing the equation that they make between them, defining the world one step at a time. After a while, they stop looking at each other; they don't need to.

"Ceiling tiles."

"Ninety-five destroyed, one hundred and sixteen partially destroyed, eighteen intact. Eighty-four."

"Chairs damaged in this classroom."

"Fifty-three destroyed, seventeen damaged but potentially repairable."

It's never been like this before. They've always been holding each other a little bit apart, divided by some reluctance to give in. When they were children, Roger didn't quite believe in her. When they were teens, she hadn't quite forgiven him. As adults, they came back together by chance (but there *is* no chance where they're concerned; there never has been, only intricate design), and still they've been holding back, afraid of giving in, afraid of needing too much.

They aren't holding back now.

"Pounds of fallen masonry."

"Seven hundred and three, in this room."

"Dust."

"Twelve thousand parts per million."

On and on they go, the shorthand becoming more extreme, the air going hot and heavy around them, like an electric storm rolling in, like another fire getting ready to ignite, a fire that needs no flame but only the constant friction between the two halves of something which has never, in all the long years of their lives, been fully realized.

(In an apartment off-campus, a woman who remembers the lab they have been allowed to forget, a woman with so much blood on her hands that she'll never, never be able to wash it clean, feels the air turn syrupy and slow, thick as molasses and just as capable of suffocating anyone foolish enough to wind up mired in it. She puts down the plate she was washing, drops the dish towel, and walks calmly to the back door. The old orange cat who hangs around out there comes running when she opens it. He feels the strangeness too, with the precognition native to the animal kingdom, and he wants nothing to do with it. He darts under the table, fur fluffed out, hiss rising in his throat. Erin sighs, drops to her knees, gathers him, squirming, into her arms. She carries him to the front door and out into the street, until they reach the small, grass-covered island at the center of their intersection, a place where nothing will fall in the chaos to come. They won't be safe here. They'll be close enough. The woman holds the beast tight and waits for the sky to fall.)

Back in the Life Sciences Annex, Roger and Dodger continue their search. Their initial goal has faded into the background, replaced by this entertaining, all-consuming new game, word for number, number for word. Roger has never understood the math that calls to her, but he feels it now, thrumming in his veins like a promise of miracles to come. Dodger has never grasped the need to put a name to the things she knows to be true, but she understands it now, and accepts the names he throws her way gladly, transforming them through the alchemy of her observations before she throws them back to him. They aren't children anymore, and were never truly children together, not in the way they both know in their bones that they should have been, but in this moment, they are playing as children play, tragedy forgotten in the face of so much joy.

So very, very much joy.

The words and numbers no longer bear any resemblance to each other to the outside ear. "Perspicacity," he says, and "Four point eight three one five," she replies, and smiles a small and secret smile, like she's just said something clever, which perhaps she has. Perhaps, in the language of numbers, she is Shakespeare, she is Eliot, she is Rossetti spinning tales of the Goblin Market and Baker giving life to the Up-and-Under. "Seven," she says, and "Celestial," he says, and his smile is as bright as hers, as matched as two peas in a pod, as two children on the improbable road, and she's laughing, and he's laughing, and everything is going to be all right. The smell of smoke and wet lingers, but the storm they're making between them has all but washed it away, replacing it with the smell of ozone, crackling bright and ready to spark.

"Blue," says Roger.

"Two," says Dodger.

"Alienate," says Roger.

"One," says Dodger, and "Zero," they say in unison, and the ground moves beneath their feet.

The earthquake begins directly below the UC Berkeley campus. Seismologists have been saying for years that the Hayward Fault, when it lets go, will rupture so as to cause an earthquake of magnitude 6.7 or above. The last time it ruptured in Berkeley, in 1870, the resulting quake was severe enough to level buildings and leave citizens trapped, some for days. Many of the quake's fatalities were secondary, caused by starvation or dehydration. The Bay Area was less populated then; the buildings, those that existed, were younger, less rigid, less primed to fall.

This quake bubbles up through earth gone static and stale over the course of decades, and it bubbles up with a fierce violence that will shock seismologists. It is the quake they've always known would come one day, that they have tried to prepare the people for. It is too much, too fast: there could never have been any preparation.

On her green island in the intersection, Erin holds old Bill as tightly as she dares and watches the apartment she shared with Dodger and Candace crumble. She could have saved some of her possessions, some of their most precious things, but how would she have explained it? No. Let it be enough that she saved herself, saved the cat, was not inside when everything that wasn't nailed down fell, the mundane turning murderous. There are so many voices around her, and all of them are screaming. She can't tell them apart. She hopes none of them belong to Candace. Let her sleep; let her die still dreaming.

In the Life Sciences Annex Roger and Dodger stand frozen, staring at one another, the air around them still electric with what they've done, what they didn't know they had it in them to do. A creaking sound warns them before a section of ceiling tumbles down. Dodger doesn't close her eyes, but Roger hears the equation in her voice as it flashes through his mind, and then she's slamming into him, her shoulder to his sternum, knocking him back, out of the way, away from the chunk of masonry and flooring that crashes into the place where he was standing.

Still the shaking continues.

The campus dances, side to side and up and down, brought to life by the seismic forces tearing at one another beneath the surface. People are screaming, running for safety. The locals find open places to stop and put their hands over their heads, checking the sky for power lines and nervously gauging the height of nearby buildings. Most will survive. The students who come from other places fare less well. They run for shelter, for doorways and for cupboards; they freeze in terror where they stand. A girl from Wisconsin dies when a chunk of falling brick strikes her head and bears her down to the ground. Another, larger chunk lands a moment later, pinning her body in place. It will take rescue crews three hours to work her free.

And the shaking continues.

The quake does not confine itself to campus, does not restrict its force to the narrow band of real estate associated with the school, but it begins there, deep beneath the Life Sciences building, and the devastation is worst around the heart of it. The walls of the library crack. The clock tower doesn't fall, but it *leans,* and that's somehow even worse; a fallen thing can be rebuilt, while a damaged, listing thing must be left until the last, until the broken glass has been swept away and the shattered foundations restored. The clock tower is the heart of campus, the landmark that leads the students home, and it is visibly broken.

Dodger scrambles to her feet, faster in a crisis than Roger has ever been; her nervous energy has become a survival skill. More pieces of ceiling are tumbling down, and the walls look as if they might cave in at any moment, turning a Nancy Drew adventure into a horror film. Roger stumbles as she pulls him up, her fingers tight on his, anchoring him, crushing flesh against bone. The pain is almost welcome. It makes the scene seem real.

"It's moving too fast!" she shouts—and why she's shouting, he doesn't know; there's no real noise beyond the low rumbling, and the sound of falling things. She could speak conversationally and still be heard. Panic changes the rules, and she's panicking as much as he is, seemingly calm, until she speaks. "I have to close my eyes!"

Roger doesn't understand what she's saying at first: it doesn't make any sense. She's the one leading the way through the falling debris. Why would she close her eyes? But she does, she does, and she's charging forward, eyes screwed shut, weaving around the rubble as it falls.

Roger closes his own eyes, too terrified to watch, and suddenly they're slamming to a stop, so abrupt that his shoulder hits hers before she screams—not shouts, *screams,* like a victim in a horror movie that's suddenly all too real, all too immediate, all too all around them—*"Keep them open, you have to keep them open!"* and he understands.

Dodger has no depth perception. She can do the math of velocity and descent in her head, dodging the debris with an accuracy any other human would be hard-pressed to match, but only if she's starting from the correct position. She needs to *see* the point of descent as something three-dimensional and true, not just figures moving on a flat surface. So long as she knows the distance between them (and she does, he knows she does; the length of their arms, the difference in their heights, those are commonplace numbers for her, the sort of math she can do in her sleep, and probably does, on the nights when she needs to ward against bad dreams), she can chart their trajectory without fail. She can get them out.

He opens his eyes. Dodger starts running again, pulling him in her wake.

Later, this will seem like a dream. The earthquake rolling on and on, tearing down walls, shattering windows, and planting cracks in foundations that could have endured for another hundred years on less seismically active soil, and the two of them running through the heart of it all, a girl with her eyes closed tight, a boy following her blindly with his eyes wide open. Outside, the open spaces have become masses of pressed-together bodies, strangers holding one another and screaming, or weeping, or doing nothing at all, just staring in wordless shock at the chaos. People have taken refuge wherever they could. The air is ablaze with screams, with weeping, and with the steady roar of car alarms, which have taken this assault for larceny, and struggle to summon their owners to save them. The air is black with smoke, with dust, and with the beating wings of panicked campus pigeons, which cannot land, but circle in endless, terrified flight.

Dodger pulls Roger around the hole that was the stairs, runs past the elevators, and hits the front door with her shoulder so hard that, if it were any quieter, they'd both be able to hear the bone break. As it stands, the pain is intense enough that for a moment, Dodger is afraid she's going to pass out. She pushes it aside as best she can, *shunting* it, and is somehow unsurprised when she hears Roger cry out behind her. She doesn't need to look to know that he's holding his shoulder. His eyes are fixed on the back of her head, and she wants to apologize, but there isn't time.

She hits the door again, *shunting*, and Roger gasps, in too much pain to scream. She doesn't feel a thing. Maybe she's damaging herself by refusing to feel the damage firsthand, but there isn't time for that, either. This door should open. It's not locked; the combination of fire damage and the earthquake has it wedged into its frame, and she can see the pressure points that will cause it to let go. It has to let go. It *has* to. Their survival matters more than a torn rotator cuff or a fractured collarbone.

She hits the door for a third time. Roger's vision goes briefly gray with pain. The door comes open, and she opens her eyes, letting her own vision take over as she hauls him out of the crumbling building, down the familiar steps, back into a world where the geometry makes sense. Things are falling here as well—tree branches, pieces of masonry, power lines—but they're more widely spaced. She has time to calculate their arc of descent before impact, time to weave between them, still pulling Roger along. He isn't in pain anymore, but he can feel its echo, filtered through her nerves. As soon as she opened her eyes she broke the connection, as much as it can be broken; their quantum entanglement is strong and getting stronger. Roger's childhood fears were more justified than either of them realized.

She wonders if he realizes it now. She wonders if he's going to pull away. And it doesn't matter now, because they're still running. Dodger takes the time out of their own escape to move a few feet to the side and knock a freshman out of the path of a snapped electrical wire; she could see the boy's hair catching flame, see his body jittering and dancing from the current, before she hit him and changed the math. No one comments on their appearance from the Life Sciences building; everyone has their own problems. Everyone is focused on their own survival.

They run until they reach a place Dodger judges safe, far enough from the falling debris that they won't be hit, far enough from the other students that they won't be overheard. The shaking is beginning to slow. The aftershocks will last for days, but the main quake, the big quake . . . that's almost over.

Roger lets go of her hand.

(Later, that's what she'll remember: she'll remember he let go of her first. She'll remember that they had each other, they were *holding on,* and then he was gone, pulling away with a finality that left her reeling. The pain still hadn't come back into her shoulder; her mind was clear. She felt him let her go.)

"Roger?" She turns to him, curious, concerned. He seems as far away as he always does, when she sees him with her own eyes: close enough to reach for, close enough to touch. But the ground between them tells a different story. It tells her he's taken a step away; if she reached out now, her hands would close on nothing. It tells her she's alone.

Someone in the distance is sobbing like their heart's been broken. Dodger feels her own begin to crack.

"Did we do this?" he asks, his voice a thin echo of her own from earlier in the morning. She'd been asking about a fire, about a death; six deaths, really, but only one she was willing to claim as their responsibility. He's asking about an earthquake, about a campus in ruins around them, about the cost in human lives. Neither of them is stupid. They both know enough about this sort of disaster to know that the death toll will be counted in the hundreds if they're lucky, and the thousands if they're not.

"Roger—" she begins, and stops dead as she sees the way he's looking at her. Like he's lost. Like she's the monster on the other side of the glass.

Like he never wants to see her again.

"Did *we* do *this*?" he repeats. "Don't you lie to me, Dodge. I'd know, so don't you lie."

She opens her mouth to lie. She stops. She can't do it. She physically can't do it. She *wants* to: can see the lie in the space behind her eyes, shimmering and perfect, a gem of prevarication and deceit. She's been practicing her lies for years. She just needs to put the words in the right order, and they'll do the work she has for them. But she *can't*. Roger has told her not to, and she can't do it.

Roger is the first of them to be afraid of what they can do together. Dodger is the first to be afraid of what he can do alone.

"I think so," she says, and her voice is a whisper, her voice is a sigh; her voice is almost swallowed by the murmuring rumble of the dying quake. The shaking has ended. The rolling has gone with it. All that remains is the faintest tremor in the ground, and in a moment, even that will be gone. "We . . . I think we did something when we were playing, and I think it maybe broke some stuff. We started the quake. But we didn't mean to hurt anybody. We couldn't have *known*."

"Now we do." He sounds sad, so sad, and she doesn't need quantum entanglement to know what he's thinking: she can see it in his eyes. He steps close again, leans forward, plants a kiss on her forehead, gentle as a farmer planting an apple tree. Then he's gone, stepping away, turning on his heel, and running, running, running into the ruins of campus, away from the thing they make when they're together, away from the consequences of what they've done. He's running, and Dodger, for once, is not; she just stays where she is, eyes open and filling slowly with tears, and watches him go.

# Report

The astrolabe spins wildly, astral bodies shuddering and twisting through their orbits.

Pluto—beautiful, jeweled Pluto, crafted from the finest platinum, studded with icy diamond chips—has begun spinning backward, racing in reverse through the mechanical cosmos. A collision seems inevitable, but over and over, it skirts past Neptune, dodges Jupiter, and continues on its implacable, incomprehensible way. The sun is the only piece of the model which does not move. It sits, motionless, in the center of the chaos. (Later review will show the astrolabe began to misbehave when the earthquake began in Berkeley, and that the sun stopped when the quake did. How this is relevant will be less clear.)

Reed stands with his hands behind his back and a frown on his face, watching the model of the universe as it attempts, one misaligned twist at a time, to tear itself apart. He didn't build the astrolabe, has never been a mechanical engineer, never cared that much about things that aren't biological, but he loves it all the same, loves it for what it represents: everything. This is what he one day hopes to control.

Everything. He coveted it the moment his mother-maker showed him her blueprints for its construction, when he was an apprentice, when Asphodel Baker was the greatest alchemist in North America, spreading her calm propaganda masked as fantasy, when it seemed like a gangling experiment in base metals turned flesh named James Reed would never be anything but a carnival miracle-peddler, capable of mixing snake oils and minor cures, but nothing more. He's lied, cheated, killed, and bargained to work his way to this place, this lab, to ownership of this astrolabe. The chaos he now oversees is either a sign that success is finally at hand, or an omen of failure yet to come.

It must be the first. He won't consider the second.

Something has happened to or with their cuckoos. The astrolabe has run in reverse dozens of times since they were sent out into the world. He remembers no timelines but this one, because he's not one of them, but the astrolabe . . . that remains his secret weapon. It's so finely calibrated, so carefully attuned to the functionality of the living universe, that it cannot help but adjust itself when something changes. A shift in the timeline is a shift in the universe. A shift in the universe must be reflected by the astrolabe, or it becomes nothing but a pretty collection of jeweled planets and glittering stars, with no value beyond that intrinsic in its component parts. Even if Reed were willing to allow that, the astrolabe would not be.

There is a knock at the open door behind him. He doesn't turn.

"Which ones?" he asks.

"Cheswich and Middleton," says Leigh. "You were right. They're almost mature."

"What have they done?"

He can hear the smile in her voice when she speaks again. Leigh has always been an admirer of destruction, when executed well and without petty complications. "An earthquake in California. The largest the region has seen in decades. FEMA is responding; the death toll is going to be in the thousands, and that's just the primary effect. Disruption to power, water, local services, those are going to kill even more. I've never killed that many people. Not even cumulatively."

Slowly, Reed turns. "And you believe they did this?"

"I know they did." Leigh is beaming. This pair isn't hers, wasn't raised according to her standards; she would order their handler to take them to pieces without a moment's hesitation, if she thought it would benefit the cause. But destruction is destruction, and she can't deny the quality of their work. "Did you read my report?"

"Refresh me."

It's not a request. Leigh feels her smile slip away. Reed is dangerous under the best of circumstances, and this isn't the best of circumstances. He's used the astrolabe repeatedly to prove that his cuckoos are maturing, citing every instance of misbehavior as proof that time has been rewritten. "Two of them have reached maturity at some point in the future," he's claimed, over and over again. "Two of them will inevitably embrace themselves, and us, when the time is right. The fact that they keep trying to put the moment off doesn't change the reality of it."

Oh, but it does, it does; Leigh knows it does, that the future is unwritten for a reason. Until they actually confront the mature cuckoos, until they see the awakened Doctrine given flesh and conscious will, it could be any of their pairs. This is why she has been pushing so hard to get him to let her start the experiment over, to push its conclusion forward. His investors wouldn't have liked the delay, but his investors are gone, dust and bones scattered over a dozen states. It's better that way. Boring, balding, hidebound old men don't deserve to change the universe. They think they do, but boring, balding, hidebound old men have always believed they deserve absolutely everything. When he proposed the Galileo solution for the second generation of cuckoos, she hadn't expected it to *work*.

They should have grown up powerless and incomplete, unable to function in the big, terrifying world of people born in the normal way rather than created as metaphors given flesh. They should have killed themselves by the age of eighteen or been drugged insensate by adults who wanted to "fix" them. There's no possible way they could have found each other, become entangled, opened the lines of communication and kept them that way for year on year, despite all the obstacles in their way. What they had done, what they've become . . . it's all impossible. It's all unlikely in the extreme. And it's all real and true and undeniable.

Leigh didn't make this mess. She still has to deal with it.

"Erin reported that Cheswich and Middleton had gone to a student, Smita Mehta, and asked her to run blood tests to determine whether they were related. She explained that blood tests wouldn't be enough; DNA testing was required. She performed those tests." Leigh's lips twist downward. "They were nearly exposed as artificial creations by a little girl with a box of toys and a fondness for sticking her nose where it doesn't belong. She found the antigen markers, she found the genetic similarities, and if she'd been allowed to continue her work, she would have found that the DNA wasn't entirely natural. She had to be stopped."

"So you had her killed."

"It's within my remit."

"Only if you could do it without attracting attention."

"There was a fire. It was very sad. Erin interviewed the girl extensively first, using a Hand of Glory for cover, and confirmed she hadn't shared her findings. I believe she was planning to write a paper about non-identical identical twins." Leigh shakes her head. "Poor fool. She had a good scientific mind, but she was out of her depth the moment she picked up the needle."

"There was nothing about the killing that could be traced back to Erin, or to us?"

Leigh shakes her head again, more firmly this time. "Nothing. You know how skilled she is. I decanted her myself; she won't have slipped. Unfortunately, the Cheswich girl has an overactive sense of responsibility. It's the numbers. All the mathematical children have shown a tendency to catastrophize and assume responsibility for things that aren't their fault. If she'd been alone on campus, it wouldn't have amounted to anything. She wasn't. She went to the Middleton boy. She expressed her concerns. He agreed to help her investigate the fire. While they were there, they somehow partially activated." A look of frustration sweeps over her face. "I don't know how. Any cameras in the building were destroyed by the fire, and Erin wasn't present. What we know is that our cuckoos entered the building, and the earthquake began eight minutes later, with them as the epicenter. They've begun to understand what they can do."

"My astrolabe supports this," says Reed. "Are they mature?"

"Erin doesn't think so." She brightens. "I could check the omens. If there's a good candidate for haruspicy—"

The entrails will speak truly only if he cares about what's being sacrificed. Some rules are older than alchemy: some rules cut all the way down to the bones of the earth. "Take one of the other experiments to the surface," he says. "Let them see the sky." That should stun whatever prize she picks long enough for Leigh to do what must be done, and an augury works best in sight of the sun.

Leigh raises her eyebrows. "Truly?"

"Truly."

"And if the entrails say your cuckoos aren't mature?"

"We leave them."

Leigh's surprise fades, leaving her stricken. "But—"

"We leave them. If they can do this much damage at the beginning of their maturation, imagine what they'll be able to do when they're fully grown. We've done it, Leigh. We've embodied the Doctrine. Keep them under supervision, and notify me if anything seems to be changing." Slowly, he begins to smile.

"Soon, we'll have everything we've worked for," he says, and Leigh says nothing at all.

It was difficult to remember exactly where Avery had been before he went away. He had taken his shadow with him, which seemed suddenly, unspeakably rude, even though Zib had never thought of it that way before. Shadows should stay behind when someone was planning on coming back, to mark the place they were *going* to be.

A hand touched her shoulder. She looked up to find the Crow Girl looking at her encouragingly.

"It's all right," she said. "He'll be back, safe and sound, you'll see."

"How do you know?" asked Zib.

"Why, because we're on the improbable road to the Impossible City, and right now, what could be more improbable, or impossible, than your friend coming back to you?" The Crow Girl smiled a bright and earnest smile. "There's no possible way it could happen, and that means it's virtually guaranteed."

Zib stared at her for a moment before bursting, noisily, into tears.

—From *Over the Woodward Wall,* by A. Deborah Baker

BOOK VII

# The End of All

Let all the number of the stars give light
To thy fair way!
                    —William Shakespeare, *Antony and Cleopatra*

Only those who will risk going too far can possibly find out
how far one can go.

                                        —T. S. Eliot

# Cost

There's so much blood.

Dodger has her back to him, one hand clasped against her side in an effort to keep some of that blood inside her body. The other hand is a blur of motion, finger-painting equations on the wall with increasingly shaky fingers. Her handwriting is losing its precision, becoming harder to read—not that he was ever any good at following her when she went deep into the math. She's in her own little world, and there's no room for him there, and there's so much blood.

He's not a doctor, but he's pretty sure there shouldn't be so much blood, not if she's planning to walk away from here—and really, that's the answer, because he knows she's not planning to walk away. She was happy before he crashed back into her world, happy with her books and her public appearances and her life, which she had crafted, one careful piece at a time, from the wreckage he'd left her in. She was happy, and then he'd come barging in with her old college roommate in tow, and he'd taken it all away. She thinks she's going to die here, and he's pretty sure she doesn't mind, because if she dies here, she never has to go through this again. She never has to worry about a knock on the door turning out to be the brother who abandoned her, coming back for one more favor that she doesn't want to grant.

Her career is over. Her ideas about the universe have been shattered. What's a life when compared to that?

He wishes he could tell her he's sorry. He wishes he could say he didn't know. He doesn't say anything. She has to finish this equation, has to finish solving them for zero, or all of this will have been for nothing—like it's been for nothing so many times before. Erin didn't want to tell him that part. Erin never wants to tell him anything if she can help it, says ignorance is bliss, or at least ignorance leads to better choices: ignorance doesn't try to account for the costs and consequences of a hundred doomed timelines every time it takes a step. He wishes he knew how it was she could remember.

And then he knows.

"Dodger," he says, and his voice is low, almost drowned out by the gunfire from outside their little corner of the ruins. Erin is holding off their attackers as best she can. She can't hold them off forever. "When did it go wrong? When, exactly, did it go wrong?"

"Like you have to ask?" She keeps painting. There's more blood seeping between her fingers now. There's so much blood. "You're the one who came to me."

"Before that. When did it go wrong before that?"

She turns her head, her fingers going still. She's so pale. She's always been pale, but there's so little blood left for her to spill. Her hair is longer than he's ever seen it, her two-hundred-dollar hairstyle ruined by gunpowder and blood and exertion. Her earrings are diamond set in platinum. She looks like an adult, and he still feels like a child.

"The earthquake, Roger," she says softly. "That's when I knew you were never going to stop leaving me. That's when I decided to stop letting you."

"I didn't mean—"

"Done is done. We're going to die here, and I'm not going to forgive you. Let me work." She turns back to the wall.

Roger goes still. Done isn't done; not according to Erin. Forgiveness isn't the key. Knowing when to forgive, *that's* the key. He can't change how he reacted to the earthquake: he knows himself well enough for that. But there are things he *can* change. There are things he can do. Here, and now, and knowing what he knows—knowing what Erin's told him, what he's seen in the days they've spent running for their lives, the blink between the last grain of sand falling and the hourglass being turned back over—there are things he can do.

He pulls the phone out of his pocket. Sets it to airplane mode. Changes the clock, until the phone believes it's ten years ago, the day of the earthquake, the day he ruined his own life in the interest of saving it. Dials a number he knows by heart. Numbers have never come easily to him, but this one, he will never forget.

He leaves his message, stuttering and stumbling over his words, feeling like a fool, watching as Dodger stops writing and turns to face him, eyes wide and bewildered. When he's done, he throws the phone aside. It isn't needed anymore. He opens his arms.

"Come on," he says, and Dodger moves toward him. She can't take her hand away from her side, but he puts his arms around her and gathers her close, smelling her expensive perfume, feeling the way she shivers.

"You ready?" he asks. How many times have they been here? How many times have they done this? A hundred times, a thousand, a million, and once, because every change begins it all again. They can do this over and over again and never really repeat a thing.

"No," she says. She tilts her head back and looks at him, eyes wide and gray and trusting. She still trusts him. Even after everything that's happened, she still trusts him, and that is the best and worst thing in the world. "Do you think this will work?"

"If it doesn't, I guess it isn't going to matter." He chuckles darkly. "If it doesn't, everything that's ever happened to us has been coincidence, and we've ruined ourselves for nothing. You can't save the world with math unless you can also change it with a question."

"Then I'm ready," she says.

There it is again, the sensation of déjà vu: unsurprising. He knows from Erin that they've been here before. At the same time there's the sensation of something new happening. He doesn't think they've been here many times before, if ever.

"Dodger," he says, and his voice is calm and clear, "don't you die, and don't you give up on me. This is an order. This is a command. This is an adjuration. Do whatever you have to do, break whatever you have to break, but don't you die, and don't you let me go. This is an order. This is—"

This is her nodding before she closes her eyes, pale and silent and so fragile-looking that he wants to protect her from the world, even the part of it that he represents.

This is the sound of gunfire going silent outside. Not tapering off; just *stopping,* like the world has been muted.

This is the world going white.

This is the end.

*We got it wrong we got it wrong we got it wrong we got it wrong we*

Avery wasn't sure he could go any further.

He was tired. He thought he had never really known what tired was before today: he had *heard* of being tired, but he'd never really *felt* it. Tired went all the way down to his bones, wrapping around them like ribbons, until his legs were lead and his arms were sacks of sand suspended from his shoulders. Tired sapped the color out of the world, turning everything gray and dull. Tired hung weights from his eyelashes. Whenever he blinked, he thought his eyes might refuse to open again.

But Zib—stupid Zib, who thought she knew everything—was supposed to be somewhere around here. That's what the Page of Frozen Waters had said, before pushing him over the waterfall. He needed to find Zib. He needed to tell her he was sorry.

There was a bundle of rags on the riverbank, covered in glittering silver dust, like fish scales or moonlight. Avery paused. Rags didn't normally have tangled, uncombed hair.

Avery found that he could run after all.

—From *Over the Woodward Wall,* by A. Deborah Baker

BOOK V

# Aftershocks

Familiarity with any great thing removes our awe of it.
—L. Frank Baum

You are an alchemist; make gold of that.
—William Shakespeare, *Timon of Athens*

# We Are

Something in the stacks falls with a clatter. Roger freezes in the act of replacing a book on the shelf, cocking his head to the side and considering the noise. Nothing audibly smashed; it wasn't students sneaking beer into the rare books aisle again. It hadn't been a meaty sound, either, so no one is passing out back there or otherwise getting up to mischief. The number of people who think library sex is a good idea never fails to astound him. Sure, he'd tried it a few times back in his undergrad days, but it had only taken one paper cut in an unfortunate place to make him realize that going back to his room was a *much* better solution.

"Kids," he says finally, shaking his head and smiling. Somewhere along the way, people who were his peers when he arrived on campus have become "kids," needing supervision, unworthy of being trusted with the rarer books in the school collection. He's found himself incapable of finding undergrads attractive recently, his mind calculating how long it's been since they graduated high school and dismissing them as too young for anything but getting himself into trouble. That's probably a good thing—he knows a lot of junior faculty who've had issues with dating students—but it still feels like one more step toward an adulthood he's not quite sure how to handle. Growing up was something that was supposed to happen to other people. Not to him. Never to him.

Roger sets the rest of his books down on the cart and walks, hands in his pockets, toward the sound. He's one of the younger professors in the UC Berkeley Linguistics department, and many of the students find him more relatable than his peers. If someone is in dishabille back there, they may feel more comfortable with him being the one to point out that the library isn't the place for such activities. And if it's another damn squirrel, he can always open a window.

The floor doesn't creak beneath his feet; the walls don't breathe as they settle. The main library at UC Berkeley is only five years old, bright and clean and new, without that smell of dust and time that eventually ensnares every good library. Parents look at the school's facilities and smile, picturing their precious children being taught in beautiful spaces, learning beautiful things, without needing to worry about black mold or falling masonry. Students like he was look at those same spaces and frown, thinking of ivy-shrouded walls, mysterious reading nooks, and the power of time. He wishes he had a way of telling them that they can be part of transforming this new place into an old one, that sometimes being the one who etches the lines in the façade is as important as choosing something already weathered and worn. But it's just a feeling, and he knows that if he were ever to articulate it, he would frighten people, so he says nothing.

Roger Middleton has grown up to be what people always thought he'd be: a college professor in khaki slacks and patched jackets, with an easy smile and a rangy walk that can take him from one side of campus to the other in under twenty minutes. Like many of the survivors of the big quake, he prefers his feet to other forms of transportation: bicycles aren't dependable on cracking concrete, cars can't swerve fast enough to avoid falling objects, but feet, ah, feet will see you to safety if there's any possible way. He rents half a duplex off-campus, and every room is filled floor to ceiling with books, except the room where he sleeps. There, although there are books on the floor and books on the bed, there's nothing on the walls that could possibly fall. Instead, the room contains several pieces of low furniture: two desks, a dresser, a bedside table.

There are three pictures on the bedside table. One of himself and his parents; one of himself and his current girlfriend; one of a girl with eyes like his, looking warily at the camera, as if she fears it might be getting ready to attack her. He keeps the picture to remind himself that he can never see her again; that together, they're a danger to themselves and others. But he misses her. Even if he no longer hears her voice in his head when he's going to sleep, even if he's almost forgotten what it is to see the color red reflected through her eyes, he misses her. He supposes he always will. He hopes somehow that will be enough to pay for what they did, for the terrible space they made together, however little they intended to.

Roger steps around the corner, and there's the source of the sound: a pile of books on the carpet, dislodged from their shelf by some quirk of the way they'd been stacked. Students are notorious for shoving books in any which way, and sometimes that creates unstable piles which inevitably collapse, replaying the earthquake in pages and volumes. This collapse happened in the Applied Mathematics section. Roger sighs, and stoops, and begins picking them up.

He has three books in his arms when he finds Dodger's face staring at him from the floor. He grimaces and picks that book up as well, turning it over to reveal the title. *You + Me: The Math of Social Networking*, it proclaims, with her name below it in smaller but equally bold lettering. He wonders what color it is, if it's as bright and candy-colored as he thinks. He wonders if she had any input on the cover design. She never finished her degree, but then, she didn't need to; not in this brave new world of computers and startups and TED talks and people looking, always looking for the next big thing. She's been doing her math in the real world since he came back to school three weeks after the quake and found her gone, leaving only a note stuffed into his mailbox.

ROGER—
GUESS IT'S YOUR TURN. IT'S ONLY FAIR. I DID IT LAST TIME.
CALL IF YOU EVER NEED ME. I LOVE YOU.
YOUR SISTER.

She hadn't bothered to leave a number, and that was like her, too: she assumed that even if he didn't want to talk to her in the space they made between them, he'd know, or at least be able to find out, how to call. He doesn't know if she was right about that. He's never tried. Every time he thinks about it, he feels the ground shift beneath his feet, hears the masonry crashing around them, and remembers that it was their fault. They're dangerous together. They shouldn't be—all the laws of physics and nature and simple linear reality tell him they *can't* be—but they are. He can't risk it. No matter how much he wants to, no matter how much he loves her, he can't risk it.

He puts her book back where it belongs, surrounding it with the other books in its category, and hopes, not for the first time, that she's happy wherever she is. That she understands that he didn't run away to save himself this time. He did it to save the world.

The rebuilding of the UC Berkeley campus was not a swift process. Even seven years on from the earthquake that reshaped the county, the signs of damage remain, etched into the architecture. Scaffolding shrouds the clock tower, concealing the process of repair. There are grad students who've never known it as anything other than tilted, a silent, solemn, broken giant watching over their daily lives. They stop as they cross the quad, looking at the sheets around the tower, and feel an obscure sense of loss, like something they thought would never change is changing, and maybe not for the better.

(The other grad students, and the faculty, also stop, also look at the tower, but their feelings are different. They are consumed by relief, like the world is finally returning to normal. Fixing a clock can't raise the dead or turn back time, but it's still a symbol of a recovery that has been a long time in coming.)

Roger walks down the broken stone pathways connecting the new library to the quad and tries, as he always does, not to notice how much around him is not what it was on the day he first came to tour the campus, a wide-eyed, hopeful freshman. The faces of the buildings are almost uniformly different. The older, more rigid trees are gone, their roots torn from soil during the great shaking. Even the pathways have changed. Most of them are made from the same artfully cracked stone that greeted him on the first day he set foot on campus, innocent and ignorant of what was to come. It was dug up and re-placed after the quake, creating a small sense of continuity in a world that seemed suddenly devoid of it. He keeps his eyes on the path. If he does that devotedly enough, he can almost pretend that nothing's changed.

UC Berkeley didn't close its doors, not for a day: barely for an hour. The campus and city were in ruins, but there were things to be done, memorials to be held, rooms to be searched, and so the campus remained a hive of activity, blazing with flashlights and ringing with voices, until the rescue crews had come and helped to move the rubble away. After that, it seemed best to just . . . keep going. Classes were held in open spaces and on the quad, anywhere that wasn't likely to collapse. Students whose work had been destroyed were helped to re-create it by willing professors and eager grad students. When the state had forgiven a semester's tuition as part of their disaster response, the survival of the school had been guaranteed. Berkeley students were among the most loyal in the world.

But not all of them. Some had transferred; mostly computer science majors who needed an actual computer lab to finish their degrees, heading for UC Santa Cruz or Stanford with apologies on their lips and the future in their eyes. Some had dropped out, traumatized by the events of that terrible, earth-shaking afternoon. Others had simply walked away. Like Dodger. One moment she'd been there, and then she'd been gone, packing up whatever of her things had survived the quake and vanishing, presumably heading back down the coast to her parents' house, but really, this was Dodger. Who knows where she ended up?

Roger has never tried to find her, not then, and not now. What they made between them . . . no. No matter how much he misses her, some things can never be allowed.

He walks across campus to Telegraph, which has been similarly sea-changed. Some of the old buildings are gone, new structures in their place; others remain in skeletal form, piles of rubble that have yet to be bought by new owners, cleared away and replaced by something shiny and new, something that's never felt the ground shake beneath it, never felt the need to fall. Some of the old businesses managed to ride out the earthquake, protected by rebuilt foundations and quirks of geography: Rasputin Records is still there, as is Moe's Books. He can't remember the low buildings on the left side of the street clearly enough to know whether the Fat Slice is original or rebuilt. They use the same recipes they always have. He supposes that's as good as having the original masonry. Maybe better.

(On some level he'll always be glad, and guilty about his gladness, that the city where he and Dodger were finally together, finally allowed to be friends and siblings and everything they should have been for their entire lives, fell down before he walked away from her. He got a fresh start. He hopes she got the same.)

He walks down to Derby, turns, and heads into the residential neighborhoods concealed behind the commercial veneer, tucked oh-so-neatly out of the public eye, where tourists and visiting parents never see them. This is the part of Berkeley where the rebuilding is the most visible, because this is the part of Berkeley that has, for the most part, refused to change. The people who live here cherish their Victorian homes, which now stand shrouded in scaffolding, being restored to life one shingle and piece of careful wiring at a time. There was an entire street that chose to go without electricity for three weeks because of the chance one of their houses could catch fire; when they were rewired by a team of electricians, they celebrated with a block party that lit up the sky for miles around. The rents here are low, if you can find someone who's willing to trust their renovated darling to a stranger.

Roger's duplex occupies the ground floor of one of those Victorians, although "floor" is a bit of a misnomer, since he only has half of one: they walk around the holes, laughing at the ridiculousness of it all, and sometimes he pretends to be a tightrope walker and sometimes he just wishes he could go to the bathroom without worrying about winding up in the basement.

There's an ancient orange cat curled up in a box on the porch, one paw covering half of his face. Roger pauses to bend and give him a gentle pat, using the motion as an excuse to check that old Bill is still breathing. No one knows how old the cat actually *is*, but he's lived longer than any outdoor cat Roger's ever known, and he's steeling himself against the day the good old fellow's heart gives up and lets him slip quietly away.

Old Bill's side rises and falls in a shallow but steady rhythm. One more day for the best cat in Berkeley, then; one more night for the best cat in the world. When Roger looks up, the front door is open, and Erin is smiling at him.

He smiles back.

"Good day at school?" she asks, reaching down to grasp the lapels of his jacket and pull him to his feet. He comes without resistance. It's best not to fight when a beautiful woman wants him to do something, he's found. It makes things more pleasant for everyone.

"Pretty good," he says, and leans in, and kisses her—a gesture she returns with enthusiasm. When he leans away again, she's smiling. So is he. "How's the congregation?"

"Congregating," she says deadpan, before laughing at her own joke.

Erin is the only one of the three people who shared Dodger's off-campus apartment to remain at UC Berkeley. Candace was killed trying to shield a group of preschoolers from debris. Dodger vanished. Erin remained. She waited outside the apartment, clutching old Bill, until the shaking stopped. Then she put down the cat and went to see what she could do to help. She turned out to be surprisingly good with her hands, citing a family history of construction and medical work. Roger ran into her three days later, outside one of the triage tents. Awkward, he'd asked how she was doing. She'd told him about Candace, about the way their apartment had shaken and crumbled in on itself, about going back to dig clothes from the rubble. He'd asked if she wanted to come back to his place, which was still standing, even if there was no running water.

She'd moved in that afternoon. When he'd moved out three weeks later, switching to someplace safer, with plumbing that actually worked, she'd come with him. Their first shared apartment had had two bedrooms. This one does too, but one of those rooms is an office, filled with all the books he won't allow in the room where they sleep. The Unitarian church where she serves as a minister is only half a mile from their current address. Like him, she walks to work most mornings. Like him, she favors feet over other forms of transit.

For both of them, on some deep level, the ground is still shaking, and always will be.

Erin kisses him again before stepping to the side and letting him in. She closes the door behind him, shutting out the world that isn't theirs, that wasn't designed to contain and comfort the two of them. "So just a normal day?"

"Someone built a book tower in the library that came down while I was doing some shelving," he says, shrugging out of his jacket and hanging it on the hook. "Oh, and I'm almost done translating that manuscript Christopher brought in. It's a really interesting Breton dialect."

"Have the walls started bleeding yet?" she asks mildly. "Because that's always what I worry about when you're translating some manuscript that's been lost to human eyes for centuries. That the walls are going to start bleeding, and then we're going to have the risen dead and a bunch of animated trees to contend with."

"I'd give myself a chainsaw hand for you," he says, and she laughs, and everything is wonderful; everything is perfect. There are pieces missing, sure, and not just in the living room floor, but whose life doesn't have a few missing pieces? Missing pieces are what makes it real, rather than just a painting of a life that could never actually exist. Missing pieces are essential.

Roger tries to tell himself that as he follows Erin to the kitchen. There's nothing in a melancholy day that a cup of coffee and a lemon scone can't fix.

She walks with a calm assurance he never quite manages to match, stepping with absolute confidence that her feet will find the structurally stable parts of the floor. She's the reason they can live here at all: the place should technically be considered uninhabitable, but somehow she found the right combination of laws and loopholes to make it home. The rules love her almost as much as he does. Her ash-colored hair is lovely in the light slanting through the hallway window, and this is home, this is harbor, this is everything it needs to be.

This may not be the life he thought he wanted, but somehow it is absolutely the life that he deserves.

It can take Roger a long time to go to sleep, but when he does, he sleeps deeply and completely, with the conviction of a child. He sprawls, revealing the true length of his lanky limbs, which he so frequently keeps tucked in close to his body, out of the way. Erin sits in the bed next to him, watching him snore.

She wishes she could love him the way she suspects he loves her. She wishes she could respond to his increasingly frequent hints about marriage, children, a home in Albany or the Berkeley hills. She wishes she could tell him it's never going to work out the way he wants it to, that she's here because she has to be, and while aspects of their relationship have been organic—things she *chose* to do, rather than things she was *ordered* to do—the relationship as a whole has always been engineered. The same could be said about the both of them. Neither came into this world the way children are supposed to. Neither is likely to leave it that way, either.

Roger wrinkles his nose, makes a grumbling sound, and rolls onto his side. Erin takes this opportunity to slip out of the bed. If he doesn't leave space for her when he rolls back over, she'll sleep on the couch. She's done it before, and he's always been understanding. That's just the sort of person he is.

Sometimes she contrasts him with Darren, her brother, who was all hard edges and sharp demands and the only other male she's ever lived with. He would have followed her out of the bedroom, asking why she was disrupting his sleep by disappearing when he expected her to be there, accusing her of screwing with the natural order of things. They would have fought, his voice low and tight and reasonable, hers arcing ever higher, until it seemed like any glassware in the area would be sacrificed on the altar of their anger. The fight would have ended when one of them admitted fault or when morning came, whichever happened first, and then they would fall asleep like puppies, tangled together in a ball of limbs and silence.

It's been long enough since he died that he shouldn't still be haunting her. She thinks sometimes that he'll haunt her until she follows him into whatever void awaits creatures such as they on the other side of the veil. If the twins are followed by the scar tissue of visions and revisions to their personal timeline, she's followed by the ghost of a teenage boy who died for no good reason in the shadow of the corn. He has no grave. She's his living mausoleum.

She sits, cross-legged on the couch, and waits. Three minutes after midnight, her phone rings. She picks it up. Brings it to her ear.

"Hello, Erin."

She nearly drops the phone.

Normally, the evening report is requested by Leigh: a serpent, to be sure, but a serpent she knows intimately, and who knows her just as well. Leigh made her, molded her, chose the color of her skin and the texture of her hair. Leigh is not her mother—more her architect— and one of them will kill the other one day, but Leigh is *familiar*. This voice . . .

This voice is softer and harder at the same time, an iron bar wrapped in a sheet of velvet, rubbing against her skin in a sickly-sweet parody of seduction. She hasn't spoken to Reed in years, not since she left the lab, but still, she knows that voice. She knows it very well.

"Sir," she manages to say through a constricted throat, with a mouth gone dry as ashes.

"You've done well keeping the language aspect of your pairing under observation. The math can't hurt anything on its own. A trigger's required if a gun's to be of use." He chuckles at his own joke, a dry, humorless sound, like bones clicking together in a tomb. When he speaks again, that small levity is gone. "Your assignment has changed. Kill him."

"Sir?"

"We have a better candidate, a pair that's managed to mature without separation, and we can't have the Doctrine's loyalties confused when it tries to take physical form. The Middleton boy has become a liability. Your service is appreciated, and you need to terminate the experiment. Clean up whatever mess it creates. We'll expect you back here within the week—oh, and Erin? Try to be more subtle this time. They can't all be electrical fires."

The line goes dead. The call has been terminated.

Erin lowers the phone and stares blankly at the hallway. At the end of it, Roger is sleeping, defenseless, unwary. He has no idea what she is, what he's welcomed into his home, his bed. He's never suspected her, not once. She could let him go like that: let him die innocent of what he was made for, of what he can do. It's the only choice she can be sure she's never made before. The odds of Dodger managing to reset the timeline on her own before she dies from disconnection shock are slim. So no, this is a thing she's never done. Every time, every timeline, every revision, she's chosen to refuse her duty. She's chosen to fight.

She's so tired. The cuckoos have the luxury of forgetting their trips to the Impossible City. Not her. She's been tangled up with them for lifetimes, and the temptation to end the story here is stronger than she expected. One knife, one throat, and she gets to be something more than their pretty little killer. She gets to go back to the lab, to the comforts of the world she was made for, and see what kind of world this would be with the Doctrine truly embodied, truly activated.

A world controlled by Reed, with Leigh at his red right hand. For the (tenth? hundredth? thousandth?) time she looks at the choice, and stands, still knowing what she's going to do, to walk into the shadows of her home.

# Flight Risk

O of!" Roger sits upright, dreams dissolving into a confused haze of fragmentary images. The color red—true red, the red he's never seen with his own eyes—lingers, and he knows he was dreaming of Dodger. (Or dreaming *with* Dodger: assuming she's still on this coast, it's not unreasonable to think their sleep cycles might occasionally align, and their subconscious minds might keep reaching out even after their conscious minds have decided to cut contact. He misses her. He imagines she feels the same.)

Still groggy, he looks down to see what hit him. It's a backpack, already half-full. He picks it up and looks inside, finding clothes, and notebooks, and his tablet.

"You have five minutes," says Erin. Her voice is cold. There's no teasing or laughter there now, only the sort of steely resolve he hasn't heard from her since before the earthquake. He looks up. She's standing in the doorway, dressed in dark gray leggings and a matching tank top. It looks like she's getting ready for a yoga class, or a run.

"What?" Roger rubs his eyes, reaches for his glasses, takes a look at the clock on the bedside table. "Erin, it's after midnight. What's going on?"

"We're getting out of here." The statement is calm, matter-of-fact: it leaves no room for argument. "This isn't the time to explain. You need to trust me."

"I do trust you, but Erin, I'm not going to get out of bed and . . . run away . . . because you had a bad dream." He schools his face, trying to look understanding when all he feels is confused. "Come back to bed. You can tell me all about it."

"You've been hearing your sister's voice in your head since you were in elementary school. I don't know exactly when it started in this timeline, since you never trusted me enough to tell me, but I'm guessing between the ages of seven and nine. You told me once that that was the 'sweet spot' for acceptance in small children." That had been another timeline, another Roger. Her memory of the conversation is hazy, but the fact that she remembers means it was important, that he told her to hold on to the information no matter what came next. She remembers him without glasses, with shorter hair, with a mustache. It's all superficial, the result of small choices gone differently, culminating in someone who was almost, but not quite, the Roger in front of her.

They destroy themselves every time they destroy the world. Their past is littered with the unburied bodies of the people they chose never to become.

Roger gapes before his mouth snaps shut and he sits up straighter, some of the old wariness coming back into his eyes. "I don't have a sister." The lie is automatic. He's ashamed of it: his cheeks redden, he presses on, saying, "Even if I did, that wouldn't make us . . . whatever that would make us."

"I know most people believe every word that comes out of your mouth, but I was Dodger's roommate before I was your girlfriend, and I'm not going to forget her. She's your sister, and if you're in danger, so is she. I had to stay with one of you, and you were the more dangerous, so you got me. We need to find her." Erin purses her lips.

"Unless you think she'd listen if you called? Give it a try. She needs to be warned. I honestly don't know if they have her under surveillance, and if they do, we could be running for nothing." She can't count on the way the other timelines have played out to give them time to get to Dodger. The trouble with starting from scratch over and over is that things can change. If they've changed too much, this is the end of the game, and she's throwing herself away on a plan that can never work.

Roger is looking at her with increasing dismay. He's a smart man. There are things he hasn't thought about for years, moments when she broke character, when she tried to warn him. She can see him putting the pieces together, finding the way they fit together, however much he wants them not to.

"Erin . . . ?" he finally says. "Honey, are you okay?"

"Dodger Cheswich is your sister," she replies. "Denial is fun, and I've encouraged it, to be fair, but the time for denial is over. You need to wake up if you don't want this to be the ending. Did you really manage to forget I knew about her—did you run away from yourself that hard? Why else would I have let you keep her picture next to our bed for all these years? Seriously, you're smarter than that. Think."

"That doesn't mean . . ." He tapers off, stops dead, and gives her a narrow-eyed, suspicious look. "Her being my sister doesn't mean any of those other things."

"Yeah, it does. We've met before, Roger, on the improbable road, and I know where you come from." The answer is so much bigger and more complicated than that, but these are the answers he can accept here and now, and she needs him to accept. She needs him *moving*. If she doesn't do her job by morning, they'll know, and they'll send someone who will. She's not their only hunter. "Can you call her or not?"

"I don't have her number."

"That's not what I mean." Erin's eyes are cold. "Close your eyes, and call her. I know you can. You know you can. We don't have the time for you to fuck with me right now, Roger, and I don't have the patience to sit and hold your hand while you work through this. I'm risking my own life to save yours. Show a scrap of gratitude, and call your damn sister."

She walks past the bed while he's gaping at her again, kneeling and opening the bottom drawer of her dresser. Pushing away a veil of lingerie and sanitary products—even though Roger has always been understanding about her periods, willing to go to the drugstore when she asks without complaining about it, something she attributes in part to the amount of time he spent with Dodger in his head, putting a box of tampons on top of something she wants left alone has always been a functional deterrent—she produces a lead-lined box. It has no latch; instead, it is sealed with a sheet of candle wax. She breaks it with one hard strike of her palm and looks over her shoulder to Roger. His eyes are still open. He hasn't moved.

"They'll know," she says quietly. "When the sun comes up and their little science projects haven't suddenly become a lot more powerful, they'll know you're still breathing. They'll assume I failed, that you were too much for me, and they'll send someone to finish what they think I started. We have until they get here and find an absence of bodies before they know I've gone rogue, and once that happens? All bets are off. So call her, before we're running."

"Erin, you need to cut this out. Whatever this is, you need to stop. It's not funny."

"I'm not trying to be *funny*. I'm trying to save your scrawny, ungrateful ass." She turns back to the box. Opens it. Withdraws its contents. Stands, and turns to face him.

Roger makes a thick *urk* noise, like he's trying to speak through a mouthful of concrete. Erin's smile is as thin as the blade of a knife, and would cut twice as sharply.

"This is a Hand of Glory," she says. "I made it from the severed hand of a murdered woman, because I knew I was going to need it eventually. I've been trying to protect you for a long time. Longer than a lifetime, even, thanks to your asshole sister. I'm sorry to drop this on you so abruptly, but it's not like there was ever a convenient moment for saying 'hey, Roger, so you know, you were engineered by alchemists who want to control the world, and they're hoping they can use you and Dodger for that purpose.'"

Roger knows that hand. It's been a long time, but there are things he doesn't have it in him to forget. The shape of Smita's fingers, long and elegant and nimble; the way she painted her nails in shockingly bright colors, as if to draw attention to her hands, which she considered her best feature. The hand Erin holds belongs to a woman who died in a fire. There's no way it should be here, no way it should still look so fresh and pliant, but it is, and it does, and the world is no longer making sense.

"Call her," says Erin. There's no love in her voice. Maybe there was never any love there at all.

Or maybe there was. Some things are difficult to fake, especially over the length and breadth of the years they've had together. There have been a *lot* of years. Their relationship, informal as it is, has outlasted marriages among his peers; there have been days when he thought they were going to be together forever. Days when it seemed like Erin was his happy-ever-after girl, like they were going to be able to build a future, one brick at a time, just by keeping one another close and never letting go. He's trusted her since the earthquake, since she stopped being Dodger's prickly roommate and became his friend, confidant, and eventually lover.

He can't throw all that away in an instant. So he takes a deep breath, trying to swallow his misgivings, and says, in his most serious tone, "Erin, I want you to explain what's going on."

Erin's eyes widen. "Oh," she says, in a small, surprised voice. "Every manifestation really does feed into every other. No wonder. No wonder. I . . ." She shakes herself like a wet dog, like she's trying to shrug off some unwanted control. "I was born in the lab that created you and Dodger. You were the pet projects of a man named James Reed, who's been trying for over a hundred years to follow Asphodel Baker's directions for incarnating a universal concept called the Doctrine of Ethos in a human body. Yours was the first generation where he began splitting the Doctrine into equal halves, both to force the hosts to be more like ordinary people, and to make them easier to control. You got language. Dodger got math."

"And you got a blow to the head if you think I'm going to believe this bullshit." Roger's getting angry. He can't help it. This is ludicrous; this is insane; this would have been impossible to swallow even if Erin hadn't gone a step too far and invoked Dodger's name. He doesn't like to talk about his sister when he can help it. He made his choice. He has to live with it.

(Under the anger is horror, slow and rich and thick as honey. Because what she's saying is impossible, yes, but so is quantum entanglement with an absent twin; so is causing an earthquake with a game. Erin is putting his life into a new context, one where things that have never been believable make sudden and absolute sense. And he does not want them to.)

"Don't you want to know what they built me for?"

He doesn't. "Sure," he says. "I'll play. What did your mad science masters design you to do?"

"Not mad science: alchemy. Mad scientists are kinder to their creations." She takes the bowl of spare change from the dresser with her free hand, tilting it forward to show its contents before she flings them into the air. Roger doesn't have time to react before they hit the ground in a grid around her. Each coin is positioned like the floor had a magnetic coil beneath it, landing at the points of imaginary squares. Every one of them is heads-up. Erin puts the dish back.

"Chaos and Order were early targets," she says. "It seems like they should be bigger than something like the Doctrine, but it turns out that because they're primal, they're also simple. They've been employing poppets of my lineage for almost as long as they've been working to incarnate yours. I am the living embodiment of Order, and I am *ordering* you to get the fuck out of that bed and follow me."

"That was a terrible pun," says Roger automatically. He can't deny the evidence of his eyes. He's always been good at justifying things unseen, but this? This is physical reality. He knows there are no magnets. This is too much for a prank.

Erin scowls. "Are you still not taking this seriously? They'll send people here when I don't check in. They'll find you. And they *will* kill you."

"Right." Roger crosses his arms. "Why are you helping me if these are the people who made you?"

"Because they made me like they made you: they made me to be a part of a pair. Chaos and Order. But we weren't as entangled as you and Dodger are—remember when she slit her wrists and nearly bled out behind her house? I remember you arguing with her, in a timeline that never existed, about whether that needed to happen. Whether that was something the two of you could revise. She said it had to be allowed to remain part of the timeline, because that event was one of the things that allowed me to convince you to come with me."

Roger's eyes have been getting wider and wider, until it seems like they're set to swallow the top half of his face. He folds his arms tighter, holding himself in a half-comforting embrace.

"You can't live if she dies, and she can't live if you die; that's how it works for the cuckoos, every last carefully designed one of you. Me, I can live without my other half just fine. Doesn't mean I wanted to." Darren had been sullen and quick to anger, rigid in ways that were almost comic, coming from an avatar of chaos. He'd wanted everything just so, following patterns he had set and only he could understand. And he'd loved her. Oh, how he'd loved her. They'd been two halves of the same coin, not brother and sister like the incarnations of the Doctrine, but Adam and Eve of the unformed universe, so suited to each other that the thought of being apart had been a painful impossibility. Until the day Reed needed a hammer to pound a stubborn nail. Until Erin needed training. Until the cuckoos needed someone who could watch over their nest while they grew, someone they would be able to accept as a member of their peer group, even though technically they had no peers. Only each other. Only ever each other.

Erin has been here before, over and over, as the timelines looped and changed around her. Darren has never been standing by her side. She suspects that, like Dodger's attempted suicide, his death may be one of the things that can't be changed: her willingness to betray Reed hinges on it having happened. She hates them for that, Roger and Dodger, who could have each other if they'd stop pushing one another away. She hates them more than she hates anything, and she'll die, again, if that's what it takes for them to stay together. She's done worse.

"I can't call her," he says. "She hasn't . . . We haven't spoken in seven years. I didn't answer when she called, and one day she just stopped calling."

"Try."

"I *can't*."

"You're going to get us both killed," says Erin, with no rancor in her voice. She reaches into her pocket, produces her phone, and throws it onto the bed. "Try the mundane way."

"I don't have her number anymore."

To his surprise, she laughs. It's a high, bright, impossibly strained sound, like glass breaking. "Oh, trust me, happy boy. That has *never* mattered. Try."

Roger picks up the phone.

Dials the number for her old apartment, the one that hasn't been there for years.

Waits.

It rings three times, four, five, and he's about to hang up when there's a click and Dodger's voice is in his ear, Dodger is *talking to him*, saying, "This is Dodger. What's your deal?"

His mouth is so dry he can barely swallow. He forces himself to do just that before saying, "Uh. Hi, Dodge."

"Roger?" She sounds puzzled. "Why are you calling me from the roof? Did you finally decide to get a cellphone?"

His mouth dries up even further. He can't speak.

(Because he remembers this; he didn't remember it a moment ago, can't even say for sure whether this is a thing that had *happened* a moment ago, but it's something that has actually and for certain happened *now*. Dodger, coming back from a trip to the kitchen for lemonade and brownies to quiz him on why he'd decided to make a prank call from the roof when he knew she was going to be right back up. Him, protesting that he didn't have a cellphone and couldn't have called her. It had been a beautiful day. The air had tasted like honeysuckle. The brownies had tasted of chocolate and marijuana. And it had happened almost eight years ago.)

She's going to hang up. He knows it, and so he swallows hard one more time, and says, "I missed you. That's all."

"Asshole," she says, with complete fondness. There's a click as she replaces the receiver in its cradle (landlines, they still used landlines back then), and he's listening to silence.

Slowly, he lowers the phone and turns his eyes back to Erin. "I just called Dodger."

"Yeah," says Erin. "Sounds like it was an old number, though."

"How . . . ?"

"Pack the backpack. Take what you need." She pulls a lighter from her pocket and flicks it on before beginning to light the fingers of the Hand. "We need to be gone by morning."

Roger stares for a moment. Then, quickly, he begins to move.

T he last thing Erin does is set the house on fire.

She does it with swift precision, touching the Hand of Glory to the aged wood of the front porch and stepping back as the flames begin to leap, growing too fast and voraciously to be ordinary. When the entire front of the house is wreathed in crackling flame, she turns and walks to the sidewalk, where Roger is waiting.

"We need to stand here for a few minutes," she says. "The Hand of Glory will keep anyone who shouldn't see us from noticing that we exist, and we want the fire to get a good grasp on the interior before we go."

"You burned the Life Sciences Annex," he says.

If Erin is surprised by the non sequitur, she doesn't show it. Instead, she just nods. "Yes. I did. With the body of your friend inside. I had to. It was an order."

"From the people you say 'made' us." His voice turns bitter at the end, twisting the single syllable in "made" until it almost breaks. "Did they also tell you to kill Smita?"

"Yes." People are emerging from their houses, pointing at the fire, exclaiming over it, ordering one another to call 911. A few seem a little too interested. They'll be the ones who have dreams of fire over the next days, the ones whose eyes get bright when they see a candle. The dangerous ones.

"Why?"

"Because your blood would have told her that you're not real. You and your sister were *made*, not born. You're too close to identical to be fraternal, and too different to be identical. She was a smart woman with a problem to work at. She would have figured out that something was wrong. The people who designed you don't want anyone sniffing around their doors. She had to be removed."

"But—"

"We've been over this. Believe me, we've been over this. I've even spared her a few times, when I thought we could risk it. You know what happened? Shit got bad faster. We wound up at the zero point faster. You had less time to get comfortable in the language of your own skin. Dodger had less time to figure out how to work the numbers. We died faster. So don't argue with me on this. It sucks that she died. I hate that I killed her. But she died quick and she died clean and we got to live in peace for this long, and on the balance of things, I'll take it. My life over hers, period."

The roof caves in with a soft crackling sound. Someone has called 911; the sound of sirens fills the air. Slowly, Roger realizes that no one is pointing at them. No one is approaching to ask if they're okay. They've lived in this neighborhood for years, and their neighbors are acting as if they don't even exist.

"What—" he begins.

"I told you," says Erin, and takes his hand, and leads him over to the nearest cluster of rubberneckers.

"Do you think they got out in time?" one of them is asking. He's in his bathrobe and nothing else, barefoot on the pavement.

"I hope so," says another. Her eyes flick past the place where Roger stands like he's not even there. For her, he isn't. "They were such a sweet couple."

"We're already past tense for these people," says Erin. "Let them be past tense for you, too. Come on. We need to find your sister, before it's too late."

Roger hasn't liked to drive since the earthquake, but that doesn't mean that a car isn't sometimes necessary. Theirs is parked on the street. Somehow, none of the neighbors notice when he starts it up and pulls away. A few even step to the side to avoid being hit, but no one points, no one says "hey, there's Roger and Erin, they're alive." They all just keep staring at the fire, and Roger and Erin drive away, shrouded by the Hand of Glory, into an uncertain future.

# Galileo

Dodger's keys jingle, juggling her purse and two bags of groceries as she unlocks the door. The sun gnaws at her back and shoulders, bright and hot and uncompromising. The drought means the honeysuckle she would normally have asked her gardener to encourage around the doorway has withered to a thin, clinging vine that provides no shade for moments like these. It's inconvenient, but a few extra bottles of sunscreen are a small price to pay for a state that's marginally less parched.

(She's done the math: the increase in showering to rinse away all those skin care products is actually greater than the water requirements of her honeysuckle. But her neighborhood is upscale enough to be snobby, and exclusive enough to be nosy. There have been a few "anonymous" tips to the water board about people whose lawns were too green or whose gardens seemed a bit too healthy. Even Ms. Stewart down on the corner has had to endure her share of "water shaming" over her roses, and she's eighty years old, with rosebushes that are only slightly younger. A few showers are also a small price to pay, this time for the prize of being left alone by neighbors with nothing better to do.)

The air inside the house is cool and dry. It smells clean, to her. On the rare occasions when she's had people over, they've found that comforting cleanness unnervingly sterile, asking her nervously whether she's just had a cleaning service in. More than anything, those reactions have taught her that she shouldn't have people in her home. It's hers, after all. She gets to keep it however she likes, as long as she's not endangering herself or others. If she were breeding cockroaches in the pantry or conducting mold experiments in the bathroom, confusion and even disgust would be warranted. She's never done either of those things. She's just kept everything clean enough to live up to its full potential. Shouldn't that be rewarded?

The door slams behind her as she makes her way to the kitchen. Some of the groceries need to be put away before they start to defrost. Others need to be put away because groceries don't belong on the counter. Once that's done, she can get back to work, secure in the knowledge that she's done her errands and interacted with humanity today. Her psychologist wants her to interact with humanity every day if she possibly can; he says her tendency to self-isolate isn't healthy and will only improve if she makes an effort.

Dodger Cheswich, self-help guru of the modern nerd, seeking help with her own self. It would be comic, if it weren't so frustrating.

She's expecting stillness, calm, and cleanness when she reaches the kitchen. She's also expecting darkness: the house stays cooler if she keeps the shades drawn when she's not home. Opening the shades would be too difficult with the groceries she's carrying, and so she goes for the easier, more ecologically wasteful option, flicking on the kitchen lights. The energy-efficient bulbs spring to life, illuminating the kitchen and dining area. Which is clean, yes, clean enough that virtually every surface is safe to eat off of, and still, yes. But it isn't empty.

Her psychologist, Dr. Peters, is sitting at her dining room table. He has a gun in his hand. The gun is pointed at her.

The strangeness of this tableau causes Dodger to freeze, expression shifting to one of profound puzzlement. Dr. Peters says nothing. For a long moment, neither does she. Then, in a politely baffled voice, she asks, "Is this a new therapy technique? Did I approve this when I signed the new insurance paperwork last week? Because I don't think I like it." She didn't approve this, she knows that much. Dodger may not be a recreational reader, but she's never signed anything she didn't understand. For someone in her line of work, that would be tantamount to career suicide.

"Put the bags down, Miss Cheswich," says Dr. Peters. "I don't want to upset you any more than I have to."

"I don't see the connection between those two statements," says Dodger, setting the bags on the counter. She keeps her purse. It's a big brown leather bag, bought with the advance from her first book. It cost more than she liked to consider at the time, but she'd run the numbers, and knew this was the sort of purse she'd only need to purchase once: it would last her entire life, classic enough never to go out of style, sturdy enough to tolerate the abuse she heaped on her possessions. She's had it for five years, and so far, it's managed to keep its side of the unspoken bargain just fine.

"You don't like making messes," says Dr. Peters. He stands. The gun is still pointed at her. "I'm afraid we're going to make a mess. That can't be helped. At least this way you'll know that your corpse was the only thing leaking on the floor."

"Ah," says Dodger. Inwardly, she's raging and frozen at the same time, fear warring with fury for control. How dare he come into her home, her space, and threaten her this way? He's her *therapist,* for God's sake. He's supposed to be one of the people she can trust. There are few enough of those in this world. How *dare* he? "If you don't mind me asking, why are you planning to kill me? I don't keep all my money in a lockbox under the mattress. There's nothing here to steal. You'd make a lot more if you just kept being my therapist."

"I'm afraid that's none of your concern," says Dr. Peters, and takes a step forward.

Dodger tilts her head.

*The room is fifteen feet long and eleven feet wide, with eight-foot ceilings.*

*Dr. Peters is six foot three inches tall, giving him a base stride of thirty-one inches. Momentum plus velocity plus kinetic absorption rate equals—*

Dr. Peters steadies his gun. His hand tenses. Dodger moves. This is *her* space, *her* place, and all she needs to know is in the numbers. She grabs a can of chicken noodle soup from the top of the bag, flinging it as hard as she can for the wall to his right. It misses his ear by inches, and he's starting to laugh when it hits the wall *just so*, finding the perfect angle for recoil, and bounces back to hit him in the head. Dr. Peters stops laughing. Dr. Peters pulls the trigger.

But Dodger isn't there. This is her space; it has no secrets from her. The house is a mathematical model, and she is the only one who knows it both inside and out, knows every angle to the slightest degree. The house is not a living thing, but it is an equation, and she moves through it with a speed that can't be matched by someone who needs eyes to see where the furniture is placed, needs to pay attention to their surroundings. In this moment, Dodger Cheswich *is* her surroundings, and she's gathering speed.

The next thing to strike Dr. Peters is a coffee mug, flying apparently from nowhere to hit him in the throat. He roars anger and confused pain. This isn't how the situation was supposed to play out. The little mathematician was supposed to cry, to beg, to apologize for the self-absorbed way she'd always interacted with him. She was supposed to say she was wrong, that she'd do anything to save herself, *anything*. This job, this whole situation, has been a trial. This is where he was meant to reap his reward. Instead, the girl is a ghost, moving from place to place like she's somehow found a way to fold the fabric of space itself.

More things fly at him. A glass paperweight, a potted succulent, a rock. Why does she have a *rock* in the damn *house*? It doesn't matter, because the more she throws, the more he'll know about where she is.

"Stop this while I have some patience left," he says. "I only have to shoot you once."

"True enough," she says, from behind him. He turns. Dodger is right there, less than a foot away. She looks . . . awake, for lack of a better word, like she's been sleepwalking through life the whole time he's been dealing with her, and has only just decided to open her eyes.

The toaster impacts with the side of his face so hard that he feels bone give way, and then he's falling into the dark, and it doesn't matter anymore.

Dodger stands over the body of her therapist, panting, the toaster clutched in her hands. It's a good toaster. Why did she never notice before what a good toaster it is? There's a dent in one shiny metal side the exact size and shape of Dr. Peters's skull. It probably won't make toast anymore. That's a pity. It was a good toaster.

Her purse begins ringing.

Dodger looks down at it, uncomprehending at first, then with dawning understanding. The phone. It's her phone. She sets the toaster on the counter and digs the phone from her purse, checking the display. UNKNOWN NUMBER, it says. A telemarketer, probably, or someone looking for a donation to a political campaign. She should ignore it. She has bigger problems.

But then, bigger problems sometimes get easier to solve when she steps back from them. She slides her thumb to the little green Answer icon, raising the phone to her ear. "Hello?"

"Oh my God it worked." The voice is breathless, excited, and so damn *young*.

The voice is her own. Dodger blinks. Frowns. Says the only thing she can, under the circumstances:

"What the fuck is going on here?"

"Oh! Uh. Hello, Dodger in the future. This is Dodger from the past. Specifically, this is Dodger from December tenth, 2008. I would have called yesterday, but the phones were pretty much out of commission after the earthquake. I hitched a ride to Palo Alto. I'm calling from our parents' place." A nervous giggle. "This is so *weird*. I've talked to the future before, but I was never the one to make the call. Do you think this counts as long distance?"

Dodger sits down, hard, on the floor. She doesn't remember making this call—quite—but the feeling of déjà vu gets stronger with every word the other Dodger says. By the time she hangs up, she's sure she'll remember the conversation from both sides. The math is changing. "Why are you calling me? *How* are you calling me?"

"Oh. Um. After Roger called us from the future, I opened our thirty-year planner and circled the first date I saw. I didn't have a way to show my work, but instinctive mathematics can be as good as practical ones if you're not being graded."

"And this number?"

"It's my number too, just not yet. I dialed the most logical combination I could think of."

None of this makes sense, and because of that, every bit of this makes perfect sense. Everything the younger Dodger is saying meshes with the older Dodger's understanding of the world, which is made of math. It's just that occasionally, the math makes its own rules. Math gets to do that, if it wants to.

"Why are you calling?" she asks.

"Don't you know?"

"I don't think I can, until you tell me," she says. "This hasn't happened for me yet. I'm the future, but I'm not *your* future until you finish the call." It should be terrifying, the thought that she's changing the equation that comprises her reality. Because this *will* change things. She knows that, as surely as she knows that every second takes away more of her slim opportunity to escape becoming the future self of a girl she, as yet, never was.

(And it's a relief, really, to know time can be revised like this. It makes so much about her life start to hang together. A good mathematician is always willing to check their work, to change the pieces that don't serve the overall equation. That's what she's doing now. Just . . . changing pieces, and making something better of herself. She would never have picked up the phone in the past if it wasn't for the sake of making a better future.)

"Roger called me," says her past self, and Dodger in the present closes her eyes and listens, silently, to every perfect, painful word.

# Long Distance

The apartment is empty when Dodger arrives. All the windows have shattered. New cracks run through its foundation. She scratches some equations into the dirt that constitutes their narrow strip of a yard—she could do them in her head, but they're easier to trust when she can see them—and decides it should be safe, if she's quick. If she smells gas or smoke or anything else that shouldn't be there, she'll get out. Until that happens, she can seek comfort in the broken familiar and gather her things.

She doesn't know yet where she's going—back to her parents, probably—but she can't stay here. Not after the way Roger looked at her, with fear and loathing and longing tangled in his eyes. Not after the way Smita died. Running away may not be the grownup thing to do, but Dodger has never put much stock in being a grownup. Sometimes logic says the childish thing is the right one.

The bookshelves in the hall have toppled over, spilling their contents across the floor. *Over the Woodward Wall* has fallen open to the center illustration, the Impossible City in gold and mercury glory.

Dodger stops for a moment, transfixed by the image. Something about it . . .

No. This isn't the time. She shakes herself free and picks through the mess, occasionally pausing to recover an especially beloved childhood treasure. There was never any real filing system here. At least the ceiling held; at least the broken glass was minimal. At least they didn't die. Roger may have looked at her like she was a monster, but they didn't die. They may still find a way through this.

She steps into her room. The damage here is even more minimal, and some of the tension leaves her shoulders. There's a dusting of plaster over everything, fallen from the ceiling; the pillow has toppled off the bed, and all her markers are on the floor. Somehow, the earthquake has erased half of one wall, reducing the equation to a black smear. She doesn't know how that's possible, but she's not in the mood to ignore the evidence of her own eyes.

Dodger walks to the bed, sits, and puts her hands over her face. The temptation to reach for Roger is enormous. She wants to talk to him. She wants to know that everything is okay. But everything is *not* okay. They made the quake. She doesn't know how, she doesn't know why, but she knows they did it, the two of them working together. They're dangerous. Maybe not individually, but together? Together, they could destroy the world.

It's not a pleasant thought. It's the only one she has.

Her phone rings.

Dodger lowers her hands. It could be her parents, checking up on her; it could be Candace or Erin, trying to confirm that she's alive. The idea that it might be Roger doesn't even cross her mind. He won't be calling her today. Maybe not ever again.

She answers the phone. (The feeling of jamais vu rises, breaks around her, because she *didn't* answer the phone, not the first time: the first time, it was voice mail and a stuttered message that was somehow enough to make things a little better, to cause the situation to repeat the next time around. This is not the first time. It's closer than they've been in years.)

"Hello?"

"Dodger." The voice is Roger's, and it's not: he sounds older, exhausted, not at the end of his rope but some distance past it, holding on through sheer force of will. "I know you're mad at me, and I know I'm the last person in the world you want to talk to right now, but I need to ask you to please not hang up."

(*this was a message last time this was a message on my voice mail; we got it wrong, we got it wrong at least once more, even after we thought we were getting it right*)

"Mad at you?" Laughter bubbles in her throat. She swallows it. "Why would I be mad at you? I'm *worried* about you. You ran away so fast, I didn't even have a chance to tell you we'd be okay. Are you okay? You don't sound so good."

"I'm not okay, really. But . . . didn't the earthquake just happen? Wasn't that today?"

"Oh," she says, things falling into place as the world goes crystalline and clear, all the numbers lining up for a change. Of course. It's the only thing that makes sense, because there's no way Roger would be calling her: not now, anyway. "You're in the future, aren't you?"

He doesn't swallow his laughter as well as she swallows hers. It seeps up around his words as he says, "You figured that out even faster than I thought you would. I've really missed you, Dodge."

So they don't make things right between them, then: so this silence that echoes in her skull, filling the space he should be occupying, becomes the new normal. She shivers. "I haven't had time to miss you yet, but it sounds like I'm going to get it," she says, forcing her voice to stay level. "I wish I didn't have to."

"Me, too," he says, and she believes him. "But I—I mean, the me in your timeline—he needs his space if he's going to accept what's going on. You've always adapted faster than I did. And he—I—needs to accept this, because it's not going away."

"I'm following the numbers. They tell me what to do."

"Sometimes I wish I'd been the one to get the math," he says, and is quiet for a moment before continuing: "The Roger in your timeline is a fool. He's not ready to accept what he needs to know, and he's pushing you away because he's scared. I can't change that. The trick that lets me call you doesn't work if I'm trying to call myself, because I'm not math, I'm words, and words can change a lot of things, but they can't break the laws of time. You're the only person I can reach this way. So please, Dodge. I want you to give him time. I want you to let him come to you. But I want you to remember that I love you. That *he* loves you, and he never stops, not for a second, not even when he's trying to convince himself the two of you were involved in some sort of messed-up *folie à deux* for all these years."

"We don't have a shared delusion," Dodger protests. "It's all real. If you take away the quantum entanglement, we'd never have met." A wave of uneasiness sweeps over her, because they *would* have met, wouldn't they? They would have met in a room she can't quite remember but can't quite forget, with bruises on their arms and the ghosts of sedatives in their veins, and they would have clung to one another and promised never to lose track again. That's where this started. That's when they learned what they could do.

But it's all vague and hazy, and she can't quite grasp hold before it dissolves into shadowy outlines and déjà vu. The feeling has haunted her for her entire life, the strong sensation that almost everything she does has happened before at least once, and maybe more. She's almost used to it at this point. Maybe everyone goes through their lives on a wave of uncertainty and false memories.

"I know," says Roger, and he sounds so tired, and she hears something in the background, unmasked by his silence—something that sounds like gunfire.

Dodger's skin prickles. "Are you okay?"

"No," he says. "I screwed up, Dodge. I ran away after the earthquake, and when I needed you, you weren't there, because you didn't . . . I don't know. Maybe you didn't love me anymore, or maybe you just got tired of dealing with my bullshit insistence that I knew best. It doesn't matter, because I ran and you didn't think I wanted you to follow, and so we're both in a bad place when I am. I need you not to give up on me, okay? That's all. When I come crawling back, I need you to remember this call, and be willing to give me one more chance. Please."

"I could never give up on you," she says, and she sounds so wounded, and so young, that it makes his chest ache. "Is there anything I can do for you? The future you who's on my phone, I mean, not the now-you. I'll give the now-you his space, and I'll be ready when he comes back to me, if you're sure he's going to come."

Roger laughs, thin and pained. "I can be a dumb-ass sometimes, and I can be an asshole sometimes, but I've never been stupid enough to run away from you forever. He'll come. I'll come. And then you can make it so this version of me never exists, because I won't have to. You can change the math."

Dodger is quiet for a moment, taking that in, along with the distant sound of gunfire. Finally, she asks, "Am I with you, in the future?"

"You are."

"What am I like?"

"Lonely."

It's just one word, but it encompasses so much, like an equal sign finishing the equation. Dodger closes her eyes, wishing she could treat the gesture the way she so often has: as an excuse to reach out and not be alone anymore. She knows she can't. Future-Roger is outside of her range, and present-Roger needs her to leave him alone if he's ever going to let her back in. That doesn't make the emptiness of her own skull any easier to bear.

"That makes sense," she says. "Tell her I'm going to make it better for us. I'm going to wait for you. I'm not going to give up."

"That's all I needed to hear."

There's a finality in his voice. Cold terror grips her, and she knows, without question, that he's about to hang up: that their brief connection, whatever it is or was or will someday be, is coming to an end. She also knows that when he hangs up, he'll cease to exist—either because he's going to die, or because he changed the equation so profoundly that he can never become. Either way, she can't let him go without telling him something.

"Roger?" she says quickly.

"Yes?"

"I love you." They don't say that as often as they should, because it's an odd love, philia and agape and distance and time. It doesn't fit the modern definitions. Neither do they.

She hears him smile. "Thanks, Dodge."

"She loves you too. Future-me. There's no way she doesn't."

"I knew that. But . . . thank you for making sure." Then the line goes dead, and she's truly alone, not talking to the future, not able to reach out to the present.

Dodger Cheswich sinks to the floor, looking at the phone in her hand, and is silent.

# Orbits

The younger Dodger stops talking. Silence falls. Finally, awkwardly, she asks, "Are you still there?"

"I'm here," confirms the older Dodger, the one who exists in 2016, the one who just hit a man in the head with her toaster. She remembers the call now. Remembers the sound of gunshots behind Roger's voice, and the calm fear that swept through her like ink through cotton, coloring her from end to end with dread.

(She also remembers going back to the house, filling her suitcase, and leaving without speaking to another soul. She remembers thinking that if he was going to turn his back on her, she was going to turn her back on him. This version of events is already going fuzzy, smearing like those earthquake equations. Soon, it will be nothing but a faded "what if?" and not her timeline at all. It should be terrifying, losing a moment that shaped so many years. Instead, it's soothing, comforting, like she's putting things back the way they should have been all along. The déjà vu that has haunted her all her life is finally starting to make sense.)

"Okay, cool," says younger Dodger. Then, in a voice filled with wonder, she says, "I really did it, huh? I called the future. That's amazing. Do we have a flying car in the future?"

"Thankfully, no," says older Dodger. "Can you imagine some of the drivers we know with flying cars? Can you imagine *Roger* with a flying car? We'd all be dead inside the week."

Younger Dodger laughs. "I guess that's true," she says. "I want to ask you about . . . oh, everything, but I don't want to create more of a paradox than I already have."

"That's probably smart," says older Dodger. "If I told you about my life, it might change the things you'd do, and then I might never exist at all."

"Better not to risk it."

"Exactly." She *needs* to exist. It's not selfishness or self-preservation that puts that thought in her head: she needs to exist because she's the version of herself with an unconscious man on her kitchen floor. She's the version someone wanted to kill. She can't risk becoming someone more trusting or less isolated. What if she'd been a mother, and he'd taken one of her children hostage? What if she'd had pets? What if she'd been a little fonder of lighting up in the afternoons, and had come home stoned and slow? No. This is the version of her that can survive the situation at hand, so this is the version of her that has to endure.

"I don't know if I can call you again. I mean, it might not be a good idea, and I don't have anything else to tell you about. Yet."

"Call if that changes; otherwise, leave well enough alone, and let this be a one-time gig," says older Dodger. "It was nice talking to you."

"You, too. I always wondered how my voice sounded to everybody else."

That seems like a good place to end it. Older Dodger laughs and hangs up the phone, becoming present-Dodger, *only*-Dodger once again. The version of Dodger who has Dr. Peters lying, unconscious, at her feet.

With a sigh, she drops her phone back into her purse and goes looking for her emergency earthquake kit. She's going to need the rope.

* * *

Dr. Peters wakes tied to one of Dodger's dining room chairs. It's sturdy oak, part of an antique set she bought on Craigslist, and the rope holding him is rated for rock climbing: he strains against the knots and is rewarded with nothing more than a bit of rope burn.

"You can open your eyes," says Dodger. She sounds annoyed, like this was in no manner the way she intended to spend her afternoon: it's the voice of a woman who has found the limits of her patience and gone past them, into the blasted hinterlands of irritation. "There's no point pretending you're still out, not when you've started wiggling around like a hooked fish."

He opens his eyes. Dodger is seated in a chair identical to the one he's tied to, legs crossed at the ankles and hands folded on her knees. He's seen that position before: she assumes it every time they have a session, confessing her confusion and sorrows to him one small, belabored word at a time. Language has never been her forte, and the language of her own inner workings is no exception. Sometimes he's wondered whether she ever stopped to listen to herself, to the contradictions and unnecessary complications she's built her life upon.

He's never asked her. That wasn't his job. He was her therapist because she needed a therapist, and because it was an easy way to keep tabs on their highest-profile project. Even Reed had been surprised when the girl had gone into publishing; she'd been pigeonholed as a researcher. The math children were always flashier than the language ones, with more striking coloration and faster movements, naturally designed to draw fire. That didn't mean they enjoyed being the focus of attention. Most of them seemed to want to disappear whenever possible, sinking deeper and deeper into their private projects, coming out only when coaxed.

Dodger has broken so many rules she didn't even know existed that he'd be impressed, if he weren't terrified. "There seems to have been a misunderstanding," he says, trying to sound earnest, trying to sound like her friend. "Untie me, and we'll talk about it."

"Was the misunderstanding you trying to shoot me, or the part where you missed?" She sounds genuinely curious.

His blood seems to chill, pulling his skin tight and trembling across his frame. "I don't know what you thought you saw, but—"

"I already called the police," she says. "I told them the neighbor kids were setting off cherry bombs in the gully. They came and went while you were passed out. Did you know I grew up less than a mile from here? I know how much like a gunshot a cherry bomb can sound, if you set it off under the right conditions. No one's going to come looking for you. It's just you and me and you telling me why you tried to kill me."

"I don't have to tell you anything."

"I guess that's true. I don't have to let you go. That's true too, isn't it? Because no one knows you're here." The words come easy because they're so sincere. She may not know Dr. Peters as well as she thought she did—and he's her *therapist*, for God's sake, he's not supposed to *shoot* her—but she knows him well enough to know he wouldn't have come alone if there'd been someone to help him. He wouldn't have come at all if there'd been someone to do the dirty work on his behalf. She's seen him telling his secretary to turn away patients whose insurance has lapsed, or whose problems are too much for him to handle. He's not shy about passing the buck, as long as there's someone he can pass it to.

"*They* know I'm here," he says, almost triumphantly.

There's nothing "almost" about the way Dodger's eyes light up. In that moment, she's won, and that means he must, somehow, have lost.

"Who?" she asks sweetly, leaning farther forward. "Because see, we're at a binary choice right now. If you tell me, I'll know, and I might not blame you as much for trying to kill me. If you don't tell me, I won't know, and I'll have to go with another course of action. I don't know how much time you have. I don't think it's much. Tick tock, as they say. Think fast."

"Miss Cheswich, I don't know what you're hoping to accomplish, but I assure you, holding me captive won't do you any good. If you let me go, right now, I promise not to press charges. You're a very sick woman, but working together, I think we can make you well again."

"Nope," she says amiably. "Gaslighting me wasn't one of your choices. You can tell me who sent you or you can keep your mouth shut, but you can't convince me that I'm crazy. Do you want to try again, or do you want to call this a binary negative? I'm happy either way."

"No one sent me."

"Someone sent you."

"I assure you, I acted alone."

"You can't even keep your story straight when you're trying to decide between martyrdom and convincing me I somehow lured you to my house and attacked you without warning. Why would I believe you when you claim to have acted alone? You're not cut out for this line of work." She leans back in her chair. "Are you even really a therapist?"

"I am," he says, stung. "I thought I helped you a great deal."

"You did and you didn't. I'm reviewing our sessions now. I always thought it was interesting how your response to my saying I was socially isolated was to tell me I needed to resolve my emotional conflicts before I attempted to make friends. I'd been expecting a referral to a support group or something, not 'no, no, be a recluse until I tell you it's time to stop.'"

"But you did it."

"I did. Because it was what I wanted to hear you say, and what I wanted to do." She looks at him calmly, and for the first time since his phone rang and Dr. Reed's voice ordered him into picking up the gun, Dr. Peters feels true fear. She's not uneasy. She's not uncomfortable. If anything, she's serene, a cat playing with its next meal. She shouldn't be like this. The math children, the high-strung, headstrong logicians, they're not like this. She should be folding, begging him to tell her what to do. A gun should not act independent of its trigger.

"Don't you think we should talk about why you'd want to be socially isolated?"

She laughs—actually *laughs*—and says, "I was a different person then. Literally. People are like equations, doctor. They can always be revised."

There's a knock at the door. She turns her head, eyes brightening, before looking back to him and saying, "Last chance. Who sent you?"

"No one."

"Suit yourself." She stands. "I'll be back." Then she walks out of the dining room, out of his field of vision, leaving him alone and helpless to do anything but wait for her return.

Dodger thinks she should be nervous. The day has been an equation of inevitabilities, from her therapist's inexplicable attack to the phone call from her past self to the knock at her door. The reasons for the call are already becoming fuzzy when she doesn't focus on them: she remembers Roger calling from the future now, and with those memories intact, she'd have no reason to call herself from the past. Living in a paradox isn't exactly comfortable. She'll still take it over the alternative. Without the paradox, this would all play out very differently.

(She can't stop the feeling that it *has* played out differently at least once: maybe dozens of times. Dozens of iterations with no careful cosine to connect the halves of the equation, no judicious cheating to make sure she'd be prepared to continue. She'll take the discomfort of the paradox over the agony of that linear but imperfect world.)

The knock comes again, more urgent this time.

Dodger opens the door. Silence falls.

Roger has gotten another gawky inch or so taller, finishing his growth as second puberty had its way with him. He's still a rail of a man, skinny bordering on scrawny. His hair is too long to be neat and too short to be elegant; it falls scraggily in his face, making the circles around his pale, haunted eyes seem even deeper. He's wearing jeans and a T-shirt that look like they were pulled out of the laundry hamper, clutching a backpack to his chest.

Erin, on the other hand, is perfectly put together, strawberry hair pulled in a sleek ponytail and face scrubbed clean. She's wearing gray spandex and a plain hoodie; she looks like trouble about to start or an accident about to happen. Her backpack is smaller than Roger's, less tightly packed. It has the look of a bug-out bag, something that's been ready for a long time. She's not frowning, but there's a darkness in her eyes that speaks of bad times coming.

Dodger barely notices. It's all data to be filed away and dealt with later. Her attention is on Roger, the way he breathes (he's still smoking; she can see it in the slope of his shoulders), the way he stands, the way he's looking at her, like she's an impossibility. A paradox. The thought would be enough to make her smile any other time. But not now. Not now. This is an inherently unstable moment, and she can't help thinking that all this back-and-forth between past and present and future has been an effort to shore it up, to make it slightly less likely to collapse. A smile could be a step too far. So she just looks at him, grave and quiet and waiting.

Erin pushes past Roger, into the house. "Snap out of it and get your things," she says, voice brusque as ever. She doesn't seem to have changed since the earthquake: she's still vital and angry, shivering under her own skin, ready to explode. "I'll explain once we're on the road, but there are some very bad people looking for you, and they're going to be here any second."

"They already are," says Dodger, taking her eyes off her brother's face and turning to face the other woman. Erin looks nonplussed. That's a nice change. She was always dismayingly difficult to throw off her stride. Dodger continues, "My therapist broke into my house and tried to shoot me. I knocked him out with a toaster. He's tied to a chair in my dining room. Want to help me make him answer some questions?"

Erin's eyebrows raise. "Seriously?" she asks. "You didn't call the cops?"

"Oh, I called them."

Erin's eyebrows drop again, into the beginning of a glower.

"I told them there were kids setting off cherry bombs in the gully, which is a fire risk, and also a valid explanation for the gunshots. No one's coming for him."

This time, Erin's eyebrows rocket all the way to her hairline as she stares at Dodger in open-mouthed approval. "When did you get so vicious?" she asks.

"When people started trying to kill me." Dodger allows herself to look at Roger again. He looks confused but not afraid. As long as he's not scared, she doesn't have to be either. "I never gave up on you, you know. I was just waiting for you to be ready."

Roger steps into the room, covering the space between them in two steps, and when he reaches her, he takes her into his arms and holds her, so tight that there's no space left between them. She works her arms free and wraps them around him in turn, closing her eyes and burying her face into his shoulder. Her vision shifts to a higher perspective, showing her hallway in less-saturated colors, with more distinct dimensions. She laughs a little at that, but the sound struggles to turn into a sob, and so she stops. If she starts crying, she's not going to stop any time soon, and they can't afford that. Not right now.

"Fuck, Dodge, I missed you," says Roger.

She pulls away, opening her eyes. Her vision returns to its normal angles, its normal limitations. "Good," she says. "I'd hate to think I was the only one."

"This is a touching reunion, but maybe we should deal with the man you have tied to a chair," says Erin impatiently. "Where is he?"

"This way," says Dodger, waving for the others to follow her. She feels strangely serene. The omnipresent feeling of déjà vu is back, but weaker, like some foundational piece of the event has changed. In all the times they've been in this hall, on this day, she suspects this is the first time she's looked at Roger and been able to forgive him for leaving her the way he did. The version of her who couldn't let him back in is gone.

She should be angry about that, demanding to know what gave him the right to pick up a phone and change the equations that make her who she is, but all she feels is relief. She needs him for the math to work properly. Anything that revises him back into her life can't be wrong.

Erin follows by walking almost in step with Dodger, her whole frame vibrating with anger. Dodger glances in her direction, frowning.

"Have you been with Roger this whole time?" she asks.

Erin nods. "Someone had to be."

Dodger doesn't have an answer for that, and then they're stepping into the dining room, where Dr. Peters has been trying to free himself from the ropes. He hasn't succeeded. He hasn't even been able to knock his chair over. He turns to glare at the sound of footsteps, and stops when he sees Erin. Slowly, smugly, he begins to smile.

"Why, hello," he purrs. "I didn't know they were sending anyone to check up on me. Come to finish what I started?" He shifts his focus to Dodger. "Shouldn't have answered the door, Miss Cheswich. You would have been better off running while you had the chance."

"I think you're working off some bad assumptions, old sport," says Erin. She walks to the table, shrugging off her backpack. She opens the central pocket and removes a mummified hand. "I don't work for your employers anymore. You could say I've joined the other team."

Dr. Peters goes pale. "What are you saying?"

"I'm saying if they wanted to control the elemental forces of creation, they shouldn't have turned us into people. People have their own agendas. Mine doesn't match theirs anymore." Erin produces a lighter and begins lighting the fingers of her terrible candle, one by one. She looks over her shoulder to Roger and Dodger. "Go pack a bag. We're going to have to run soon, and I'd rather not hold your hand through this whole thing."

"What are you going to do to him?" asks Dodger.

"What you can't. If he knows anything I don't, he'll tell me. If he doesn't, he won't tell anyone else you got away. Take what you can't bear to lose. I'll burn this place before we leave."

Dodger blinks. "What?"

Roger's hand settles on her shoulder. She looks up at him, and he shakes his head. "I'll explain while Erin works," he says, voice thick with loathing and regret. "Let's get you packed."

"My room is this way," she says, and the two of them walk away, leaving Erin alone with Dr. Peters.

"*Dodger!*" Dr. Peters yells after her.

She doesn't turn around.

Dodger's room is large, spotless, barren: the only furniture is an island of bed and desk in the center of the floor, pressed together so she can roll over in the night and wake up her laptop, getting to work before her eyes are fully focused. The room is also claustrophobically small, thanks to the writing on the walls. The equations begin next to the door and cover every inch of available space. Most are plain dry-erase marker, but a few are scrawled in red, and others are surrounded by boxy outlines, isolating them.

Roger looks at the room and feels himself relax in the alien face of it all. "I guess some things never change, huh?" he says.

"I guess not," Dodger replies. "Are you planning to tell me what's going on, or am I supposed to pack a bag and trust you after seven years?" She may be a paradox walking, revised by her own hand, but she's still angry at him, under the forgiveness. That's almost a relief. She's changed some of her math; her core equations remain intact.

"Dodger . . ."

"I never gave up on you. I waited for you to call me. I waited for *seven years*. Do you have any idea what that's like? I almost started playing chess again, just so I'd have something to do with my time." Instead, she's written books, taught classes, traveled the world; tutored high school students who needed help with math, spoken to groups of girls hoping to go into STEM, done work for some of the biggest tech companies in the Valley. She's kept busy, because she's had to. As she glares at her brother, she knows she would have given it all up to spend those seven years on campus, arguing about whose night it was to pick the pizza place.

Roger looks at her for a long moment before he turns away and says, "I'm sorry. I couldn't deal with what we were when we were together."

"You mean the earthquake."

"I mean the earthquake." He pauses before he asks, "Don't you think we caused it?"

"I know we did." She shrugs. "I did some consulting with the USGS a few years ago. They wanted mathematical models of probable quakes in this region, and I had a new way of mapping faults that seemed like just the thing. They gave me access to all their data. That quake began directly underneath us and involved a fault that's never given way in that spot before. We created something we didn't understand, and it hurt a lot of people."

"It's our fault all those people died."

"No." Dodger sounds surprisingly serene. "It's the fault of the people who made us."

Roger stops for a moment before he asks, "What do you mean?"

"We're a government weapons program gone wrong, or some mad scientist's pet project, or *something,* because there's no way we happened naturally. We're too Midwich for that." Dodger looks at him levelly. "Someone made us. Someone made us, and then they separated us because we were dangerous when we were together."

He laughs. It's all he can think of to do. "How did you figure this out on your own? Erin had to tell me, and I'm still not sure I believe her."

"It helps that I spent part of today talking to myself from seven years ago, right after she spoke to you in the future," says Dodger. Roger stares and so she explains, telling him about the calls, telling him how the world rewrote itself to account for this new data. History is an equation. It can be changed under the right circumstances. It should be terrifying, but it's really just wonderful, because it means so many of their mistakes have been curated ones, deemed necessary by themselves in the future.

When she finishes, Roger sits heavily on her bed and says, "You'd better pack. Erin will be almost done with Dr. Peters by now, and she doesn't do patient well."

"Why is she part of this? Why is she *here*?"

"Because the people who made us made her too. She was assigned to keep an eye on us while we were at college. I think . . . I think she was supposed to make sure nothing like the earthquake happened." That's the charitable interpretation. The more probable one says she was supposed to *guarantee* the earthquake, because the earthquake was what had proved they were growing into their full potential. Without it, they would never have run away from each other, but without it, they wouldn't have needed to.

In a vague way, Roger is starting to realize that the earthquake, terrible tragedy that it was, probably saved their lives. Without it, they would have become experimentally uninteresting before graduation.

Dodger blinks. "That makes sense," she says finally. "Is she really going to burn my house down?"

"She burned ours down."

That's new data. Dodger blinks again before she asks, "Girlfriend?"

"Yeah. Since a couple months after the quake." His laugh is small and bitter. "I guess without you to be her roommate, she needed to find another way to maintain her cover."

"And they had Dr. Peters ready to start watching me," says Dodger. "You got a girlfriend, I got a therapist. I'm not sure who got the better deal."

"You did." The words are small, and absolutely final: they leave no room for discussion.

"She *really* burned your house down?"

"She did."

Dodger pauses, adding these facts to the data she already has before crossing to the closet and opening it. There's the rest of her things: she has two dressers in there, face to face, so that she can open one by flattening herself against the other. Clothes hang from the rack, and there are several bags shoved into the very back. She digs through them, finding a hiking backpack and tossing it out before she asks her next question: "Did she kill Smita?"

"Yes," he says. "The people who made us didn't like Smita digging in our DNA. I guess it could have . . . told her things they didn't want anyone to know. Not even us. Maybe especially not us. And there wasn't any other way to make her be quiet."

Dodger stops, her arms full of clothes pulled down from their hangers, and just looks at him. "She killed Smita and she's going to burn my house down and you're okay with this? You don't see a single thing wrong with the idea?"

"Your therapist tried to shoot you. I think that lends some credence to the idea that someone's out to get us, and Erin is trying to keep us alive." And he's called the past, and she's received calls from the future; time is malleable where they're concerned, unstitching itself one impossible idea at a time. "She says it was alchemists who made us, and that they've decided we're not necessary anymore."

"What?" Dodger stares at him. "Why?"

"Because you weren't the only pair they made from your template, and they have another one that's performing better," says Erin from the doorway, wearily. Both turn to face her. She's somehow managed to keep the blood from touching her clothing, but whatever strange technique she used wasn't enough to keep her hands clean. They're red from fingertips to palm.

She looks at them with calm resignation, and says, "I wish you'd stayed together. I hate explaining this shit. Dodger. You were designed in a lab by an alchemist who thought he could follow Asphodel Baker's instructions, harness the Doctrine of Ethos, and use it to control the universe if he put it into a pair of malleable human bodies. The earthquake was proof that the two of you *could* channel the Doctrine, and the separation was proof you *wouldn't*. So he's continued working with his other cuckoos, trying to find the ones who'd get him to the Impossible City and world domination. Now one of those pairs is ready to manifest the Doctrine fully, which means all the others have to die, to make absolutely sure that none of you are holding part of the Doctrine in abeyance and keeping it away from them."

Dodger frowns. "They're treating the Doctrine of Ethos as a single divisible whole, with the theory being that if we exist, we have part of it trapped, and it can't be unified?"

"Yes."

"And so they're planning to kill us."

"Yes."

"How do we make them stop?"

Erin looks at her gravely, and says, "You manifest first. I think they're wrong: I can see the universe falling into place around you, and when I see something, it's usually true. Like calls to like. The first pair to claim the Doctrine will call the rest of it home and have dominion over the entire thing. If you manifest, it belongs to you, and they won't be able to touch you."

Roger stands. "How do we do that?"

"See, that's the problem," says Erin. "I haven't the faintest idea."

# Glory

They leave by the light of an inferno, shielded by Erin's Hand of Glory. She washed the blood off her fingers before reaching for the matches, but the faint iron smell of it still surrounds her. She doesn't look back. Neither does Dodger, whose life has been reduced to a single pack slung across her shoulders, to two people who walk beside her. It's almost freeing, the knowledge that there's nothing to go back to. Even the laptop with all her research notes is gone, sacrificed to the blaze.

"I need to call my parents when we stop for gas," she says, once they reach the car (sensibly parked two blocks over, in case the house was under surveillance).

Erin shakes her head. "You can't. They have to believe you died in the fire."

Dodger feels her eyes widen. "But—"

"Your parents don't work for the alchemist who made you, Dodger. You were a legitimate adoption. That means they're vulnerable. If you make contact, they could wind up dealing with someone like me—someone who's acting on orders." There are worse things than Erin in Reed's bag of tricks. The thought of the Cheswiches meeting Leigh is chilling. She doesn't want Dodger to live with the knowledge that she was responsible for the death of her parents. That's already happened too many times. It's not necessary.

She doesn't think it's necessary.

She hopes it's not.

"Wait," says Roger. "Why did you phrase it like that? That she was a 'legitimate' adoption. What are you saying?"

"Only one of you was placed in a civilian household, and it's not safe for you to contact your parents either, but for a whole different set of reasons." Erin holds up her free hand. "Give me the car keys. The two of you need to catch up, and that'll be easier if you're not trying to pay attention to the road."

Roger and Dodger exchange a look, expressions unsure. Erin sighs.

"I wouldn't have saved your fucking lives if I was going to drive us off a cliff," she says. "But you need to get tangled up in each other the way you used to be—don't look at me like that, I was assigned to watch you, remember? I can tell when you're sharing one head instead of living in two. You're not supposed to be completely separate. I need you to manifest as fast as possible, and this is where it starts. With you, in the car, making it right."

"You keep using that word," says Dodger. "'Manifest.' What do you want us to *do*?"

Erin continues to hold out her hand for the keys. "I want you to do what every molecule of your bodies was designed to do. I want you to embody the Doctrine of Ethos. Once you do that, once you become the living force that holds the universe together, they won't be able to touch you. They might try, but it isn't going to matter, because you're going to be more than they can handle. If you don't manifest, that's it: this is the end of the line. They're going to figure out that I've turned, if they haven't figured it out already, and they're going to send someone else to clean up my mess. And if we defeat that person, they'll send another, and another, and the whole time, they'll be trying to force their new protégés to manifest the Doctrine. This is a race. Do you get that? This is a race, and if you lose, you die."

Roger and Dodger stare at her. Roger finds his voice first, asking, "Why didn't you tell me any of this? You've had *seven years* to tell me this."

"I love that we live in a world where that's the confusing part and not, I don't know, everything else," mutters Dodger.

Erin ignores her. "I didn't tell you because I didn't have to, and because I was hoping you'd decide to make things right with your sister in your own time, and because I didn't have any way to prove it. I could do the thing with the coins, but that's not proof; that's a parlor trick. The whole 'phone calls to the past' gimmick was a Hail Mary. I didn't know for sure that she was going to pick up until she did. Time is her thing, not yours."

"Wait, what?" asks Dodger.

"Time is math made manifest in the physical world," says Erin. "Time is your thing."

"What's mine?" asks Roger.

Erin's smile is more a grimace, baring all her teeth. "You got everything else, and you got her. Now will you give me the damn keys and get in the car? This Hand of Glory isn't going to last forever, and I don't have time to make another one. Once it runs out, we're going to be a beacon for anyone who's looking for reality distortion. I'd rather not be here when that happens."

The wax of the dead woman's hand has run down, taking her fingers with it; three of them are merely stumps, and one has guttered out completely. Her thumb still burns steadily, but it's only a matter of time before that runs down as well. As they watch, the flame on her pointer finger goes out.

"Here," says Roger, tossing Erin the keys.

She snatches them out of the air with a sarcastic "*Thank* you" and climbs into the driver's seat, setting her Hand of Glory in the passenger's place. Roger and Dodger exchange a look before getting into the back. She's right about one thing: they need to get tangled up in each other again, the way they used to be, the way they've been running away from since they were children.

Dodger waits until Erin starts the engine before asking, voice low, "Do you really think she's telling the truth?"

"I called you," says Roger. "I mean, I picked up the phone and called you before the earthquake happened. I called you in the *past*. I talked to you. I hadn't heard your voice in seven years, and I called you, and I talked to you."

"I think you also called me from an alternate timeline," says Dodger.

He looks at her blankly.

"It was the day of the earthquake. I was back at the apartment, trying to figure out how much could be saved and how much I was going to leave behind—I didn't know about Candace yet—when my phone rang, and it was you, from the future. But not *this* future, because this version of you wouldn't need to say the things that version of you said. When we touch the past, we change it. We revise ourselves. And it's not something we can take back. I can't refuse the changes you made when you called me from the future, even if I wanted to. Which I don't. I was on the verge of giving up on you until you told me not to."

She smiles beatifically, and Roger fights the urge to squirm. She got numbers: she got time. The one commonality in all the instances of phone calls across time is Dodger, and he knows without being told that he'd get nothing but dead air or a stranger's voice if he tried to call his childhood home and speak to his adolescent self. Time doesn't bend for him the way it does for her. *Reality* bends for him. When he asks for something, he usually gets it, because the world listens when given commands.

Time rewrites itself, but words are what trigger the transformations in people. It's a bigger responsibility than he could ever have asked for. "Erin, you keep saying you want us to manifest," he says, turning toward the front seat. "Is there any way to do the opposite? Is there a way for us to *refuse* the Doctrine, to just give it up and let them have it back?"

"You can die," she says. "Remember what I said earlier: if you make this choice, you're making it for both of you. You can't survive without each other. You're too tangled up inside."

Roger, remembering the seizures he experienced when Dodger attempted suicide, says nothing. Dodger, on the other hand, shakes her head.

"We can't give this up," she says. "Even if that were somehow an option—and I'm glad it's not—we *can't*. Who would you even be without the words, Roger? Who would *I* be, if you took my numbers away? I've needed sleeping pills for years, because my head's too empty. We're not supposed to be apart. She's right. And remember the earthquake."

Roger will never forget the earthquake. Part of him will be going through the earthquake forever.

"Do you want the sort of people who would send someone like Dr. Peters to kill me to have the sort of power that it took to make the earthquake?" Dodger's voice is earnest, accompanied by her hand, offered to him across the backseat. "They don't deserve what we have, and we don't deserve to die. We have to make this right."

"We have to try," Roger agrees, and puts his hand in hers, skin touching skin for the first time in so damn long. Their eyes widen in tandem before they collapse in their seats, bodies going limp, heads lolling to the sides.

Erin watches all this in the rearview mirror, waiting until she's sure they've lost consciousness before she rolls her eyes and guns the engine.

"Amateurs," she mutters, and drives on.

Everything is darkness and everything is light. There is a flash of pink in the distance, at the contradictory edge between the two states, and Roger knows that he is, at least on some level, sharing headspace with Dodger: his memory of the colors he can't normally distinguish from one another has been getting fuzzy as the years slipped by, the distinct shades beginning to blend together into something beautiful but indistinct.

"Roger?" Her voice is inside and outside his head at the same time, coming from far away and from so close that it's as much a part of him as his own skin. It's unnerving. It's so welcome that it's almost like a physical ache, a cruel reminder of how alone he's been these last seven years, even with Erin by his side.

"I'm here," he says.

"But where's 'here'?" Dodger sounds frustrated. "What happened? All I did was touch you—"

"After seven years of *not* touching me, when we were close enough to whatever it means to manifest that we nearly leveled Berkeley," he says. It's amazing how reasonable he can sound when he has someone else to worry about. Maybe that's the real reason there had to be two of them. So he'd always have someone else to worry about, and couldn't just run rampant, revising the world to his liking. "I think this is the Doctrine trying to force us back together."

"You think?"

"I don't know. How would I? This is as new to me as it is to you."

"Couldn't we be the living proof of Euler's identity? That seems a lot less dangerous."

"What's Euler's identity?"

"It's basically the prettiest equation in the world. It's the Helen of Troy of mathematical ideals." She sounds like she's getting closer as she speaks, like the math is drawing her to him. He doesn't interrupt, and she continues, almost dreamily, "It contains three of the basic arithmetic functions, it links five mathematical constants . . ."

He turns and there she is, standing behind him on this endless black-and-white plane. She blinks, and pink and red lines flare around the edge of the horizon. Wherever they are, they're sharing visual inputs. He can see the color of her hair, the shadings of the freckles on her cheeks, and when she smiles, he sees how pale she is. Nervousness has stolen much of her color, and even its absence is a revelation to him now. He smiles back, matching her anxiety with his own.

"See, I always knew we'd figure out how to find each other again," he says.

"But is it safe? A lot of people died last time, Roger. No matter what some weirdo mad scientist built us to be, we can't bring those people back. We can't change what we've done."

"You and I both know that's not true."

Dodger is quiet for a moment. Then, finally, she says, "Posit a time-line in flux."

"Done."

"If we can modify our pasts to change our futures, who's to say we haven't been doing it all along? That everything that's happened, good or bad, hasn't been changed because changing it would result in an even worse overall situation?" She catches her lower lip between her teeth, worries it for a moment, and finally says, "Erin says if either one of us dies, the other dies too."

"Yes."

"But you didn't call from the future and tell me not to kill myself. I didn't call from the future and tell me it was going to be okay, we were going to wind up in the same place for grad school, and you wouldn't be better off without me. What if . . . that's because we needed to *know* she was telling the truth? So neither of us would say 'forget this, you're on your own' and refuse to go? We're taking a lot on faith, but we're taking it partially because it matches what we already know. She isn't contradicting the existing numbers, she's adding to them by putting the equations we have into context. Conservatism bias writ large."

Roger frowns. "What's worse than that quake, Dodge? We killed so many people because we didn't know what we were doing. What could possibly be so bad that letting the quake stand is necessary?"

"Letting the sort of people who'd build biological weapons and put them out into the world to experiment with their powers have control of the fully manifest Doctrine of Ethos," says Dodger, and there's sudden steel in her tone, like she's figuring out the shape of the problem one function at a time. "According to Erin, we'll be stronger when we're manifest. Earthquakes will be *easy*. But we didn't mean to do it. We didn't mean to hurt those people. What happens if someone who doesn't care that much gets that sort of power? Anyone who would make us is not someone who can be trusted. The earthquake tells us that. The earthquake says 'this is horrible, now manifest, because otherwise, something even worse is going to happen.'"

Roger is silent. Dodger stays where she is, waiting. She's the cold one: she's the one who can reduce everything to numbers, weighing lives now against lives later. It's not a part of herself that she's proud of or has ever truly embraced. Here, now, it's the most important thing she can be.

"Isn't there a way we could make it not happen?" he asks finally.

"I think we have to see the whole equation before we can decide," she says. "We're not there yet. We're in the middle of the problem. If we get to the end, if we manifest, maybe we can revise more than we can right now."

And maybe they can't. She doesn't say that part, but Roger hears it anyway: it's implicit in the pause between her sentences, sculpted out of silence and hesitation. He doesn't want to hear it. The unspoken pieces of language are sometimes the most painful.

"How many people have to die for us?" he asks. "How can we pretend to be important enough to be worth that?"

"How many more would die if we took ourselves out of the equation and let someone else have this sort of power?" she counters. "I know you're a good person. I hope I'm a good person. We won't break things for fun, or because someone tells us to. We're not perfect. We're the best choice I can see."

Roger sighs. It only takes one step to close the distance between them, one step before his arms are around her and his face is against her shoulder. She holds him tight, and they are matched in both placement and position, two halves of the same platonically ideal whole. They should never have been separated; they had to be apart, or they would never have been able to become individuals, would never have learnt how to span the missing places in their own souls.

"All right," says Roger. "We'll do it."

They continue holding each other, eyes closed, until the shared mindscape fades away, and they are only two bodies in the back of a car, tangled together like a thorn briar, impossible to separate, dangerous to touch.

Erin, in the front seat, smiles and keeps on driving.

# War

I understand," says Leigh. "Comb the ashes: look for anything that tells us where they're going. If you find Erin's body, contact me. We need to know what we're up against."

She hangs up the phone before Professor Vernon can object. The man is old, almost used up, still trying to earn his share of the Philosopher's Stone: he's an excellent mathematician and was instrumental in their figuring out the necessary invocations to embody the Doctrine of Ethos, but he's never been a good alchemist. Without the aid of Reed and his clever connections, Vernon would have given up the discipline entirely. No big loss. He's unlikely to survive any confrontation with the cuckoos, and that's fine too, as far as Leigh's concerned. One less mouth to feed in the new world can only be a good thing.

Her skin feels like it's on fire as she leaves her lab, walking fast, hands balled by her sides. Most of the rooms she passes are empty, their subjects long since flown. She's taken a few of them apart herself, using their blood and organs in alchemical tinctures that have taught them a great deal about the universe. The subjects would probably think it was an unfair exchange, but that's why none of them have ever been given a vote.

Reed stopped actively pursuing anything apart from the Doctrine years ago. The other manifest forces are too easy to create and refine. Other alchemists have snatched some of them up, pinning them in place; others have been able to manifest on their own, with no alchemy involved. Only the Doctrine has defied him, and so only the Doctrine matters: it is the alkahest, the universal solvent that dissolves everything else and allows the universe to be remade.

Leigh's footsteps echo in shadowed halls, and the few who walk here this close to the plan's fruition scurry to avoid her wrath. She is the monster in their midst, and not one of them wants to face her when she walks with such purpose, such anger, such intent.

Reed is in the observation lounge, standing in front of a wide glass window looking in on a room containing two teens. The male is balled on their shared bunk, his arms gripping his knees, his face hidden from view. The female sits beside him, one arm draped protectively around his shoulders, glaring at everything around her like she could make it all go away through sheer force of anger. His hair is dark blond, like wheat; hers is almost white, almost green, the color of fresh cornsilk in the light.

"It's fascinating, isn't it," says Reed, without turning, "how their natures change the activation of their genes? The math children are always so much more strikingly colored than their fellows. I think it's because they can handle more damage without compromising the Doctrine. It's protecting itself, in them, by making sure people will aim first for the math children. The language children can always order them to change things, as long as they're breathing long enough to do it. Anyone aiming at these two will shoot her first, every time."

"We've lost Cheswich and Middleton," says Leigh.

Reed goes still.

"Erin was instructed to terminate the male; the shock of losing him should have killed the female, but just in case, we dispatched Peters to her location. Both cuckoos are missing. Both their homes burnt down—a favorite tactic of Erin's, if you recall. One body was found, in the female's home. Peters. Either Erin has switched sides, or they've managed to subdue her."

Reed turns. Still he says nothing. Leigh looks at him with bland fearlessness. He can see the anger in her eyes.

"It's possible the male is closer to manifestation than expected and was able to talk Erin around into working with him," says Leigh. "If that's the case, his influence will wear off at some point, and she'll finish her job. He doesn't know what he can do. There's no way he's given her instructions that would compel her loyalty on a permanent basis. It simply wouldn't occur to him at this stage in his development."

"And if he has?"

"Then he has her, and we'll never get her back." It doesn't matter at this point. If they did get her back, if they did have her loyalty returned to them, Leigh would still take pleasure in taking her apart. An agent compromised is no longer an agent who can be relied upon, no matter how well that agent may have performed in the past. As an avatar of Order whose Chaos has long since been recycled for parts and knowledge, Erin has been living on borrowed time for years. Her debts are finally coming due.

"I see." Reed straightens, seeming to grow tall and terrible in the light coming through the two-way mirror. He has always been tall; he has always been terrible. He is simply putting the masks aside. "What are you going to do about this, Leigh?"

"Me?" Her eyes narrow. "This was your project. This has *always* been your project. You're the one who wouldn't let me terminate them when they got entangled, the one who said I couldn't send someone to collect them and get them safely under lock and key. You're the one who's defended this pair of flawed avatars every step of the way. Why am I the one who has to clean up your mess?"

"Because *I'm* the one who's going to make us immortal," he says, gesturing toward the window, toward the tired and trembling teens on the other side. "*That* is our future. *That* is absolute control of the forces that bind this universe. I need to prepare them for what they're going to become. I need to anoint and uplift them, and you need to remove the competition from their path. Take whatever you need. Men, weapons, anything. Go to California. Fix this."

Leigh looks at him in silence for a count of ten, eyes narrowed, assessing. In her breast, the ghostly wings of the carrion birds that were used to stitch her wounded flesh back to life beat against her ribs. Finally, she says, "You're still following a dead woman's blueprint. Haven't you ever wondered what you could have become if you'd broken free of Asphodel's design?"

"It became my design when I killed her."

Did it? She wants to ask the questions he has forbidden, questions of purpose and motivation and reason, questions of how much of this has been his own idea and how much of it has been Asphodel Baker mapping her own path down the improbable road. Can a dead woman claim the Impossible City?

Perhaps soon, they'll know. "I can't guarantee any of them will survive the recovery," she says. "Killing half a pair kills the other in all but the most extreme cases, and I'm not what you send into the field when you want something done subtly."

"I'm aware."

"Then I'm gone. Just remember, when you turn on the evening news, that this was what you asked for." Leigh turns on her heel and walks away, not looking back. She doesn't want him to see the color rising in her cheeks, or her growing excitement at the idea of being released from the lab that has been her home and her prison for so very long.

She's an experiment too. And like any experiment, she wants to be free.

Reed watches her go before turning to the window. On the other side, the boy is crying again, and the girl with the almost green hair is trying to comfort him, still glaring daggers at everything around her, as if she could protect him through the sheer application of her hatred.

"You're going to change the world for me," he says.

In the silence that comes after his words, he thinks he can smell Asphodel's perfume.

# Science

Roger wakes first. For a horrifying moment, he doesn't know who he is. His body fits wrong. The moment passes, and then he doesn't know *where* he is. There's a woman in his arms, too tall and lanky to be Erin, who has always been a compact, comforting weight when she curls against him. He realizes the light is coming from all around him as the landscape slides by outside the car windows, and that the woman clinging to his side has red hair. Dodger.

He pauses. Blinks. And in a slightly strangled voice, asks, "Why am I seeing colors?"

"You are? That's good news." Erin doesn't sound like she thinks it's good news. Erin sounds grim, like the world has been canceled while she drove. "How many colors you don't normally see are you seeing right now?"

"Red. Um. Purple, pink . . ." Roger swings his head wildly around, looking at everything. "Lots. All? Lots." They're faded around the edges, like whatever's allowing him to see them isn't fully integrated with his senses yet. "What's going on?"

"You're starting to re-entangle, is what's going on. See if you can get Dodger off you. Don't push her out of the car, just stop touching her."

"What?"

"She's touching you. See if you can make her stop." Erin's gaze flicks to the rearview mirror, regarding him with black amusement. "You're good at letting go. Do it again."

Roger gapes at her, the woman he thought he loved, the woman he thought loved him. Then, with exquisite care, he turns to the sister he hasn't seen in years and begins prying her off his arm.

It's hard. Dodger has an incredibly strong grip for someone who's never done a day's physical labor, and he doesn't want to wake her; he can't shake her or pull for fear that it will put her over the edge and open her eyes. He's not ready for that. When he was running from a burning home and into her presence, everything was moving too fast for him to stop and consider what he was doing. Now he's here, and she's here, and he doesn't know how to talk to her. If she wakes up, he'll have to figure it out. The awkwardness between them will pass—if nothing else, Erin's still driving like she expects to be attacked at any moment, and somewhere between her producing Smita's severed, mummified hand and her setting the house on fire, he's stopped doubting her—but right now, awkwardness still reigns.

Finally, he manages to get untangled from Dodger's grasp. The new colors fade out of the world. Not all at once: no switch has been flipped, no filter has been removed. They just . . . fade, like someone is adjusting the balance on reality.

"The red's gone," he says, resisting the urge to lean over and take Dodger's hand, to see if the color comes back. Everything seems gray without it, sapped of meaning and potency. He's been without color for most of his life, and now it feels like he can't live without it for another moment.

"That's because you're not fully manifest. When you are, you probably won't even need to be touching to see things the way she does—or vice versa. She'll get depth perception, you'll get color, it'll be a wonderland for everybody." Erin's voice has gone bitter.

"Erin? What's wrong?"

She laughs brutally. "Everything. You get her back, okay? Be grateful for that. My other half is gone forever, and what he gave me, he took with him when he went."

"What . . ."

"I'm the living manifestation of Order, Roger. I see chaos everywhere I look. If it's out of place, if it doesn't belong, that's all I can see. I live in a world that can never be harmonious, because the only person who could describe actual order to me is gone." Erin's fingers drum a hard staccato on the steering wheel. "Wake her up. We need to figure out our next move, and she's a part of that."

"Why—"

"Just do it. We don't have much time."

He could argue. He could try to make her explain. But she'd have to explain again after Dodger was awake, and he doesn't *want* to talk to her without his sister to act as a buffer between them. Part of him still insists on looking at her as the woman he's loved for the last seven years. No amount of telling himself it was never real is going to make the adjustment any faster.

He'll probably hate her when this is over. He wishes the thought weren't such a relief.

He turns to Dodger, putting a hand on her shoulder (red rushes back into the world, *red*; he can't resist stealing a quick glance at Erin, seeing the strawberry color of her hair for the first time in years, and wishing he didn't find it quite so beautiful) and shaking gently.

"Hey," he says. "Dodge. Wake up. You've been asleep long enough."

She makes a small mumbling noise and slaps at his hand.

Roger smiles. So much has changed, about both of them. After seven years, he figures it will take a while before he feels like he knows her. But this, at least, has stayed the same. On the rare occasions when she slows down enough for sleep to catch her, she *hates* waking up. He shakes again.

"Wake up," he says. "We need to let my terrifying ex-girlfriend tell us how we're supposed to manifest a primal force of reality before asshole alchemists set us the fuck on fire."

As a sentence, it shouldn't make any sense. It does, though: he's proud of that.

Dodger opens her eyes. "What," she says flatly.

"*There* you are!" He shouldn't be smiling. This isn't the situation for smiling. He can't help himself, because she's awake, she's here, and they're talking again. They're *together* again. They can figure everything out from here. "Erin, she's awake."

"Fine and dandy," says Erin. She looks at the rearview mirror, studying the cuckoos in her backseat. Dodger is groggy and disoriented; Roger is smiling like his entire world hasn't just been turned on its head. She suspects that's a sign of shock. None of this is real for him yet. "Dodger, where are we going?"

"What?"

"We're on the improbable road, and you're the one with the head full of numbers and the compass where your heart ought to be. Where are we going? If you give me directions, I'll follow them."

Roger sits up straighter, suddenly remembering a long-ago night in the fog. One second it's not there; the next it is, flooding his mind in living color. "You called me Jack Daw."

"So you remember now. I don't know whether that's good or bad, but I guess we're going to live with it either way. I called you Jackdaw because that's *what* you are, and Jack Daw because that's *who* you are, or who you'll become. She"—a nod toward Dodger in the mirror—"is a Crow Girl, but she can mature into a Rook if you help her. If the Page of Frozen Waters isn't already on her way here, she will be soon."

"What's with all the Up-and-Under imagery?" asks Dodger. "We're not six. You don't need to turn things into a children's book."

"Ah, but see, the Up-and-Under was never about the children. It was always about the symbols, and you both got them, all the way down to your bones. Bones the Page would very much like to get her hands on, by the way. She'll fold them into herself without a moment's hesitation, and come away even harder to destroy." Erin pulls the car onto the shoulder of the freeway, putting on her hazard lights before she twists to face them. "You don't want to be out in the open when she gets here, kids. She doesn't play fair."

Dodger looks at her dubiously as she wipes her eyes, like the motion could somehow chase the fog of sleep away. Then she stops, blinking at her hands. Slowly, she brings them closer to her face before pulling them farther away. "Whoa."

"Depth perception: gotta love it," says Erin. "Asphodel Baker was the greatest alchemist of her age."

Dodger lowers her hands. "What," she says. There's no question there: the word lacks emphasis, intonation, anything but a flat drop into the world.

"She brewed miracles. She found ways to use electricity and modern methods to speed the production of gold and alkahest—she even perfected the elixir of life. She thought alchemy would bring about a paradise on earth, a world where no one would need to work, or age, or die. Everything about life would be a choice, not a predestination. A remarkable amount of her work lapsed into animism, which she thought was a vital part of the alchemical art, one that had been ignored for too long. She pointed to the existence of natural incarnate forces—Winter, Summer, the Sun and Moon, all those notable assholes—as proof that anything could be embodied, if the alchemist working the process wanted it badly enough."

"Natural incarnate forces?" asks Roger.

"What," says Dodger again, still flat, still not asking any questions: she's protesting something unfair and untrue, and her eyes on Erin are like knives, utterly unwilling to forgive.

Erin sighs. "We don't have time for this. I need directions."

"I'm not giving them to you until you start making sense," snaps Dodger.

"Roger, tell her to give me the directions." Erin switches her attention to him. "This isn't the time for childish tantrums."

"Sounds like you're about to have one." Roger folds his arms. "Keep going."

This time, Erin's sigh is deeply aggravated. "Baker spent some time trying to bring other American alchemists around to her way of thinking. She wanted them to stop warring with each other and guarding their secrets; she thought if they worked together, they'd be able to gain more ground and uncover more of the secrets of the universe. They saw this as a bid for power, since she was—at the time—the only one of them to have harnessed electricity to her whims. They were sexists and traditionalists, and they joined ranks against her. They began poaching or assassinating her students, to keep her ways of thinking from gaining too much credence with the masses. In the end, desperate, she began encoding her teachings in fiction, hiding them in plain sight."

"The Up-and-Under books are secretly alchemy primers?" asks Dodger.

Erin nods. "They were intended to show the enlightened mind the way to expand its reach and grasp. The Oz books are similar. Baum was trying to suppress Baker with his own alchemical wonderland. He succeeded—his readership was wider—but he also failed."

Dodger stares at her for a moment before reaching for the handle on her door. "Okay, that's it," she says. "I'm out. If you'll both excuse me, I need to go explain to my insurance adjusters how my house spontaneously caught fire, and why it wasn't arson."

"James Reed was Baker's final creation and only surviving apprentice. James Reed is, in an alchemical sense, your father. He used his own blood and Asphodel's bones and the body of a living woman, and he crafted you to be his tools in the world to come."

Dodger stops mid-reach.

"Reed killed his maker, but not before she finished her masterpiece. All the rules of alchemy, all the trials of the student, the process of purification and reconstitution of the universe into whatever form you chose, she preserved them in her books. And in her notes, of course. All the things she hadn't had time to encode. Reed took those notes and continued where his master had left off. But where Baker dreamt of a world that would belong to all—an Up-and-Under, a paradise, a fairy country where no one would grow old, or get sick, or die—Reed dreamt of power. Of *control*. That's why he's been working for so long to force the Doctrine into flesh. It's such a big concept, such a big part of the universe, that it didn't want to come quietly. It didn't want to come at all. He needed help. He recruited other alchemists, some through flattery, some through force. He let them work at embodying lesser ideals, to give him more and more control over the world. He's killed and lied and stolen. You're not the first of your flesh. He's set Jackdaws and Crow Girls on this road before, let them get almost as far as you have, and then he's had them killed, for one reason or another. They've all been imperfect. *You're* imperfect. You entangled too early, and you didn't develop exactly along the lines he had set for you. He wants you dead. He's said so, in as many words, because your successors are ready to take the iron shoes and rainbow ribbons and wish you right the fuck out of the Up-and-Under. I don't know how many ways I can say this. You leave, you die. You stay with me, you listen, maybe you live. Probably not. I don't think the odds are ever going to be in our favor. But at least with me, you get a maybe."

"What does any of this have to do with the Up-and-Under?" asks Roger.

Erin groans. "Oh, God, I should have found a way to start teaching you this crap years ago. Look: when Baker created the Up-and-Under, she split it into four countries, representing the four stages of the alchemical path—novice, apprentice, journeyman, and master. Hyacinth, Meadowsweet, Aster, and Crocus. More accurately, Water, Earth, Fire, and Air. They match the four Humors that control the body, and the four Temperaments that determine everything we do. For a while, this whole damn country matched her map, because she had that much power. She embodied part of the Doctrine in *herself* through sheer sympathy with its existence, and she got to set the definitions. When her rivals attacked her, that embodiment was the first thing they sought to undermine. They couldn't undo it completely, not with the number of children who read and believed in her stories, but they were able to break some of the fundamental laws she'd tried to impose on the world. That's where Baum came in. *His* fictional countries changed the orientations. Reversed them, cast them into alchemical flux and moved them into sympathy with Oz. The alignments have been switching uncontrollably ever since."

"Meaning what?" asks Roger.

"Meaning we don't know whether we're currently in the master's territory of Fire and the Choleric, or the novice's territory of Water and the Phlegmatic. And that makes all the difference in the goddamn world if we're trying to beat a hundred-year-old alchemist at his own game!" Erin's cheeks are flushed and her eyes are overly bright.

Roger and Dodger stare at her, united in their dismay. Finally, Dodger asks, "Why should we believe you?"

"Aren't you the one who said she talked to her own past?" counters Erin. "You should believe me because if I'm lying, you're losing your mind. That's a genuine concern of yours, isn't it? Little number girl who's never been able to figure out how humans work, who hears the voice of her brother in her head when she's scared or lonely. Are you even sure he exists? Maybe he's something you made up."

For the first time, Dodger looks alarmed. "Of course he's real. He's right here."

"So am I, but you seem awfully eager to dismiss everything I'm saying, even though it answers the questions you've been asking your entire life," says Erin. "Baker was an alchemist. Reed follows her teachings, in a twisted way. You're the product of an alchemist's desire to control reality, and while I realize this is a lot to dump on you all at once, all you have to do is think about what I'm saying and you'll understand how true it is. It's a single equation that explains your entire life. If you don't want to accept it, there's not much I can do for you."

Dodger stares at her. Erin glares back.

Dodger is the first to look away.

"If we're going to fight them—and we're *going* to fight them; we don't have a choice, unless the two of you want to roll over, show your bellies, and die the sort of death I wouldn't wish on a dog—we need to figure out whether we're in Hyacinth or Crocus. There isn't time to get to one of the stable countries, and the Impossible City is out of the question."

"Why?" asks Roger.

The look Erin gives him is one he remembers all too well from his childhood, when adults accustomed to dealing with a smart kid would be disappointed by his occasional flashes of childish ignorance, like the word "prodigy" was supposed to have been somehow accompanied by a direct download of the encyclopedia into his brain. His cheeks flare with the ghosts of old embarrassments.

"The Impossible City is Reed's territory, even if he's never been inside; he controls the walls," she says, words slow and careful. "We're not ready to take it yet. Maybe we never will be. They say you're going to manifest if you're not stopped, and I'm banking on that, but that doesn't mean I know what it means. No one does. Maybe you'll just become too troublesome to kill, without actually having the power it would take to stop the greatest alchemist of his age. You could be the new Stormcrows, living in exile while you wait for the King of Cups to weaken enough for you to take him down. There's only one way to find out, so if we could stop fucking around and get moving, I'd be awfully grateful."

"What do we have to do?" asks Roger. He can see that Dodger will be a while in coping with this information. It's all words, all piled on top of each other: there's no clear equation for her to complete. This is on him.

Erin shakes her head. "We need to hide. We need to figure out where we're going. We need to get there. You need to manifest, and you need to do it fast."

"You keep saying that but not saying what it *means*. What do you want us to do?"

"I think the closest you've come to manifestation was the earthquake. God, the earthquake." Erin looks wistful as she focuses on Roger, like she's thinking about good cake or better sex. "I knew it was coming because it's happened before. There was so much scar tissue around that moment that the air was like molasses. If you'd kept going, if you'd continued to tell her what to do and she'd continued to feed back the numbers . . . you could have manifested right then and there. I still don't know why you never do."

"You can feel the timeline changes?" Dodger shoves her way back into the conversation—literally. She plants one hand on Roger's chest, pushing him aside to get closer to Erin. "How? Why? I can't feel them."

Roger says nothing. He's too busy staring at the world around him, at the colors that intensified by a factor of ten as soon as she touched him. So many words make sense when things look like this. Color is a kind of magic. He hopes people who have it understand that, and don't take it for granted.

"Of course not. You cause them." Erin looks levelly at Dodger. "Every time the timeline has changed, it's been because your brother told you to make the old world go away. You're a thermonuclear device on two legs. You're the flash flood that sweeps people into the Up-and-Under. But him? He's your trigger. You can't do most of the things you're capable of without someone to set you off."

Dodger blinks, taken aback. "That's a little misogynistic."

"Reed didn't pick which of you got which half of the Doctrine: you did that yourselves, while you were incubating. Don't ask me how fetuses pick anything. You were little science projects with the same genes, only one chromosome apart, and you decided how those genes would manifest. Firstborn gets language, second gets math. Second also gets all the recessives turned on, because the math kids are the expendable ones: they get to be targets all their lives. As long as there's breath in a math kid's body, the language kids can order them to reset the timeline to a point before shit got bad. Of the pairs I know of, it was split about fifty-fifty which kid got language and which got math." Erin never met any of the other incarnate Doctrines: they were given into the care of other handlers, when they were allowed outside the confines of the lab in the first place. She's grateful for that, in an abstract sort of way. Just this once, in her entire life, she's pulled the good card. She got the pair who might make it out alive.

"I think I've seen this movie," says Roger. "I make a lousy Aladdin."

"Oh, you've got your share of party tricks. When you're fully manifest, no one will be able to go against you. If you ask for something, you'll get it. You could rule the world if you wanted to. That's part of why it was so important that I stay with you, guide you toward academia, let you embrace your love of dead languages and not being an asshole. I didn't switch sides just to replace the old bastard with a new bastard."

Both of them are gaping at her now.

"I know this is a lot."

"You *think*?" demands Dodger.

"I know it's hard to take in."

Roger snorts.

"But we're out of time. We need to hide, and we need to figure out our next move, and the two of you need to decide whether you're going to believe me, or whether you're going to die. Choose, because you're not getting a third option."

Roger and Dodger exchange a look. It's still uneasy, the space they make between them, packed with the ghosts of seven years and the shaking of the ground beneath their feet. Dodger finally appears to realize that she's touching him; she yelps and pulls away, back to her half of the backseat. Some wounds don't heal in an instant. Some wounds don't heal at all.

Erin hopes this one isn't that kind of wound. If it is, they're all doomed. She twists back around, puts the car back into gear, and pulls off the shoulder. "Tell me where to go."

"Uh," says Dodger. "Left?"

"Roger? Activate her." This is it: this is the real test of how much attention they've been paying, how willing they are to follow her under the undertow and into the Up-and-Under. She's no Niamh, no daughter of the sea, but she's the best guide they're going to get, and she's betting more than they can know on what's about to happen.

"Don't you dare," says Dodger.

"I'm sorry," says Roger. He sounds like he genuinely means it, which makes it worse, somehow, when he continues: "Dodger, tell us where to go."

The air in the car changes, becoming thick and electric. It's like the charge they made between them when they summoned the earthquake, but subtly different: it's brighter, cleaner, more aware of itself. Dodger sits up straight, eyes going wide and glassy for a count of ten. Roger isn't even sure she's breathing. She looks like she's somewhere else, somewhere better.

When she blinks, crashing back into the present, he feels almost bad for her. Then she shoots a glare in his direction, poisonously mad, and his feelings shift into an odd mixture of self-pity and guilt. He didn't know it would work. He hadn't been *sure*. How can she blame him when he wasn't *sure*?

"Dodge—" he begins.

She cuts him off. "Take the next exit, and turn left at the bottom of the off-ramp," she says. "We need to leave the car."

Erin smiles to herself and hits the gas.

They leave the car in a Fremont Park-and-Ride, stuffing bills into the machine until it produces a parking ticket good for twenty-four hours. Dodger snatches it from Erin's hand, darting off into the maze of vehicles and returning a few minutes later with a different ticket clutched in her hand. This one is good for only eight hours. She sticks it to the windshield, glancing at Erin and saying, "Anyone who looks at this car will think it's been here for more than half the day already. It can't be how we got here."

She's not just describing physical concepts anymore, although she may not realize that: she's in shock. They both are. This is the sort of thing that should be presented gradually, a little bit at a time, easing the subjects into their new reality. Instead, Erin has shoved them into the deep end of the pool and is counting on them to figure out how to swim.

And they are. Dodger is right about the tag, about the car. There are ways for someone like Leigh to track them to this parking lot, even after they leave the vehicle behind. The Hand of Glory guttered out somewhere on the freeway, leaving them visible to both mundane and metaphysical surveillance. They're going to be found. But when Leigh gets here, she'll find a trail that's been cold for sixteen hours, because all that time has been shunted somewhere else. All that time has been *moved*.

Dodger doesn't know what she's doing. That isn't going to stop her from doing it. Once they get moving, the children of the improbable road act on instinct, and their instincts are rarely wrong.

"All right," says Erin. "Let's go. We need to figure out where we are, and then we need to get wherever it is we're going."

They're in Fremont, California, in the San Francisco Bay Area; all of them know that, and all of them know it doesn't matter. Where they really are is the Up-and-Under, and in the Up-and-Under, sometimes the hardest thing to find is the road that takes you home.

The woman was impossibly beautiful. She looked like sunshine on a Saturday, like chocolate cake and afternoons with no homework. She had a smile like a mother's praise, all sugar and softness, and Zib stared at her, wanting nothing more than to throw herself into those welcoming, unfamiliar arms.

*If you trust her, you'll never get home,* whispered a voice in the back of her mind, a voice that sounded so much like the Crow Girl that Zib nearly looked over her shoulder to see if she'd been followed. That was silly. The Crow Girl was with Avery, looking for a lock to fit their skeleton key. Avery couldn't be left alone. He was delicate.

Zib had never been allowed to be delicate. From the day she was born, she had been told to be tough, to be bold, to pick herself up and dust herself off and keep running. Sometimes she wondered what it was like, to be allowed to fall down and stay fallen.

"Hello, little girl," said the incredible woman. "What's your name?"

"Zib," said Zib.

"They call me the Queen of Swords. I would very much like to be your friend . . ."

—From *Over the Woodward Wall,* by A. Deborah Baker

# Up-and-Under

Forgive me, my children, but I will never know you.
—A. Deborah Baker

I became insane, with long intervals of horrible sanity.
—Edgar Allen Poe

# Coal Dust

Midnight greets Leigh Barrow as she steps off the plane and onto Californian earth for the first time. (But not for the first time, never for the first time; there are so few first times for someone like her, a mosaic, a palimpsest of a woman; there are too many souls woven into the depths of her. Somewhere deep, a woman she once was rolls over and cries in restless slumber, remembering the scent of eucalyptus on the wind, the taste of sea air, the cries of the gulls that flew, white-winged and bright, above the California coast.)

She shivers away the feeling of the ghosts at her foundation stirring and strides toward the car sent to do her bidding. The man behind the wheel is an alchemist, a student of Reed's art who realized long ago that his survival would be more certain if he was well outside his master's ever-questing grasp. The other man, the one who opens the door for her without a word, is a construct, mud and frogs and clever science. Leigh spares a smile for him, poisonous and sweet.

"How long ago did you make him?" she asks, once she's settled in the backseat, belt buckled across her waist, pistol resting in her lap.

On the tarmac, the private jet which brought her here is taxiing away, heading toward the hangar where it will wait for her return.

"Six years, ma'am."

"Clay, native amphibians, and . . . ?"

"Railway iron, ma'am. Stolen from the tracks. I had to trade any chance of speech for the additional resilience, but you could hit him with a bus and he wouldn't notice."

"Hmmm," says Leigh speculatively. The massive construct gets into the front passenger seat, not bothering with his own seatbelt; it wouldn't stretch across the barreled expanse of his chest. "We'll have to see about that."

The alchemist behind the wheel goes as silent as his construct. No one who works with or for James Reed doesn't know about Leigh Barrow: where he found her, what she is. For a manikin to outlive their creator . . . it requires an immense amount of power.

"Have you found them?" The question is asked lightly, almost sweetly. In that moment, Leigh could have been anyone, harmless and looking for her friends.

"No, ma'am," he says.

"Why not?" The moment has passed. Her voice is a promise of pain unavoidable, and his hands clench on the wheel.

He knew when Reed called that he probably wouldn't survive the night. He had no way to refuse. Until this moment, he was still holding on to hope. Hope is gone now; hope has fled.

"They left their car. I can take you there."

"Do that," she says, leaning back in the seat. "And drive quickly. I'm not feeling patient tonight."

"Yes, ma'am. Clyde?"

The construct opens the glove compartment and withdraws a Hand of Glory. This one is very small. The owner, when living, couldn't have been more than six years old. Leigh doesn't comment. The refusal of some people to use Hands of Glory made from children has never made sense to her; a murdered child will not magically be un-murdered if you refuse to exploit the resources they've left behind.

Meat is meat. Meat exists to be used, and anyone who thinks differently is deluding themselves about their place in the world.

The construct lights the Hand. The car fills with the sweet smell of wax and burning flesh. Leigh breathes deeply, and the nameless alchemist hits the gas, accelerating beyond the speed limit, hidden from the watchful eyes of the police, as he drives toward the illusion of salvation.

It takes less than thirty minutes to travel between the private airfield and the lot where Erin's car is hidden. Leigh steps onto the sidewalk and looks dismissively around. This is a small town aspiring to become a city, still connected to the people who forged it; they no doubt remember the names of their founders, celebrating them every year, as if creating a settlement were something special and unique, and not the human urge to propagate writ large. Better to celebrate the people who came after the sweet rush of newness, the ones who fought their way through floods and famine to build a functioning municipality, an infrastructure worth sustaining. Better to support the ones who fought and died in the name of something that would never be theirs, would always belong to some sainted, long-dead founder.

The Up-and-Under belongs to the Averys and Hepzibahs, but it's the Queens of Wands who will be remembered. It's not fair. That's how it goes.

Leigh walks away without looking back; doesn't see the still-nameless alchemist heave a sigh of relief. He's a boy who imagines himself a man. He'll be dead before morning. She knows herself and knows what this search will require in the way of alchemy, of science, of murder. His heart will fuel a tracking tincture, his hands form the cloaking devices to keep her from being seen. He is, at his core, expendable, and she doesn't have the time or energy to spare in making him aware of that fact. Instead, she walks, steps quick and fleet as a hunting hound's, nose turned to the wind, looking for traces of alchemy. Like speaks to like, and Leigh Barrow is a woman made of many women, bone and feather and soil. She can no more overlook the signs of a working than she can grow wings and fly, the crow beating in her breast notwithstanding. She weaves between the cars, and she never stops, and she never looks back.

The air cools as she approaches a green Honda. She steps closer, and the scent of wax caresses her nostrils, identifying her target. That doesn't explain the coolness: the coolness is something she's never felt before. It's as if the behavior of the air has changed, the molecules slowing down, losing some of their excitement.

The doors are locked. That's never been a problem for her. One quick application of her elbow later, the window is shattered and she's letting herself into the car, where the air is even colder. A great working has happened here, a working she doesn't know or recognize. The thought is chilling in a way the air is not. If they're beginning to manifest, if that *bitch* Erin has found a way to coax them toward their destiny . . .

(Will they be tame creatures, under her control? Will Erin find a way to reduce phoenixes to firebirds, turning burning things into something manageable, something that wants to be commanded? Or will they blaze out of proportion to the fuel available, igniting and destroying the world? Leigh won't lie, not even to herself: the thought is beguiling, attractive in a way almost strong enough to overcome her lingering loyalty to the man who holds her reins.)

She shakes herself as brutally as a hound shakes a rat, chasing the too-tempting, too-terrible thought away, and bends to pluck the discarded Hand of Glory from the footwell. The wax is still soft and malleable; the fire can't have burnt down more than a few hours ago. Reaching into her pocket, she produces a handful of coal dust streaked with glints of silver. The coal came from a mine where a disaster claimed the life of over a hundred men; the silver, melted down from the jewelry of a woman whose husband had choked the life from her body before bedding his mistress in her marital bed. It's a subtle, complex thing, is alchemy. Reed isn't half the alchemist

Baker was, but he's smart enough to know when he should give his employees their freedom. Leigh's art was refined under the tutelage of the man who made her, a man who recognized that the aspects of alchemy belonging to the dead were best practiced by the dead themselves. It wasn't until that man died (she will not even think his name) and her leash was pressed into Reed's hand that she began to flourish. Where the dead are, so is she, and where she is, she can work miracles.

She spreads the dust thinly across her palm, purses her lips, and whistles five notes of a threnody written to honor the death of Abraham Lincoln. The coal dust moves; the silver does not. Leigh frowns. According to the candle, the car has been here less than an hour. According to the humors of the air around it, the car has been here all night and for the better part of a day, drinking in sunlight and moonlight alike, growing ripe with potential. The contradiction shouldn't be possible.

But there is a chill in the air, and the Doctrine is half made of time. Leigh's hand snaps shut, nails digging into her skin until it splits, allowing dark, sluggish blood to seep forth. The smell is sweet, like decaying meat.

They're manifesting.

When she climbs out of the car some five minutes later, her face is smooth, her shoulders relaxed; her hands dangle by her sides, fingers pointed daintily downward, betraying none of her dismay. She walks back through the maze of cars to her ride. The construct stands outside his vehicle, keeping watch, guarding against the dangers of the night. She knows herself for the greatest of those dangers, and she smiles without pleasure at the thought.

The alchemist rolls down his window when she gestures for him to do so. "Ma'am?"

"They were here. Now they're not. They have no car. What are their transit options at this hour of the night? Don't gawp at me, we don't have time. Where could they *go*?"

"The trains aren't running. Not for another three hours. They'd have to either steal a car or find something that stays open all night."

Leigh has monitored the missing cuckoos since the cradle. Dodger doesn't drive: Roger does, but can hardly be considered mechanically inclined. Her smile is a terrible thing. "Good," she says. "Then they're stuck, and we can move them."

The alchemist says nothing.

# Up All Night

As Leigh Barrow's plane taxis to a stop on the runway, Dodger walks briskly down a sidewalk, with Erin and Roger in close pursuit. The bag holding everything she has left in the world is slung across her shoulders, both too heavy and too light for her to bear. How can it be everything when it's so *small*? How can her life, her world, be compacted into something she can carry without trouble, lift without strain?

It's the sort of thought that can drive a person mad. She shunts it to the side, focusing on the task at hand. "BART doesn't start running until four, and there's no all-night bus in Fremont," she says, not slowing, not looking back. "We don't have a car, and I at least don't know how to steal one. Erin?"

"What, because I'm an arsonist I must also be a car thief? No. I can't help you there."

"Maybe you should have spent more time picking up useful skills and less time fucking my brother," says Dodger. "I don't know where we're supposed to be, but I know we're not supposed to be here. Can either of you ride a bicycle?"

"No, and right now, you shouldn't be riding one either," says Roger. Still she doesn't turn. "Why's that?"

"Because your hair is red," he says.

That stops her. She twists around, frowning in his direction. "What the hell does that have to do with anything?"

"If I'm getting the color of your hair, you're probably getting depth perception through your own eyes for the first time in your life," he says. "I'd crash the first time I saw an orange cat. You wouldn't even get that far. You'd get distracted by the shadows on a curb and ram yourself into a plate glass window. Honestly, I'm amazed you can walk."

"You'll both adjust, given time, assuming you have any, which is why it's *so important* you stop screwing around and *manifest*," says Erin sharply. "Dodger. You need to get us someplace safe. Unless you think what we're looking for is in Fremont?"

"I don't even know what we're looking for," she says. "You haven't told us. You've spouted a lot of crap about the Up-and-Under and A. Deborah Baker and killer death alchemists, but you haven't followed it up with 'and we just need to find the magic Denny's where they sell the coffee of conjuring and everything will be hunky-dory.' It's like playing D&D with an unprepared dungeon master. You're the one who knows the rules to this bullshit game."

Erin blinks. "Good call," she says. "I think it's about a half mile that way." She points, as both Roger and Dodger stare at her.

"What is?" Roger asks, after a moment's bewildered silence.

Erin grins. "The Denny's. Come on."


Three creations of terrible alchemy sit crammed into a booth in the all-night Denny's, pressed against the red vinyl seats, looking at their menus. "Maybe it's a sign that this has all been too much for me, but pancakes sound really good right about now," says Roger.

"Get whatever you want. Just keep in mind that we can't use credit cards," says Erin. "I have plenty of cash."

"Maybe don't say that so loud?" Dodger glances nervously around. "Some of the people in here look like they'd mug their mothers for fun."

"I'd like to see them try." Erin's grin is feral. "Remember: you were made to control the universe, and I was made to make sure you'd get that far. I'd *love* a good, easy mugging right about now."

"Are you sure you should be mentioning the 'control the universe' thing in here?" asks Roger.

"People don't listen," says Erin. "Everyone thinks of themselves as so important, so integral to the human condition, that someone must be hanging on their every word, but that's not true. It never has been. Maybe when there's a witch trial on, I guess. No one's listening to us. Which is sort of funny when you consider how important the two of you *are*. No. We need to hide, we need to lay low, and part of that is being completely natural and open about everything. It keeps people from looking at us too hard. No one with anything to lose would be sitting in Denny's after midnight, eating pancakes."

"This is so weird," says Dodger.

"Isn't it great?" Erin smiles again—more normally this time, lips drawn tight over teeth—and goes back to looking at her menu. "I think I'm going to have a milkshake."

Dodger's phone rings.

All three of them go silent, turning to look at her backpack as if it's suddenly revealed itself to be full of venomous snakes. The phone continues ringing. In a light, pleasant tone laced with menace, Erin asks, "What part of 'we're trying to lay low' means 'leave your phone on'? If there's a GPS locator in there, I may as well kill you both and hope Reed will believe me when I tell him that this was a long game to let me determine how close to manifestation you were."

"I *did* turn it off," protests Dodger, rummaging through the backpack until she comes up with the small box of her cellphone. The screen is blank. She rummages deeper, and produces the battery, which she slides across the table to Erin. "See? I took the fucking battery out."

The phone is still ringing. Roger looks at it nervously. "When did you get a fancy battery-free phone?"

"I didn't."

Erin picks up the battery, turning it over in her hand before fixing Dodger with a hard look. "You're not lying to save your own skin?"

"I don't understand enough of what's going on to lie to you." Dodger pops the back off her phone and holds it up, still ringing, to show Erin the empty cavity where the battery ought to be. "This isn't scientifically possible."

Roger laughs. He doesn't say anything: he just laughs, helplessly, sinking lower and lower in his seat, until his head is almost level with the top of the booth.

Dodger sighs. "Right. Should I answer it?"

"There aren't many people who could call you on a dead phone. You're one of them. Pick up."

Dodger nods, and presses the button on the side of her phone before raising it to her ear. Roger stops laughing.

"Hello?" she says.

L eigh hasn't spoken to the Cheswich girl since she was a baby, red-faced and squalling whenever taken more than five feet from her brother. Still, she's heard recordings, has seen pictures, and she knows the voice of a cuckoo when she hears it. She smiles, eyes half-lidded, and leans back in the chair she's commandeered for her use.

"Why, Dodger," she purrs. "You sound like such a big, grown-up girl. How old are you now? Twenty-nine? Almost an old maid, and nothing to show for it but a lecture tour and a few books that have already being remaindered in some stores. I read your first one. You should be proud of your scholarship. That's one thing I'll never try to take away from you: you have a brilliant mind. It's a pity you didn't do more with it while you had the chance."

"Who is this?" Dodger's voice is low and tight with fear. Leigh's smile grows. All the math children are like this, wary and easily frightened when they assume the danger is to themselves. Threaten their other halves and the response is very different. That's why it's important to come at the problem sideways, putting pressure on the weak link.

The math children will die to defend the language children. Many of them have. Most of them have had no capacity for defending themselves. It isn't part of what they're made of—and Leigh knows very well what they're made of. She was one of the people who did the making, after all.

"My name is Leigh Barrow. I assume you're with Erin. I want you to lower the phone and say my name. Watch her eyes. You'll understand how serious I am. Once you've done that, come back to me. Oh, and Dodger? If you let her take the phone away, I'll hang up, and you'll never know what I've done."

Dodger doesn't say anything. Leigh keeps smiling, and listens. In the background, she hears Erin's startled, wordless exclamation, followed by a run of words too fast and too distant to be understood. That's all right. She doesn't need to know what her creation and former protégée is saying to know that it isn't anything good, because no one ever has anything good to say about her or the things she does. Not even Reed, who supposedly values her contributions to his work. Leigh doesn't mind. Being universally feared and disliked has its advantages, and she is legion; she needs no one's company but her own.

"Hello?" Dodger's voice, querulous and—yes—afraid. Oh, good. That will make things so much easier.

"Hello, dear. Where are you?"

"No."

A simple refusal, flat, nothing to latch onto or exploit. Leigh's smile grows. This is going to be *fun*. "I don't think you understand. You know who I am. You know what I am to you. Not mother—that questionable honor was reserved for a farm animal who got more than she deserved when I slit her kiss to crotch—but midwife. I was there when you were born. I yanked you into the world screaming, covered in blood and mucus, and I've always hoped I'd have the opportunity to send you out of the world the same way. You know *what* I am. If you want me to be merciful—which isn't easy for me, I'm not going to lie to you—then you need to tell me where you are, and let me come to you."

"No," Dodger says again, and it's so stark, and it's so simple, and it's never going to be enough. Maybe if she'd been the firstborn . . . but if she'd been the firstborn, Leigh wouldn't be calling her. Always go for the weak link in a hunt, if there's any possible way.

"You don't have to be so stubborn, you know. We could be friends."

"That's not going to happen."

"Oh no? I have something I can offer. Something I think you'll want very much."

Dodger pauses. She knows the importance of barter, of bargaining; the math children always think they can get something for nothing, or for not quite as much, if they play their cards correctly. "What's that?"

"An easy death. I'll kill you so gently, Dodger. I'll slit your throat before you have a chance to blink, and you'll bleed out on the floor still waiting for me to strike. If I do it fast enough, there won't be any pain—not for you. Erin may even be able to keep your brother alive, if she uses everything I've taught her. You could set him free. I know you've tried to do that before. I know that's all you've ever really wanted to do."

Silence.

"Oh, but I haven't given you any reason to go along with my proposal, have I? Here's a reason: your parents are dead."

"What?" The word is half-gasp. Leigh can picture the look on the girl's face. The horror, the anger, the fear, all mixed together in a delicious cocktail of pain. She wishes she could actually see it, but hearing it is almost as good.

"Your parents. They're dead. I killed them, in case you were hoping this was about a car crash or something of the sort. You see, I couldn't find you anywhere—and I've been looking *ever* so hard. I assume you've been twisting time around yourself to muddy the trail. That's not very nice of you, you know. You've been *denying* me. I don't like to be denied, so I took a little trip to the address where Reed placed you."

Dodger finds she can't breathe.

"I rang the doorbell. Your mother answered. She was wearing a pink robe with blue satin trim. Very out-of-date. It soaked up the blood nicely when I stabbed her." The blade sliding between her ribs, slicing flesh and organs indiscriminately. Her lung had deflated like an old balloon, no longer capable of holding air or sustaining a body. It was a simple move, and one Leigh had practiced many times, on many bodies. "Did Erin ever tell you how she killed your little Indian girl after you and Roger were stupid enough to request a DNA test? She learned that move from me, and I showed it to your mother tonight. She didn't even have a chance to scream before she was on the floor. You'll be happy to know that her body's going to be donated to science. My science. I always need more parts."

"You're lying." It's the whisper of a wounded child. There are voices behind it, loud ones, raised in exclamation and dismay.

Leigh leans back farther in the chair, letting the weathered leather wrap around her like a lover's arms, and closes her eyes. It's a good chair. A pity about the bloodstains, but all things must come to an end in this world. "Am I? Or do you simply not want to listen to the truth? I admit, it's a painful truth, but it's the one we have, and it's not negotiable for people like you and me. Your brother, he can argue with the truth, within reason . . . but he can't raise the dead. Only a very good alchemist can do that, and believe me when I say you wouldn't appreciate the results. They're rarely pretty. Even when they are, there's always a cost. Everything costs."

"You're *lying*."

"Your mother answered the door, and when she didn't go back up the stairs, your father came down. I shot him. Men get so aggressive when they see their wives dead, and his hands are intact. You'll never see me coming. Do you believe me now? Or do I need to walk through your childhood home, describing everything I see to make you understand that I'm not a liar? Because I'll be honest, Dodger. I'm getting tired of you calling me names I haven't earned."

A soft squeaking sound, and then silence. Leigh opens her eyes.

"Come home," she says. "Leave them, or bring them with you. Try to take me by force, try to ambush me, come for *revenge,* I don't care, just come home. Come close enough for me to give you what I've promised. The people who took you in, raised you, and claimed you as their daughter are dead, little cuckoo, and all because you wanted to see the Impossible City. You could have spared them. You could have spared so many people. Come home, and leave the rest of the people you care about among the living. Because I assure you, it doesn't end here."

"I can't . . ."

"Your mother's blood tasted like candy, little girl. Don't fuck with me. Come home."

Leigh hangs up the phone and stands. The nameless alchemist is standing in the hallway, his construct a dark shape behind him. She looks at the pair with narrowed eyes. "Well?"

"I have them both laid out in the dining room like you asked."

"Good." Her smile has nothing to do with happiness. "Let's arm ourselves, shall we?"

Back in the diner, Dodger drops the phone. She stares at it, eyes huge in her pale face, and for a long moment, no one says anything. Finally, Roger reaches for her, and flinches when she pulls away.

Her head snaps up, attention zeroing in on Erin. "Was she lying?" she asks. Her voice breaks on the last word.

Erin is more concerned about the rest of her breaking, for good. "No," she says, quiet, implacable. "If Leigh Barrow says she's killed someone, she's killed them. That's how she operates. She can lie, but she rarely sees the need. The truth hurts so much more."

Dodger stands. This time, it's Erin who moves, leaning across the table, putting her hands on the other woman's shoulder, and shoving her back down into her seat.

"Let me *go!*"

"And what? You'll call an Uber and run off to Palo Alto to get yourself killed? You die, Roger dies. You want that?" Erin glares. It's the last weapon she has. She belonged to Leigh once: she knows how the woman operates because she operates in much the same way. There's power in the truth. It's an alchemy of its own. "If she told you any lies at all, she told you there was a way for you to die without killing him. His body might keep breathing for a while after yours stops, but it won't do a damn thing to save his mind. You die, he dies, and no matter what, your parents don't come back."

Dodger's eyes widen again, flaring with sudden hope. "They could! They could. The timeline, we . . . we can reset the timeline. We can go back and try to warn them."

"It doesn't work that way. It's never that precise."

"It has to be!" Dodger turns to Roger. "Please. She said you're the one who has to tell me what to do. So tell me what to do. Let me change the timeline."

"I think we need to listen to Erin right now," says Roger quietly.

"Dodger, don't you think if we could do this without losing your parents, we would have already reset the timeline to do it that way?" Erin tries to make the question as gentle as she can. "I know you've accepted that the earthquake had to happen to make you believe me. What if—as much as it hurts—what if this is where your parents have to die, because otherwise, they're going to suffer something much worse? Not everyone can be saved."

Dodger stares at her. "You're fucking kidding, right? They're my *parents*."

"His parents work for Reed," says Erin, indicating Roger. "They trained him like a puppy to be sure he'd take the correct shape. At least your parents truly loved you. Take that, and avenge them by manifesting the way you're supposed to."

Roger says nothing.

Dodger looks between the two of them, eyes going wider and wider, before she moves, again, to stand. This time, Erin doesn't stop her. "You people are both insane," she says. "I'm going home." She steps out of the booth, moving toward the door.

Roger jumps to his feet before he can stop to think, lunging after her, grabbing her arm. "Don't go. Please."

She looks back toward him. "My parents," she says.

"I'm know. Dodger, I'm so sorry, I—"

"Really? Because we just found out you lost your parents, too. Maybe this is symmetry. Maybe this is the numbers balancing. Only, you never really had yours. There was never anything there to subtract." She's being cruel. She knows it; he can see that in her eyes. That doesn't keep the barb from hitting home.

He lets her go.

Dodger takes another step away.

Erin looks at him. "It's on you now," she says.

He can't hesitate or they'll lose her, and if they lose her, they'll lose everything. The world will lose everything. She'll forgive him. He holds tightly to that thought as he says, "Dodger, stop."

Dodger stops.

"Come back."

She turns, face a mask of fury and dismay, and walks the three steps back to the booth, where she stands, vibrating with rage. "Don't do this," she says.

"Sit down," says Roger.

Dodger sits down.

"I'm sorry, Dodge," says Roger. "I can't let you leave."

Dodger turns her face away and says nothing. Erin sighs into the silence.

"Oh, isn't this going to be fun?" The question is blessedly rhetorical. None of them would have an answer if it wasn't. She picks up her discarded menu, opens it, and says, "We need to eat. We may not get another opportunity."

Roger stares at her, aghast. "What?"

"You heard me." She lowers the menu and looks at him. "This is war, Jackdaw. I kept you out of it as long as I could, because I needed you to have as much time and knowledge under your belt as possible, but that doesn't change the fact that it's been going on for over a hundred years. Baker thought of you, Reed created you, and now that you're here, the whole world gets to keep you. Both of you. This isn't something you walk away from. Smita wasn't the first person I killed on Leigh's orders, and the Cheswiches won't be the last people she kills on her own. Are you with me *yet*? All you can do by running away is play straight into her plans."

"Aren't we even going to call the police?" Dodger's question is small, meek, the question of a child. There's no anger in it. All the anger is reserved for her expression. Her glare in this moment could melt steel.

"And send them to their deaths? Are you sure that's what you want to do?" Erin meets Dodger's glare unflinchingly. "That's assuming they'd find the house. She'll have Hands of Glory burning by now, making the whole place obscure. She's not an amateur. She taught me everything I know—but as the cliché goes, she didn't teach me everything *she* knows. She's a monster trying to bait you into meeting her in her den, and we can't let you go. I'm sorry. We can't lose you, or we lose everything."

"She's not a monster. She's a woman. Women can die."

Erin shakes her head. "She was crafted from a dozen corpses. Half her bones are carved with protective runes, safe below the skin, where no one can see to counter them. The alchemist who made her died at Reed's hand; there's no one living who knows every trick that woman has squirreled away. She's dangerous. She's deadly. If you want to stop her, if you want to avenge your parents and make things as close to right as they can be, you *must* manifest. I don't know how many ways I can say this. You have to find the heart of this country we're in, whether it's Munchkin or Hyacinth, and you have to get us there, before it's too late."

Dodger holds Erin's gaze locked on her own. "When this is over," she says, in a perfectly reasonable tone, "I'm walking away, and I'm never speaking to either of you again."

"We'll see," says Erin. "Now figure out what you want to eat. You're going to need to keep your strength up."

# Ham and Eggs

TIMELINE: 4:13 PDT, JUNE 17, 2016
(THIS DAMNED DAY).

They linger over their midnight meal (which reaches the table sometime after one A.M.; misnomers and inaccuracies abound in this liminal space between the night and day) until Erin glances at the clock on the wall and says, "The trains have started running. We should go."

"Go *where*?" asks Roger. "We don't know where we're going. We just know there's a killer out there looking for us, and we've spent the whole damn night sitting in this Denny's, eating eggs and not running for our lives."

"Eggs can be a lifesaver," says Erin. She turns her eyes to Dodger. "If you want to know where we're going, ask your Crow Girl. She's the only one who can get us there, if she'd start playing along."

Dodger hasn't said anything in hours. She glares at Erin and holds fast to her silence.

Erin sighs. "Sulking doesn't bring them back, but it might get us killed. Roger, talk some sense into your damn sister."

"It's like spiders," says Dodger.

They both go still.

"When he gives an order I don't want to follow, it's like spiders in my brain, and I *can't say no.*" She virtually spits her words. "No matter how much I want to not do it, I have to, because he told me to, and it's like spiders running their spider legs all over the inside of my brain. You told him to do that. You made him use me like a puppet."

"Dodge—" Roger begins.

"Don't think you're getting out of this," she says. "She told you to do it, but she's not you. You don't have to listen to her the way I have to listen to you. So you're not clean either."

"It's nice to know you can still sulk like a teenager, but this isn't getting us anywhere," says Erin. "If you want to be mad at me, it's not like I can stop you. I want you to remember one thing, though: I didn't make you. The man who did, the man who sent a killer here to take you down, he's out there. All of this is at his feet. He's been chasing this dream for a long time. The only way we stop him is by taking it away from him."

"Alchemists can raise the dead," says Dodger suddenly.

"Yes," says Erin. She doesn't say any of the other things, the things about the costs of such an action, the reasons most people would never dream of doing such a thing. Sometimes when the facts speak for themselves, they do so by telling blatant, beautiful lies. "But if you want to be able to make an alchemist do what you want, you need to manifest. You need to know where we are."

Dodger looks at her flatly before she reaches across the table and grabs the salt and pepper shakers, removes their lids, and dumps their contents onto the Formica, stirring the mess with her fingers until it has been inextricably mingled. (The resulting blend looks distressingly like the coal dust and ground silver Leigh favors. Dodger doesn't know this. Erin does, and she shivers.)

"We need to determine the properties of the set in order to define the quadrants," says Dodger. "You said this is either water or fire, correct?"

"Yes," says Erin.

"Assigning values to the four possibilities, with water standing at

negative two and fire standing at positive two, we begin by subtract-
ing air and earth from each . . ." Dodger's fingers continue to move
as she speaks, drawing lines and equations through the mess she's
made, sinking deeper and deeper into her own little world.

The air around their booth is getting colder. What Dodger is doing
isn't math in the truest sense of the word, and at the same time, it's a
deeper, truer arithmetic than she's done in years. It is the instinctive
math of children weighing parental disapproval against the rapidly
setting sun, and the heartbroken math of sailors measuring the holes
in their boat against the distance to the shore. This is the math that
moves the universe, the measure and countermeasure that dances
over and around the numbers. Dodger holds this kind of math in her
bones, and her fingers dance through the blend of vegetable and min-
eral scattered in front of her, separating them from one another with
almost thoughtless swipes. Bit by bit, the figures she is pulling from
the bone and char blending are becoming paler, losing the charcoal
tint of the pepper.

When she's done, she has separated the salt and the pepper. It
should have been impossible. She doesn't even appear to realize it's
happened. Dodger taps the table beneath her last line of incomprehensible figures and says, "Water. That's why we're having this
drought, or part of it. Whatever Baker's enemies—I can't believe I'm
saying this—whatever Baker's enemies did to unmake her work, it's
still going on, and part of it is trying to deny the quadrants their
essential natures. So you take as much of the water away from the
place that's supposed to represent water in the equation as you can,
and hope eventually it gets so unbalanced that it can't hold together
anymore."

"Makes sense," says Erin. "Baker purified the elements when she
divided them. She tied each of them to a concrete anchor point, but
nothing in nature wants to be pure for long. If someone wanted to
destroy the Impossible City, they'd begin by destabilizing the elements. That's what Baum was trying to do, with his mixed and muddled Oz. The old bastard."

"I don't care about your dead alchemists and their stupid plans," says Dodger. She stands. This time, no one stops her. "We're in the element of water, and if you can give me the dimensions of its borders and the alchemical flux that attends them, I can lead you straight to whatever serves as its center. *Now* can we go?"

"There's just one more thing we have to do first," says Erin.

"*What?*" demands Dodger.

Erin smiles implacably. "I have to pay the check."

Even under the circumstances, Roger can't keep from laughing.

They walk the mile and a half to the BART station, through abandoned business parks and silent residential neighborhoods. Erin takes the lead at first, with Roger behind her and Dodger bringing up the rear. Dodger is muttering to herself, taking quick, tight looks around, like she's measuring things. Roger keeps looking back at Dodger, reassuring himself that she hasn't run away. Finally, he turns his face forward and closes his eyes.

"Hey, Dodge."

The sound of Roger's voice echoing in her skull is enough to make her jump. He's still walking. She narrows her eyes. "You're going to trip and fall."

"I'm not." Being this close to his body while he's in her head gives his words a strange echo effect, inside and outside layering over each other to create something entirely new. "I learned this trick from you. Remember, during the earthquake? You closed your eyes and kept running, because you had mine to look through. It was pretty clever."

"It's almost like I'm smart or something," she says bitterly. "This isn't the way to have a private conversation. Your *girlfriend* can still hear us."

"She's not my girlfriend anymore," he says. "I don't know if she ever was. Dodge . . . we have to find a way to get through this without losing each other. I don't think I can handle it."

"You should've thought of that before you let her use you to put me on a leash," she says. "It's not safe to be around you."

"I won't do it again without your permission. I promise." He pauses. That doesn't seem like enough. "I *swear*," he amends, and it's more childish, and that makes it more sincere.

"I don't think that's a promise you can keep. I don't want to be apart from you, but I don't believe you when you say you won't hurt me. You're going to hurt me."

"Of course I am. I'm your brother. I'm going to hurt you and annoy you and drive you crazy, and you're going to do the same to me. So what if I got super-persuasion powers? You can break *time*. That's pretty badass, Dodge. But it only works if we stay together. I'm tired of feeling like something's missing. I'm tired of wondering what color my apples are. Stay with me. Sure, we'll probably hurt each other, but no one else will ever hurt us again." That's what she's always wanted, isn't it? For no one to hurt her.

Dodger is quiet for a moment. Then, in a soft voice, she says, "I'll kill you if you break your word. I can do it. No matter how strong you get, I can do it."

"I know."

She smiles to herself, nods, and says, "Get out of my head."

Roger opens his eyes and feels her hand slipping into his. He glances to the side and there she is, walking beside him, eyes still fixed front.

"If this Leigh woman is as smart as you say, she'll be watching for us to get on the BART," she says. "It's the easiest way to get around the Bay Area once you give up having a car. So we need to do something else."

"Something else like what?" asks Erin. "You still haven't told me where we're going."

"Because I still don't know," says Dodger. "But I know we need to get to the water. Do you have any more cash on you?"

"I always have cash on me."

"Good." Dodger's smile takes on an almost feral edge. It's the sort of smile that gives children nightmares, and Roger is obscurely relieved. If Dodger is giving other people nightmares, she isn't too weighed down by her own. "I hope you have a lot, because we're taking a taxi."

"To where?"

"Far away."

"Far away" turns out to be Berkeley: they're back where they started from, in the city where the ashes of the house where Roger and Erin shared so many happy years still smolder. The air feels electric when they step out of the cab, and Roger realizes it's partially because it's been so long since he was here with Dodger, who takes his hand as soon as she's out of the vehicle. The last time they were together in this city, they killed more than a thousand people, and destroyed landmarks that should have stood for another hundred years. Now, they're just two cuckoos on the run, two more supplicants on the way to the Impossible City. The moment should have more weight to it, should matter more. It doesn't. This is just a way station. This was only ever a way station.

"The Transbay bus picks up from the Albany BART station," says Dodger. "We'll take that as far as the Financial District. There's a bike rental kiosk near the bus stop. We can get where we need to go from there."

"And where do we need to go?" asks Erin.

"I still don't know."

The cab dropped them three blocks from the station, at Dodger's insistence. It's a paper-thin ruse; it won't cost Leigh and her people more than a few seconds. A few seconds is better than nothing. They walk to the station and stop, looking at its bright lights, its modern lines. This is what normalcy looks like. This is the life that they, for better or for worse, have been forced to leave behind.

"We need more time," says Dodger abruptly. She turns to Roger. "Order me."

"What?"

"I don't know what to do, and we don't have time to stand around waiting for me to figure it out. It's only spiders in my brain when I don't want you to do it. I want you to do it. Tell me to buy us more time."

Erin steps back, folding her arms, and watches. They need to do this, to find the empty spaces between them and determine the best ways to fill them. She *remembers* this, or something very much like it, from other timelines, attempts to manifest which ended in failure, and in everything being set back to the start. She doesn't know when Roger told her to remember it, but remember it she does: she knows this is important. She will not interfere.

It still aches. She remembers the hurt she felt the first time she realized she'd never be part of their closed circle, their nation of two. Reed might have split the Doctrine into two bodies, each with their own thoughts, personality, and desires, but he was never strong enough to make them independent of each other. They'd always come back together, and when they did, they'd always form a single whole, without a crack between them to let anyone else slither in.

Roger grimaces. "Are you sure?" he asks, voice unsettled.

"I am," says Dodger. "Tell me."

He takes a deep breath. "Dodger," he says. "Find us more time. That's an order."

The air around them seems to plummet four degrees as Dodger's eyes widen and go glassy. Behind them, her mind is working double-time, making connections and throwing them aside at a speed she wouldn't be capable of on her own. Then, without a word, she starts to walk away. After only a few steps, she breaks into a run.

Erin and Roger run after her, following her into the bright open-air lobby of the BART station. She digs in her pocket, pulling out a crumpled twenty-dollar bill, and feeds it to the machine, punching a series of keys that shouldn't do anything but confuse the poor computer. Instead, it spits out a hail of golden dollar coins and three tickets, each set to the value of a one-way trip to Fremont. She fills her pockets with dollar coins, keeps one ticket, and holds the other two out toward her companions.

"Take them," she says, when they fail to move.

They do.

She licks her ticket on the side without the magnetic strip, and gestures for the others to do the same. They do, and she snatches the tickets from their hands, running away across the station. Roger and Erin stare after her.

"Do you know what she's doing?" Roger asks.

"Not a damn clue," says Erin.

Dodger returns at a trot, hands empty. "Gave them to some homeless kids looking for a place to take a nap," she says. "The tickets are ours. Everything about them says 'ours.' Breath and spit and purpose. As long as they're in the BART system, anyone running the numbers to try and find us is going to get a false positive off those tickets." She hesitates, face falling. "Leigh wouldn't . . . she wouldn't derail an entire train to take us out, would she?"

"No," says Erin, before Dodger can run to try to reclaim the tickets. She says it so firmly, with so much certainty, that it's almost possible to believe she's not lying. "That's too public. She'll avoid that sort of thing if there's any way."

"Great," says Dodger. "The bus leaves in five minutes. We should be on it."

They are.

The sun won't be up for another hour. The bus slides through the darkness, all cool, processed air and drowsy commuters. They can't sit together and so Erin sits apart, easing herself back into the reality where this is her natural condition: where loneliness is not only a consequence but the water in which she swims, melancholy mermaid never more to come to land. Dodger takes the window in the seat she shares with Roger, and he closes his eyes, letting her watch the trip for both of them. His color vision is coming, but it's not as nuanced as hers. Seeing San Francisco by night with her depth and complexity of color is . . . it's amazing.

It's amazing.

They glide through the fog clinging to the Bay Bridge, long, snaking thing that it is, incongruous palm trees waving to their left, rooted in soil suspended over water (there's alchemy in those trees, in earth over water, surrounded by air and the hot steel combustion engines of the cars; now that he knows this force exists, is not just a children's story, he's beginning to see it everywhere). Then the fog breaks, and there is San Francisco, glorious in the darkness, lit up like a beacon to the weary and the lost. Dodger's hand tightens over his. Roger goes still.

Every city is the Impossible City, when a savior is needed badly enough. When that's where the road of alchemical enlightenment leads.

"Can we survive this?" asks Dodger, eyes still on the window, and Roger doesn't answer her, and maybe that's for the best. Maybe some questions don't need to be answered.

The bus stop is cold and industrial, surrounded by the sleeping giants of the Financial District. The Greyhound depot isn't far away. Dodger vanishes inside, returns with three tickets to three different destinations, repeats the trick with saliva and strangers. When Leigh goes looking, she'll find that not only are they on the BART, they're also heading for Reno, Nevada; Portland, Oregon; and Seattle, Washington, all places where the lakes are liquid and water's claim might be seen as stronger. There's a chance she'll see all four options and deduce that none of them is true, but she's smart enough to know that they'll have considered that possibility, and might be banking on it. She has to check at least one of their false leads. Dodger has done what she promised. She's bought them time.

They move across the parking lot and down the street, a silent trio of refugees running from a war that can't be real. The bicycle rental rack is bolted to the street in front of a deli, automated, no humans involved. Dodger feeds it golden dollar coins until it surrenders three bikes, all new and white and glossy. Even the tires have been scrubbed clean.

They take their bikes and stand there, unmoving, all three of them clutching their handlebars hard. Erin speaks first.

"Now where?" she asks.

"Don't you know?" asks Dodger.

Erin looks at her and shakes her head. "I'm the living incarnation of the force of Order," she says. "I didn't get cosmic knowledge or the ability to change the universe. I got the urge to organize your CDs. It's on the two of you. Where are we going?"

Roger and Dodger exchange a look.

"Mathematically, this place is water," she says.

"We need something on or near water, that was standing when Baker was alive, or she wouldn't have used it as an anchor point," says Roger. "Leave out natural landmarks—she was hung up on the idea of the Impossible City and finding a way for man to coexist with nature, so she won't have used something no one built."

"Which is good, because if she'd gone for natural beauty, we'd need to get ourselves to Santa Cruz," says Dodger. "Natural Bridges is Baker's sort of place."

"The monarch migration alone would have sealed the deal," agrees Roger. "It would have been something manmade, something she thought would endure—"

"—so nothing that looked temporary or like a passing thing," says Dodger. "Golden Gate Bridge is tempting, but I think that's why it doesn't add up. It's a false flag—"

"—too much of a tourist attraction to risk using, and not *about* water. It's about being *above* water. I'd almost buy it for fire, if you told me it had to be a landmark, but it feels less like our destination and more like one of—"

"—the ways to get there. Add the sum of the bridges, subtract the average distance traveled, and the date . . ." Dodger stops slowly this time, breaking the rhythm of the theory they've been tossing between them. Her eyes widen. "It's gone. Whatever it is, it's gone."

Roger blinks. "Show your math," he says, because that's always been the one thing she's happy to do, no matter what else is going on: she'll always, always stop to show her math.

"Reed's been trying to undo everything Baker did. He has to have known where the anchors were, because he probably helped Baker *create* them. So we need something that fits the parameters, matches the math, and isn't there anymore."

"Ah," says Roger, understanding. He pinches the bridge of his nose, trying to concentrate.

History is a form of language. It tells the story of an area, of a city, of an idea (because all any civilization is, really, is a string of ideas tied together in a shining cord, tangled sometimes, frayed, but continuous and beautiful, even when it's not). It's never been his specialty. Still, he picks things up. Sometimes he feels like he picks them up straight from the city itself. And who knows? Maybe he does. Maybe he does.

"1896," he says. "Erin, what was Baker doing in 1896?"

"Gathering apprentices, teaching elementary school, laying the seeds of her philosophy," she says. "She knew what she wanted to do with the Up-and-Under, but the first book hadn't come out yet. She wasn't sure it could be accomplished."

"And she banked on the belief of children to act as an anchor for the more extreme ideas," he says. "The Sutro Baths were opened to the public in 1896. They were supposed to be a permanent fixture of the city. Dodger, what do the numbers say?"

Her eyes go glossy again. He may never get used to that, and maybe that's a good thing. A sister should be a sister first, after all, and not a search engine for the wonders of the cosmos.

"Opened 1896, burned to the ground 1966. Arson. Edison made two films there. They were considered a miracle of modern engineering, electricity . . . people. So many people. Divide by the number of people, subtract the deaths by water, add babies conceived on the grounds behind the maintenance shed, where no one was looking . . . yes." Dodger is nodding, slow at first, but gaining speed. "Yes, the math works. The Sutro Baths were the center of this quadrant. They still are. When Reed's people burned them, they didn't move the capital, because they didn't want things to stay anchored."

"Can't take the Impossible City until you take everything else," says Erin. "How far?"

"Not far," says Dodger, and slings her leg over her bike. "Let's end this."

The sun won't be up for another half hour. Only the moon watches them go.

# Water

The air off the Pacific is freezing, and there is no coastline: there is only fog, all-encompassing, all-devouring. None of them are dressed for this. They shiver uncontrollably as they ride down the final short slope to the cliff's edge, looking out on the remains of the Sutro Baths.

There's something timeless about the ruins, something ancient about the great concrete blocks that jut from the sounding sea, the long, smooth foundations being beaten by the waves. The tide is low enough that the shape of the structure is clear, even if there is no obvious way—no marked way—down to its beginning. Signs posted by the state warn against urban exploration, threaten with legal action or death by water for those foolish souls who choose to go any closer, to look any deeper than they can from the safety of the shore.

"Can you get us there?" Roger asks, looking to Erin.

And Erin, who sees the weak points in the world—the chaotic places, the things that are getting ready to give way, like the loose earth of a foot trail down a sheer cliff face—nods.

They descend in a line, Erin first, Dodger behind her where her still-developing depth perception won't be a danger, Roger in the rear, ready to grab and steady should either of them slip or, worse, fall. The cliff is steep and unforgiving, even though the distance to the concrete foundations is not so great. This was never intended to be climbed on foot, not by God, not by man, and not by the alchemy that arranged for the Baths to burn to the ground.

*(In Fremont, three homeless teens are watched by a nameless alchemist whose planchette insists they're the cuckoos he's been seeking. None of these children stand upon the improbable road. He knows that as surely as he knows Leigh would kill them for wasting her time. When he calls in, it's to say the tickets rode alone, no human hands to hold them, and that their targets are not here.)*

*(A bus bound for Reno is pulled over by a state patrolman who has driven this stretch of road, under a variety of identities, for over sixty years. Immortality does not carry with it the skills to change professions, and owing that immortality to a man like James Reed does not leave many opportunities for study or learning a new trade. The three men sleeping at the back with tickets that resonate as someone else's are left to slumber without incident.)*

*(There is value in the loyalty of subordinates. There is mercy in their betrayals.)*

They descend by inches, by feet, by years. The air goes flat around them, losing the resonance of the wind, even as it continues to grow colder. At the same time, the cold loses its power. Roger and Dodger walk straighter, stand taller. Only Erin shivers, and when she looks back at them, she can barely focus on their faces. They don't have individual features. They are one and they are neither, and they are so close to one of the focal points of the world that there is no difference between those two ideals.

The door is gone. The stairs are gone. There is only the foundation, gray and cold and blackened in places where the fire had its way. Erin steps aside when she reaches the first of the great implacable stones. Dodger steps forward, head cocked, looking at the structure like she can see it as it was meant to be. And she is Time and she is Math and maybe she can; maybe she sees what was, instead of what truly, terribly is.

"The blueprints would have put one of the stairways here," she says, and takes a step into empty air. She does not fall: logic has been suspended. Instead, she shifts her weight onto a step that isn't there, a step that glimmers mercury silver and purified gold in the shivering sea air. She takes another step, and another, and the steps remain sketched spectral and true behind her.

Roger and Erin exchange a look. Roger speaks first.

"Dodger seems to be walking into a building that doesn't exist."

"Sure looks like it."

"The building isn't *there*."

"Nope."

"But she's going up the stairs anyway. The stairs that aren't there either."

"Yup."

"Can *we* walk into the building that doesn't exist?"

"There's only one way to find out."

Roger turns to look at the glimmering ghost of the stairs, and says, with a firm certainty, "The stairs are there. The stairs are real. The stairs will support our weight without dropping us into the ocean to drown or die of hypothermia."

The glimmering stairs lose some of their shine, silver and gold replaced by half-visible concrete, like they're becoming solid again; like he's called them back into the world. Roger takes his first cautious step. As with Dodger, the steps hold him; there is no give to whatever he stands upon, whatever he's called more truly into being.

His sister is almost to the top. He hurries after her, and Erin brings up the rear, and all is silence, save for the beating of the sea against the shore.

The stairs end abruptly. Dodger puts out a foot, testing the air, and there's nothing there: only emptiness, and the fall that waits beyond it, looking for another body to claim. She pulls her foot back, balanced on the thin ribbon of almost that has carried her this far, and looks over her shoulder to where Roger is hurrying up behind her.

"There aren't any more stairs," she reports.

"What comes after stairs?" He stops on the step below hers, putting his hands on her shoulders. Color blossoms back into his world, deep and bright and limitless. "Look for it."

Dodger turns back to the empty air in front of her, looking at it with new eyes—eyes that see how far it is to the horizon, that can trace and factor every line. She blinks once, hard, and says, "This is where the landing was, where they moved into the body of the Baths. There would have been a short entryway, to keep the saltwater from getting inside, and then the door. The door would have been right here."

She steps forward, into the empty air, already reaching for the doorknob. Roger starts to tighten his grip on her shoulders, certain that she's going to fall . . . then he stops, and lets her go. They've already come so far, done so many things that shouldn't have been possible. What's one more? So he lets her go, and trusts the air to hold her.

Dodger doesn't fall.

Her hand finds the doorknob where there is no doorknob, and the door blossoms into being around it, spiraling out in a fractal bloom that grows almost too fast to follow, meeting up with the blooming patches of solidity spreading outward from her feet, drawing a floor to hold her and walls to justify its existence. They start glimmering and thin, mercury and gold, before the gray and brown race in, sketching them into real things, solid things. She opens the door. She steps through. Roger follows, and Erin follows him, and all of them stand there, breathless and unbelieving, as the fractals rush ever outward, drawing walls, windows, deep bathing pools. Re-creating the past.

"Whoa," says Dodger.

"Ditto," says Roger.

"Fucking finally," says Erin. She moves past them and the floor beneath her feet is solid; they have called this place far enough back into being that it can support her. She looks around as she walks, taking the measure of her surroundings. "We're going to need to find a place where you can work. I don't know what manifestation entails, but if you're going to do it, you're going to do it here—and you need to do it *fast*."

"Why?" asks Dodger. She doesn't take her eyes off the ceiling, a domed lattice of glass and steel and electric lights that are beginning to flicker on, one after another, pulling on a grid that isn't real to activate circuits that no longer exist. They are standing inside a ghost. The weight of it hits her like a blow. They are *standing* inside a *ghost*, something she called back into being and Roger turned solid around them. This can't be happening. This is happening.

"Because something this big is going to be like a goddamn signal fire to the people looking for us. You bought the time to get us here. Now you need to make it count for something." Erin's face is grim. "You need to make it matter, or all this was for nothing."

# Fire

Leigh Barrow is on the phone with James Reed when Dodger steps into the air above what used to be the foundations of the Sutro Baths. Leigh stops mid-word, mouth going slack, eyes fixing on the horizon, where a beam of golden light illuminates the sky. It looks like a castle spire, like a tower, like a beanstalk stretching up toward some distant country in the sky. She hates it. She hates it like fire. She would tear it down with her bare hands if she could.

Reed is shouting. She snaps out of her fugue, bringing the phone back to her ear.

"The sky just turned gold," she says, ignoring whatever he's trying to tell her. Either it's about the manifestation, in which case she knows better than he does what's going on, or it's not, in which case it doesn't matter anymore. The cuckoos have found their way to the castle. It's not the Impossible City, but it might as well be, because like calls to like, and where they are, where they're standing, they have access to everything the Queen of Wands—everything Baker—ever knew. "They've found the capital. They've started. Reed, I know you hate to share, but you need to tell me where to go, and you need to tell me *right now*."

Silence, punctuated by heavy breathing. Then: "You forget your place, Leigh."

"My place is by your side in the new world, doing the things you don't want to do, killing the people you don't want to kill. Your hands have always been too clean. If you want that new world to happen, instead of just being a cute idea you used to talk about before you let two fucking cuckoos *seize the Doctrine,* this is where you tell me where to go."

"I could have unmade you the moment you fell into my hands."

"Sure. But you didn't. You knew what I could do for you, and kept me as I am instead of breaking me down for parts. Right here, right now, I am what you have on the ground; I am what you have that's capable of stopping these wayward children. Tell me where to go."

Reed's sigh is deep and tired. He's never allowed himself to sound that weary in her presence before. Leigh hears her death in that exhalation. She has proven too difficult. When she returns to Ohio, he's going to have her killed.

*You'll have to see me before I see you, old man,* she thinks. The Doctrine is still there for the taking, embodied in those skinny teenagers he has captive at the lab. She can control the forces of an unthinking universe just as well as he can, and her reign will be a lot more fun. Blood will fall from the sky; seas will burn; bodies will litter the streets.

So much more fun.

"Baker anchored California around the Sutro Baths," he says. "She thought the damned things were an architectural miracle, a temple to the idea of water that would never fail, never fall, never lose its luster. She tied the country she was trying to create to a bathhouse. I only wish she could have seen the damn place burn."

"Got it," says Leigh. She moves to hang up, and is stopped by Reed's voice.

"Leigh."

"Yes?"

"Bring me their bodies. I want to take them apart."

"Can I have the heads?" she asks lightly, even though she knows she'll never receive anything from James Reed again, save perhaps for a knife between the ribs and a bullet to the heart. Killing her will be difficult, but she's sure he'll be willing to put the effort in.

"Of course."

"Then of course. Now, if you'll excuse me, I'm going to save the world." She hangs up her phone. After a moment's consideration, she drops it to the street and grinds it beneath her heel, shattering the screen, destroying the delicate internal circuitry.

"Oops," she says.

The nameless alchemist has returned from his attempts to run down the misleading BART tickets (and she knows he found their holders, and let them live; under the circumstances, she has better things to concern herself with). Leigh walks to his car, opens the passenger-side door, and climbs in.

"Can you see that?" she asks, pointing to the column of golden light in the sky.

He follows her finger. His eyes widen. "Where the fuck did that come from?"

"The Sutro Baths, and that's where we're going. You'd better floor it," she says, voice serene. "We've got some cuckoos to kill."


Commuter traffic is just starting to get under way, but they're a "high-occupancy vehicle"; they qualify for the carpool lane. Between that, some impressively defensive driving, and a glorious willingness to violate traffic laws, it's a little over an hour before they're pulling up to what the GPS claims will be the ruins of the Sutro Baths.

There are no ruins here. There is only a dome of glass and steel glittering in the sunrise, lit from within by electric bulbs and lit from without by the entire sky. The structure glows with mercury light. It will be visible to alchemists for a hundred miles, a bright and welcoming beacon telling them that all is forgiven, that Baker's dream has endured.

Leigh hates it as she's hated little else in her life. She climbs out of the car, producing two pistols from inside her jacket and holding them low against her thighs, where they're less likely to be seen by passersby. She doesn't expect that to be a problem. Something like this—the reappearance of a historical landmark, the discoloration of the entire horizon—should have attracted dozens of onlookers by now. Since that hasn't happened, she assumes the working in progress shares some aspects of its function with the Hand of Glory. No one is here because no one can see what's happening. No one who isn't already a part of this fight.

"Kill anything inside that moves and isn't me," says Leigh, looking to the nameless alchemist. "There may be a little strawberry blonde with a trustworthy face. I'd prefer to kill her myself. I understand that may not be possible. If it's not, make sure it hurts when you take her down. Make sure she suffers. All right?"

"Yes, ma'am," says the alchemist.

"Good boy. Maybe I won't kill you after all."

There's no need for them to walk down the cliff: the Baths are back, fully material, glittering in the sunlight. Leigh Barrow walks straight through the front door.

# Concrete

There isn't time to explore the Baths, much as each of them would like to, for their own reasons. Roger is enchanted by the history of the place, by the idea that they've somehow turned word into deed into material reality. Dodger can't take her eyes off the angles, the mathematical perfection of the construction, the concrete glory of math become clear and present all around them. Erin simply wants to know the best places to hide when Leigh arrives—because Leigh is *going* to arrive. This is why they don't have any time (*there was never enough time*).

Dodger leads them through the Baths, eyes half-closed and one hand held in front of her like a dowser looking for water. The others follow, saying nothing. Distracting her would cost time (*there is never enough time*).

They walk through vast chambers filled with empty pools, into a long, L-shaped room. The furniture flickers in and out of being, not quite stable; it appeared to have been a sitting room, once upon a time. Vast windows look out on the Pacific, watching the water beat against the rocks. Dodger stops. Roger and Erin stop in turn, watching her.

"Here," she says, and heads for the wall, ripping at the wallpaper. It comes away easily, in sheets, weakened by the sea air and by its own unreality. This is a thing that burned years ago. Of course it's malleable now.

Roger takes a step toward her, to join her, and stops a second time when Erin catches his elbow. He looks back to find her watching him gravely.

"If this gets bad, you need to tell her to take you back," she says. "She won't be able to refuse. Tell her it's an order. Tell her it's a command. Tell her it's an adjuration. She'll do it, and if you word it just like that, you may take something back with you that helps us next time."

"How do you—"

"Because you told me." Her smile is more of a pained grimace. "Order, remember? I see the frayed and broken spaces. I see the *scars*. Both of you get to be ignorant of how long we've been doing this, but I don't. I don't have to remember everything, thank God. I think I'd kill you both, and stop this, if I did. I still get more than you do. And sometimes you tell me, explicitly, to remember things for the next time."

"Like what?"

Her smile fades. "Don't ask me that, Roger. You've signed off on things you don't want to know about. Dodger's the chess player, but you're the one who's said 'this is a sacrifice for the greater good.' If I tell you what you've told me not to change, you're going to remember, and you're going to hate yourself. So don't ask me. For your sake. For her sake. Let it go."

Roger looks at her in silence for a moment before he glances toward Dodger. "How bad?" he asks.

"Bad enough."

"Okay. I don't like it, but . . . okay."

"Good. Go help your sister take over the universe. I'm going to go keep you alive long enough to do it."

"How?"

Erin smiles sharply, a blade in a woman's skin, and pulls the gun from inside her shirt. "I'm going to fight back." Then she's gone, turning on her heel and walking out of the room, leaving him alone.

No: not alone. Dodger is there, writing figures on the wall with a Sharpie produced from her overstuffed backpack, lost in her own little world. Watching her write on a wall is its own form of time travel: he blinks and they're in her off-campus apartment with the whiteboard walls, both of them laughing, content, *together*. He blinks again and it's a chalkboard seen through borrowed eyes, a stick of chalk in her hand and the stinging smell of chalk dust in her nostrils. He knows the words—nostalgia, longing, regret. He also knows that the only way forward is through.

He goes to her.

"I love you," he says.

"I know."

"I'm sorry," he says.

"I forgive you." She doesn't take her eyes off the wall. "I'm sorry, too."

"You don't have to be," he says.

"Never leave me again?"

"I won't."

"Good. The numbers add up. The math is good."

"What can I do?" he asks.

"Describe the Baths," she says. He does, and as he speaks she writes faster and faster, turning his words into numbers, reducing the history and splendor of the place to a chain of figures.

"Describe California," she says next, and he does, and again, she writes, filling the wall and moving on to the next, the universe in figures and functions, an equation that could solve the world, if only they had time to describe and document every piece, every aspect of something so vast that it should be without limit. (And they *do* have time, they *do*: for the first time, Roger realizes that their twisting of their own timeline means they can finish anything, if only they can remember beginning it.)

Next is America; after that, the world. The air in the room grows colder and colder, and the mercury glow returns to the walls, glittering and bright. Her Sharpie is still just a Sharpie, black ink and the chemical smell of the marker, but the marks it leaves behind shine like glass, like silver. The rules of reality are turning malleable.

The first gunshot sounds right after Dodger has asked him to describe the house where he grew up. Roger jumps. She looks up, expression sharp.

"We can't stop now," she says. "We're so close. Keep talking."

"Dodger—"

*"Keep talking."*

So he does. His house, and his impressions of her house, and then himself, Roger Middleton, who was supposed to be ordinary and turned out to be something . . . else. The gunfire continues. Some of it is close; Erin, holding back whoever has come to attack them. That Leigh woman, he assumes. She's got backup. The cacophony is too much to be coming from just two firearms. There's an army out there, or maybe only a small mob, and they're so close, and these walls aren't really here. These walls are *thin*. How long can this go on?

He knows the words: doubt, disbelief, skepticism. He knows their power. He hasn't considered his own power, here and now and in this place where the walls glow mercury bright, where he's feeding the words that make up the world to the sister-cuckoo who hatched with him from the same egg. He sees the walls flicker. Only for a moment.

A moment is long enough for him to begin to move, hands outstretched, mouth forming a word that will never come.

A moment is long enough for the bullets to break through.

Dodger screams.

# Showdown

Erin keeps her back to the pillar as best she can, ducking around it only to aim, fire, and retreat again. "It's over, Leigh!" she shouts. "They're *going* to manifest! Run now, and maybe you'll be too far away to worry about by the time they get around to cleaning up Reed's mess!"

"You stupid idealistic child," Leigh replies. "They're not going to manifest. Reed's already taking the Doctrine from them. You've chosen the wrong side. I thought better of you."

"I chose the wrong side when you killed Darren." She ducks around the pillar one more time, fires one more time, following the chaotic threads of combat through the air. This time, her shot is followed by the heavy cement-sack sound of a body hitting the floor.

For a moment—a tiny, trembling moment—she allows herself to hope that this is it; that it's over, that she's won. Then Leigh says, in a voice dripping with disgust, "You just shot a perfectly good alchemist, and we don't even have the facility to take him apart. This is why you're useless, Erin. You're wasteful. You were never going to be anything other than a tool."

Her voice is getting closer. Erin breaks cover and runs for the next pillar, moving just ahead of the shining strips of chaos that would put her in the path of Leigh's bullets. The battle is a grid. She can't see her own shots true—that would be too much like order—but she can avoid the bright and biting places where the order breaks down. She can keep this up forever.

She hopes she can keep this up forever.

"Stop running and face me!" Leigh is starting to sound angry. Good. Angry people make more mistakes, more errors; they drop things, they lose their focus, they lose their drive. Leigh has been calm and cool for long enough. Erin is ready for her to stop.

"No!"

"I don't understand why you have to be so unreasonable. I didn't raise you like this."

Erin stops, ducks around her pillar, fires two shots at Leigh, who somehow steps easily to the side. "You didn't raise me at all!"

"I may as well have!"

Too late, Erin realizes she's being herded. A heavy hand lands on her shoulder, and she looks up into the blank face of a manikin. She struggles to break away, watching Leigh Barrow walk toward her, calm and cruel as a hunting cat. She's still struggling when the wall in front of her thins and all but disappears, becoming a shining screen of silver.

Erin's eyes widen. She can't stop herself.

Leigh smiles. In a motion so smooth it looks practiced, Leigh turns and fires through the thin golden screen of the wall, pulling the trigger twice before the stone snaps back into solidity.

"There," she says, looking back to Erin. Her smile is smug and unwavering. "Looks like that may have cleared things up nicely, doesn't it? Now. Where were we?"

Avery took a step forward. His knees were shaking. His teeth were chattering. His whole skeleton felt like it was coming apart at the joints, like it was going to fall into so many bones on the floor. He wanted to turn. He wanted to run away. He didn't belong here.

But Zib was clinging to the bars of her cage, and he could see the black feathers pushing against her skin, trying to burst free, to turn her into a Crow Girl like all the others. She wouldn't be Zib if he let that happen. She'd be something else, something wilder and stranger and not his at all. He hadn't known her long enough to care as much as he did. He cared anyway. He couldn't let the Page have her.

"You have to give her back," he said. "She's my friend, and she doesn't belong to you."

The Page of Frozen Waters smiled. "Why should I?" she asked.

"Because . . ." Avery took a deep breath. "Because I asked, and because I'll cut you into ribbons if you don't."

—From *Over the Woodward Wall,* by A. Deborah Baker

# The End of All Things

Now the number is even.

—William Shakespeare, *Love's Labors Lost*

It is a callous age.

—L. Frank Baum

# Outcome

There's so much blood.

Roger didn't know there could be so much blood. It's everywhere, hot and red and bitter. Dodger is on her knees, eyes wide and glassy, one hand clasped over the hole in her shoulder. This, then, is where the slightest change changes everything; the length of the words he has given her have dictated her place along the wall. He can see where shortening the equation would have kept her safe, where lengthening it would have put the bullet through her heart. It's too complex. They cannot win.

His own heart is beating out of rhythm, starting to surrender to the sympathetic pull of Dodger's pain. He'll last longer than she does—he has the distant feeling that he always lasts longer than she does when she's the one who's hurt; that it has to be like that for them to have any chance—but if she dies, he won't be far behind. They walk the improbable road together, all the way to the end.

She's not moving. She's just kneeling, blood pouring down her arm and soaking into her jeans, and they're going to die here.

No: not necessarily. He can always tell her to take them back. Erin was clear about that. He knows the words to say, the instructions to give; he can get them out of here.

Dodger lifts her head.

"Wow," she says, in a voice gone pale with pain. "This hurts a lot. I mean, wow. I did *not* know how much this would hurt. I need to . . . add this . . . to the equation . . . Roger?"

"Dodge." He finally moves, hurrying to prop her up. There is so much blood. It's getting everywhere. They're both going to be covered, and he doesn't care, he doesn't *care,* because she's the one doing the bleeding; she's the one turning everything as red as her hair (no, redder, so much redder; he can see the color as clear as day, and for the first time, he doesn't care about that either).

"Tell me to finish."

He stops. That isn't the order he was expecting to give. Can he even give two orders at the same time? If he tells her to finish, will he be able to make her stop long enough to reset the timeline? Even for them, there are limits.

"Please." She closes her eyes, grimacing. "It hurts. Can't focus. You can make me focus. *Please.* I'm so close to done. I can see the shape of it. I can see . . . I know how to finish. I don't think I've ever gotten this close to finishing."

Roger pauses. "Do you remember being here before?"

"No. But the math does. It's in the imaginary numbers. They have echoes, places where the unfinished equations influence the way they hang together . . . please. I think I can finish."

He's killing her if he does this. He knows that. He might be killing both of them. Or he might be saving them both. "All right," he says softly. "Look at me."

Dodger opens her eyes.

"Finish the problem, Dodger. This is an order. This is a command. This is an adjuration. Finish the problem."

She smiles, even as her eyes go glassy with something more than pain. Her Sharpie is ruined, and so she doesn't reach for it; she dips her fingers in her own blood and begins writing on the wall, finger-painting like a child, slowly at first, but with gathering speed as the command and her own nature take control.

Roger straightens, stands. He needs to buy her some time, and he doesn't have much currency left. But he has one thing.

Dripping with his sister's blood, shaken to the core of himself, he turns and walks to the door, opens it, and steps out into the Baths.

It takes a moment for the scene he's walked into to make sense. There's Erin, held in place by a hulking mountain of a man. There's a dead man on the floor. There's a small, smiling woman who looks like she's just stepped out of a beauty pageant, or a horror movie, pointing a gun at Erin's chest. He knows Erin sees him; there's no way she could not. She does not betray him. Her eyes do not widen, her gaze does not waver. She's brought them this far, knowing her death may be the final coin to pay the ferryman's fee, and she won't waver now. There's something noble about that. More importantly, there's something stupid about it. Roger *wants* her to betray them.

Apparently, he has to do some things himself. "Hey!" he calls, waving his arms in a semaphore gesture of look-at-me. "What are you doing over there?"

The beauty queen turns. It's all he can do not to recoil. She's lovely, yes, but her eyes are a dead woman's, so cold and so flat that he can see the death of stars reflected there, even at this distance.

And he's seen her before, when he was a child, when she came to terrify him into giving up his sister. Until this moment, he didn't really believe his parents had betrayed him, but she's the proof. She always has been.

She frowns. "Roger?" she asks.

(Part of him remembers that voice, deep down and tucked away in a corner of his mind. He remembers every voice he's ever heard, on some level, because that too is a part of language. This voice was the first voice the world contained. This was the voice that pulled him from his mother's womb and said, "Oh, I think you'll do," like he was a tool, a piece of meat, and not a human child. The part of him that's never forgotten Leigh Barrow shies away from the reality of what he's about to do, and he is glad to let it go. Some things are easier for the unprepared.)

"Ayuh," he says, hitting that syllable with as much New England scorn and blank-faced disdain as he can muster. "You've got a friend of mine there. I'd prefer you didn't shoot her."

"Who, Erin?" Leigh gestures toward the captive woman with the barrel of her gun. "She's no friend of yours. She's been watching you on my orders for years. You know that, don't you? She was never your friend, never loved you, never cared one bit about what happened to you. She was just there to wait for the day when I'd tell her to pull the trigger."

"Roger, get *out* of here," snarls Erin, bucking against her captor. He holds her fast, hands like manacles, arms like chains. She can't escape from him. She never could. "Run!"

*(and they have been here before they have been exactly here before, Erin held captive, Roger emerging to beg for medical assistance—but no, they have* not *been here before, because he's come to beg for nothing; for the first time, he begs for nothing)*

"Not going to do that, Erin, sorry," he calls, and focuses back on Leigh. "Seems she changed sides at some point. Maybe when you told her to spend seven years sleeping with me. Even the best agent's going to start to waver when they get too close. Let her go. Let her down. If you'll do that, we'll think about letting you surrender."

Erin's eyes widen. Leigh's gun finally swings around to point at him.

"Oh, you stupid little Jack Daw," she says, almost sweetly, and pulls the trigger.

"*Miss!*" shouts Roger, and ducks to the side as the bullet whizzes harmlessly past his head. Leigh scowls and fires again, and "Miss!" he shouts again, and the bullet misses him, again. Roger grins, continuing to dance away from Leigh's probable line of fire.

"Can't hit when your bullets won't obey you, huh?" he asks. "We're manifest. You should give up while you still can."

"You're not manifest," she snaps, all fury and frustration. "You're wading at the edge of an ocean, and you're going to drown. Where's your sister, if you're so manifest? She's bleeding out in a room that doesn't exist, and as soon as she dies, you're powerless. If you even survive. I hope you do. I want to take you apart while you're still struggling to look me in the eye." Leigh fires again. The bullet misses again.

But it hits the wall. It goes through the wall.

Dodger is on the other side of the wall.

Roger hesitates. He can't help her. Going back in there would just distract her, give her something else to worry about, and she isn't calling for him. He can save Erin, if he tries. "Why don't you try to take me apart now?"

"She doesn't like it when the meat fights back," says Erin. "That's why the only people who'll work with her willingly are made of *mud*." She kicks the leg of the man who holds her. For the first time, Roger sees the strange smoothness of his skin, the blankness of his eyes. He's a constructed thing, and not a human being at all.

Dodger is a constructed thing. So is Erin. So is Roger. What does that make them?

Leigh turns her attention back to her captive, eyes narrow and body vibrating with fury. "That's it. I'm sorry, dearest, but you're fired."

She takes aim, the gun trained this time on Erin's forehead. A bullet at that range . . . there's no chance Erin will survive. No chance. Unless . . .

Roger closes his eyes. "Dodge, I need you to help me," he says, voice low, words quick. He's disrupting her train of thought. He knows that, and he's sorry, but some things can't wait. "Leigh has Erin captive by the far wall. There is a lot of water between her and me. I'm on a different section of floor. Can we . . . let that other piece go?"

"*Show me.*"

He opens his eyes. There's a flicker in his vision, the sense of someone else looking through his eyes (has the feeling ever been that strong? Has it ever been that easy to *know* when he's not alone, when one has become two has become something that is not a number, but is instead an inevitability?), and then, so soft that it barely qualifies as a whisper:

*"No. Brace yourself."*

The walls are not smooth. There is a delicate filigree to them, lips and ridges; the natural sort of refinements one puts into a bathhouse designed for the amusement and entertainment of legions. Roger jumps, grabs the nearest bit of protruding wall, and holds fast. It's a childish activity, dangling by his fingertips. There was a time when this would have kept him amused for hours, jumping up, hanging until he got tired, and then dropping down again. This time, he doesn't dare let himself fall. The feeling of Dodger watching through his eyes recedes.

The floor goes with her.

Not a section of floor, not a piece or portion: no. That would require too much finesse, and this is not a time for finesse. This is a time for brute force. The entire floor disappears, revealing the distant concrete ruins that are all that truly remain of the Sutro Baths, and the cold, cruel sea that beats itself against the shore. Erin has time to scream. The man holding her falls without a sound. And Leigh . . .

Leigh turns, glaring venom, and looks at him as she falls. She hits the waves and is gone. All of them are gone. Roger is alone, hanging by his fingertips above the distant, jagged shore.

*"Dodger!"* he howls. The crashing waves take his voice and claim it as their own. That doesn't stop him. *"Bring the floor back! They're gone, you have to bring the floor back!"*

The mercury glow returns, laced with timid gold. Then the gold overwhelms the silver, and the floor surges back, growing in the same fractal spiral as before. The glow fades, and there is concrete and carpet and the deep wells of empty bathing pools in its place.

Cautiously, Roger lowers himself down to test the solidity of the floor. It holds his weight with no more give than should be expected of good construction. He lets go of the wall, and still the floor holds him.

Erin is gone. He should feel worse about that. He should feel *more* about that, should feel anything at all. Instead, he's . . . numb, like this was a somehow-inevitable consequence, sad, yes, even heartbreaking, but no more or less tragic than everything else that's happened. Maybe he's a bad person. Maybe he's always been a bad person, and this is just the world finally proving it to him.

Or maybe the weight of what they've done here today will hit him one night a month from now, jerking him out of a sound sleep as he remembers the resignation on the face of a woman he'd believed himself to be in love with as she fell to her death in the deep, lightless waters of the Pacific. That's all in the future. The future is Dodger's department.

Dodger. His eyes widen for an instant before he closes them.

"Dodge?"

There's no reply.

He remembers to open his eyes before he breaks into a run.

The room where he left his sister and her math has been transformed into a chamber of horrors. There is blood everywhere. On the walls, the ceiling, the floor; there is blood in places blood should never be. It is brilliantly, violently red, so red that it attacks the eye, shaming and scarring it. And at the center of it all is Dodger.

She has never looked so small, or so pale. With all the blood, it seems impossible for her to be this pale. She should be a rose garden, drying in a hundred different, subtle shades of red. Instead, she is bone and wax and soapstone, she is snow and teeth and goose feathers. There is no color in her skin at all. Her hair is almost offensively bright next to the wrung-out rest of her.

Roger runs across the room. He knows the words—exsanguination, hypovolemia, hemorrhage—but he's never known them like this, as real things, tricky and tangled as venomous snakes. The words can comfort him. The words may be the *only* things that comfort him. They can't make things better.

Or maybe they can. The Sutro Baths are still all around him, solid and real. He's still here. Erin said he'd die if Dodger did, and he believes her, because he remembers that terrible day when Dodger tried to take herself out of the world. The edges of his vision are becoming riddled with those little black dots that came before the seizures, all those years ago, but they're *small,* they're almost something he can overlook. She's going. She isn't gone. Not yet.

He drops to his knees beside her. The blood is so thick that it squishes like jam on toast, gelatinous and warm and somehow obscene. He swallows his nausea, gathers her in his arms. She is so still. She is so cold.

But the walls . . .

The walls are covered with equations. No: not equations. With *equation,* one single string of formulae and functions, all leading toward an inevitable sum. It's beautiful. He doesn't understand it, and still, he knows it's beautiful. Dodger has reduced the world, the situation, them, to one room, filled with the quick, arcane figures that, for her, have always equaled reality.

"Wow," he whispers, and looks down at her. "You finished. Dodge, you finished. You did the whole thing. You finished it. Wake up now, okay? You finished, and that means you get to wake up, and we get to win."

She does not wake up.

He shakes her a little. He can't help himself. "Come on. I need you to tell me what this means. I need you to read it to me. Wake up."

She does not move, does not react, does nothing, in fact, but lie in his arms and bleed, growing colder and paler with every second. There can't be that many seconds left for her, and when she goes, he goes too. He has to reset. He has to tell her to take them back. They can go again, they can try again, and maybe next time—

Maybe next time they'll wind up right back here again, with all their ghosts still dogging their heels, and all their mistakes made for the second, or hundredth, or two hundredth time. No. He can't. It might be the right thing to do, and yet still, he can't.

Dodger got the math. He got the words. That was how this was sup-posed to work, right? He looks at the writing on the wall again, the figures and forms that mean just shy of nothing to him, and takes a breath. They did this once before. He knows what to do. He knows what the consequences might be. That doesn't mean he has a choice.

"Light," he reads, letting the symbols on the wall tell him what they want to be, what they want to *mean*. "This is the light of dark places, the light defined by its own absence, and through definition, becoming darkness; weight, mass, the cessation of emptiness—"

The building shakes as he reads, becoming the epicenter of its own unending, private earthquake. The walls glow gold and the sky is filled with blazing mercury light, sending a beacon up, up, ever onward into the heavens, into the ceaseless sky.

Look.

Look.

Look at the boy from Cambridge, Massachusetts, always too thin, now so tired he can barely move. He's uninjured, but that doesn't matter; he's still wounded. He holds the body of his sister, and if she's alive, it's only barely, survival measured by the thinnest of margins. His clothing is stained with her blood. His hands ache with splinters and with their own stillness, as if through motion he might have redeemed her and, by redeeming her, redeemed himself.

Look at the girl from Palo Alto, California, so motionless that it's clear how close she is to the transition from person to past. She is crumpled and cast-aside, exhausted from her own efforts to become something more than a consequence. The wound in her shoulder has crusted over; the bleeding has stopped. That doesn't matter. There was more than enough damage done to take her to the edge, and over, into what waits beyond. She is ready to return to the Up-and-Under via the graveyard path. When she goes, she knows she will not go alone.

On and on Roger reads, telling the story of the writing on the wall, and this, too, is something that goes back to the birth of mankind, the storytelling ape, the fire burning in the dark places: humanity has always yearned to interpret the signs around it. He looks at his sister's math, which he knows describes a universe, and he describes what he sees in ever-grander terms, feeling her body chill in his arms, watching the black spots gather at the edges of his vision, wiping the world away one fragment at a time.

It's too late for a reset now. She couldn't hear him if he called.

It's too late to go back and try again. For the first time, their story's ending.

"... and their names were Roger and Dodger, because they were named by people who should never have been allowed anywhere near children," he reads (*describes*), and squeezes her to his chest, like he would give her half of his own heartbeat, fill her veins with his own blood. "They grew up sort of weird and sort of wonderful and they found each other and lost each other over and over again. But this time, when they found each other, they came as close as they could to the Impossible City. They walked the length of the improbable road, and the girl wrote down everything she knew about the universe, and the boy read it all aloud, and everything was okay. Everything was fine. They got to be together."

He stops, looking down at Dodger expectantly. She doesn't move.

"Dodge, come on. I read your math."

She doesn't move.

"Come *on*." He shakes her, and still she doesn't move. Desperate, he looks back at the wall, searching for something—anything—he might have left out. That he might have missed.

There's a thumbprint next to the final figure. It could, under the right circumstances, be interpreted as an asterisk. She must have left it before she fell. So he reaches for her hand, and takes it firmly in his, and reads the ending.

"And they both lived."

Dodger opens her eyes.

# Spindrift

They walk out of the fading ghost of the Sutro Baths an hour later, Dodger leaning on Roger's arm, her eyes closed, letting him see the world for them both. They no longer need to reach to make that connection: closing their eyes is enough. Right now, neither of them can be truly alone; every time they blink, the other is there. No loneliness, no risk of separation. No privacy. They'll worry about that later, when Dodger is stronger, when Roger is less overwhelmed by the language of the world around him.

Both of them had believed themselves connected to their chosen disciplines. That was before. Before the sky turned to mercury: before the world cracked open and offered them its secrets. When Roger takes the lead, everything has a name, and he can all but see the story of the world hanging in the air. When he closes his eyes and Dodger opens hers, everything is numbers, surrounded by the calm calculation of angles and surface areas. This, too, will take some adjusting to. This will need to be worked on.

The Baths vanish behind them, gone again as they have been for decades. Dodger lets her head loll against Roger's shoulder, and smiles.

"I liked it there," she says. "We should live there."

"We can't live in a giant bathtub."

"Well, then, we should find someplace *like* there, and live in that place instead."

"Someplace that isn't real?"

"Someplace that used to be real but stopped for a while."

Roger nods. "Whatever you want, Dodge. We can live in a castle that got burnt down a thousand years ago, if it'll make you happy."

She nods, eyes half-closed. "It will."

"Good." He's been steering them toward the beach, walking around the driftwood and rocks littering the shore. Someone will spot them soon and call the Coast Guard or something. He's almost looking forward to that. They can take a nice ride in a boat and get Dodger someplace where she can be looked after. He's pretty sure her body would be thrilled to get a little more blood into it, and he knows he's a compatible donor. It's just a matter of finding someone with a needle to spare.

They walk down the shore, water lapping at their shoes, and somehow it's no surprise when a bundle of spindrift and kelp resolves into the body of a woman, lying, Ophelia-esque, in the foam.

"Dodger, can you stand on your own?"

"I can try," she says, and steps away from him, opening her eyes and wrapping her arms around herself. She's looking better. There's some color back in her cheeks, and when he moves out of her reach, she doesn't wobble. She's rebuilding herself, one simple cell division at a time, and biology is in many ways a mathematical function. She's going to be fine.

The same cannot necessarily be said of Erin. She's pale, but lacks the waxen bloodlessness Dodger so recently displayed: her skin has a faint greenish tinge, like she's lingered too long in the chambers of the sea. Human voices did not wake her. Her clothing is torn, but her limbs seem straight and strong, and she has no visible wounds.

"Erin." Roger kneels beside her, lifting her head tenderly from the sand. Dodger, watching, can finally see how they were lovers; can see the delicate hyperspace they sketched between them, before Erin's betrayal shattered it forever.

He cups her skull with his fingers, looking at her closed eyes, and smiles, because he can see the story of her. She finally makes sense.

"You're okay," he says. "Open your eyes."

There's nothing to contradict him, no reason she *shouldn't* be able to survive the trauma she's endured. His words are put before the universe, and after a moment, the universe agrees with him. Her eyes open. She blinks, twice, before she gasps, taking a huge, sucking breath of air. Roger takes his hands away as she begins to cough, rolls onto her side, and vomits a lungful of water onto the sand.

Dodger tilts her head. "What, you can raise the dead now?" she asks. "Fancy."

"Hey, *you* were almost dead what, fifteen minutes ago? Shut your face."

"I'll shut *your* face," she says, smirking, amused. She quiets, and watches Erin continue to vomit what seems like half the sea out of her body. There is more water there than woman, or at least it looks that way. Maybe Roger *can* raise the dead.

Dodger hugs herself and shivers, and wonders whether that's a good thing.

Finally, Erin is finished vomiting. She pushes herself unsteadily upright in the sand and coughs, once, before she smiles. "You did it," she says, looking from the blood-smeared Roger to the blood-drenched Dodger. "You manifested."

"That and a cup of coffee will buy us a night in a holding cell if we don't get off this beach," says Dodger. "Someone's going to call the Coast Guard soon, if they haven't already, and since we're probably being looked at for arson right now, maybe that's not such a good thing? As a thought?"

"You don't understand how much things have changed for you," says Erin. She shifts her weight to her feet, tottering into a standing position. She looks weak as a kitten. "No one's going to arrest you, or try to put you in jail. No one's going to touch you, ever again, if you don't want them to."

For a girl who just maybe-drowned, she's remarkably spry. Roger watches her, an uneasy sense of responsibility spreading through his bones. This is his. He made it, made *her,* when he called her back from her watery grave. "So we're done," he says.

Erin looks at him. "Not quite. There's still one person out there who knows what you are, knows what you can do, and knows enough to want to hurt you."

"Reed," says Dodger, in a voice like a sigh.

Erin nods. "He knows you've manifested. When you found yourselves, it was like a signal flare for the people who knew what to watch for. He's going to be marshalling his forces. If you want to stay alive— if you want to stay free—you need to take this to him. You need to *stop* him."

"And then what?" Dodger is pale and weak-looking, but her voice cracks like a whip. "Is there another dungeon we have to crawl through, another dragon we have to defeat? Don't look at me like that. I was a nerd kid, I played D&D. Just answer the question. If we do this, do you throw another boss fight in our path, or do you walk away and leave us the fuck alone?"

"This is the last one," says Erin. "We stop him, and the Up-and-Under is safe, at least until some other asshole comes along and decides to destroy the house that Baker built."

"Well, when that happens, it's going to be someone else's problem," says Roger firmly. "We'll do this, because we deserve to be left alone. And after that, you're *going* to leave us alone. You're never going to see us again."

"Deal," says Erin. She smiles a skeleton's smile, all teeth and pallor. "He's never going to see us coming."

Roger looks at her, and hopes she's right.

Avery and Zib stood hand-in-hand, looking at the great towers of the Impossible City. The buildings here weren't like any other buildings they had ever seen. They *moved*, changing shape and form and function according to the needs of the people who walked on their high walkways, moving between them like dreams.

Beside them, Niamh sighed.

"What's wrong?" asked Zib.

"I lived here once," said Niamh. "I never will again."

"Why not?"

"Because drowned girls are very possible, and the Impossible City only welcomes impossible things. Girls like me happen too often to ever make it home . . ."

—From *Over the Woodward Wall*, by A. Deborah Baker

# After the End

It's mathematics, the ultimate code,
And the universe was singing in my favorite mode . . .
—Dr. Mary Crowell, "The Doctrine of Ethos"

Everything is measured in the span of a second.
—A. Deborah Baker

# Cost and
# Consequence

Leigh is dead and the cuckoos are in the wind and the only thing
Reed can't understand is how it's all gone so wrong so *fast*. They
were weak, separated, in denial: their only use was in keeping the
Doctrine contained until their replacements could mature enough to
take it as their own. None of this is in keeping with the plan, and he
doesn't have time for it.

He would regret the loss of Leigh, if there was time. She was a liability, yes, and he had been planning to kill her, absolutely, but she
had been loyal in her way, and she had deserved to die a victor, not . . .
whatever this was. What was the point of traveling to the Impossible
City, only to fall before the doors were even opened? It was unfair. It
held no resonance. Asphodel would have called it narratively unsat-
isfying for one of the heroes to die this close to achieving their goals.

(The thought that Asphodel would not have called Leigh a hero,
would not have called *him* a hero, never crosses his mind. This is his
story, has been since he wrested it away from his creator, and of course
he's the hero. How could he be anything else?)

They'll be coming for him next. They must. They're manifest, and they'll be seeking the City now, seeking it with all the zeal of their conflicted cuckoo hearts. More, they'll know that he alone, in all the world, holds the keys to their unmaking. So they'll come for him and, through him, for the Impossible City.

There is little time left. Subtlety, such as it is, must fall by the wayside. There is too much left to do.

The box, which left Reed's hands not three hours prior, is placed before the High Priest of the American Alchemical Congress with the reverence of a sacrament, who looks at the paper—dull lead scribed with platinum sigils—and frowns.

"What is this nonsense?" he demands.

"An apprentice of Master Daniels found this in the walls of the old master's house," says the alchemist who carried the box into the room. He is slight, slender, and shivering.

The others dismiss his shaking as awe. Who wouldn't feel awe, in the presence of the greatest of the American alchemists? They have peers around the country, but none of them can compare to the presence and power in this room.

Perhaps if they looked closer, they might see that it is not awe but terror that puts the tremble in his hands. Perhaps they might ask themselves why he comes to them now, with so little fanfare; why the box was found now and not years ago.

Here is a secret about powerful men, one they would prefer go unspoken: their arrogance is one of the greatest forces in the universe. Even the most paranoid among them see what they want to see, believe what they want to believe, and this creates cracks through which the clever may insinuate themselves, changing the story around them.

The alchemist who carried the prize here, to these men, these powerful, greedy, terrible men, closes his eyes. He has to tell himself that his lover will be safe: that Reed will keep his word and let the man go. Every war, however slow, however understated, has its crossfires, and he was, in the end, unable to keep the man he loved above all others out of the way.

His love will live and he will die, and in this moment, that seems like the only way this could have gone.

The seal on the package is broken by a greedy master's hands, unable to scan through the lead paper with any accuracy: the mechanism inside bursts, spraying alkahest from one side of the room to the other, and all that remains is the screaming.

Soon, even that is done, and the rest is silence.

# Ghosts

They cross the country as ghosts: silently, swiftly, leaving no footsteps. Buses let them board without tickets; trains do the same, although the number and variety of the conductors means either Roger or Dodger has to be awake at all times, to smile blithely and work their own version of the strange magic surrounding them. (Roger pulls what he insists on calling "Jedi mind tricks," telling the conductors their tickets are in order. Dodger produces bits of paper—receipts, movie stubs, old index cards—and holds them up for inspection, nodding solemnly when they're taken for valid tickets. It's penny-ante stuff, the sort of tricks that will be beneath them before much longer, and yet they can't conceal their glee when it works. Here it is: the proof that they are what Erin said they were, and more, that they're getting stronger, more capable, by the day. It won't be long before no one will notice them if they don't want to be noticed, if they tell the air to keep them hidden, the world to keep them safe. Roger thinks this is a quiet tragedy. Dodger thinks this is a miracle. Both of them are right.)

They're getting stronger. They're still holding themselves back. Erin, who knows more than they do, even if she's never been here before, refuses to tell them what to do. They have to figure it out on their own. This time, every time, if she wants it to work, she has to let them figure it out on their own.

But oh, they're moving so slowly, and oh, she's so afraid they won't be fast enough when they need to be.

The last bus lets them off in Ohio, where the air is hot with summer and the sky is bruised with the promise of a storm. There are cities here—they've seen them, even passed through a couple, when the bus routes curved just *so*—but this is the country, the kind of wide, flat country neither of them has ever seen. They were born here. That doesn't make it home. They are children of the jagged, coastal places, the spots where the land drops away and the sea comes up to catch it. This grand flatness, this tornado-catcher of a country, has never belonged to them. The man they are on their way to meet made sure of that.

"Not too late," says Dodger, and she's lying.

"Always was," says Roger, and he's not. He takes her hand, and together they follow Erin into the corn.

They are less than a week into their manifestation and already the signs of it are clear, for anyone with eyes that know how to see, with ears that know how to hear. They stand taller, walk straighter, move with more ease. Dodger shows no signs that she's barely recovered from a life-threatening injury; if anything, she looks healthier than she's ever been, walking fast, moving faster, her every gesture an attack on the world around her. She's fully integrated her new depth perception into her vision, and has stopped running into things quite so often, although she still runs at them like she expects everything, even walls, even mountains, to stand aside.

Roger, on the other hand, ambles through the world. Let Dodger race ahead; he'll always catch up. He moves smoothly, easily, and everything around him rearranges to let him pass. He is comfortable in both his own skin and his place in the world. It's a terrifying combination, for those few who can look at it and understand what it means. Erin supposes that, after they have faced down Reed, for better or for worse, the people who can tell what Roger and Dodger are by looking at them will never trouble them again. Some risks are too dangerous to take when there's any way for them to be avoided.

The corn rustles around them, husks rubbing one against the other like the legs of a thousand insects. Dodger wrinkles her nose.

"This is very outdoors," she says. "I don't *like* outdoors. That's where you get sent when you've been bad."

Roger, who has started hearing the echoes of the things she doesn't say, hears the words "where your parents send you," even though they go unspoken. He reaches for her hand, takes it, squeezes it, and keeps walking.

(He can raise the dead, but he needs something *to* raise, and there was nothing left when Leigh was done. Her parents are as lost to her as his are to him, and he wishes at least one of them had been spared.)

"Reed wants to be well concealed," says Erin. "He likes to think of himself as a spider, sitting in his web, pulling his strings and keeping things hidden. The new King of Cups."

There's so much Roger wants to say. He says none of it. That Reed must die is certain. That Erin, not Dodger, not him, will be the one to pull the trigger is equally certain. All of them have people they want to avenge, deaths they want repaid. But Dodger's never killed anyone, and the only people he's killed—Leigh and the man of earth—were killed in self-defense. However necessary this is, it's still murder.

They wade through the corn until it seems like the world is nothing *but* corn, gold like the Impossible City, like the Sutro Baths. Maybe this is the true essence of the Up-and-Under, of transmutation, of everything: the purification of the base materials of soil and sky and water into golden kernels, growing sweet and patient on their stalks. Erin darts ahead, and suddenly there's a shack in the middle of the corn, small and listing to one side, made of corrugated tin. Someone has painted it with silver paint, until it shines like mercury in the sun.

Roger and Dodger both stop and blink at the shack, nonplussed.

"Is that it?" asks Dodger.

Erin opens the door and smiles, quick and tight. "It's a long way down." Then she's gone, vanishing into the gloom inside the shack, and they have no choice but to follow. She is their only guide, now that they've committed themselves to walking the improbable road all the way to the King. They can't afford to lose her.

The shed door swings shut behind them, and all is silence. Silence, and the corn.


Erin wasn't joking when she said it was a long way down: a hatch in the shed floor opens on a spiraling staircase descending down, down, into the darkness below the corn. They descend until it begins to feel ridiculous, until Dodger—who grew up in earthquake country, not twister country—is sticking so close to Roger's side that he's afraid he'll trip over her and send them both tumbling down into the dark.

The stairs *are* dark. There are lights every ten feet or so, but they're barely enough to split the gloom. They've descended almost fifty feet before he realizes the lights are getting brighter, matching the adjustment of their eyes. This system will keep people disoriented for as long as humanly possible, rather than letting them fully adjust to either dark or day. He'd be impressed, if he weren't so angry.

The light brightens. The stairwell opens up as it drops away. The last fifteen feet of the spiral stair winds through the open air, descending into a room that looks more like an airplane hangar. The walls are tin, like the shed upstairs; the floor is industrial linoleum. Dodger looks around, eyes narrowed, assessing everything. Roger wants to ask what she sees. He doesn't dare speak aloud.

Erin quickens her pace. They do the same, and the three of them reach the ground still alone, still without pursuit.

"Now what?" whispers Dodger.

"Now we tell Daddy dearest that we're home—don't look so alarmed, Roger. I'm an adoptive sibling at best, and a distant, distant, *distant* cousin at worst. You didn't screw your sister."

"Ew," says Dodger.

Erin chuckles—a quick, bitter thing—before she cups her hands around her mouth and shouts, "James Reed! We're here for you!"

When she lowers her hands, Roger and Dodger are staring at her. She smirks, shrugs.

"He's going to know sooner or later. This is better than skulking around the place, running into all his old experiments." Erin's face darkens. "There are things here you should never have to see. That *I* should never have seen. Consider yourselves lucky that you won't have to."

"But they should have," says a new voice, a man's voice, calm and level as any professor. That's what he sounds like: a teacher, someone to be trusted without question. The sort of man who would grade fairly on the curve, who would take the time to clearly explain the material and make sure the entire class is on the same page.

Roger and Dodger turn. Erin doesn't. She's seen James Reed before. She has no need to see him now.

He's tall, as has always been the fashion for men with voices like his, in positions like this one. Baker was a performer, after all. She knew the importance of things like height, like looking the part. So Reed is tall, and Reed is handsome, with a smile that would have made parents worry about the virtue of their daughters when he was younger, when the world was simpler, when virtue was considered something to be lost. His hair is the color of desert sand, and his eyes are like a viper's, bright as jewels, constantly calculating.

He is smiling, and both of them are wise enough to see the danger there, and neither of them knows how to turn it aside.

"I saw what you did, you know," he says conversationally, walking closer, like a man out for an evening stroll. "I think every alchemist in the world probably saw. You painted the sky like a canvas, and wasn't it a lovely shade of gold? Which one of you figured out what to do, by the by? My little cuckoo-children, sent into the world to fend for yourselves. I always knew you'd fly back to the nest. Back to me."

Dodger's hand tightens on Roger's, grinding their fingers together until it hurts. "I didn't fend for myself," she says. "I had parents. Heather and Peter Cheswich. You had them killed."

"Don't take that tone with me, Dodger; if you had a father in this world, it was me, and little girls shouldn't speak so to their fathers." The mask slips. Only for a moment, but long enough for them to see through into the chasm on the other side. He's dangerous, this jovial humbug of a man, and he'll kill them if he can. Then the mask snaps back into place, and he says, "I didn't have them killed, Leigh chose to kill them. There's a difference there, if you feel like having a productive conversation. I can't control who my subordinates choose to kill. Why, if I could, you wouldn't have dropped three of my best people into the ocean just because you were having a bit of a sulk."

"They were trying to kill us," says Roger.

"I'm not one of your people," says Erin.

"Saying you were one of my best wasn't enough for you?" Reed clucks his tongue. "Kids these days. But you're not the matter at hand, are you? No, no. Not at all." He shifts his focus back to Roger and Dodger, continuing to walk toward them. "You could have been perfect. You still could be. Hand me your reins. Let me bind you to my service, be my children, let me love you, and I will let you live."

"No," says Roger. "We're not here to work for you. We're not tools."

"Oh, but you are, Roger. You always have been. I am a master craftsman, and you're very much your father's son." Reed shakes his head. "If you're not here to work for me, I assume you're here to return what you've stolen from me. That's awfully good of you, all things considered."

"We don't have anything of yours," says Dodger.

Roger says nothing, but he tugs her back, making sure their shoulders are aligned, that there's no way for them to be separated without seeing it coming. She's the better liar. The flipside is that he's better at telling truth from lies, at least when he hears them coming from other people. He knows what Reed wants.

"We can't surrender the Doctrine," he says. "We *are* the Doctrine. The only way we could let it go is to . . ."

Roger stops as Reed begins smiling the slow, vicious smile of a man who believes he holds all the cards.

"That's right," he says. "You're going to have to die. I'd apologize, but well. You must have seen it coming."

Dodger laughs.

All the others turn to look at her. Erin is annoyed; Reed bewildered; Roger amused.

"Oh, man, really?" she asks. "We, like, walk in here as the living embodiment of a cosmic force *you* felt the need to pin down and incarnate, and you think you can just waltz up and *kill* us? How were you planning to do that?"

"By distracting you," he purrs.

Leigh drops the Hand of Glory, appearing out of nowhere. The metal rebar in her other hand is long enough to catch them both in the back of the head at the same time. They are still flesh; they are still mortal. They fall. Erin snarls, reaching for the gun in her belt, and stops as the barrel of someone else's gun is pressed against the base of her skull.

"Please don't make me," whispers a young female voice, green as grass, as springtime, as any usurper's daughter looking at a throne she doesn't want and never asked for. Erin goes very still. The other math child, the chosen contender for Dodger's place.

"As you can see, my dear, cosmic power doesn't make a person clever. It just makes them sloppy. Never count a construct out until you've seen the body. Leigh came home two days ago. Damp, battered, and angry. You should have been more careful." Reed steps daintily over Dodger, kneeling next to Roger. "He has my chin . . . Thank you, Erin, for delivering them to me. Now's where you try to convince us you're still loyal. We won't believe you, of course, but it might be fun to hear what you have to say."

"I betrayed you both," says Erin. "What you're doing, what you're trying to do—it's wrong. I won't be a killer for you anymore."

"The little girl behind you has no such compunctions."

The nameless girl makes a small whimpering sound. Erin thinks, but does not say, that she has plenty of compunctions. She just has too much to lose to give them voice.

Leigh drops her rebar with a clatter. Erin's eyes flick to her.

"How are you alive?" she asks, in an almost conversational tone. Anything to keep them talking and keep herself breathing. Roger doesn't have the skill to put her back together after she takes a bullet to the brain. He will someday. He's not there yet.

"You can't drown a dead woman," says Leigh. There's a new rasp in her voice, a deep gurgle that speaks of water in the lungs. She narrows her eyes. "How are *you* alive?"

"You made me to see the chaotic places in everything. I'm sure the side effect of me hating the world was an accident. Doesn't matter. I hit the water seeing all the spots where it was wildest and most likely to hurt me. I swam around them." It was a small way to describe a big, terrifying moment, one that ended, inevitably, with her inhaling a lungful of water and washing up on the shore for Roger and Dodger to find. But she'd done it. She'd made it out of the sea without being battered into pieces on the rocks. Under the circumstances, she can't see that as anything other than a victory.

Leigh looks, briefly, almost impressed. "I suppose we did an excellent job with you, your betrayal notwithstanding. I'll make the next one along the same lines. She'll be loyal."

"If you wanted loyalty, you shouldn't have killed Darren."

"I'll keep that in mind," says Leigh. She looks to Reed. "Can I kill her now?"

"Kimberley can pull that trigger if you like. I'm sure she's eager to get down to the business of stripping the Doctrine from these unworthy hosts."

Leigh frowns. "I want to do it myself."

"You want to do everything yourself. Learn to delegate." Reed lets go of Roger's chin, straightening as the other man's face hits the floor. "I want them stripped, cleaned, and brought to the lab. It's time to begin." Then he walks away, whistling.

Leigh and Erin both glare hatred at his receding back. In that moment, if in no other, they are united.

The moment passes. Leigh turns back to Erin, and smiles.

"Bring her, Kim," she says. "It's time she learned the penalty for going against her betters."

\* \* \*

The lab where Erin is placed is familiar: she grew up here. She knows every line and color, every piece of well-worn furniture. She can close her eyes and picture Darren anywhere in this room, a smirk on his lips, trying so hard to look cool, even when neither one of them had any idea what "cool" was.

*"Hey, Erin, you know what?"*

*"What?"*

*"When we get out of here, I'm going to take you someplace so swank it doesn't seem real. Like Disneyland."*

*"I believe you."*

She did. She does. If Darren were here, if Roger could call him back from dust and bones the way she'd been called back from the sea, he would untie her and take her someplace so swank it wouldn't seem real. He always kept his promises, right up until he promised never to leave her. But that was a foolish promise, wasn't it? He should have known better. They both should have known better.

The children made here never know better. She's banking on that.

As she has since she was left here, alone, tied up tight as a Thanksgiving turkey, she scans the air, looking for patches of chaos. Air in an enclosed system like this one will always trend toward order, becoming invisible to her. Storm cells are an impossible, painful beauty reserved for the world above.

This time, her patience is rewarded. There's a patch of chaos toward the center of the room, a place where the air has been thrown somehow into disarray, even though there should be nothing there. "I see you," she says, in a calm, carrying voice. "You can put the Hand down."

As she'd hoped—prayed, even, although she's never quite sure what she's allowed to pray to—a Hand of Glory appears on the table nearest to the disturbance, flames freshly blown out, and a teenage girl with hair so white it verges on pale corn-silk green is there. Unlike the Hand, she doesn't appear: she's been there for some time. She was simply, prior to this moment, difficult to see.

She is too thin, dressed in tattered clothes twenty years out-of-date, shivering in the warm air of the lab. She watches Erin like a fawn, all enormous eyes and unstoppable twitches. Erin looks calmly back at her, face composed, unmoving.

"How did you know I was there?" the girl asks, finally. "I had . . . I had a Hand . . ."

"I didn't," says Erin, and smiles. "Kim, wasn't it? Untie me, Kim. I have unfinished business with the man who made you."

"I can't. They have my brother."

He's gotten smarter, Reed has: he's figured out that a hostage is a better lever than a corpse. If only he'd learned that lesson a little sooner, Erin might have stayed loyal. She shakes her head.

"You can't let that give them the power to control you," she says. "Do you know who the people I came here with are?"

"Usurpers," says Kim. She doesn't sound like she understands what the word means. She probably doesn't. Reed has never been a fan of well-informed subordinates, and she's not the one with a dictionary where her heart ought to be.

"They're the living Doctrine of Ethos. They're what Reed wants to turn you into. He can't control them, so he wants to kill them. If he does, if he succeeds, the Doctrine will pass to you and your brother, and you'll never be free, ever. Do you understand that? He'll keep you here forever, and he'll do whatever he must to prevent you from breaking free. You'll never have your brother back."

Kim's face twists in sudden rage. "Oh, what, and you'll give him to me? Timothy is *scared* and he's *alone* and you're trying to trick me into letting him get hurt, because you're racing Mr. Reed for the universe. If we become the Doctrine, we'll be safe."

"No, you won't," says Erin, keeping her voice calm. "If you become the Doctrine, you'll be pawns, and a man who'd do the sort of things Reed has done will be able to control the universe. Roger and Dodger don't want to hurt you. They'll do their best to protect you, but they can only do that if they're alive and free. Untie me. Let me help them. Let me help you."

"He has my *brother*."

"He has Dodger's brother, too. She's a math kid, just like you. She sees numbers everywhere she looks. She's also a prissy princess who doesn't like anyone talking to her precious Roger, but she fights it down okay. We're not friends. I think the two of you could be. I think you could learn a lot from each other. What are you, sixteen?"

"Fifteen," admits Kim.

"Having a mentor who actually understands might do you a world of good. Timothy's all about language, isn't he? Well, so is Roger, and he's the sweetest, kindest, most generous fool you'll ever meet. These are the people you should be throwing your weight behind. Not a humbug alchemist and a dead woman dressed up in her Sunday clothes." Erin shakes her head. "Untie me. I'll get your brother back."

Kim takes a hesitant step forward. "Promise?"

"Promise to try."

Kim hesitates. Erin looks at her, trying not to focus on how easy it would be to snap her neck, how quickly one small motion would put Reed's plans into the grave. Timothy—"Tim," as she's sure they call him—would die without his other half. There'd be no appropriate second vessel for the Doctrine. Even if he managed to kill Roger and Dodger, freeing the Doctrine from the confines of their flesh, it would be another fifteen years before he could try for an embodiment. All she has to do is kill a child, and she'll have time for her revenge.

All she has to do is become Leigh's monster daughter, and not just her science project.

When Kim unties her hands, Erin flexes them to bring back the circulation, but she doesn't reach for the girl's throat. When Kim unties her arms, Erin begins pulling the ropes away of her own accord, but she doesn't lunge. Let Leigh be the monster of the piece. Erin will find another way. She knows there has to be one. There's always another way.

The Hand of Glory is still half-potent, good for an hour or more of concealing light. She slides off the table, picks it up, and looks at Kim. "I can tie you up if you like," she says. "They'll think I tricked you. They won't be angry. Not at you, anyway."

Kim shakes her head. "I need to get to my brother."

"Suit yourself." Leigh always kept the matches on the workbench, next to the henbane. Erin grabs them, touches one to the Hand's primary wick, and is gone from all human sight.

Kim stands where she is for a long moment, looking at the place where Erin isn't. Then she runs for the door. "I'm coming, Tim," she mutters, wishing he could hear her, knowing she's alone. "Hold on, because I'm coming."

# Birthright

Dodger wakes naked on her back in a strange room, held down by ropes of braided silk. She blinks at the ceiling, which is a perfect astronomical map of the night sky. Then she closes her eyes.

"Roger?"

"Here." The voice is close and distant at the same time. She opens her eyes, breaking their temporary connection, and turns her head—all she can easily move, at the moment—to see Roger on a table she assumes is much like the one she's tied to. Like her, he's naked. Like her, he's tied down with silk rope. Presumably also like her, his entire body has been painted with mercury runes. She squints. Their meaning is obscure, but she can see their mathematical value, which trends, inexorably, toward zero.

"Why aren't we dead?"

"Because we are the Doctrine."

Silence from Dodger. Roger swallows the impulse to sigh. She's not being intentionally slow: she doesn't understand. He wishes he didn't, either.

"We have the Doctrine and those kids of Reed's don't. If he kills us, we take the Doctrine with us, and he has to start over." A whole new generation of—what? Science projects? Children? Clones? It doesn't matter. They end this here and now, or they condemn another series of children just like they were to play out this little drama, over and over, forever.

"Oh." Dodger's voice is small. "He needs to subtract so he can add, instead of just wiping us off the board."

"Yes. Can you see how I'm tied?"

Dodger answers with a question: "Am I covered in weird squiggles?"

"Yes," he says.

"What do they mean?"

He's too far away for her to see the fine points of his expression, but he's not too far away for her to catch the flash of fear when he replies, "Reduction, removal, extraction. I was awake when they were painting us."

"All those things mean 'zero' to me. He's going to use them to siphon off the Doctrine."

"Yeah." He doesn't mention the bucket he saw them carry in, the bucket full of what they call "alkahest," the universal solvent. It can dissolve anything. Even a universal constant.

Dodger didn't see the bucket. He can't hear her thoughts, but he knows what she's thinking: it wouldn't be so bad to lose the Doctrine, would it? They'd go back to being the people they were before they followed Erin into a building that didn't exist and solved the universal equations. She'll still love math. He'll still love words. They just won't be tied to those things on a cosmic level. They'll be able to get out of each other's heads, to do whatever they want with their lives, to be *people*, instead of ideas.

Even as she thinks it, she knows it isn't possible. The math doesn't work. They aren't people who somehow inherited a cosmic force of logic and definition: they *are* that force, made incarnate by someone who should have known better, should have done better, should have *been* better. They're ideas who dreamt of being people, and now that they're waking up, it's too late for them to be anything else. The children Reed intends to put in their places might still be able to turn human. She and Roger . . . no. Not anymore.

She knows without asking that Roger reached the same conclusion before she woke; he was just waiting for her to catch up. She closes her eyes. "We need to get out of here."

"Got any ideas?"

"Aren't we supposed to represent the base forces of the universe?"

"Yeah, but that doesn't come with a Penn and Teller starter course."

He sounds so frustrated that she laughs a little. Eyes still closed, she says, "Reed wants to strip us to our base components and instill them in our replacements. Which ends with us dead and them pretty screwed-up. I wouldn't want a mad scientist shoving something into me just because he thought it should be there. There has to be something we can do."

"Can you math your way out of being tied up?"

Dodger's eyes open, widen. She stares at the ceiling for a second before she smiles and says, "That's not a bad idea. Hang on." She squirms, getting a feel for the rope around her, before looking back to Roger. "Okay. The tables are thirty-six inches in width and four inches thick. That means each loop around the table itself, not including us, involves eighty inches of rope. Adding our geometry—"

She talks faster and faster, until Roger is no longer following what she's saying. She gets like this when there's math involved, and he's not going to interrupt, because he can see the shape of what she *means*, and what she means is "I can get us out of this." He watches as she twists just so, shifting her shoulder up, shifting her arms a fraction of an inch to the side. She's working at the knots without ever touching them, using the physics of the rope and the math of the situation as a whole to get herself free. He isn't sure she can do it. It shouldn't be possible. But then, when has anything about them been possible?

This, too, is a manifestation. He's starting to see how they can walk in the world when all this is over. Magic doesn't have to be flashy and huge. Sometimes, it's the subtle things that are the most effective of all.

"—and pull and *ha!*" Dodger sits up, the rope falling loose around her. She's still naked and covered in silvery runes, but some things are less important than freedom.

Roger averts his eyes as she runs to his side, and keeps them averted while she's untying him. Then he sits up, and they look around the room. It's bigger than it seemed at first, with a floor painted in constellations, like a strange mirror of the starry sky above them. The walls are stained glass, each panel showing a scene from one of Baker's books, but subtly changed. The King of Cups holds a staff in one hand and a chalice in the other. The Stormcrow Princess is still charred gray, but she wears the robes of a rival wizard, and the color of her skin is clearly the result of chemical poisoning, flesh blistered by things she was never meant to steal.

Through all the panels move Avery and Zib, the students, learning at the hand of the master. Water runs through their hands and is transmuted into blood; dust is transmuted into air. Maybe he could have just . . . asked . . . and the ropes would have gone to wind and nothingness.

"We need to stop thinking like there are rules," he says.

"These people are *bonkers* and I want my clothes," says Dodger.

"Agreed," says Roger. "The door's this way. Come on."

They cross the room with quick, economical steps. It's remarkably easy to walk without looking at each other; they just keep swapping off whose eyes are closed, letting them both stay anchored in the present without risking seeing something they shouldn't.

The door slams open just before they would have reached it, and there is Leigh Barrow, grinning like a skeleton, a bone saw in her hands. "Did you think you were going somewhere?" she asks, in a voice like oleander honey, like every poisoned poem the world has ever known. "Lay down. It'll hurt less if you lay down."

Dodger breaks away from her brother. Dodger, who has always attacked the world, who has approached every opportunity as the chance to challenge for dominance, and win. Her shoulder hits Leigh in the center of her chest, and then the two are falling, a writhing mass of limbs and deadly edges as Leigh waves her saw, trying to make contact with Dodger without cutting herself.

"*Stop!*" shouts Roger, and he doesn't believe it will work, not here, not against the woman who has been the monster in the back of his mind since he was born, since she came to his house and threatened everything he'd ever known. He doesn't believe it will work, and he's still growing into the space of his own skin: in the face of his doubt, nothing happens. Leigh continues to thrash. Dodger, who was never his target, continues to fight.

"*Run!*" Dodger shrieks.

He knows she's not asking him to abandon her: this request, made here and now, is a cry for help, for him to find a way to save them both. He still hesitates long enough for Leigh's saw to draw first blood before he runs deeper into the silent compound, looking for an answer.

Nothing here is familiar. Everything here is familiar. The déjà vu that has defined his life haunts him in every hallway, even places where no one would ever take an infant. He's seen this place before in other timelines, other attempts to manifest. It's enough to make him wonder how many times they've supposedly "won," only to follow Erin into the dark and die here, miles below the fields of golden corn.

Then a body is running toward him down the hall, and he skids to a stop bare seconds before he would have collided with a teenage girl whose hair carries surprisingly green undertones, like she grew from the corn herself. She makes a small squeaking noise when she sees that he's naked, her cheeks flaring red, and tries to run past him.

He grabs her arm before she can. "Who are you?" he demands.

"Kimberley," she says. "Please. I have to find my brother."

Of course. "His name is Timothy, right?" She nods, eyes wide. "I'm Roger. My sister, Dodger, is fighting a woman we thought was dead. I need to stop her. Can you help me?"

Her wide-eyed gaze turns wary. "You're them. You're the ones who stole the Doctrine."

"No, honey, we're not. We're the ones who earned it, and we're the ones who want to save you. Unless this is what you want your life to be?" He waves his free hand, indicating the tunnel around them. "If we get away, so do you. You're just a kid. You deserve the chance to be something more than everything."

"That's what the other lady said, before she stole my candle."

Other lady . . . "You saw Erin? You gave her a Hand of Glory?" God, when did all this start making sense? When did these become the building blocks of an ordinary conversation, on an ordinary day?

Kimberley nods tightly. Roger sighs.

"All right. Erin's . . . going to do what Erin's going to do. Right now, we need to save my sister. Can you help me?"

"Mr. Reed says when we're the Doctrine, we won't need anybody to help us."

"Mr. Reed is wrong," says Roger. "You're always going to need people. Please. Let me need you now."

"Okay," she whispers. He lets go of her arm. She offers her hand and he takes it, only jumping a little at the jolt that passes between them. It's not the same as the space he and Dodger make when they're together, but it's similar enough that he knows this girl is of their kind; she and her brother both are their kin, and must be protected at all costs.

"Guess the family just got a little bigger," he says, and lets her lead him into the dark.

They haven't gone very far when they break back into a run.

D odger and Leigh roll around the floor for almost a minute before the bone saw scores a bright line of pain down Dodger's back and she breaks free, retreating to a safe distance. Leigh is laughing, delighted by the whole exciting digression from the original plan.

"Oh, little cuckoo, you are a wonder and a delight and a nuisance," she says, shifting her bone saw to her other hand. A bit of blood has dripped onto her arm. She lifts it to her mouth, running her tongue along the stain and smiling. "I am so going to enjoy taking you apart."

"You stay the hell away from me." Dodger retreats farther. She needs time to do the math, time to find the numbers that will set her free. Roger says she needs to let go of the rules, but rules are what make the numbers *work*. There will always be rules, for her. That's probably a good thing. Without them, she would unmake everything just to make him happy.

There is equipment piled against the walls, where they had missed it in their hurry to escape. Long benches of beakers and vials, the tools of the alchemist's trade. But no knives. No convenient hacksaws or axes. She grabs a few beakers, holding them to her chest as she backs away from Leigh. When the other woman advances, she flings, calculating the arc of momentum and descent with unconscious ease. They burst against Leigh's chest and shoulders, making her laugh even harder.

"Really? This is how you fight me? With flung glassware, and the idea that good will triumph? This has never been about good and evil. This is about power. Who has it, who doesn't. Who knows how to *use* it. Right now, you have all the power you could want, but you don't know what to do with it. There are a thousand ways the Doctrine could get you out of this room, and you aren't smart enough to find any of them on your own. You are the incarnate force that powers a universe, and the best you can do is throw things at me."

Dodger keeps backing away. Her heel hits something that sloshes, and she risks a glance to see that she's almost put her foot into a bucket of clear liquid. Water, or cleaning fluid, no doubt. If she were alone, she'd take this opportunity to wash the markings off her skin, slowing the ritual they're intended to be part of just that little fraction. But she's not alone, and Leigh is coming.

"Your math is bad and I refuse to let it stand, and I can throw other things," she says, and grabs the bucket, barely noticing the rows upon rows of alchemical symbols etched around its circumference as she tosses its contents onto the advancing woman.

*(she is a child of the Up-and-Under, but that is not the only story here, and there is a history of trapped girls throwing buckets of liquid on witches in Oz, and "witch" is just another word for "alchemist" when the frills are removed; there is a tradition behind her motion, even if she has little understanding of what she does, even if her hands are*

*guided by all the Dorothys who came before her, gowned in gingham*
*with silver slippers on their feet; by all the Zibs who couldn't make it*
*quite this far, their hair full of tangles and their hearts full of a boy with*
*a smile like a country funeral)*

The three treasures of alchemy are the transmutation of base
materials, the creation of the panacea, and the distillation of the alkahest, the universal solvent which can dissolve virtually anything.
Baker found all three treasures and made them easier to call from the
walls of the world. For something such as the creation of a host for a
universal force, or the removal of that force from an unwilling host,
all three were required. The bucket falls from Dodger's suddenly
nerveless fingers. A few drops of liquid bounce free when the bucket
hits the floor, and she unconsciously maps their trajectory, stepping
backward, never getting a speck of the solution on her.

Leigh, drenched from head to toe, is not so lucky.

She screams as she dissolves. Dodger backs away farther, and
thinks she will hear that sound, the wailing of a dozen dead women
finally consigned to the grave, until the day she dies.

"Dodger!"

She turns, and there's Erin in the doorway, Erin with a Hand of
Glory so freshly extinguished that its stubs are smoking, and she's
never been so glad to see anyone in her life.

"I killed her," she says, in a dazed tone. "She . . . she *melted*. I *melted*
her." She wraps her arms abruptly around her stomach. "I think I'm
going to throw up."

"Don't throw up," says Erin. "Where's your brother? We need to
get you out of here."

"He went looking for help. He should be back any second."

"Great. We'll find your clothes, and we'll go. This was a terrible
idea. I'm so sorry. I—" Erin stops, mouth moving soundlessly.

Dodger screams when the knife emerges from the front of Erin's
shirt, when Dr. Reed shoves the living (*dying*) incarnation of Order
into the room like so much trash. She's still screaming when he advances past the threshold, glancing almost disinterestedly at the
smoking remains of his second-in-command.

"You killed Leigh," he says. "Fascinating. I never expected one of you to have the guts. You've done me a favor, in a way. She was getting ideas above her station, and killing her would have been difficult for me. We were simply too much alike."

Dodger stops screaming. Reed smiles.

"That's better," he says. "Now, where were we?"

Dodger dances backward to the workbench. It's too much to hope that she'll find another bucket of acid, so she grabs two beakers and holds them like baseballs, ready to throw (*the odds say she won't find two deadly weapons in one room, but the odds are her playthings, and if she throws, the man will die*). "Stay the *fuck* away from me," she snarls.

Reed looks at the beakers, narrow-eyed and nervous. "Is that any way to talk to your father?"

"You're not my father."

"I may as well be. I made you. Built you, one piece and particle at a time. I contributed half the base material to grow the form you occupy. Oh, don't look so shocked. You knew you were human, on some level. Did you think we'd managed to sprout you from a seed?" Reed steps forward.

Dodger steps back. "I don't care if you were the sperm donor. That doesn't make you my *father*. Now get out of here before I take away the math that makes you."

"Dodger, Dodger, Dodger." He shakes his head, clucking his tongue apologetically. "I named you, you know. I made you and I named you and by the standards of any empire that's ever risen, that makes you mine. You belong to me, body and soul, and you owe me the bright light you hold captive in your breast. It was never meant to be yours."

"If it wasn't meant to be mine, why did it choose me?"

He frowns. "It didn't. You got in the way. It was meant to belong to another girl. A good girl. A tractable girl. You would like her, I think. You have a great deal in common."

"But not pants, which is a little creepy if you're going to insist that we're your children." Roger's voice is a delight and a salvation. Dodger looks past Reed to where her brother stands in the doorway, a pale, frightened teenage girl by his side. He's found sweatpants somewhere. His bare chest is still covered in mercury and gold sigils.

He's holding a gun.

Reed stops when he sees it. He puts his hands up, suddenly conciliatory; a gesture ruined by the bloody knife he still holds. "Now, son, let's not go doing anything you'd regret later."

"Like letting you go?" Roger takes a step into the room, eyes never leaving Dr. Reed. "Dodger, you okay?"

"I just melted a woman. Other than that, I'm dandy."

"No one's hands are clean." Roger shakes his head. "We came here because we needed to save these kids. But I want you to remember that we would have been happy spending our whole lives never knowing what we were. We would have been *fine*. You forced our hand. You made this."

"I'm Baker's last living student," says Reed. "I'm the only one who remembers all her teachings, who truly understands her great work. Do you want all that knowledge to be lost?"

Roger hesitates. Then, beatifically, he smiles.

"Should've thought of that before you made me the living incarnation of language," he says. "Nothing is ever lost. It just moves into a different tongue. And you? You stopped existing a long time ago. You're a story without a storyteller. We don't need you anymore."

"Boy, you'd best stop right there—"

"You're not real," says Roger, and pulls the trigger.

The alchemical shields that should stop the bullet are gone, reduced to fiction and wiped away. There is nothing to interfere with its flight. The sound of the shot is like a sigh.

Blood trickling down from the hole in his forehead, James Reed, son and student and creation of Asphodel Baker, the greatest alchemist of her age, falls, and is still, and all is quiet.

# Pants

They find Erin's body, but they don't find her pulse; everything took too long. In the end, they leave her where she lies. This will be her tomb, and there is something so right about the idea that they do not question it. Their clothes are in a room three halls over. The sigils covering their bodies vanish when Roger whispers them away, naming and denying them one by one. Some residue is left behind: they are gilded, but no longer prepared to catch the attention of a universal transfer they want nothing to do with.

Timothy—Tim, as he shyly says he prefers to be called, and of course he does; of course it's Kim and Tim; when Reed named them, he hid their parallels under the sort of subtlety that has to be learned through experience—was locked in another small room, quite close to the room with their clothing. The locks worked on mathematical principles. Dodger didn't even have to touch them for them to spring open, ashamed that they even considered keeping her out. Kim is with him now, the two packing their scant belongings and preparing for a life aboveground.

"We have to keep them, you know," says Roger, giving Dodger a sidelong look, gauging her reaction.

"You always did like taking strays," she says. She pauses. "Did old Bill . . . ?"

"He survived the earthquake. That cat's unkillable. Erin put him in the neighbor's yard before she set the house on fire."

Dodger snorts. "Wow. The world is so weird sometimes."

"Tell me about it."

The four of them seem to be alone in this vast, echoing compound. There were other alchemists here once: that's plain from the number of labs they find, the number of empty rooms that must have held specimens, just based on their layout and design. Reed may have let them go when he thought he was nearing his goal . . . or there may be a reason that the corn here grows so gloriously green.

Roger and Dodger walk the halls of the place where they were made, hand in hand, looking at everything with silent care. They will not come here again.

They reach the door to Reed's office. There is nothing else it can be: it is too ornate, too extravagant to belong to anyone else. They stop there for a moment, looking at it gravely.

Roger speaks first. "We could start over."

"We could."

"Erin says we've done this at least a dozen times, and I know I've been here before. So we could start over, finally knowing how to win, and try for an ending that saves her. That saves a lot of people."

"We could," Dodger repeats, and lets go of his hand, and reaches for the door. There's a keycard lock. It's all just numbers. She looks at it coldly and it flashes green, allowing the door to swing open, revealing the splendor of Reed's astrolabe. "I want to do a lot of math first. We need a clearer path through this."

"Of course," says Roger, and falls silent at the sight of Reed's lab.

Gold and copper worlds dance, jeweled and filigreed and beautiful. They are spinning in perfect harmony, and for a moment, the sight is enough to take their breath away. They enter the room, walking in opposite directions around the edge, gaping up at the planets as they spin.

It is Dodger who reaches Reed's desk first, who finds the ledger with the golden orbital spiral stamped on its cover. She opens it, looking at its contents first with curiosity, and then with growing, horrified understanding. "Roger?"

"Huh?" He looks away from the spinning worlds. "What is it?"

"We can't start over until we've checked every variable. Until we know we can do it *perfectly*. I'm only doing this one more time, and it has to be flawless."

"What?" That's enough to make him hurry to her side, wonder forgotten. "What is it?"

"The astrolabe began showing errors the day we were born. Running in reverse, stopping, backing up. Leaping from one time to another. It's the resets. Some of these columns are describing the ones who didn't manifest, but I . . . I know these dates." She taps a column. "This is where we made contact. See? The last time on that day, that's when I gave up. Or when you told me not to. It's all through our lives, all these little corrections, all the times we went back and started again. But I can't reset without you, and you didn't know to tell me to reset when I was *five*."

(*five years old, and she runs into the street where a truck hits her, putting her into a coma that will last for twenty-five years, until a man she never got to meet is brought to her bedside by a scowling woman with strawberry blonde hair, until the man gives her an order at the woman's cold command; five years old, and she lived to be thirty, and she never lived at all*)

He doesn't fully understand. She can see that, and be frustrated by it, even as she forgives him. Sometimes she won't understand him either. That's why they have to stay together. They have to explain the universe for one another.

"Every time we've reached the Baths, or whatever else we could use to call the Impossible City into being, we've tried again," she says. "Maybe sometimes we've tried again from someplace that looked a lot like this, but it almost never happens until now. Until we're almost thirty years old. But Roger, *the stars haven't moved*. Erin said the Doctrine was a universal force. She meant it. We've been resetting the entire universe, because otherwise . . ."

". . . the stars would have jumped thirty years out of place every time we reset time," he says, with dawning horror. "Does he say how many times? How many errors he recorded?"

"This last time was lucky number thirteen—"

"That's not so bad."

"—thousand."

Almost half a million years of looping the universe through their lifetimes, of using their own needs as a lever on which to turn everything that is or ever has been. Roger stares at her. For the first time he can remember, words have no meaning. The numbers they describe are too big; the offense they contain is too much.

Finally, in a choked voice, he says, "Yeah, let's not fuck with time any more until we're sure we're doing it for the last time."

"Yeah."

"Let's do something else."

"Yeah."

"Farmer's market?"

Dodger blinks before smiling slowly, wearily, but with a depth of joy he hasn't seen from her in a very, very long time.

"Sounds good," she says. "I think we've earned some potatoes."

He laughs, because there's nothing else to say.


See them now:

They walk through the corn, a cluster of four moving two by two, brothers holding fast to sisters, sisters keeping their brothers close. They are not a family, not yet, but they will be; the inevitability of it is written in the too-similar lines of their faces, in the way they share certain small mannerisms, certain subtle ways of holding themselves. They come from the same place. They share experiences that no one else will ever understand, nor should be asked to.

And they are beautiful. There is nothing arrogant or cruel to their beauty; it's a fact of existence, as plain as the noses on their faces or the smears of mercury and gold paint still showing on the skins of two of them. They've traveled through the Up-and-Under, perhaps the last to make such a pilgrimage, and the things they've learnt from this journey will be with them always. For better or for worse, there is no going back to where they started. Not for any of them.

"California," says Dodger, and "California," Roger agrees, and "Anywhere but here," says Kim, in a voice like a sigh. Tim says nothing. Tim simply looks around with eyes like saucers, drinking in the world.

But this is not the entire ending. Look:

In a room beneath the earth, in a place where nothing good endures, a woman left for dead, a woman whose pulse had fallen so far below the threshold needed for saving, stirs. She opens her eyes. She is weak, wrung almost to the point of breaking, but she is alive.

All she sees is chaos. That isn't unusual: Erin has always seen chaos, everywhere she looks. But this chaos is almost soothing, because this chaos means it's over. This chaos means it's done. Most of all, this chaos means this time, they're letting things roll onward. For better or worse, they've found a timeline they're willing to preserve for a while, and they're willing to let her rest. The idea is almost intoxicating. Rest. What a glorious, impossible goal that seems.

Rest.

Hand over hand, Erin drags her near-bloodless body to the Hand of Glory. She digs a match from her pocket, sets it to the fingers, and watches the light return. Her eyes are so heavy. She is so tired. Still, she smiles as she lets the Hand brush fire onto the nearby table, watching the flames consume the silk rope that had been used to bind Roger, then move onto the wood, eating it in greedy gulps. Flames lit from a Hand of Glory will burn almost anything. Best of all, until the Hand itself is consumed, no one will notice the fire. No one will come to stop it.

Everything will burn.

She closes her eyes before the flames can reach her. There is Darren, smiling, hands outstretched, offering to lead her somewhere far away, somewhere better than this, somewhere they can be together. For the first time since she began to understand what her life was meant to be, Erin lets go.

By the time the flames come for her, she's long, long gone.

There is a strange heat at their backs when they reach the edge of the field. They turn, and see that the hut has become a tower of flame; the corn has become a blazing beacon, lighting up the sky. For a moment, they just stare.

"Erin," says Roger, and his eyes sting with tears he doesn't know how to shed. "She wasn't . . ." His voice trails off. They could have saved her. They still can, once they figure out how to revise the world. One last time.

But not today.

"She had a Hand of Glory," says Dodger. "She always did like lighting fires."

Roger laughs. He can't stop himself; he doesn't try very hard. Dodger glances at him, at the firelight dancing on his face. Then, wordlessly, she offers her hand to Kim, who takes it with matching silence, and holds fast, and does not let her go.

They have to learn what they are. They have to learn what that means. They have so much left to do, and so little of it is certain, or clear, or simple. But as the firelight filters through the corn, the world is the color of mercury, and the embers from the all-consuming flame are like an improbable road leading upward, ever upward, into the infinite and ever-forgiving sky.

"Where will we go?"

"Anywhere you want."

"Will you stay with me?"

Avery reached for Zib's hand. She let him take it, and they tangled their fingers together like the roots of a tree, so tight that they might never come untangled.

"Always," he said.

They started to walk. The improbable road was there to meet them.

—From *Over the Woodward Wall,*
by A. Deborah Baker